MATHEY GIRLS

a novel

Melody Chu

Redleaves Books

To Erica

Part One

1

Esther Hsu waited at the table set for six, arms tented over her plate, fingertips pressing against each other. She had booked an outside table, because she wasn't sure who was still being cautious, and the weather had played nice. Yes, there was a breeze, but the last snow had melted away, spring acknowledging its inevitable abdication to summer.

The doors to the patio began to swing out and Esther craned her neck in anticipation. The opaque glass opened to reveal a waiter in a white oxford and black pants. He scowled as he walked onto the patio; catching Esther's disappointed glance he forced his face into a placid mask. Embarrassed at seeing his discontent, she turned to survey her empty table. She reached over to straighten a fork, surprised at its weight.

The restaurant sat in Brixton, a wealthy suburban enclave northwest of Philadelphia, on a street of trendy boutiques, a yoga studio, an independent coffee roastery, and strategically placed shade trees. The shops here were active and open for business—no shuttered storefronts or For Lease signs as in Esther's downtown neighborhood. Brixton had survived Covid, it seemed.

Only half an hour until Claire was scheduled to arrive, and none of the other Mathey Girls were there yet; Esther opened the *Baby shower for Claire?* WhatsApp chat.

I'm at the restaurant, she said. *What are your ETAs?*

I'm in the car from the airport, Maggie said. *I hardly slept at all on the plane. So excited!* Maggie had taken a red-eye from San Francisco to arrive that morning, leaving the next afternoon, to minimize time away from her children. She had always been devoted to her kids, but the pandemic had tied her to them so closely that trying to pull her from the kids only made the knot draw into itself that much tighter.

Esther was glad Maggie had agreed to the trip, for Claire's sake. Claire wouldn't feel the same if Maggie wasn't with them.

Waiting for Uber at the rental house, Wendy said. *Should be there in 10.* Unlike Maggie, Wendy had absolutely no qualms about leaving her son in Chicago.

Neither Serena nor Valerie replied; they were probably both using the train ride down from the City to work. They were constantly on their phones or laptops, just like Esther used to be, and a part of her missed that feeling of always being busy, always in demand.

Esther sent a separate text to Lazarus, Claire's husband.

Any chance you can stall Claire? Others not here yet.

I'll do my best, Laz said. *How much time do you need?*

10-15 mins? Not too long bc you still need to put up the decorations.

SO MANY DECORATIONS.

Was it that much to set up? Just the streamers, the banners, the wall decorations, the photo backdrop, the themed plates and tablecloths and utensils and napkins, the balloons (mylar and latex, standalone and arch), the helium tank. It was a lot, but Claire's house was enormous, and Laz would have the entire duration of the brunch to set up before the shower guests started arriving.

Three months ago, when they had asked her in the *Mathey Girls* chat, Claire had said she didn't need a baby shower. They had held one for her when she was pregnant with Hannah almost a decade earlier, back when they were all young and having a baby was new, a miracle. This baby, a surprise, was a blessing for sure but Claire was older now, she and Laz settled and established, and she had already bought everything she would need for baby number two (whatever his name might be).

Esther, Wendy, Maggie, Serena and Valerie had discussed amongst themselves on a new *Baby shower for Claire?* chat. They had to do something, right? It had been, what, almost three years since they had all seen each other, though it felt so much longer. The past two years had unmoored everyone, making it painfully clear that life had changed, was changing, would change, and they needed to celebrate while they could. (Later on, Esther would recollect this underlying hum of anxiety—had they known in their hearts what would happen? Of course not, how could they have known. It was just the lingering stress of the pandemic, the continuation of two years of WHEN WILL

IT END, the coming to grips with IT WILL NEVER END.) Claire's pregnancy was the best possible reason to revive their near-annual gatherings, and the birth of another child in their group after so many years warranted something extra. They decided on a surprise brunch, Mathey Girls only, with a larger surprise baby shower immediately following.

Esther, desperate to be useful and productive, had volunteered to take the lead in organizing. Aren't you too busy, her friends asked, and she didn't tell them that she had all the time in the world. She told them instead that she should do it since she lived in Philly, not too far from Claire, so it was the easiest for her to arrange everything.

Today was the culmination of weeks of Esther's calling and emailing and messaging and buying and coordinating, a tidal wave of anticipation building to its crest. She had done her best with what she could, and she was ready to let fate take over now, to ride the wave with arms open.

The patio doors opened again; it was the restaurant hostess leading a young couple to their table. Dammit. Esther took a sip of her water, the outside of the glass already wet from sitting.

A part of her was afraid of what would come after today, of the void that she would face once everyone went back to their ordinary lives. But no need to think about voids, not today. Today the Mathey Girls would be together; they would celebrate Claire and each other.

It was Maggie who named their group chat *Mathey Girls*. The name was a tongue-in-cheek reference to the fact that they all, except for Val, had lived in the Mathey residential college at Princeton (as Serena would say to non-Princetonians, *It's pronounced Mathey as in Matt-y, not math-y. Think white bro, not Asian nerd*). Mathey Girls, despite the fact that none of them was anywhere near a girl anymore, each of them near or already at forty. Mathey Girls, a very Princeton name, despite the fact that, as a group, they had never been very "Princeton." Their band of three Chinese American women, one Singaporean Chinese woman and one white woman had always looked out of place on campus. Somehow, they had settled into the name Mathey Girls, though their identification with that name was far removed from the cluster of Gothic dorms where they first met.

Esther was reviewing her baby shower spreadsheet one last time when she heard a bellowed "Hullo!"

Wendy! Esther jumped up to greet her. A cascade of emotion washed over Esther as she took in the familiar physical presence of her old friend. At five foot one, Wendy was the shortest in their group; short but solid. She wore a navy dress with a polo collar.

"Esther, are you crying?" Wendy asked with a laugh. "You're that happy to see me?"

"No, no," Esther said, brushing her fingers over her eyes.

Wendy surveyed the table and then Esther, giving both a nod of approval before sitting down. "And how are you?"

"I'm fine," Esther said, her automatic response, and she realized that in that moment she actually was. "I'm so glad to see you—you look exactly the same."

"Ha," Wendy said. "Don't lie. I've gained ten pounds over the pandemic, and I have so much more gray hair. But thank God I can get my hair dyed again." Wendy ran her fingers through her bob, thick and lustrous as it had always been. "You don't seem to have much gray. Your freelancing must be going well—no stress."

Esther chuckled weakly. She hadn't been stressed by work in a long time—not because her freelancing was going well, but because she didn't have work to do. She hadn't told her friends or family that her clients had stopped giving her new projects, that her only productivity these past few months was planning today's baby shower. If anything, she should be stressed about not having any projects lined up, but she was keeping that firmly repressed for now.

Ever pragmatic, Wendy launched into a very Singaporean analysis of the small house that Esther had booked for the Mathey Girl out-of-towners. "Overall, the house you reserved was a good choice," Wendy said, and she started discussing its pros and cons (distance from Claire's house, having a decent common area, lacking proper curtains but thank God she had brought her sleep mask, etc.) while Esther murmured in solidarity.

Esther's phone buzzed with a message from Claire. *Hey, I'm sorry but I'm running late. Hannah is complaining of a bad stomachache and Laz just spilled an entire box of cereal on the kitchen floor?!? I'll be on my way soon.*

A smile crossed her face as she imagined the shenanigans at Claire's house, and the smile spread into a grin as she saw who came through the patio door.

Maggie, draped in a billowing taupe caftan, red hair unkempt, dragging her suitcase behind her like a witch dragging her broom.

Serena and Val, behind her, excitement on their faces. Some of the patrons stared at the striking couple. They attracted attention not simply because of their ethnicities (Chinese American and African American, respectively), but because of the confidence and ease they exuded despite their physical differences. Serena, lanky and angular, was wearing a black top and pants (she always wore pants) and Valerie, soft and curvy, wore a brilliant emerald column dress.

"Ladies!" Maggie whooped as she flew to give hugs to Esther and Wendy. "Thank God! We made it before Claire!"

Serena raised her hand in greeting. "Yo."

Valerie enveloped Esther in a pillowy embrace that smelled of vanilla. "I missed you. Thank you for organizing all this."

"I missed you too," Esther said into Val's shoulder. "And I'm glad I could help."

"So when is Claire coming?" Serena asked as the women sat down around the table.

"Soon," Esther said, and she explained how Laz had stalled by spilling the cereal.

"Heh. Nice," Serena said.

"You really thought of everything," Maggie said. "For all of this. The brunch, the shower."

"I really appreciated your spreadsheet," Wendy said.

"Nerd," Serena said.

Valerie swatted Serena's arm. "It was a very lovely spreadsheet," she said to Esther. "With all those colors."

Esther blushed and was about to both downplay and defend herself when a scream rang across the patio. They, and all the patrons and waitstaff, turned to see Claire in the doorway.

"No! No way! Oh my gosh! What are you all doing here?" The Mathey Girls rose as Claire waddled toward them, arms opened wide. Claire had always been cute, with her small frame and heart shaped face, but beaming with elation in a polka dot maternity dress, she was adorable.

Their table rang with a chorus of squeals and laughs, arms reaching long to hug Claire over her giant belly. "Did you plan this?" Claire asked Esther, her hand shooshing the tears away from her eyes.

"For me?"

"Surprise," Esther said. Her cheeks were unused to smiling, she realized, but it was a good kind of hurt.

"And all this time, I thought you didn't want to see me," Claire said.

Esther started to explain but Claire laughed. "I'm kidding, Esther, thank you so much for organizing this. This is amazing." Claire kept her hand on her belly, as if she needed to hold it in before she exploded from all the emotion, and the friends beckoned for her to sit as they settled back at the table. "Everyone looks so cute! Val, I love your dress. And Maggie, did you take a red eye? You must be exhausted," Claire said.

"No, I slept on the flight—it's kind of nice to have a break from the kids," Maggie said. "I mean, I miss them, obviously—"

"But it feels good to get away, right?" Wendy asked.

"Wait," Claire said, "aren't you coming back in like three weeks for Reunions?"

"Ha ha, yes, that's the plan," Maggie said.

At the mention of Reunions, Serena gave just the slightest of eye rolls, and Val gave Serena just the slightest of nudges to be nice. Maggie had originally proposed holding the baby shower the weekend of Princeton Reunions, as her family hadn't gone since before the pandemic, and they were excited to resume their annual pilgrimage. The other Mathey Girls rejected the idea immediately. It was too close to Claire's due date in late May, and what if she was having the baby right when they all flew in? More importantly, Serena argued, Princeton Reunions were fundamentally nauseating and there was no way she was going to be roped into the searing heat, the hordes of drunk alums, the celebration of the very decrepit and very white elder classes. I was just kidding, Maggie had said, but Esther knew that she wasn't.

"I haven't been on a plane since the pandemic started, and now I'll be flying twice in a month," Maggie said. "You know, I was surprised that there were so many people not wearing masks on the flight."

"Do people still wear masks in California?" Wendy asked.

Maggie shrugged. "A lot of people do."

"Hardly anyone wore a mask on the train," Serena said. "We don't usually, anymore."

"But don't worry," Valerie said. She reached across the table and put her hand on Claire's arm. "We wore masks on the way down."

"It's fine," Claire said. "But I appreciate the thought."

Esther hadn't considered that pregnant women needed to worry more about Covid. Did they? She hadn't thought of that while planning the shower. Crap.

"Enough about masks. Claire, how are you feeling?" Maggie asked, and the pregnancy talk began. Maggie, Claire, Wendy chattering away about weight gain and fatigue and nausea and cravings. Serena and Valerie and Esther exchanged knowing looks and let the others sate themselves with maternal discourse. They had been through this before, and they were happy to let the pregnant member of their group revel in the sisterhood of pending motherhood.

Their waitress, a young woman with a shaved side cut and a row of mini studs lining her exposed ear, approached the table. Just as she started to ask for orders, Wendy said to Claire, "You know the secret to dealing with hemorrhoids?"

The waitress took a step back, as if to escape, but Maggie apologized and told her it was fine, they were just talking about pregnancy things, if she didn't understand now, she might understand someday. After taking the orders, the waitress left with a smile and the Mathey Girls broke into laughter. They were used to their group being seen as a little ridiculous in public.

"You just wanted French toast?" Val asked Esther. "With all the fancy food on the menu?"

"Just French toast. I haven't had it in forever." At this point, it felt like years since she had eaten in a real sit-down restaurant at all.

"So Midwestern of you," Wendy said. As a Singaporean who had long ago settled down in Chicago, she liked to bond with Esther, who grew up in Cleveland, over 'Midwestern' things.

"Is French toast a Midwestern thing?" Serena asked. "Isn't it French? Or is it like 'French fries' French?"

"It's actually French," Maggie said, "in origin. *Pain perdu*. A way to use stale bread."

"I meant it's very Midwestern to order French toast instead of something like short ribs eggs Benedict," Wendy said.

Esther shrugged. "I just like French toast."

"Great," Claire said, "we've established that Esther likes French toast. But seriously, I need to know, what's the secret to dealing with hemorrhoids?"

With a laugh the Mathey Girls returned to their chatter. Through the rest of the brunch Esther let herself be carried away, gleaning updates, laughing at her friends' jokes, commiserating at her friends' complaints. She had thought it would be an adjustment to meet as a group in person again, that the physical proximity of others might feel uncomfortable. She had forgotten how easy it was to feel easy when she was with the Mathey Girls, and this hadn't changed despite the pandemic.

Over her French toast, Esther learned that Serena and Valerie were considering buying a brownstone and had begun looking at places; that Wendy's brokerage firm was doing well despite the pandemic, and that their transition to remote working was surprisingly seamless; that Maggie's kids were now 15 and 11 and 6, a fact that everyone—Maggie included—seemed to find hard to believe, and they were ecstatic to be back at school in person even though they still had to mask.

"And what about you?" Claire asked Esther. "How have you been?"

"I'm fine," Esther said.

"How's work?" Valerie asked. "Still busy with the freelance stuff?"

Esther nodded and slipped her fingers along the edge of the napkin on her lap. She didn't want to ruin the occasion by telling everyone that she hadn't been working.

"After all this time, I still don't know what you do," Maggie said. The others laughed, as if they all thought freelance management consulting was a big mystery. "Actually, I don't really know what any of you do, except for Claire—economics professor, easy. Wendy, on the other hand, you've explained it to me a million times but what really is a commodities brokerage business? And you two lawyers—" she wagged her finger at Serena and Val, "I mean, you're lawyers, but what do you do exactly, all day?"

"I would say the same thing to you," Serena said. "What do you do all day? Especially if your kids are all back at school?"

Maggie paused, as if weighing whether to be offended. Esther glanced at the others, who were also waiting to see how Maggie would react. She hoped that they wouldn't argue. There had been many barbs thrown between Maggie and Serena over the years, and by now it was Maggie's choice whether to take Serena's bait.

After a moment, Maggie threw her hands in the air in surrender. "Point taken."

Claire shifted her body toward Esther, pivoting to clear the air. "Are you still as stressed out as before, when you were at that firm?" Claire asked. "I hope the freelancing gives you some time to slow down once in a while. At least a little time to breathe."

Esther shrugged. A silence settled on the group as they looked at her. "It's been fine," she said. "Manageable." She didn't want to lie to her friends, not face to face like this, but she couldn't tell them the truth.

Claire patted Esther's hand. The group waited to see if Esther would share more, but she didn't, and they didn't push. She had always been the quiet one, she knew, and her friends understood her preference to float in the waters of their friendship, not agitate or make waves. Others at the table would be more than happy to do that.

The Mathey Girls finished their food and lingered over conversation. As they sipped their coffees and mimosas, Esther received a text from Laz: *The guests are arriving*.

"So, Claire," Esther said, trying her best to be nonchalant, "Laz said it would be okay if we go to your house after brunch. To see the renovations you did over the pandemic."

"Of course!" Claire said. "Oh, I hope he cleaned up. Do we have plans for today? Tomorrow? How long is everyone staying?"

"We're all heading out tomorrow and as for plans, we're playing it by ear," Serena said, signaling for the check.

Their waitress came back to the table. "Your bill has already been paid," she said, tilting her head towards Wendy. Her earrings flashed in the sun.

"My treat," Wendy said.

"Did you pay when you went to the bathroom?" Claire asked, and Wendy gave her a sly smile. "So Asian. We'll split it and Venmo you."

"Nonsense," Wendy said. "And I purposely don't use Venmo for this very reason."

Before the waitress could leave the table, Maggie asked her to take a picture of the group. She took the phone and set up the shot, like an expert, and the women straightened up and smiled wide. Phone returned, Maggie immediately sent the picture to the *Mathey Girls* chat and everyone examined their phones.

"Aww," Maggie said. "We look so cute together."

"Separately, we're old and haggard," Wendy said. "But together we're not bad."

"I've gained so much weight," Claire said.

"You are so cute right now!" Esther said, and the others agreed.

"We're like a perverse Benetton ad," Serena said. "I mean, look at us. Chinese, Chinese, White, Chinese, Chinese, Black, everybody all dressed up."

"Nothing perverse about that," Valerie said.

"You know what I mean," Serena said.

"Ladies," Wendy said, rising from her seat, "I think it's time to get our perverse little group back to Claire's house."

2

"Someone must be having a party," Claire said as she turned the car onto her street. "Everyone's celebrating today!"

In the backseat, Wendy glanced at Esther with eyebrows up. Esther grimaced at the cars lining the length of the road. At least everyone had followed instructions and stayed out of Claire's driveway.

"Your house is so beautiful," Maggie said from the passenger seat. "Can we go through the main entrance? I want to see this foyer renovation in all its glory. And let's wait for Serena and Val's Uber to get in so we can go in together so we can get that full effect. You said that the contractors took three months longer than they planned?"

Another glance from Wendy to Esther as Maggie distracted Claire with talk of home renovation struggles during the pandemic. Smooth. Soon the Mathey Girls were fully assembled on the front stoop, Claire turning the key in her lock. She was looking back at Maggie, saying something about Covid price inflation, when she pushed open the door.

"SURPRISE!"

Claire's hands flew to her face, and then to her belly. "What? WHAT? Ahhh!"

Esther had known that over twenty women other than the Mathey Girls had RSVPed Yes for the shower, plus a handful of Maybes. Still, she was unprepared for the sight of all of these women, all strangers to Esther, crowded in the foyer, some holding wine glasses, some masked, and many with at least a little gray in their hair.

Laz took Claire's hand and brought her inside.

"No way! You did all of this?" Claire asked with wide eyes before giving her husband a kiss.

Laz pointed between himself and Esther. "We did it," he said.

Laz and Claire's daughter Hannah had festooned the kitchen, living room and dining room with the baby shower decorations that Esther had bought. Bunches of blue, silver and white balloons, streamers leading from room to room, garlands hanging from doorways announcing, "IT'S A BOY" and "WELCOME BABY", giant stacked cardboard blocks in the entry spelling out B-A-B-Y. It was over the top, the Chens' Brixton mansion converted into a baby shower decoration showcase.

The women hugged and laughed and cheered and then Maggie said, "Now Mr. Chen, it's time for you to leave!"

The Mathey Girls playfully pushed Laz toward the door, and out of it. "Wait, I have to leave?!" he asked, pretending he didn't know. As Esther gave him one last shove on his shoulder, caught up in the merriment, they locked eyes, and he lifted his chin to say thank you. Someone pushed the door closed.

Esther followed the others back to the women clustered around Claire. Esther had prepared games and ordered snacks and done everything that the internet told her she should do, and she was pleased at how everything came together, but also overwhelmed.

She wandered through the first-floor rooms, picking up napkins and crumbs. The other Mathey Girls mingled with the strangers, slipping into easy conversation with Claire's friends and colleagues, letting Claire enjoy her moment without crowding her. They knew that after the shower, once everyone had left, they would have Claire to themselves again.

Esther decided to help people get refills on their drinks. Like a caterer, which she hadn't thought to get, because she really didn't think this many people would show up. She armed herself with bottles of white and red and traveled between clusters of people topping up their glasses.

"Silly Esther," Maggie said, accepting another pour of white. "Come chat with us."

Esther cast an eye over the group of women that Maggie was talking to and she shook her head with a shy smile; she didn't feel up to chatting with strangers. She walked on and saw Claire surrounded by a different group of women she didn't recognize. Maybe one of the women looked familiar, maybe she was in one of her classes way back when. Claire and Maggie had always been more connected to the rest of the Princeton community; Esther's college days were so cloistered and small in comparison. Just the Mathey Girls—minus Val, because Serena hadn't met her yet—had been enough back then. As the years went by, she told herself that they were still enough, as she tried and failed to make friends who could possibly be as close as these women were to her.

As Esther headed back to the kitchen with the empty bottles, she passed a room with a closed sliding door. She could see through the frosted window that someone was inside. She set the bottles on the hall table and knocked on the door.

Slowly, it slid open. It was Claire's daughter Hannah, somber in a pink dress, thin arms dangling down, and she blinked hard before offering a quiet "Hi."

Esther knelt down. "Hi, Hannah. Do you remember me? Auntie Esther?"

Hannah nodded slowly, but it was unclear if she actually meant it. She had that haircut that so many little Asian girls had, blunt bangs reaching her eyebrows, shoulder-length straight bob. She looked very neat with that haircut—how many Asian girls were stereotyped as being neat and docile simply by having that particular hair? Hannah wasn't exactly docile, as Esther knew from Claire, but she definitely looked the part.

It had been over two years since Esther saw Hannah in person and the transformation was startling. The last time Esther had seen her, when she had gone to the Chens' for dinner, there were only rumors of some new virus in China, and Hannah had presented her with a gaping hole where her two front baby teeth had been. Now the adult teeth had grown in, enormous, and her face had lost some of its pudginess.

"How old are you now? Eight?"

"Nine," Hannah said.

She looked so small, so serious. Esther was sure that when she was nine, she was a happier girl. At that age, she hadn't yet been introduced to sadness.

Esther and Hannah stared at each other for a moment, and then Hannah started to slide the door shut again.

"Wait—" Esther said. "Did you want to get some snacks? I bought a lot of cookies and no one's eating them."

Hannah looked at her skeptically, but when Esther held out her hand, she took it. Esther gave herself a moment of self-congratulation for luring the little girl out of her cave.

Soon they were in the kitchen, munching on fancy sugar cookies shaped like milk bottles, prams and rattles, covered in matte blue frosting that shattered against Esther's teeth when she bit down.

"There you are," Wendy said as she entered the kitchen. "Maggie says it's time to do the games." Wendy held out her hand to Hannah. "Hi, Hannah! It's Auntie Wendy. I haven't seen you in ages. You've grown so big!"

Hannah eyed Wendy and her outstretched hand, unsure.

"Okay, well, let's go," Wendy said after a moment.

"You guys are going to lead the games, right?" Esther asked. She had sent the game instructions to the *Baby shower for Claire?* group so that someone else could take charge.

"Don't worry," Wendy said. "We've got this."

***

"Hit Me Baby One More Time!"

"Baby Love!"

"Baby Got Back!"

"Be My Baby!"

"ICE ICE BABY!"

The women cried, frantic, their hands gesturing wildly, their laughter uproarious. In the living room the Mathey Girls held court, leading Claire and the guests through a series of silly baby-related games—baby trivia, a price guessing game, a name-that-baby-song game.

Through the commotion, Hannah had parked herself on the couch next to Claire, receiving intermittent squeezes and kisses on the head. Esther could guess why Hannah looked so solemn. After nine years she was going to share her mother with a baby, and not just any baby, a baby boy, and from what Claire had told the Mathey Girls, this was a big deal to the Chen family. Not that Laz cared, but his mother in Taiwan most definitely did.

After the games, it was time to open presents and Esther helped by moving the excess packaging and torn wrapping paper off to a giant pile behind the couch. On handing her one particularly awkward empty box, Claire gave Esther a very knowing smile of appreciation and a whispered thank you. Warmth spread inside Esther and out to her cheeks, and she shook her head as if to say, it's nothing really.

"You all are so lucky to have such a tight knit group," an elderly white lady said to Esther after the presents were opened and the women were all chatting in loose clusters again.

"Yes," Esther said, trying not to stand too close. The woman was wearing two masks, and Esther wasn't wearing one at all.

The woman said something that started with "Your friends..." and ended getting trapped somewhere between mask one and mask two.

"I'm sorry?" Esther asked, trying to lean forward to hear better without leaning so far forward as to infect the woman with any virus she might be carrying.

"You are all friends from college?" she asked, slowly and loudly.

"That's right."

The woman seemed to want to chat more, but Esther wanted to escape, so she pretended that she heard someone calling her and fled.

She went to the room with the sliding door, where she had found Hannah earlier; it was empty now. Esther slipped in. When Esther had last been in the house, this room was a guest room with a futon, but over the pandemic it had evolved into an extensively organized playroom. The toys ran the gamut from all sizes of plastic horses to massive Lego structures to boxes labeled *Barbies, Art supplies, Puzzles (small), Puzzles (>500 pieces)*.

Hannah came into the playroom holding a cookie shaped like a teddy bear, its bottom feet bitten off. Her lips were pale blue from the icing.

"Do you mind if I'm in here?" Esther asked.

Hannah shrugged, taking a chunk out of the teddy bear's torso, observing.

"This is a lot of toys," Esther said.

"I don't play with a lot of these anymore." Hannah surveyed the

16

wall in front of her. "I guess the baby can play with these someday, if he wants, and that's why we still have them."

"Are you excited for your little brother?" Esther asked. Hannah just looked at her and didn't respond. Stupid question.

"Why are you in here?" Hannah asked. Esther heard this as a question of curiosity rather than antagonism and chose not to take offense.

"Sometimes I get overwhelmed with a lot of new people. And it got worse over Covid," Esther said. "I'm not used to it."

"It's very loud," Hannah said.

Wendy arrived with a knock on the door. "People are starting to leave," she said.

Esther and Hannah looked at each other and then at Wendy, who suggested they go say goodbye. At the front door a departure line had formed, stalled by hugs and thank yous and promises to meet up again soon, this was so fun, it's been too long, good luck with the delivery, make sure to update us when the baby is born.

After all the other guests left, the Mathey Girls sat Claire down on the sofa and began dismantling the decorations, transforming the house back from baby shower showcase to regular old mansion.

"You don't need to do that," Claire said. "I can do it later."

The friends laughed and shushed her.

"Can we keep some of the decorations up?" Hannah asked, eying the balloon garland draped above the fireplace.

"Well, honey," Maggie said, "we're taking things down now, while we're here, so your parents don't have to worry about it later. Your daddy is so busy, and your mommy's body needs to take care of your baby brother."

"I know," Hannah said. "But we could take the balloons down later. I could help too."

"That's so sweet," Maggie said. "Okay. Let's leave the balloons up today, and we can take them down tomorrow before we head back home?"

Hannah gave Maggie a long look and then skulked away.

Esther and Serena went to the kitchen to tidy up. "There's so much food left," Serena said, surveying the remaining platters of cookies and canapes.

"I wasn't sure how much to order," Esther said. She squeezed her hands together. "I was afraid there wouldn't be enough."

"Ha. How many people did you think were coming? Fifty?" Serena rummaged through Claire's kitchen for storage containers. The cabinets that lined the walls were cavernous, occupied by a plethora of small appliances, utensils, crockery, cooking implements, and dishware.

"So... much... stuff," Serena said. "I don't know how they could possibly use all this stuff."

"They need to fill the cabinets," Esther said, but Serena didn't laugh.

Eventually they found a drawer in the massive island with all sizes of plastic bags and the two women set to work.

"You did a good job organizing the shower," Serena said without looking up.

"Thank you," Esther said without looking up either.

"So you've been alright?"

"Yes, I guess."

"It doesn't seem like you're as crazy busy as you were before, right? When you were with the firm."

Esther felt an accusation lurking. "I haven't been looking too hard for new projects," she said. "Not recently."

Serena leaned her filled bag against the bag that Esther had already placed on the island. "I would say something snide about some people not needing to work for money but, given that I'm pretty much living off my sugar mama, I can't be one to judge."

Of all of them, Serena was the one most likely to judge, but all Esther said was, "But you work very hard."

Serena raked her hand through her hair, short-cropped and peppered with gray. "My work is a labor of love, and sometimes hate," she said. "I couldn't live the life I live without Val's financial support, and I recognize my privilege."

Esther didn't know how to respond. Serena and Valerie were always something of a mystery to her. They had met in law school, Serena on a warpath to fix the world—she now worked for a nonprofit dedicated to the advancement of Asian American legal causes—while Valerie prepared to infiltrate the echelons of corporate

Biglaw where she was now a partner. Somehow despite their different races, different career goals, different personalities, they had united wholly and completely. Esther loved and deeply respected Serena but couldn't imagine committing to a lifetime of her as a spouse. Valerie had tamed Serena, over the years, and Esther was grateful to accept Val as an honorary Mathey Girl for that reason alone.

"But I hear that you have a nice apartment," Serena said, as if she wanted to make amends.

"It's an old building," Esther said. A thought flitted somewhere across the back of her mind. How Chinese it was, to downplay the positive. Or maybe it was just her personality.

"Claire told me it's in a really good location. Close to Penn?"

"Just a few minutes' drive," Esther said.

"But you didn't really see Claire, even though you were so close to her office?"

"I mean, we met up a couple of times. I was busy at first, and then there was the pandemic, and you know..." Esther tried not to wilt under Serena's gaze. Serena had always demanded the best from her friends, her high standards unspoken until someone like Esther inevitably came up short.

Esther had bought her apartment in Rittenhouse Square in 2012 as an investment property. In March 2020, when everything was shutting down, her then-tenant fled back to Oregon, and Esther decided to leave Manhattan for the hopefully safer environs of Philadelphia. She had thought—they had all thought—that Esther and Claire would see each other all the time. They didn't. Instead, Esther cocooned herself in her apartment, busying herself with work to get through the worst of the uncertainty and panic. She had her job; she had her apartment; she had grocery and meal delivery. As each wave of pandemic anxiety crested and subsided, Esther held onto the safety of her one bedroom, her small but adequate kitchen and adjoining sitting area. Her family and friends floated in their separate pods, and as long as everyone was safe, she didn't need to be afraid.

She had actually almost paid off her mortgage before she got fired from her longstanding job at Centridge Consulting. The apartment was the only thing that Esther had now, the only decision that she could deem wise. The building was old, yes, but her view was magnificent. Her living room looked out onto a corner of the Square; to see trees, real trees, outside her window instead of the grungy brick of the building next door still felt like an accomplishment two years after moving in.

"Well," Serena said, eying Esther as if peeling layers off of her skin, "I'm glad that we did this. It's been good to see you again."

"Yes," Esther said.

"Thank you for organizing," Serena said, and she gave a nod as if writing a check mark next to Esther's name on her mental friendship evaluation form.

Esther blushed. "I think I should text Laz and let him know he can come back," she said. "I need to go find my phone." She fled the kitchen, before Serena might change her mind as to whether Esther was good enough or not.

***

The house tidied, Laz back from wherever he had escaped to, the Mathey Girls sat in Claire's living room and enjoyed each other's company. They had always been able to entertain themselves with very little, busying themselves with board games, chatting about current events, replaying memories from college, each new sentence uttered by one of them adding to the Great Wall that was their lifelong friendship.

As always, Laz stayed at the edge of the group. He too had known all of them since college; the Mathey Girls had walked with Claire through every step of her relationship with her husband. The spouses of the group fell on a spectrum of in and out. Valerie had been accepted as one of them early on; Laz had always gone along with them but only as an appendage of Claire; Maggie's husband Jeremy was tolerant but generally uninterested; Wendy's ex-husband had never really liked them and had even told her that he thought they were a bad influence. (No one had liked the ex, and they were pleased he was back in his native Singapore, far away from Wendy and her son.)

By the end of the night, the women were falling, hard, into nostalgia and sentimentality. Claire leaned on Maggie's shoulder and let out a slow sigh. "Thank you, ladies," she said. "To be honest, I was a little scared when I found out I was pregnant."

"Why?" Wendy asked.

A layer of tears formed over Claire's eyes and threatened to spill out. "We still weren't sure what was going to happen with the pandemic, and even though Laz and I had our vaccines, they didn't have the vaccine for Hannah yet, and Laz was going into the hospital every day..."

"Everything has been worse with the pandemic," Wendy said.

"Especially for parents," Maggie said, and Esther could see the trauma flash across the faces of her friends who were mothers.

"But you're almost at the finish line," Val said. "You don't have anything to be afraid of."

Claire gave her a smile. "Yes, almost at the finish line. And then I only have to take care of a little baby, in my late thirties, during a pandemic."

"Well, according to the Republicans, the pandemic is over already," Serena said, and everyone laughed a little too forcefully.

"Remember that guy, the super Republican guy who tried to ask Serena out?" Maggie asked, and the seriousness dissipated from the group as they delved into their past, trying to remember all of the guys and girls that Serena had rejected those four years in New Jersey.

They had been thrown together at random, five young women out of a hundred female freshmen in Mathey, five young women out of five hundred in their Princeton class, five young women out of the thousands who applied that year for a spot in that class. It felt like magic how they had coalesced into a friendship as freshmen, so easy and natural that it must have been destiny. The hours they spent together—in their dorms, in the dining halls, in the library, at Chuck's Spring Street Cafe off campus, at Quaker Bridge Mall, four years of college, innumerable meetups and trips after graduation, hour after hour after hour together—built something unbreakable.

Later, thinking back on that Saturday evening, Esther would remember looking from face to face, drinking in each of her friends at their closest to each other and to the group. This weekend would be the last time they would hear Claire's clear and generous laughter, see the crow's feet emergent around her eyes, feel the warmth of her presence. They didn't know this, could never have guessed it, but after Claire died Esther often thought back to that last visit and wondered if she could have somehow made it more special for Claire, if she could have done better.

21

3

Esther first met Claire in the Mathey dining hall their second week at Princeton. At the entrance, it seemed like a regular cafeteria with the usual thick plastic trays, the lines, the registers. Then a turn into the dining hall proper, tray in her hands, and Esther faced a single extended aisle with an impossibly long runner covering the stone floor. The walkway was flanked by rows and rows of wooden tables fortified by wooden chairs. The tables at the start of this gauntlet were usually full, all the way through the middle, the dining hall ringing with the clamor of students reveling in their newfound freedom and community. The space didn't start to empty out until the back where a handful of loners would sit, purposely detached from each other.

As she walked down the long aisle that night, Esther didn't look up at the high arched ceiling, the faux-medieval flags hanging from the rafters, or the Gothic chandeliers. Instead, her eyes swept left and right and ahead, trying to identify a space where she could be by herself—if necessary—without it being too obvious.

Two weeks in, and she hadn't made friends yet. She was amicable enough with her roommate Amanda, but Amanda had made other friends immediately upon arriving at campus and wasn't often in their dorm. Same with the people in their RA group; smiles were freely given and received, but everyone seemed to know what they were doing in terms of a social life and parties and being away from home.

Esther missed her family—her parents and even her little brother —and her home in Cleveland. She was overwhelmed by the classes, the architecture, the exuberance and entitlement emitted by her fellow students. The color orange was everywhere. She had thought by now she would have gotten her bearings, but no, she was still walking down the dining hall aisle afraid that she wouldn't find anyone to sit with, or that she would find someone to sit with but they wouldn't really want her there.

Someone she had talked to in a Mathey event met her eye and nodded, and she nodded back, but she wasn't invited to sit so she kept moving. She resigned herself to sitting toward the back of the dining hall, past the middle but not quite as far as the loners.

Then she saw the two girls—the Asian one with an open face, dusky skin and glossy hair in a ponytail, and the white one, her red hair in the loosest of top knots, her body lanky. Esther didn't see them at every meal, but whenever she did, they were together, just the two of them. Always alive and alert to each other, often in deep conversation, sometimes chortling with laughter, seemingly oblivious to those around them. She had seen them walking in the courtyard, arms linked. Esther wished that she could be the kind of girl who could befriend someone so closely despite being so different.

Their heads were bowed as if in prayer, and when the Asian girl lifted her head, she surveyed the cafeteria. Then, to Esther's surprise, the Asian girl smiled and held up her hand in a wave. Esther looked behind her, but there wasn't anyone there. The Asian girl beckoned her over. *Sit here,* she mouthed, pointing to the seat next to her.

Even as she placed her tray on the table, Esther had doubts whether she was meant to be there.

"Hi, I'm Claire," the Asian girl said.

"I'm Esther."

"And I'm Maggie," the white girl said, putting out her hand for a shake.

Esther was surprised; she hadn't really shaken anyone's hand before, but she obliged and slid into the chair next to Claire.

"Thank you for sitting with us," Claire said. She and Maggie laughed.

"What do you mean?" Esther asked.

"People don't seem to want to sit with us," Maggie said. "We're not sure why."

"Oh," Esther said. She didn't want to admit that she had seen them together before, had noticed their camaraderie and assumed it was exclusive.

"Do you live in Blair?" Claire asked, referring to one of the Mathey dorms.

"No, Campbell," Esther said. "You guys are in Blair?"

Maggie nodded and took a bite of her pasta.

"We're roommates," Claire said. "Are you Chinese? I'm Chinese."

"I am," Esther said. "My parents were born in China, but they came to the US from Taiwan."

"Mine too," Claire said. When she grinned, a dimple appeared on one cheek. "I'm from California. You?"

"Ohio," Esther said.

The girls considered this, as if trying to place Ohio on a map, and Maggie said, "We noticed that you sit by yourself a lot."

Esther flushed.

"No, don't be embarrassed!" Claire said. "We just thought you might like some company."

Was it that obvious? Did she seem that desperate? "Oh, I'm okay," Esther said. "But thank you, for inviting me."

Maggie went back to her pasta, but Claire took a moment to offer Esther another smile.

After that first meal, Esther started to sit with Claire and Maggie when she saw them in the dining hall. Their schedules didn't always match up, and there were meals where Esther sat alone, but she was no longer afraid when she stood at the head of the long aisle, tray in hands, looking for open seats.

It was Claire who introduced her to Serena, whose dorm was next to Claire's, and to the Asian American Students Association where they met Wendy. It was Claire that the Mathey Girls had intuitively coalesced around, the star to their planets. She drew them in with her warmth and her insight, the way she would spend that extra second to offer one more smile when it might make all the difference.

***

Two short weeks after the baby shower, when everyone had gone back to their busy or not so busy lives, Claire texted the *Mathey Girls* chat group. Her water had broken, she wrote, and she was at the hospital in labor. When Serena asked how it was possible that she was chatting so calmly with them, Claire explained that she had had her epidural and was being induced, because the delivery was not progressing as quickly as the doctors wanted it to.

Are you excited? Maggie asked in the chat.

Yes! Finally time to get this baby out! Claire said.

Wendy responded to Claire's message with a heart emoji.

Who's watching Hannah? Maggie asked. *Did Laz's mom arrive yet?*

She just got here, Claire said. *Just in time too. And of course she was mad that my water broke early. I mean, seriously?? And of course she brought the confinement nurse!* (silly face emoji)

Claire's mother-in-law had flown in from Taiwan to help the family when Claire was having the baby, and for the month afterward. She had insisted on bringing a traditional confinement nurse with her, whose job would be to take care of Claire and the baby for a full thirty days after delivery.

Esther thought it was crazy what Claire had agreed for that first month: no leaving the house, no showers, no washing her hair, no touching any cold water, and she would have to eat kidney and liver every day. Claire had refused to do this after Hannah was born, and Laz's mother had blamed the lack of the traditional one-month confinement for Claire's two subsequent miscarriages. Now, with the baby boy, Mrs. Chen had insisted.

OMG the confinement nurse, Serena said. *I can't believe they're actually going through with this.* (angry face emoji)

At least you'll be able to get some rest with the baby, Wendy said. *But make sure they bring him to your breast whenever he's hungry! Otherwise you won't have adequate milk supply.*

Got it, Claire said.

Esther watched the text conversation unfold on her phone as she lay in her bed. *Good luck,* she said. (heart emoji)

Claire replied with a heart emoji.

I should try to get some rest, Claire said. *It's going to be some hours still until the baby comes.*

Let us know when he's out and about! Wendy said.

We're looking forward to seeing pics of the baby! Maggie said.

Claire replied with a thumbs up.

Love you guys, Claire said. *Good night!*

That night, Esther dreamed that the Mathey Girls were shopping at Delia's. Back in college, the five of them (pre-Val, though Val was with them in the dream) regularly visited the trendy juniors' clothing shop in Quaker Bridge Mall off Route 1. The group's collective campus jobs —dining hall server, mail sorter, research assistant, peer tutor—didn't provide enough funds to shop at the upscale stores on Nassau Street in Princeton itself. They were too old for some of these clothes, they knew, but they were too young for regular women's wear, and Delia's offerings were cheap and fun.

In the dream, the six Mathey Girls were their current old ages, but they were in the late 90s Delia's. Two bored sales attendants chatted at the front of the store, uninterested in the group of women browsing together. As they did two decades earlier, Esther and her friends took their time going through the circular racks, fingers brushing against pink polyesters and distressed denims as plastic hangers clacked against each other.

What were they shopping for? Did it matter?

"There's no maternity clothes," Claire said, picking up a tiny tank and placing it against her chest. Perched above her swollen belly it looked like a bikini top.

"That could be for the baby," Wendy said.

The Mathey Girls started looking for clothes for the baby, as if the baby were going to be a girl and as if the baby would fit these clothes. They were disappointed that the store had mostly clothes for early aughts clubbing. Tight crop tops, low rise black stretchy pants with flared bottoms, chunky boots.

Eventually they found some dresses, long prom gowns, that the baby could wear.

"I don't know if I can pay for all this," Claire said, running her fingers down a row of silver sequins.

"I can help," Maggie said, and then the Mathey Girls all offered to chip in.

"You guys are the best," Claire said. "She's going to love them."

Esther woke from the dream with a fuzzy sense of contentment and reached for her phone to check the *Mathey Girls* chat.

At two a.m. Philadelphia time, eleven p.m. San Francisco time,

Maggie had said: *Any update?*

At three a.m. Philly time, midnight San Francisco time, Maggie had said: *Hope everything is going swimmingly! I need to go to sleep now but I look forward to good news in the morning!*

At seven a.m. Philly time, Serena had said: *How is everything @Claire?*

It was seven-thirty now, and Esther texted Laz: *Everything okay with Claire and the baby?*

She waited twenty minutes, uneasy, and after she didn't see any replies, she messaged the baby shower chat group. *Has anyone heard from Claire or Laz? I texted Laz and no reply.*

After she hit send, she stared at her phone, willing it to give her some good news. When it didn't cooperate, she decided to take a shower and think positive thoughts. The steam and hot water helped wash away her foreboding. Toweling herself off, she pictured an exhausted Claire holding a chubby baby boy in her arms—Claire had told them that the doctors thought the baby was going to be big.

After throwing on some clothes, Esther checked her phone and saw a missed call from Maggie and a text. *Call me ASAP.*

***

Esther had never heard Maggie this way. She was blubbering, gasping for breath. At the same time, she didn't want to wake her kids or her husband, so she blubbered and gasped in one of her downstairs bathrooms. On the other end of the line in her Philly apartment, Esther's heart exploded.

Claire was dead.

Claire was dead.

She was gone.

An amniotic embolism, Maggie said.

Maggie had woken up early, a heavy feeling in her heart, and had seen Esther's message to the baby shower chat group. She crept downstairs, trying not to make any noise, and called Laz from the bathroom. He was sobbing when he picked up.

The doctors tried everything, Maggie said. They couldn't stop the bleeding and now Claire was gone.

27

"But..." Esther said. She didn't understand. It was impossible to understand. "She was fine, just last night?"

Maggie tried to find the breath to explain. This was possible, apparently, but it had never happened to anyone she knew.

"But she was in a good hospital..." Esther said.

It didn't matter.

"But Laz is a doctor, and this still happened?"

It didn't matter.

Tears were running down Esther's face and she too was gulping for air. "And the baby?" she asked, a croak, a last attempt to wrestle something acceptable out of this moment.

Maggie sniffed. "The baby is alive. But he's in the NICU."

Esther lay down on her bed with the phone pressed to her ear. She didn't say it, and Maggie didn't say it, but they may have been thinking the same thing. If only Claire had lived. They didn't really care about the baby. They cared about Claire.

They stayed on the line, weeping across the long distance between them, until Maggie heard one of her sons calling.

"Oh, God, I need to go," she said.

Esther didn't want the phone call to end. She didn't want to face a world without Claire.

"Esther, would you be able to tell the others?"

"Tell the others..." Esther said.

"I don't think I could handle it," Maggie said.

"I don't know..." Then Esther thought of Maggie, and her three kids, and the fact that Maggie had had to hear the news from Laz, and she could hear Maggie's panicked breathing on the phone. "Okay," she said. "I'll tell them."

Maggie gave a sob and said a quick goodbye before hanging up.

Esther gave herself a moment before opening the *Mathey Girls* chat. Her heart had solidified to lead.

@wendy @serena @val - call me. ASAP.

She went to the bathroom and tried to throw up. She wanted to empty herself of her leaden heart, but all that came up was a hint of bile. Back on her bed, blanket around her, she closed her eyes and waited for the calls to come in.

Serena and Val called, and then Wendy, and so Esther put them on conference and was spared having to tell them one by one. It was still horrible. Armed only with the meager information that Maggie had given her, she struggled to make it make sense.

No, she didn't understand the ambiotic—amniotic? Yes, amniotic —embolism either.

No, she didn't know exactly when it had happened.

No, she hadn't been in contact with Laz.

No, she didn't know what was happening with the baby, or with Hannah, though they knew that Laz's mother was in town with that confinement nurse; surely they could help.

The women floundered in their grief, stunned, and then Valerie cleared her throat. "I'll reach out to Laz and see what he needs, what we can do," she said. "Claire was like my sister, but you guys knew her the best and the longest and I know this will be harder on you guys than me." Esther could hear the quiver in Val's voice.

"Thank you," Esther whispered.

"And I will give Maggie a call and make sure she's okay," Val said.

"You don't have to do it all," Wendy said in a hollow voice, monotone.

"No, it's fine," Val said. "Let me take this one."

"I love you," Serena said.

"I love you too," Wendy said. "All of you."

They said their goodbyes and, alone again, Esther let out a wail. The cry filled her room, her apartment, maybe Rittenhouse Square, maybe the city of Philadelphia. It wasn't enough though. Claire couldn't hear it.

***

Esther entombed herself in her apartment. Crippled, cut down, decimated, obliterated, pulverized by grief. Claire was the sun at the heart of the Mathey Girls, and her death was a merciless black hole. Valerie posted updates to the chat which Esther took in like punches to the face. She said that Claire hadn't suffered much. She had bled to death on the operating table where she had had an emergency C-section, her last conscious moments holding Laz's hand. She had seen her son, now named Jasper, and given Laz a weak smile. Her last words were that she didn't feel well.

Jasper was in some kind of baby hibernation unit, under a cooling blanket that lowered his body temperature so that he was effectively in a coma. There was the possibility that when they woke him after several days, there would be brain damage.

Laz had asked Valerie to ask the Mathey Girls to pray for the baby, and for him and Hannah.

Esther tried to dredge up her old Christian self and pray for them. It didn't work.

She raged at God for killing Claire, then she remembered that she no longer believed in God, and got angrier that Claire did believe in God and her God let her die.

Laz was not doing well, Valerie said in a later message. Maybe Esther could pay him a visit?

Esther ignored the request. The thought of leaving her apartment made her ill.

Wendy sent Esther a separate message asking if she was okay, she hadn't been saying much in the chat group, did she want to talk?

No, Esther said. She didn't want to talk. She was okay, she said. As soon as she sent the message she felt disgusted with herself. She wasn't okay. To be okay would be disrespectful to Claire.

A part of her life had been ripped away, and she didn't know what to do with the fabric left behind. She had known Claire since they started adulthood, and Esther had expected that their lives would continue together for decades more. She told herself that she was almost forty, she was an adult, this wasn't her first exposure to death, but still—to have Claire alive one day and gone forever the next. Esther's older brother Caleb had died when she was a child, after a long period of illness. Claire's death was nothing like that. This was incomprehensible. The horrific ridiculousness of a healthy, vibrant woman dying—*dying*—while giving birth, in 2022.

At some point, Esther's little brother Didi called. She watched her phone buzz. Didi—his real name was Andrew, but Esther only ever thought of him as *didi*, Chinese for *little brother*—left a somber voicemail saying that he'd heard about Claire, he was really sorry, he wanted to make sure she was doing okay.

Didi called again later that day and left another voicemail; he sounded as if he had been crying. He said that he had always thought of Claire like a sister, ever since she took him under her wing when he was a freshman at Princeton and they were juniors, and he had felt so lost, and he would never forget how kind she was.

Esther heard the second voicemail and thought about calling Didi back. She decided she wasn't ready.

Her parents called, but didn't leave a voicemail. Didi must have told them about Claire.

Esther wanted her mother to comfort her, to be the type of mother that could. But she wasn't. And maybe Esther didn't deserve to be comforted, not yet.

She could have spent the last two years differently. She could have taken up Claire's offers for dinners or weekend visits to her house. She could have reached out more on her own, but instead had been bogged down by the stress and shame of her spiraling work situation. She had used Covid as an excuse to isolate herself, and now it was too late.

4

The baby is awake, Valerie told the group. *And so far he seems healthy. He's going back home in a couple of days. No word yet on the funeral.*

The fourth day after Claire's death, Serena called Esther, repeatedly, until Esther picked up.

"You haven't been answering my calls," Serena said. "Are you holding up okay?"

"No," Esther said. "Not really."

"Well, I guess none of us are. But I'm glad you picked up this time. I think Laz is having a really hard time. Val and I are planning to go down this weekend to see him and the baby. Can you come?"

Esther shuddered. "I don't know."

"We can pick you up, we can all go together. I think it would mean a lot to him."

"I don't..." Esther said.

"Esther, I know this has hit you hard. It's hit all of us hard. But think of how Laz must be feeling right now. Do this with us, for Claire's sake."

Three days later, for Claire's sake, Esther took a shower, put on clean clothes, made herself presentable, ate a piece of toast over a plate so she wouldn't get crumbs on herself.

For Claire's sake, she was sitting in the Uber with Serena and Val, on their way to Brixton. Val was in the front, chatting with the driver, and Serena and Esther looked out their respective windows under a blanket of silence.

Over the past few days, Esther's grief had morphed and mutated, an ocean of sadness, some moments harrowing, others deceptively calm. The grief she felt for Claire was distorted by the experience she had when she was younger—she was eleven when her brother Caleb died. She knew what it felt like to have a loved one taken too soon. But her experience as an adult was different, and her brain was trying to understand why.

She had known Claire longer and more intimately than she had known her brother. Yes, Caleb had been a constant presence in her life, at least until he went to college when she was ten. Yes, she had adored him. He was, in young man form, her parents' hopes and dreams and happiness—this was clear even to her juvenile self. Her relationship with Claire, though, was on another level. Claire was a sister, a peer, an equal. Claire wasn't someone Esther aspired to be; she was a part of Esther herself. Claire understood her in ways that no one in her family ever would.

When Caleb had died, Esther at eleven had known that he was gone, but she didn't quite understand what this meant. Back then, she believed in heaven, and she thought that she would be reunited with him one day. His death was a loss, and Esther had been sad, but the effect on her had more to do with his absence from the family, and the hurt it caused her parents, than the type of piercing grief that arose from Claire's death. As an adult she understood too fully that Claire would never be in her life again.

Esther was pulled from her rumination by the touch of Serena's hand. "We're almost there," Serena said.

The car wound through the hilly turns of Brixton. Ancient trees stood guard on the sides of the road. The massive houses sat distant and distinct, each protected by a carefully curated landscape.

Esther met eyes with Serena; they were both on the edge of crying and Serena looked away first, as if pulling apart a magnet.

"Nice house," the Uber driver said as he pulled into the driveway. He was young, scruffy. He glanced in the rearview mirror and, taking in Serena and Esther's faces, quickly looked away.

Esther followed her friends to the front porch of the Chen residence. Tall columns lined the landing, and a broad white wooden door loomed. The women wiped their eyes and smoothed out their faces, and Valerie rang the bell.

It was Mrs. Chen who opened the door: thin unnaturally black hair pulled back into a bun, gaunt face retaining shadows of its former plump glory, no doubt due to expensive Japanese or Korean skin creams. She was small but entirely commanding. Serena and Esther recognized her from Claire's wedding, and they had spent decades disliking her on Claire's behalf.

Esther wasn't sure how to address her. Her Chinese was limited to basic household vocabulary and whatever remained of her college Mandarin classes; she didn't know the terms or protocol for condolences. She decided to call her Auntie and hoped this was acceptable.

"*Ayi hao*," Esther said, nodding with an awkward half bow, and Serena followed suit.

Mrs. Chen eyed the women and said something in Chinese. Serena looked to Esther for clarification, but Esther wasn't sure what she said either. Before Esther could ask Mrs. Chen to say it again, the old woman turned away and shouted for Laz in Chinese. She beckoned them in, pointed at the pile of shoes near the door (as if they wouldn't know to take off their shoes).

As Esther stepped into the foyer, Claire's entryway, the breath left her body. The space was too much, too empty, and she grabbed the wall to steady herself.

"Hi guys," Laz said, appearing from some far room of the house. He looked like he had aged ten years with his dark and swollen eyelids, his pallid and puffy skin, the way his body seemed to have already given up trying. The women hugged him, and Esther was crying again, they were all crying again.

He led them to the living room and sat on the couch. Esther chose the armchair, letting Val and Serena sit on opposite sides of Laz. She had wanted to stay out of the way, but she realized that she was sitting directly in Laz's line of sight.

"Thank you for coming," he said in a low voice, looking down.

"Of course," Serena said. "I…"

Esther waited for her to continue, but she didn't say anything else.

"It's hard to find words, Laz," Val said. "We're just so sorry."

Esther gripped the armchair, her fingers digging into the fabric. She wanted to say something, but what would she say?

A ruddy Chinese woman in her fifties came in with a tray of cut fruit. Mrs. Chen followed, holding Jasper high as if bearing a gift. She placed him in Laz's arms.

"He's so sweet," Valerie said, and she asked to hold him. "What a handsome boy." As she cradled the baby, her eyes welled.

"Eat some fruit," commanded Mrs. Chen in Chinese. She and the other woman, who must have been the confinement nurse from Taiwan, stood watch as the group admired the baby.

It was Esther's turn to hold Jasper, then, and she took him because that's what they all seemed to want her to do. He couldn't have been more than ten pounds, but Esther felt laden with his weight in her arms, heady with a sweet and milky smell. With chubby rosy cheeks and fat closed fists, he wore an elephant onesie that she recognized from the baby shower. She was overwhelmed with the thought that Claire never even got to hold him. He would never know his mother.

"Poor baby," she said without thinking.

"Esther!" Serena hissed, taking the baby from her.

Esther reddened and sat on her hands. She was supposed to coo over the baby, not pity him. No one else acknowledged what she said, and she hoped they hadn't heard.

"Jasper's healthy, thank God," Laz said. "They weren't sure if he would have brain damage from the birth. The cooling blanket saved him."

In Chinese, Mrs. Chen remarked that the baby needed to eat, and the confinement nurse gathered Jasper in her arms.

After they left, Laz rubbed his face, leaned forward. "I tried to go in, you know."

"What do you mean?" Serena asked.

"Claire wouldn't stop bleeding after Jasper was born. It all happened so fast. Jasper was born, he wasn't responsive, he was taken to the newborn ICU, and Claire was just bleeding and bleeding. She told me she didn't feel well; I told her to hold on, to stay with me, then the surgeons put her under so they could operate. They made me leave but I could see the monitors through the window. I... all I could do was pray, then, with Claire in surgery and the baby in NICU." Laz looked up, meeting Esther's eyes, but Esther felt that he was looking through her. "I've never prayed so hard."

Esther wanted him to look away, but she knew that he needed to keep going, and she nodded just slightly.

"At one point a Code Blue was called," he said. "The residents came running. I tried to go in, then, tried to run in and help. They pushed me out. Said I couldn't be in there. Pushed me out and shut the door, and all I could do was wait."

"Oh, Laz," Serena murmured.

Laz started to sob. "I'm a doctor, and I couldn't do anything."

"Don't say that," Esther croaked out. "Don't think like that."

Serena nodded her agreement. "You can't think like that."

"I don't know why I'm here and she isn't," he said, trying to gather himself.

Val drew him to her, and resting against her shoulder he seemed to settle.

The weight of grief in that moment brought Esther back to similar moments, heavy in her memory, with her family decades ago. "How is Hannah doing?" Esther asked.

Laz looked up and blinked slowly. "Hannah?"

"Where is she now?" Val asked.

"She must be around here somewhere. I don't know." He pushed himself up but then sank back down again, as if he wasn't strong enough to resist the pull of the sofa.

"I can find her. I'll check on her," Esther said, getting up and escaping the living room.

In the hallway Esther leaned her hand against the wall and took a long breath. As she walked, her shaky fingertips gliding across the paint, its stability was her anchor.

Light shone through the window of the closed playroom door. She knocked and when the door remained shut, she slowly slid it open.

Hannah was attacking a mandala coloring page with a colored pencil. She had started in the center of the page and was moving outward, all blues and purples and greens.

"Hi," Esther said.

Hannah didn't look up.

Esther sat down on the floor, near Hannah but not so near that she could reach out and touch her. She sat and waited, the only sound the scratching of the pencil's angry strokes on the page.

Eventually, Hannah paused her offensive against the coloring book. She stared at Esther, like Laz had earlier, as if she were looking through her.

Esther didn't know what to say. She realized that Hannah was the same age that Didi was when Caleb died. She tried to remember Didi in those days, but she drew a blank. All she could remember of that time was her heartache and, most importantly, the heartache of her parents.

Hannah went back to her work.

"I'm so sorry about your mom," Esther said. Hannah's hand stayed for just a second, then the sound of pencil against paper fell to a steadier *shrr*. "Do you need anything?"

Esther waited for what felt like ages. She took one of the colored pencils and wrote her name and cell number on a piece of scrap paper on the table. "Here. If you need anything, you can call this number. I live nearby, well not too far. You can use your dad's phone, or if you have your own phone, no I remember your mom said you were too young—" Esther clamped her mouth shut for a moment. "You can use your dad's phone if you need anything. Like I remember that you like ice cream, right? I can take you for ice cream some time if you want."

Facing Hannah's continuing silence, Esther crept out of the room and slid the door closed. As she approached the living room, she could hear Serena's voice, sharp and clear. "No—you can't let her take your kids, Laz. That's insane."

***

The idea seemed preposterous to Esther, that Hannah and Jasper would be sent to Taiwan to live with Laz's family.

"I know it sounds crazy," Laz said.

"And you would just live in Philadelphia, by yourself?" Valerie asked.

"Yes, I think so, until things settle down, I guess."

"What do you mean, settle down? What's going to change for you?" Serena asked, a challenge.

Laz just shook his head. "I can't raise them by myself, can I?"

The women glanced at each other. How many times had Claire mentioned how busy Laz was, how he never seemed to have time for Hannah? The Mathey Girls had seen Claire pull double duty as a professor and mother for years; Claire was willing to take up the slack given his job—she had known it would be like this and supported his decision to be a doctor, after all. But, some of the Mathey Girls would argue, he was a research doctor with a lab, not a surgeon with a call schedule.

"Did you find Hannah?" Laz asked Esther.

"She was in the playroom coloring," Esther said. "But she didn't want to talk to me."

"Does she even speak Chinese?" Serena asked.

"No, but she can learn," Laz said, "and there's an international school that teaches in English."

"Your sister has kids, right? You're thinking she would take Hannah and Jasper too?" Serena asked.

"Peipei can't take the kids, or doesn't want to. They would live with my mom. And I would go with them, at first. It's not that unusual, you know, for Chinese grandparents to take care of the kids while the parents work." He addressed this to Valerie, then looked to Serena and Esther for confirmation. "Right?"

Esther just shook her head. She wasn't familiar with this kind of arrangement.

"No—that's for like first-gen immigrants who just arrived and started their careers," Serena said. "Not for parents who have lived in the US for ages. Not for kids who have already started growing up here."

"Could you be a doctor in Taiwan?" Valerie asked. "That way you could be with them. Not that we want to see you go."

"Maybe," Laz said. "I don't know. I wouldn't want to."

"Is Hannah okay?" Esther asked. "I mean, of course she isn't. But how is she?"

Laz considered. "She's been very quiet. She hasn't talked much. But she hasn't cried much either."

"Wait—it's only the middle of May—Hannah's not on summer break yet, right?" Val asked. "What's going to happen with school?"

"She still has a couple weeks. But I'm not sure when she'll go back to school. I don't know if she's ready. It's all... a lot."

Again, the women looked at each other, transmitting concern.

"But the kids—you want to be with your kids, right?" Esther asked.

"Yes, of course," Laz said. "But how is this going to work? Without..."

"Claire would be mortified that you're even thinking about this," Serena said.

"Hey," Val said, gently. "This is difficult for everyone. Let's take a breath here."

"It's just an idea," Laz said in a low whisper.

"It's a terrible idea," Serena said.

The moment hung heavy. "You're right," Laz said, after a moment. "It's not a good idea. I'm not thinking straight these days."

Serena was about to say something, edging forward on her seat, but Val lifted her hand and shook her head.

"How long before your mom goes back?" Esther asked.

"She's going to stay the month that she originally planned for the baby," Laz said.

"So we don't need to make any decisions right away," Val suggested.

"Right," Laz said dully.

"It's a real question though," Esther said to Val and Serena when they were back in an Uber. "How is Laz going to take care of the kids?"

Serena narrowed her eyes. "He has to figure it out. He's their dad."

"I don't get how Laz's mother could take care of a baby and a nine-year-old girl who doesn't speak Chinese," Valerie said.

"She would pay someone to do it," Serena said. "She has the money, I'm sure. She would hire some kind of ayi to raise them."

"*Ayi*, is that an aunt?" Val asked.

"It's the same word in Chinese, for aunt, helper, or nanny," Esther said.

"Couldn't we do that—find a nanny for the kids? I'm sure we could," Val said.

"It would need to be someone that Mrs. Chen approves of," Serena said. "She's definitely pulling the strings here."

"We would probably need to find someone who speaks Chinese," Esther said.

"At least we have a couple weeks before Mrs. Chen goes back," Serena said. "I think we could find someone, somehow."

Esther tried to picture Hannah, coloring, in an apartment in Taipei with Mrs. Chen watching over her. The ancient etched lines around Mrs. Chen's mouth turning down as she looked at the little girl who missed her mother. "You were right, though, what you said to Laz. Claire wouldn't want her kids to be sent away," she said.

"Definitely not," Serena said. "We've got to find help for him here."

"In the meantime, maybe I could do something," Esther said.

"What?" Serena asked.

Valerie turned her body towards the back seat. "What are you thinking?"

"I don't know. Maybe I could help watch the kids." Esther reddened as she realized how stupid this sounded.

"Oh Esther," Val said. "That's very kind of you to offer. Aren't you too busy with work?"

"I'm in between projects... I have some time."

Esther saw skepticism on Serena's face. "Do you even know how to take care of a baby?" Serena asked.

"Hey," Val said. "Be nice."

"Maybe not the baby," Esther said. "But maybe, I mean, I could help with Hannah. Keep her company some of the time, like when Laz goes back to work. Hannah's only a little older than my nephew."

Val and Serena exchanged looks.

"If you wouldn't mind," Val said, "I think it would really help the family."

"I don't mind," Esther said.

Serena got out her phone and paused. "You're sure?"

Esther nodded.

"Okay," Serena said. She started typing on her phone, and soon Esther and Val's phones dinged. Serena had created a new WhatsApp group called *Mathey Help*: Serena, Valerie, Esther, Maggie, Wendy and Laz. Serena sent quick messages in succession:

Laz, thank you for letting us come visit today. Our prayers are with you and your family.

We would like to help in any way possible, especially with the kids. We can look for a nanny for when your mom leaves, and until then Esther can visit Hannah, help her open up maybe.

Esther felt a twinge of doubt as she looked at her phone. Someone like Maggie or Wendy, with kid experience, would know how to deal with Hannah. If only one of them lived closer.

"Hey," Val said, observing from the front seat, "it's going to be okay."

"And what if I don't have what it takes?" Esther asked.

"I mean, Hannah should be easy to take care of, I think," Serena said. "And Val and I won't be far."

They dropped Esther off at her apartment; they were returning to New York that night. She was glad they didn't ask to come up. As she stepped out of the car, she heard Valerie say, "Stay strong, and we'll see you at the memorial." She didn't look back as she hurried into the building.

Esther opened her apartment door to a billow of fetid air. She scanned the kitchen, the dirty dishes, the stray cups, the wadded greasy napkins that hadn't quite made it into the trash can. Her living/dining room was no better. She ran to the windows at the back wall and opened them wide. A faint breeze drifted in.

She needed to clear her apartment of the sadness that had festered for the last week. Being in Claire's house, with its wide airy spaces, showed her how pathetic her apartment was. Especially when it stank of an unwashed, grief-imprinted recluse. Claire wouldn't want her to live this way.

She let shame fuel her determination and cleared her apartment of the visible debris. Then, standing next to her open windows, she texted Laz: *I hope you saw Serena's message. I am here for you, and Hannah, and whatever you might need.*

After she sent it, she felt conflicted at how easily she was able to be productive and functioning again, despite her best friend's death. And—it felt wrong, somehow, texting Laz now that Claire was gone.

She was spraying down her kitchen counters when her phone chimed with a reply from Laz: *I thought about your offer, to help Hannah.*

Esther waited, watched the three blinking dots tell her that he was writing.

She was supposed to be at home with Claire and the baby this summer, he

41

said. *We didn't sign her up for anything.*

Esther understood. In past summers, freed from her teaching duties, Claire had ensured that Hannah had a healthy mix of time with mom and enriching and interesting summer camps. *No camps?* she asked.

No camps. I think it might be too late to sign her up, Laz said.

I will do some digging, see if I can find anything, Esther said. *Anything you were thinking of in particular?*

It took a few minutes for Laz to write back. *I'm not sure.*

Maybe I should speak with Hannah to see what she might be interested in, Esther said.

Oh, he said.

She isn't talking much, he said.

I see, Esther said.

Maybe you could come over again some time and maybe she will open up, he said.

I can come tomorrow, if that works, Esther said.

Thank you. Yes.

Esther wanted to reassure him that things were going to be alright, that they would figure it out together, that he wasn't alone. I can try to help you, I understand how lost you feel without Claire right now, she wanted to say, but her thumbs stayed still, paralyzed by their inability to translate this much feeling into mere lines of text on a screen.

5

Over the next few days, some basic survival instinct dragged Esther out of her initial swamp of sadness. In halting, staggered steps she brought herself to a place where she could conjure good memories of Claire and smile instead of tear up, where she could wake up not mired in grief. Most importantly, she was able to take a shower in the morning and some time during the day go over to Laz's house to see Hannah. Esther had gone three times, and while Hannah still wasn't talking to her, she didn't take it personally; Laz said that Hannah had barely spoken since Claire's death.

Despite the silence, Esther felt like Hannah was warming up to her. She would sit in the playroom or accompany Hannah to the living room if she went to watch TV. She always had a book in her bag, so if Hannah seemed particularly uninterested in her presence she could read or pretend that she was reading. She would stay for an hour or two, providing silent support, then check if Laz or Mrs. Chen needed anything from the store before heading home. Her trips to the Chen house meant that she was having more regular interaction with other people than she'd had in years.

By her fourth such visit to the Chens', Esther knew to go straight to the playroom after greeting the confinement nurse at the door and taking off her shoes. Hannah was engrossed in finishing a jigsaw puzzle when Esther entered.

"Wow, you did that all by yourself? Three hundred pieces is a lot."

Hannah gave a small smile, causing Esther's heart to skip a beat.

"Could I do one?" Esther asked. She surveyed the offerings on the puzzle shelf and pulled out a generic fairy and unicorn scene with 500 pieces. "Maybe this one? I loved doing puzzles when I was a kid."

Hannah nodded and Esther took the puzzle to an empty space on the playroom floor. She opened the box, started looking for edge pieces, and in the periphery of her vision she saw that Hannah was watching her. Without looking up, she said, "You could help me, if you want."

Esther kept working, slowly and methodically, plucking out edge pieces and laying them to the side. A small pile amassed, and then Hannah was at her side, trying to match the edge pieces together. Esther didn't say anything, simply continued to search for edge pieces and set them in a pile next to Hannah when she found them.

Once Esther had trouble finding edge pieces in the box, she began to work on piecing together the edge opposite from the one Hannah was working on. They worked silently until they had nearly completed the frame of the puzzle.

"How do you think we should do the middle?" Esther asked in a quiet voice.

Hannah took the box lid and pointed at the unicorn dominating the picture. Together they started pulling white pieces out of the box. They took turns without touching each other—but they were very close.

As Hannah started to piece the body of the unicorn together, Esther's phone buzzed with a message from Didi asking if he could stay at her apartment when he came for Claire's memorial service, which was happening at the end of the week.

Esther held her phone close to her chest and walked to the corner of the playroom, hoping that Hannah hadn't seen the message. Her first instinct was to tell Didi that he didn't need to come to the memorial—neither of them was good with things like funerals—but if he really wanted to come, it would be better for him to stay at a hotel. She knew this was cowardly, though, so she didn't respond to his message immediately.

When she went back to Hannah, she saw that the unicorn was nearly completed. "I could really go for some ice cream," Esther said softly. Hannah looked at her and seemed to be wrestling with something inside. "Would you wanna get some? Get out of the house for a little bit?"

Hannah started to shake her head no, then she gave the smallest of nods.

"Hold on," Esther said.

She went to the living room where she found Laz and Mrs. Chen discussing the memorial service. "Would it be okay if I take Hannah to get some ice cream?"

"Yes, of course," Laz said. "She wants to go?"

"I guess so," Esther said. "Oh, and before I forget to tell you, I finally found a therapist for her. I made an appointment for his first available, not for another three weeks, but better than the months that others mentioned."

Mrs. Chen looked at Esther as if evaluating her intentions.

"He has a high rating on Google," Esther said.

"Thanks, Esther," Laz said. He took his keys from his pocket and held them out. "To take her to ice cream."

In the garage, Hannah stiffened when she saw Claire's green Prius. Esther thought of the many trips Claire and Hannah would have taken together in that car, how many little chats they would have had, how many glances in the rearview mirror Claire would have given to Hannah, each moment both special and mundane.

Esther put her hand on Hannah's shoulder and guided her to the other side of Laz's BMW.

At the ice cream shop, Hannah pointed at the cotton candy flavor, and they ate sitting on the benches outside. Esther was glad that she had thought to ask Hannah if she wanted sprinkles. Hannah ate slowly, deliberately, and Esther could tell that she was struggling with how much to enjoy it. She recalled that feeling from her childhood well.

When they went back after ice cream, Mrs. Chen asked Esther if she wanted to stay for dinner, but Esther politely declined. She was happy to spend time with Hannah, but dinner with Mrs. Chen was another thing entirely.

Esther was waiting for her Uber when Laz joined her on the landing outside.

"Thanks for coming again," Laz said.

"No problem." She studied his worn face. She was never sure what to say around Laz these days.

"Did she... say anything to you today?" he asked.

"No, but we did a puzzle together. And I'm pretty sure she enjoyed the ice cream."

Laz glanced down and smiled at the ground briefly before looking back up. "I asked her last night if she wanted to get ice cream after dinner and she point-blank refused—without words, of course. She seems to just want me to leave her alone most of the time."

"I'm sure that's not the case," Esther said, unsure.

"Well, anyway. She was willing to go with you today. That's a good thing. Oh, your car's here," Laz said, pointing.

In the car, Esther savored her progress with Hannah that day. She had known that Hannah didn't mind her company; maybe she actually enjoyed it. She would order some puzzles online for overnight delivery, she decided. This could be a thing they did together.

Her phone buzzed. It was Didi, texting again. He had booked his flight and a hotel near the airport.

Cancel the hotel, she wrote. *You can stay with me.*

***

Esther had always suspected that Didi had a crush on Claire during college. A lot of boys did, though by junior year, when Didi came to New Jersey, Claire was thoroughly taken by and attached to Laz.

By junior year Esther was finally on solid ground at Princeton. Her sophomore year had been a mishmash as she tossed away her pre-med dreams and tried to figure out what she really wanted. By the end of sophomore year, she had decided to major in economics because why not, a lot of people were doing it, it wasn't crazy hard as long as she didn't do the math track, and it left her options open. Banker, consultant, lawyer, whatever. An econ major declaration at Princeton University in the early 2000s was an announcement that she didn't have a passion for anything in particular, wasn't excellent at anything in particular, and she was okay with that.

Junior year was different, because she had finally settled on a major, yes, but also because the Mathey Girls were no longer living in Mathey. Gone were the days of the coddled *Don't worry parents, we'll take care of your precious children* residential college. Claire, Maggie, Serena and Esther were living in Spelman, the only block of upperclassmen housing where the dorms had kitchens. In other words, the dorm for the weirdos who weren't joining eating clubs—the mansions lining Prospect Avenue where almost all upperclassmen drank, ate, socialized, networked, and bonded.

The Mathey Girls had a ready list of reasons they didn't join eating clubs. Drinking alcohol made Esther throw up; eating clubs were expensive and her fees would be subsidizing everyone else's poison. Serena was appalled by the idea of students, often with higher levels of melanin, serving other students, mostly students with lower levels of melanin, the gross extenuation of class privilege. Claire objected on conservative Christian grounds. Maggie just really liked to cook. Wendy, who lived in a single dorm nearby, didn't care one way or the other about the eating clubs but why would she join a club if her friends wouldn't be there? So, the Mathey Girls pretended to be mini-adults, cooking dinners and avoiding the alcohol, class privilege and 'un-Christian' behavior down on "The Street."

Far away from the center of campus, Didi had started as a freshman in Forbes College. It was the newest and nicest residential college, but it was also removed from everyone else. At the time, and still, Didi and Esther were both close and not close. They shared trauma as siblings, but their opposing personalities kept them from building on that connection to grow a deeper relationship.

Esther was glad that Didi was in Forbes, that he was pre-med and, unlike her, actually seemed to belong there. She checked in on him because her parents asked her to and invited him for dinner once a week. Her roommates took to him right away, calling him Didi instead of Andrew, because that's what Esther called him. They saw him as an extension of her, and they loved her so they loved him, but it was also true that Didi got along with people in a way that Esther never did. Claire told Esther that Didi seemed lonely, that he could use some sisterly guidance, and Esther was happy for her friends to act as big sisters to him too.

Now Didi was coming for Claire's memorial service. It would be awkward going with Didi, but maybe it would be a little bit comforting. And, Esther reasoned, they didn't have to talk about their last funeral together. They didn't have to talk about their brother Caleb.

***

By the time Didi got to Esther's apartment the night before the memorial, it was past eleven. His flight had been delayed two hours and the delay showed on his worn face and wrinkled clothes. Still, he arrived with a smile and hug for Esther, and she was glad to see him.

"Nice place," Didi said. "It's bigger than I thought it would be." He surveyed Esther's living/dining room and took a deep breath in. "And it smells like a forest."

"That would be the cleaning stuff I used," Esther said. "You're good with sleeping on the couch, right? It's comfy. I've slept on it before."

Didi nodded and pulled his suitcase to a corner.

"Sit," she said, motioning to the small dining table. "Do you want some water?"

"I could use a drink," he said.

"Oh, shit," she said. "I don't have alcohol. I don't drink. Should I go get something?"

Didi grunted. "I forgot. No, it's fine, water's good."

Esther brought him water and two packs of Tastykake Butterscotch Krimpets, the small highly processed frosted cakes wrapped in cellophane that had been his favorite in college.

"Nice," he said, opening a pack. "This takes me back. I used to get these all the time from the Wa." Like Esther, during college Didi had stocked up on Tastykake Krimpets at Wawa, the ubiquitous East Coast convenience store that everyone on campus called "the Wa".

Esther took the second cake from the open pack and took a bite. "These are sweeter than I remember," she said.

"If I lived here, I would eat these all the time," he said. "Crystal would kill me."

"How is Crystal?"

Didi's face lit up. "She's great. She's killing it at work, Section Head of her group at the Clinic now, which keeps her busy but also lets her have more control of her patient time and the executive decision-making stuff she likes."

Esther let Didi brag about his wife. She and Crystal were friendly, but they weren't really friends. "And Mom and Dad are okay?" she asked.

"They're fine," he said. "They miss you. They told me to tell you that."

She chose not to respond to that particular comment. It had been a while since she called and years since she had gone home to Cleveland to visit.

"You seeing anyone?" Didi asked. "Mom and Dad told me to ask."

"Ugh. No, not currently."

"Whatever happened to Lewis Chang?"

"I broke up with him like a decade ago, Didi."

"I thought you guys might get married or something, back then."

"Things didn't work out." Esther recalled how difficult it had been with Lewis, both of them trying to find time in their schedules, fighting over last-minute cancellations due to work trips or calls, gradually giving up as they realized they were only trying to make their families happy by committing to a serious relationship.

She steered discussion back to Didi's work, and then they moved on to his young children Benjamin and Bonnie, his airplane delay, and the weather in both Cleveland and Philly.

They didn't mention Claire. Esther had decided that she would let Didi take the lead—if he wanted to talk about her, she would, but otherwise it would be as it always was between them. Cordial. Pleasant. Familiar, so deeply familiar that harder topics could be understood without being discussed.

A moment came where Didi opened his mouth and paused. Esther waited, expecting him to say something about Claire. "About—about the memorial tomorrow."

"Yeah?" Under the table Esther clenched her fingers together.

Didi stood up. "Do you have an iron? I need to press my suit. Or maybe I'll do it in the morning. I'm pretty tired."

"Right. You should get some sleep," Esther said, gathering the sticky Tastykake wrappers in her hand and crumpling them into a ball. "Let me get the sheets."

6

Esther and Didi arrived at the memorial hall early, to help as needed, but there were already dozens of people, and empty seats for hundreds more. At the front of the long room, on the podium, were Claire's ashes. The urn sat between a picture of Claire, alone, smiling, radiant, and a picture of her with Laz and Hannah. In each of them, she looked at the camera, unashamed to be alive. There was no fear in her eyes in those pictures.

Esther stood frozen by the photos until Serena brought Hannah to her.

Hannah was wearing the crushed velvet dress Esther had bought at Macy's two days ago. Hannah hadn't wanted to go shopping, so Esther had picked it out for her. In the Macy's girls' department, she had debated between two versions of the dress: black and dark purple. She had texted the Mathey Girls asking if she absolutely had to pick the black. It was so somber and foreboding. The purple should be okay, Valerie had said, and Esther was glad that she had been given that permission.

She took Hannah's hand, and they went to their seats at the end of the front row. It would be Esther, then Hannah, then Laz, then Mrs. Chen, then the confinement nurse with Jasper. Mrs. Chen and the confinement nurse were wearing surgical masks, as were most of Claire's extended family sitting behind them. An aunt and some older cousins that Claire had never talked about had traveled from California, but Esther couldn't see enough of their faces to see any resemblance to her friend. Laz's sister Peipei had flown in from Taiwan, leaving her husband and children behind.

The rest of the hundreds of seats would be filled with others who cherished Claire. No blood connecting them, no legal obligations, just love and respect. There would be many from Penn, from the

Economics Department and other departments: professors, students, support staff. There were old classmates from Princeton, people Esther hadn't really interacted with because she had the Mathey Girls, but whom Claire had still loved and appreciated. People from Claire's church, people from her time at Yale as a grad student, people from who knows where.

As the seats behind them filled, the murmuring and shuffling crescendoed. "Are you doing okay?" Esther asked Hannah.

Hannah didn't reply; she was staring at the picture of her mom to the left of the urn. Her black eyes were soaking in the blown-up portrait, pixels too obvious as close as they were. Esther didn't know the context of the picture; it was taken outside, in autumn, beautiful enough to be mistaken for a professional portrait if not for the pixels. Laz had probably taken it. Imagine taking a picture of your wife at her most radiant, not knowing that it would be used at her memorial service.

Esther and Hannah sat alone in their row, waiting. The Mathey Girls came to check on them, one by one, and Esther was happy to see them, but she was also struggling with too many feelings inside. This was the first funeral-type event that Esther had attended since Caleb's, having made excuses for all the others. For Hannah's sake, Esther was glad that Mrs. Chen had insisted on cremation. Esther remembered too well her brother Caleb in his casket at the funeral. The mask of funeral makeup had horrified her. She had touched his hand, not thinking, and not only was it icy cold, but she had smudged some of the makeup. She remembered looking at her finger, at the smudge of makeup she had stolen from her brother's body.

She pulled herself away from the unwanted memory and turned to look at the rows of chairs filling behind her. She saw Didi at the back of the room with someone who looked vaguely familiar, someone from college, and she was surprised because Didi was crying. This morning at her apartment he had been his normal, collected, easygoing self. But now he was being pulled into an embrace by the Princeton guy, his body wracked by a sob. Esther realized that Hannah had turned to follow her gaze; she guided Hannah's shoulders back to looking at her.

"It's going to be okay," Esther said, and Hannah nodded.

When the service was about to start, Laz came to sit down. He ran his hand over Hannah's hair and gave Esther a meager smile. "Thank you," he said to her, and let his body fall, heavy, into his seat.

Claire's pastor, a man who looked to Esther too young and too scrawny to be a Man of God, began the services. Esther had almost forgotten how religious Claire was. She had always been respectful of Esther's own complicated relationship with church and God, never pushing her own views. But of course Claire's memorial would be a religious ceremony. She would have wanted that.

A hymn was sung, then the pastor gave his eulogy for Claire. He praised her brilliance, her generosity, her optimism. She was beloved, he said, and Esther felt a hurt jealousy. Yes, Claire was all of those great things, and yes she was beloved, but had he really known her? Did he understand how magnetic she was? She was so competent, at everything, but she never came across as arrogant.

Then the Dean of the Penn Economics Department said something and again Esther was aggravated by how superficial his assessment of Claire was. Claire was more than smart, more than kind. She was more than a great teacher. She was special, and her pastor and her colleagues weren't doing her justice.

It was the family's turn, now, and since Laz had told Valerie that he didn't want to say anything, his sister Peipei went to the podium. She talked about how Claire had made her little brother so happy that even though he was far away from his family in Taiwan, they were peaceful knowing that he was taken care of.

Esther snuck glances at Hannah, who sat on her hands as she stared unblinking at her aunt at the podium. Esther put her arm on the back of Hannah's chair, without touching her, to let her know that she was there, that Hannah wasn't alone.

To the right of Hannah, Esther saw that Laz was just a larger version of his daughter. Each of them sat upright, facing forward, staring ahead, a forced formality providing them with a sense of control. Laz's lips quivered and the muscles stiffened in his cheeks.

And then it was Serena's turn to speak.

I first met Claire when I was eighteen years old, a freshman at Princeton University, in the Mathey residential college. I lived in a quad dorm, one entryway from the dorm that she shared with her roommates Maggie, Victoria and Misha. From the first time I met her, at an icebreaker for our RA group, it was obvious that she was smart, brilliant, but also surprisingly generous and empathetic. She greeted life with open eyes and greeted people with open arms. Literally. She was probably the most prolific hugger I have ever met. (laughter)

I have had the privilege of being one of Claire's closest friends for the past twenty years. Claire was, in many ways, the center of our group of friends—organizer, reuniter, empathizer, even conflict resolver. In every role that Claire was in, she acted with generosity and grace. I cannot express how much I miss her, how much we will all miss her. (Valerie handed her a tissue.) *Thank you. I swear, I don't usually cry in public. Or ever.*

This memorial service has been very bittersweet. We mourn the loss of our friend, sister, colleague, the special presence that she was in every sphere of her life. But we have to celebrate that we had Claire in our lives for even this short period. We have to celebrate the beautiful family she had with Laz and Hannah and now baby Jasper. We have to be grateful that we were touched by her kindness, that we can live our lives with her memory and the blessing that she bestowed on us just by her presence.

I believe that Claire is in a better place now, looking down at us. I also believe that that better place has been made even better by having Claire in it. We love you, Claire.

Esther turned once again to Hannah and her father beyond her. Laz was crying, bent over, head in his hands. Her own eyes welled, but she saw that Hannah was watching her now. Hannah, who still hadn't cried, though her eyes were red and her face was flushed. She wrapped her arms around Hannah, rubbed her back, and she felt Hannah loosen and bury her face in her dress.

After another hymn, the pastor announced that the service was over, with the family's gratitude to everyone who came and refreshments available for the guests.

"Thank you for speaking for us, today," Wendy said to Serena.

Serena nodded with pursed lips.

The Mathey Girls had moved a row of chairs into a haphazard circle. Everyone looked aged and tired, and Esther knew that she looked the same.

"It was good to see Didi," Maggie said. "Claire was always so nice to him."

"She was so nice to everyone," Serena said.

"I hope Laz's family appreciates how amazing Claire was now. I mean, it's too late, but..." Maggie blew her nose.

After a pause, Wendy cleared her throat. "Laz's sister isn't how I thought she'd be, given how Claire described her," she said.

"What do you mean?" Val asked.

"She seems very intimidated by her mother," Wendy said.

"Everyone's intimidated by her mother," Valerie said.

"Laz isn't afraid," Wendy said. "I suppose it's because he's the boy."

"Remember when Hannah was young, and Mrs. Chen would always ask Claire when she was going to have a boy?" Serena asked.

Esther turned to look at Hannah, who was standing with Laz and the rest of the family in the receiving line. Laz was holding her hand, and she was gazing at her shoes. Esther didn't remember the receiving line at her brother's funeral. But that one had been different—after the ceremony they had gone in the funeral car to the cemetery to lower the casket. She remembered how it had been raining that day, how her mother had wailed when the casket descended into the earth, and how she had clutched Didi's hand.

***

The night of the memorial, Didi wanted to go for drinks, and the Mathey Girls agreed on a bar near Penn to drown their sorrows. Didi asked if he should text some other Princeton people in town for the memorial, but the Mathey Girls said no, just them please. He was free to join his other friends if he wanted, they said. Didi stayed with them.

Valerie texted Laz, told him they would be waiting with open arms if he wanted to get out, but they didn't expect him to come. He was functioning—replying to texts, answering questions, making arrangements—but he seemed empty, as if he had collapsed within himself.

"To Claire," Wendy said, holding her glass up, and their glasses met.

Esther was drinking a cranberry soda with lime. Everyone else had the privilege of alcohol to ease their pain, to help them loosen up in their grief.

When she was working, Esther had gone to countless drinks as the reliable, sober colleague, letting everyone get sloshed and transform into totally different people while she stayed the same, promising not to tell anyone what she heard and saw, listening to secrets, hearing confessions, pretending to engage in sane debate with someone who was slurring both words and ideas. At the end of the night, she made sure people got into cabs back to their hotels or their houses, or sometimes back to the office. More than once, she had accompanied young women to their apartments, supported them up stairs and in elevators, helped to unlock doors when keys fumbled in locks, held hair back, prepared wet washcloths, fetched cups of water, rummaged for Tylenol, taken off shoes, tucked into bed, and crept back out once her charges were safe and reasonably clean and asleep.

Drinks were exhausting for someone who didn't drink.

Esther wished her metabolism would cooperate, just once, where she could obliterate herself along with the people around her, let someone else take care of her for a change.

"I can't cry anymore," Maggie said, looking down at her glass. "I think I've cried out all my tears."

Wendy put her arm around her. Maggie was the first to lay claim to Claire's friendship; four years of living together and then decades of sisterhood. Unlike most of the Mathey Girls, in the years since college Claire and Maggie had talked almost every week.

The music in the bar was too loud for a group conversation; no one had the energy to shout across the table, so they retreated to their drinks. They drank as if drinking would bring their friend back, just for one more hug, one more smile.

At one point, Maggie put her hand on Esther's shoulder to steady herself. "Claire was better at life than I was," she said, tilting slightly forward. "She made it all work, with her job and her family." Her eyes welled, her tears coming back after all. "I feel like a failure. But Claire said I wasn't a failure. She said I was just as good as she was. But I'm not."

Esther didn't know what to say, so she gave Maggie a hug.

Didi was talking to Serena and Wendy across the table, loud and sloppy. "I thought I was in love with Claire in college."

"Poor Didi," Wendy said.

"I thought I wanted to marry her someday, even though she had a boyfriend."

Serena clapped Didi on the back. "We all knew," she said.

"He's a great guy, Laz," Didi said, slurring the z. "And I figured it out, I figured out that I didn't want to marry Claire. I just wanted to have her as my sister."

"Shh," Wendy said.

"Sometimes Claire was nicer to me than my own sister," Didi said, a stage whisper, as if Esther wasn't across the table listening to this very conversation.

Wendy and Serena looked at Esther to see if she had heard. *It's fine*, Esther mouthed to them, but it stung.

Valerie, who still looked fairly sober, pulled Esther close. "He doesn't mean it," she said.

"He might be right, though."

"No," Valerie said, wagging a finger, and Esther understood that Val was more drunk than she looked. "You're a great sister."

Esther knew this wasn't true, and how would Val know, but she nodded anyway.

"And," Valerie said, "everyone had a crush on Claire. I think Claire was the person that made Serena realize she was gay."

"What?" Serena shouted. "I heard my name."

"Claire made you know you were gay," Valerie said.

"Claire made me gay," Serena said, laughing, and the Mathey Girls shared a round of bitter laughter.

Esther knew that she could never repeat what she heard from Valerie or Maggie or Didi, or any of the other Mathey Girls tonight. She was a receptacle of the truths that the alcohol had unleashed, an unwilling trash can.

Later in the evening, Laz came after all. By that time the bar was filling up, and they didn't see him until he was almost at the table.

Laz, face puffy and discolored under the dim lights, wearing the same button-down shirt he had worn at the memorial service, its wrinkled untucked edges now hanging over jeans. He was greeted with hugs and sad shouts of welcome. "I couldn't sleep," he said, sitting down between Serena and Didi.

"We got started without you," Maggie said. "But we'll get you caught up."

Shots were ordered, downed, re-ordered.

Esther tried to remain inconspicuous. Laz wanted to be drunk, everyone else wanted him drunk, and she didn't want to distract from their mission.

It didn't take long for everyone to grow weepy and sodden. After a couple of drinks Laz's face was a deep red. "We did it," Wendy said, pointing to his cheek.

Claire wouldn't have wanted to see this, Esther thought. She had let Laz drink, but not too much, and the extent of his Asian flush, redder than all of them, was proof that he had drunk too much. But then, Claire would have wanted Laz to be happy. But then, Esther thought, Claire would never have wanted to die, to leave Laz and Hannah and the baby.

Didi and Laz were huddled together now, Didi in earnest confession, Laz nodding and saying it was okay, and the two men crying, arms around each other.

By 1 a.m., stillness had settled over the group. Wendy and Didi were still talking to each other, somehow. Valerie was looking at her phone. Serena was asleep, face flushed and mouth open as she leaned against the booth. Maggie and Laz had finished reminiscing, musing about Claire back in college, and sat looking at nothing, each in their private fog. The bar was full now, and loud.

A white guy stopped as he passed their table. "Hey, why so sad?" he shouted. "It's Saturday night!" He lifted his two hands, holding beers.

Valerie sat up. "What the fuck," she said. "Who are you to tell us how to feel?"

The white guy started back. "Hey, everyone in here is happy except you."

"Fuck you," Valerie shouted. Everyone was watching now.

"Fuck you, bitch," the white guy shouted back, and Esther stood up to block Valerie's line of vision.

"Our friend just died," Esther said.

"What?" the white guy asked.

"OUR FRIEND DIED. HER MEMORIAL SERVICE WAS TODAY," Esther shouted.

The white guy backed up, bumped into someone else who told him to fuck off, spilled some of the beer. He looked at the stricken faces at the table, his gaze resting on Laz and Didi. "Sorry bro," he said. "Sorry for your loss." Then he was gone.

The group looked at each other, stunned into near sobriety.

"I think it's time to go home," Laz said.

7

When Esther arrived at the Chen house two days after the memorial service, it was Hannah who opened the door. As soon as Esther took off her shoes, before she had a chance to line them up against the wall, Hannah grabbed her sleeve and led her to the playroom.

Hannah slid the door shut and motioned for Esther to sit by the wall farthest from the entrance.

Standing over her, Hannah took a deep breath. "Don't freak out," she said.

"Holy shit," Esther said. "Sorry. Oh my gosh. You're talking again."

"Only to you."

Esther wanted to give Hannah a hug, a high five, shout some kind of congratulations, but the look on Hannah's face stopped her. "What's wrong?" she asked.

"Don't let her take me," Hannah said.

"What do you mean?"

"She wants to take me to Taiwan. Auntie Peipei."

"What the… they still want to do that?"

"You knew?" Hannah asked. "Why didn't you tell me?"

"I thought your dad decided it was a terrible idea. And it's not like the two of us were having conversations."

Hannah fell back into a beanbag and looked at the ceiling. "Auntie Peipei told me last night that she wanted me to go back with her. She has a dog and two kids; the kids are older than I am, in high school, but she says I can get a lot of new toys." She sat up. "I don't want new toys. I don't want to go with her."

Esther studied the wall, trying to process. "What does your dad think?"

"I don't know," Hannah said. "I haven't talked to him."

"But you can talk to him now, just like you're talking to me,"

Esther said.

Hannah closed her eyes. "It's weird now. I didn't want to talk, at first, and so I didn't, and then I wanted to talk, but I didn't, and now it's weird."

"It doesn't have to be weird," Esther said, but Hannah was shaking her head. Esther remembered Claire mentioning how stubborn Hannah was, how black and white.

Esther was about to say something when Hannah bolted upright in the beanbag, jabbed her finger toward the door then brought it to her lips. *Shh*, she mouthed. Esther turned and saw a shadow at the door, someone about to come in, or listening in. Esther and Hannah remained quiet and eventually the shadow moved on.

"I think that was Auntie Peipei," Hannah whispered.

"When is she going back to Taiwan?" Esther whispered back.

"I don't know. Soon."

Later, as Esther was getting ready to head back home, Peipei asked if she wanted to join her for bubble tea. Esther looked into Peipei's face, a mixture of Laz and Mrs. Chen, and found she couldn't say no.

Peipei hadn't gone to Claire and Laz's wedding, so many years ago, saying that she needed to be with her babies, she couldn't leave them in Taiwan. The Mathey Girls had understood that this was just an excuse. After all, Laz had told them how Peipei had two live-in nannies for her kids, plus a housekeeper. Poor Claire had tried to conceal her disappointment when she talked about it. An only child, Claire had hoped that her sister-in-law would be like a true sister, a trusted friend and confidante. It turned out, she told the Mathey Girls, that they were her real sisters, after all.

As Esther understood it, Laz had fought his family to marry Claire and stay in the United States after medical school. His grandfather on his mother's side had founded a hospital in Taipei, and the family had wanted him to assume the mantle once his education was complete. Instead, he had decided to marry an American—true, she was Chinese American and could speak some Chinese, but still, she refused to move to Taiwan—and Peipei had shown her disapproval by avoiding the wedding, avoiding Claire and even avoiding Hannah in the early years.

Now, Esther wanted to think the best about Peipei who was, by blood, the closest mother-type figure in Hannah's family. She looked kind, unlike Mrs. Chen, and Claire had said that Peipei had apologized to her during Claire's first trip to Taiwan, that Peipei had genuinely seemed to adore Hannah on that trip.

Peipei and Esther were getting into the BMW in the garage when Laz opened the door to the backseat and slid in. Esther glanced behind her, confused, but neither Laz nor Peipei said anything. As Peipei backed the car out of the garage and drove down the long sloping driveway to the street, Laz crouched down, near sideways in the footwells. A few blocks from the house, Peipei pulled over to the side. She and Laz opened their doors.

"What's going on?" Esther asked. "Am I being kidnapped?"

Neither Peipei nor Laz laughed as they switched seats so that Laz could drive.

"Sorry," Laz said. "We didn't want my mom to know I came along."

"And why is that?" Esther asked.

They drove past a bubble tea shop and Esther trailed it with her finger. "There's the bubble tea place..."

Peipei scoffed. "That's not real bubble tea. That's like water. We're going to a real place." Peipei sounded much more Chinese than Laz. Both of them had been sent to the US for high school and college, but the subsequent years in Taiwan meant that Peipei's accent was more pronounced. While fluent, her English sounded as if it had been mangled and rebuilt. Almost right, but not quite there.

They passed another tea shop and soon they were on I-76. "We're going to Chinatown," Peipei said, answering Esther's question before she could ask it.

At the bubble tea shop, Peipei paid for their drinks, and they sat in a small booth in the back. Esther gripped her lemon yogurt slush, felt the cold emanating through the flimsy plastic of the cup.

"First of all," Peipei said, "I want to say thanks for helping with Hannah. She is not talking to us yet, but I heard you guys talking in the playroom, so I'm glad that she is getting better."

Laz raised his hand. "Wait, Hannah talked to you? Were you going to tell me?"

"It was a surprise to me too," Esther said. "I was going to tell—"

"Shh, Lazarus," Peipei said. "Let me finish."

Laz nodded.

"You know my mom?" Peipei asked, as if this were a question. "My mom really wants the kids to go back to Taiwan. At first, she thought she could take them, but now she wants me to take them because she thinks I can do a better job of taking care of them. Maybe, maybe not. But I know Lazarus doesn't want them to go."

Laz was rubbing his fingers across the top of his forehead. "No, I don't," he said.

"So, what do we do?" Peipei asked. "I love the kids—I would be okay if they came back with me. We could find an ayi and everything for them. We have the space. But, if Lazarus wants them to stay, and they want to stay, which seems like Hannah does, then it's a different story."

Esther took a sip and let two boba pearls rest on her tongue.

"The question is what is best for the kids, and for Lazarus," Peipei said.

Esther chewed and swallowed. "And what do I have to do with this?" she asked.

Peipei looked at Laz. "Peipei needs to go home soon," Laz said. "And I'm going back to work, and my mom and Lin ayi are scheduled to go back a week after. I need to convince my mom that I can take care of the kids on my own. The problem is that I don't know if I can."

"No, he cannot," Peipei said. Laz dropped his head. "We need to hire some nannies as soon as possible. I can find a Chinese ayi for the baby. Hannah is harder," she said.

"But even with a nanny..." Laz said, "I don't think my mom is going to believe that my kids are okay."

"I can help look for a nanny," Esther said. "No problem."

Laz and Peipei glanced at each other. Peipei leaned forward. "Lazarus says you're taking a break from work."

Esther blushed. "I mean, I've been freelancing—"

"But you're not working now?" Peipei asked.

"I was going to look for new projects this summer."

Peipei took a sip of her milk tea and studied Esther as if waiting for Esther to understand what she wanted her to understand.

"I can... be Hannah's... nanny?" Esther asked.

Peipei laughed sharply. "You went to Princeton! You won't be anyone's nanny." She leaned forward again. "But we can tell my mom that you will be helping to take care of her, right?"

"I mean, I'm happy to visit," Esther said, uneasy.

"We can pay you for your time," Peipei said.

Laz looked at his sister in consternation. "Peipei."

"It's not a problem," Peipei said.

Esther looked to Laz for help. "I'm not sure exactly what you're asking me to do."

"I'm not sure exactly what Peipei is thinking either," Laz said, "but it would mean a lot to me if you would keep visiting Hannah, being a part of her life, just until we get everything settled down."

"Of course," Esther said. "Did you think I wouldn't?" As she asked that, though, she realized that she hadn't given much thought to how many more daily visits she would give Hannah. At some point, she had thought, Hannah would talk, the Chens would find a nanny, things would normalize, and they could continue their lives without her intruding.

"Just for now," Peipei said. "Maybe through the summer."

Esther turned to Laz. "Whatever happened with Hannah's school? Is she going back?"

"I called the school last week," Peipei said. "Hannah doesn't need to go back to school."

"She doesn't want to," Lazarus added. "I tried to tell her it might be good to see her friends, her teachers, and she refused. Had a fit. More than once."

"It's okay. They'll send some homework for her to do. They'll work with us. That school is so expensive, they better work with us!" Peipei laughed, then settled her face to match Esther's. "Hannah will be fine. She just needs some special attention right now. And she likes you, even talks to you."

"I'm just so glad she's talking again," Lazarus said. "Thank you, Esther."

"I mean, I want to help," Esther said. It was true. How could she not help? "But I don't know anything about taking care of a kid."

"Just spend time with her," Peipei said. "That's all."

Esther considered the hope on Laz's face. "I can spend time with her," she said. "Of course I can spend time with her."

"Just let Lazarus know how much we should pay," Peipei said, "and I'll take care of it."

Esther shook her head. "I don't think that's necessary."

"Are you sure?" Lazarus asked. "If it takes you away from your work?"

"Money's not the issue," Esther said. "I have some savings." She had been chipping away at her savings for months now, but she could last a while longer.

"Esther's not the type of girl to spend her money on expensive things, you can tell," Peipei said, eying the faux leather satchel that hung on the back of Esther's chair. Esther wanted to defend herself, but it was true, that purse was something her mom had found at TJMaxx and given to her years ago.

"Okay. You know, it doesn't matter what you do with Hannah," Peipei said and, seeing Esther's surprised expression, added, "I mean, all that matters is that my mom believes that Hannah is in good hands."

"And that Hannah actually is taken care of," Esther said. "Right?"

"Of course," Laz said.

"Of course," Peipei said, but her face remained impassive. "I'll talk to Mom and let her know."

***

For her new non-official non-job as Hannah's non-nanny, Esther got herself a used car and drove it up to Brixton the following Monday morning. In the open garage, Laz was heading out for his first day back at work, and it was strange to see him in his dress clothes again, put together. He wore a red tie with a blue striped shirt; Esther guessed that if he had tried to wear that combination before, Claire would have steered him to change one or the other.

He was a hematopathologist, which Esther understood meant that he looked at slides and dealt with cancer patients rather than autopsies of the dead like a regular pathologist. When Covid had first struck, and everyone had gone remote, the Mathey Girls were grateful with Claire that he didn't need to deal with Covid patients, that he wasn't one of the ones who had to go to the trenches and expose himself to the mysterious deadly terrifying scourge.

Laz was a doctor, but he was a scientist and an academic, and in that way he and Claire had been very similar. Scientists, but not entirely scientific. Academics, but also truly interested in people.

"You have a car now?" Laz asked when she got out.

"Yeah, I got a used one." She had chosen a Civic because it would be reliable and easy to maneuver and park in the city. It was black, because that was the color that they had in the lot, and it was ready to go.

"I forgot," Laz said. "You used to drive a lot during college."

Esther nodded. She had made the long drive between Cleveland and Princeton many times, often alone—dreamy, contemplative eight-hour trips where she listened to music and let her mind wander over everything and nothing. After graduation Didi kept the car, and as a consultant, she was never in one place long enough to justify buying her own.

"You didn't buy this car for Hannah, did you?" Laz asked.

Esther started to deny it but settled into a shrug. Seeing the question on Laz's face she added, "It's fine, Laz. I have savings. And it was used."

"I would have let you use the Prius," Laz said, and then shook his head no. "Maybe not." He threw a backward glance at the Prius before looking past Esther. "I guess I will need to get rid of that car, at some point. Claire loved it, though."

"Are you ready for your first day?" she asked, hoping to divert him from his sorrow.

Laz looked at her with a wary hope. "I'm looking forward to getting back to normal life. Not that life will be normal, you know, I'm not saying life will ever be normal." And just like that they were both tearing up again, and Esther gave him a hug.

He felt very thin. She smelled his cologne, and it seemed wrong for him to try to smell nice when his wife was gone. "You'll be okay," she said, the words forced out of her throat, husky.

As Esther watched his BMW retreat down the driveway, it struck her how lucky he was that he could drive away from this very moment. She felt a pang of nostalgia for the days when all she had to think about was work, when the pressure of her job had eaten all of her free emotion and energy, when she was a consultant super engine dedicated to her mandate, her clients, whatever project she was staffed on.

Inside the house, Esther tried to entice Hannah away from the TV. "Just think—now with a car we can go all around the city. Like to museums, or new parks. It's so nice outside."

Hannah kept her eyes on the screen, but Esther could tell that she was listening.

"How about the children's museum," Esther said.

"You mean the Please Touch Museum?"

"Yeah—it's supposed to be really fun."

Hannah shook her head after a moment. "No... I'm too big for it now."

"Art Museum?"

"Too boring."

"Franklin Institute?"

"Too crowded."

"How about just a new park, one farther away?"

"I've been to all the parks," Hannah said.

"There's no way you've been to all the parks. In all of Philadelphia."

At this, Hannah looked at Esther as if she wanted to say something, but she didn't.

Then Esther understood. Claire must have taken Hannah to the museums and the parks, many times. Maybe Hannah was scared, and she was trying to protect the memories she had of those places with her mother.

"Still," Esther said, "I don't think we should stay at home and watch TV all day."

"Why not?" Hannah asked.

Because your mom wouldn't like it, Esther thought. "We could work on your homework packet," she said, but Hannah shook her head no. Her school had sent Laz a packet of worksheets that Hannah could complete in lieu of returning to school. When Hannah had first seen it, she had flicked through it with disdain.

"I guess we could do one of the new puzzles," Hannah offered, rising from the floor. She glanced back at Esther as she left the living room. "Coming?"

In the rest of the house, Peipei, Mrs. Chen and the confinement nurse Lin ayi roamed like loud, discontented ghosts. Mrs. Chen had decreed that the door to the playroom should remain open, so Esther and Hannah heard Peipei shouting in Chinese on the phone; Mrs. Chen scolding Peipei or Lin ayi; Jasper crying and Lin ayi making shushing sounds.

Esther could tell from Peipei's exasperated phone calls and rants to no one in particular that she was having a hard time finding a good nanny for Jasper. She and Mrs. Chen were on the hunt for someone from Taiwan, who knew the Chinese ways of raising a baby boy, but only the good ways, like the right foods and the right amount of clothing, not the bad ways, like creating entitled little princes.

As they were finishing up with lunch that day, Peipei jabbed her chopsticks at the air. "How hard can it be to find an ayi?" she asked Esther, but Esther had no idea. She had never tried to find an ayi before.

Mrs. Chen clucked her tongue and reminded everyone in Chinese that there were plenty of qualified ayis in Taiwan.

"Mom, you know that Lazarus wants to keep the kids in America," Peipei said in Chinese.

Mrs. Chen then said, in Chinese, that Laz and Peipei were both stupid and she was just waiting for them to realize that she was right.

"Did Grandma just say Auntie Peipei was stupid?" Hannah whispered to Esther.

Peipei turned and glared at Hannah before grabbing her bowl and taking it to the sink.

"Let's go outside," Esther said, shuttling Hannah out of the room. In the backyard, Hannah roamed on the hulking wooden play structure in the far corner. It was in the shape of a pirate ship, with a rustic feel despite its imposing size, and Hannah had a recently rekindled interest in it.

"But why is Auntie Peipei so mad?" Hannah asked, walking slowly across the planks of the mini bridge, arms outstretched as if she were a tightrope walker.

"I think she wants to go home," Esther said. "But she can't until she finds a good nanny for the baby."

"She probably misses her kids," Hannah said.

Esther nodded, though she suspected that Peipei just wanted to get away from Mrs. Chen. In Taiwan, she had told Esther, Peipei was busy and successful as a co-owner of a line of skincare spas incorporating the latest in Korean facial techniques and products. Peipei had mentioned her business multiple times but, at least to Esther, had never really mentioned her kids back home.

Esther's phone dinged with a message from Wendy in the *Mathey Help* group.

Success! Wendy said.

?? Esther asked.

I found a nanny. Maybe. I'll give you a call to discuss.

Wendy had asked around her personal Asian American network, and one of her connections in New York put her in touch with an ex-banker in southern Jersey who was planning to become an ex-ex-banker as her children were old enough to go to school and she no longer needed her full-time Chinese ayi.

"There's one potential problem, though," Wendy said on the phone. "Zhang ayi, the nanny, is from China. And Laz had said they were looking for someone from Taiwan."

After the call, Esther went to relay Wendy's message to Peipei and Mrs. Chen in the living room. Peipei translated into Chinese for Mrs. Chen.

"A mainlander? That won't work," Mrs. Chen said in Chinese. "You can't find anyone from Taiwan?"

People from Taiwan had certain conceptions about people from Communist mainland China, Esther knew, and those views could differ depending on whether the person from Taiwan was a descendant of families who had lived in Taiwan before 1949 like the Chens, versus families like Esther's parents' who had fled mainland China in 1949 when China became Communist. Esther had grown up understanding that many of the older generation from Taiwan saw themselves as more honest, more sophisticated, and truer to traditional Chinese culture than mainlanders.

"Isn't it better to have someone who is Chinese than someone who isn't? We don't have any other options," Peipei said in Chinese. Before Mrs. Chen could say anything, she added in English, "Let's set up the interview and give her a chance first."

The next evening Zhang ayi came to meet the family, and Esther was asked to stay to meet her as well. Despite Mrs. Chen's warning that this mainland ayi might be very different culturally, Esther found that Zhang ayi gave off very similar vibes to Lin ayi, the confinement nurse from Taiwan. They wore the same type of cheap rayon shirts, untucked, with loose pants. They had the same graying hair, not quite put together, the same mottled skin, the same air of heartiness and motherliness and domestic helper-ness.

The miracle was that Mrs. Chen actually approved. It turned out that Zhang ayi's mother was from Fuzhou, that she spoke the mainland dialect closest to Taiwanese, and that she could cook Fuzhou food which was similar to Taiwanese food. Somewhere they had shared ancestors, as hundreds of years ago Mrs. Chen's ancestors had left Fuzhou to be fishermen on the small island that would become Taiwan. As Zhang ayi revealed her family history, Mrs. Chen dipped her head in recognition, Lin ayi smiled and nodded with her mouth open, and Peipei clapped her hands in satisfaction.

Esther took Hannah to the backyard while the adults made arrangements.

"What do you think?" Esther asked.

Hannah walked up the plank of the wooden pirate ship. She leaned her arms on the side of the boat, looking like a very serious and tiny sea captain. "I don't think she speaks English," she said.

"Probably only a little."

"You'll still come over, right?" Hannah asked.

"Of course," Esther said. "I'll come over every day if you want."

"All day?"

"Sure, unless I have other things to do." Not that I ever have anything to do these days, Esther thought. "But I think you're going to get tired of me."

Hannah looked down at Esther with a furrowed brow. "Weren't you going to try to pick up some more work projects this summer?"

Esther forgot when she had said this in Hannah's presence. "Um…

maybe in the fall, when you're back in school."

"I see," Hannah said. She rested her face on her arms.

Later, an elated Peipei told Esther the terms of Zhang ayi's engagement. She would come to live at the Chen house next week, before Mrs. Chen and Lin ayi flew back to Taiwan. She would get Sundays off, but since her closest relatives were in New York they didn't expect that she would do much outside of the house. She would take care of Jasper, cook for the family, do light housework in between the regular cleaners. She would also help watch Hannah as necessary, but the understanding was that Esther would be with Hannah much of the day. Peipei would pay Zhang ayi a ridiculous amount of money —no need to worry Laz and Mrs. Chen about how much, she said.

"The best part," Peipei said, "is that I can go back to Taiwan tomorrow."

8

Peipei left, and Esther didn't understand why Mrs. Chen and Lin ayi stayed; now that Zhang ayi was there for the baby, Mrs. Chen and Lin ayi did nothing all day except talk about the meals they (Lin ayi, mostly) would prepare for Laz when he came home from work. They didn't even want to go to the Chinese grocery store, so Esther and Hannah went to pick up the groceries for them.

Now they were walking slowly down the aisle of the store, Hannah holding the list that Lin ayi had made. Esther had used a combination of Google translate and her own diminished Chinese skills to translate each item. The lighting in the store was just barely sufficient, the cleanliness of the floors subpar. The cart had a squeaky wheel and veered slightly to the left when pushed.

"Old soy," Hannah said. "I don't know what that is."

Esther stopped the cart. "*Lao chou*. Old soy. I think it's a kind of soy sauce?" Before them stood four shelves of soy sauce and soy sauce variants: Chinese, Taiwanese, Cantonese, Korean soy sauce; light, dark, seasoned, unseasoned soy sauce; soy sauce paste; soy sauce glaze.

"Can I look at snacks?" Hannah asked.

"Sure. Stay close."

Eventually, Esther found what she was looking for, she thought, but it was a large glass bottle. Sixteen ounces seemed too much of whatever this was, when Mrs. Chen and Lin ayi would be leaving soon, so she looked for a smaller version. She was afraid that if she bought the big one, Mrs. Chen would think that she was being too extravagant. With Peipei gone, Mrs. Chen watched Esther and Hannah more aggressively, like a predator watching prey, waiting for opportunities to criticize.

Esther saw a very small bottle of *lao chou*, in a section with smaller bottles of things, mystifyingly far from the larger version. Was this one too little? She could always come again if they used it all up before they left, right? She put the large bottle back on the shelf, grabbed the small one.

She found Hannah in the aisle of sweets, a pile of snacks at her feet.

"Whoa," Esther said.

Hannah looked down at the pile. "What?"

"That's a lot. That's like six different kinds of candy."

"You said I could get what I wanted," Hannah said.

"I did?"

"Yes, in the car. You said I could get what I wanted." Hannah paused. "I also want chips. I haven't gotten there yet." She eyed Esther, waiting for a reaction.

Esther felt a latent Chinese American frugality arise within her. She understood, vaguely, that this must come from her own childhood trips with her mom to the single Cleveland Chinese grocery store, where she was allowed to choose one thing at most—and only if her mom was in a good mood. "It's too much," she told Hannah.

"My grandma is paying for it anyway. Why do you care?"

Esther started at her tone. "Actually, your Auntie Peipei is paying for it, but in any case, it's too much." Peipei had given Esther a prepaid debit card for expenses before she left, despite Esther saying it wasn't necessary.

"I hardly ever get candy anymore," Hannah said. Her eyes welled. As her face grew red, Esther started to panic.

"Okay," Esther said.

Hannah sniffled.

"Fine. You can have that stuff. Maybe put one thing back."

"Okay!" Hannah said, placing the cookies and creme Pocky back on the shelf. She turned back to Esther with a bright smile. "And I can still get chips?"

It frightened Esther how easily Hannah changed. Her eyes were still watery, but she was happy now—was this all a trick? Was Esther being played?

No. Hannah lost her mom. Hannah could have the treats.

But Claire wouldn't have wanted Hannah to eat so much junk food.

But Claire wasn't here.

"A little bit of each," Esther said.

Hannah looked at her in victory and went to plunder the other aisles.

"How could you buy so much?" Mrs. Chen asked in Chinese as she inspected the five plastic bags, full and covered with yellow smiley faces and red thank yous, resting on the kitchen island.

Lin ayi started to unpack the groceries. Mrs. Chen oversaw the process, and Esther watched in hopeful anticipation as the two women chattered in Chinese.

"Good, she found fermented bean curd," Lin ayi said.

"The Chinese watercress is old," Mrs. Chen said.

"It's not that bad," Lin ayi said. "Better than when your son bought it last time."

Mrs. Chen laughed. "Well at least she can do better than my son."

I can understand you, Esther wanted to say. I can understand everything you say, almost.

At the table Hannah opened a bag of salted egg yolk flavor chips and popped one into her mouth. "Yuck," she said.

"I told you they sounded gross," Esther said.

Hannah put the chips aside and opened a bag of shrimp chips.

"Hey," Esther said. "Can we at least finish one bag of chips before starting another?"

"Try them," Hannah said. "They're gross."

A sting of chemical umami attacked Esther's tongue as she bit down on a salted egg yolk chip.

"Look at how much junk food she bought her," Mrs. Chen said behind them. "She's going to get fat."

"She's too skinny," Lin ayi said. "She needs to gain some weight."

Esther sat with Hannah and started eating the shrimp chips.

Then she heard a sharp laugh. Lin ayi was holding the bottle of *lao chou* and looking at her.

"How did you find a bottle this small? It's too small!" Lin ayi crowed.

Esther blushed. In mangled Chinese, she tried to explain. "The big bottle was too big. I didn't want to waste."

"It's fine," Mrs. Chen said to Lin ayi. "We're going home soon. She can always go to the store again and get more if we need it." She flicked her hand as if waving Esther away, as if Esther and her time were disposable.

***

"I win!" Hannah said, putting her last tile down. "You should probably check your phone." They had been playing Rummikub, and Esther hadn't wanted to break the flow of the game, ignoring the multiple dings in short succession.

Esther uncrossed her legs and rose from the floor with a grunt. Hannah tossed the tiles back into the box, sharp clacks of plastic ringing as Esther got her phone from the table.

You hanging in there @Esther? Wendy had asked in the *Mathey Girls* chat.

I hope the new nanny is working out, Maggie said.

Tell Hannah we said hi, Serena said.

In the conversation history, a few minutes had passed, and then Maggie added another message. *I miss Claire so much.*

Me too, Wendy said.

Us too, Serena said.

They gave each other care emojis and sad emojis and now, ten minutes later, Esther wasn't sure how to respond.

We are doing okay, she said. *Of course I miss her too.*

Hannah had finished putting Rummikub away and was examining her game collection for whatever they would play next. Esther thought that maybe she should talk to Hannah more about Claire, and how Hannah was doing emotionally, but it never seemed the right time. She was trying to find the words to broach the topic when the doorbell rang.

"I'll get it!" Hannah said and ran out of the playroom.

At the front door, Mrs. Chen was trying to communicate with a UPS delivery man. He wanted her to sign but she didn't understand. Instead, she beckoned with her hands as if inviting him in. Hannah was bouncing up and down near the door, adding to the confusion.

"Hi," Esther called out to the UPS guy.

The UPS guy looked past Mrs. Chen to Esther. "I need a signature," he said. He shook his head at Mrs. Chen. No, he was not going to come inside. He looked at Mrs. Chen as if she might have Covid, as if she wanted to give it to him in the comfort of her home.

Esther reached past Mrs. Chen and signed on the device. The UPS guy picked up the box from the floor and tried to give it to Esther, but Mrs. Chen pushed her way forward.

"It's heavy, ma'am," the UPS guy said.

"Too heavy," Esther said in Chinese, and Mrs. Chen stepped to the side in frustration.

Esther took the package, staggering under its weight.

"Come, come," Mrs. Chen said in Chinese. She tottered toward the kitchen.

The package had been sent from Taiwan and was addressed to Laz in the same handwriting that Esther's parents used for English, neat and slanted. She didn't recognize the characters in the sender's name; she hardly remembered any characters from the two years of Chinese she had taken in college despite all of the work the classes had required.

In the kitchen Mrs. Chen approached with an industrial size box cutter, waving it in the air. Esther stepped back instinctively. She recalled that Claire had told them about the massive box cutter she had bought during the pandemic, when they all started receiving packages all the time, buying and buying to reassure themselves that they were still connected to the world, albeit through commerce, and safe from consumer goods shortages.

Mrs. Chen attacked the box with fervor, and Esther was afraid that she would cut herself or damage whatever was inside the box or both. The tape was soon cut through, and Mrs. Chen ripped the sides open with triumph. "Wah," she said, a sound of satisfaction. She pointed to the contents. "It's for you," she said in Chinese.

Esther, surprised, took a hesitant look into the box.

It was books.

Books to learn Chinese, for children.

As Esther tried to get a closer look, Mrs. Chen began to lift them out of the box—they were actually very thin, almost like pamphlets, with lesson books and workbooks all part of the same series. The titles were in English, but there were traditional Chinese characters under the English and on the covers as decoration.

"Heritage Chinese: Learn Chinese Together" was the series name.

"For Jiejie," Mrs. Chen said in Chinese, using Hannah's new Chinese nickname. When Jasper was born, Hannah had stopped being *Meimei* (*little sister* or *little girl*) and become *Jiejie* (*big sister*) in the family. "You teach her Chinese."

Esther stepped away from the box and let Mrs. Chen continue unpacking.

"Peipei sent them," Mrs. Chen said, smiling to herself.

"But Peipei..." Esther said in Chinese and then realized she didn't know how to say what she wanted to say. She wanted to say: Peipei has way overestimated my Chinese skills. And she's only been gone a few days, how did these books get here so fast?

"Jiejie!" Mrs. Chen called. Nothing happened. "Jiejie!" Mrs. Chen called again, louder, sharper, and Jasper started crying upstairs.

Hannah came into the kitchen. "What?" she asked. She looked at her grandmother clutching a slim stack of the books.

"She will teach you," Mrs. Chen said in Chinese. She looked at Esther. "Tell her. Tell her you will teach her Chinese."

Esther just shrugged and turned her hands up. She didn't want to disrespect Mrs. Chen and say no, of course she wasn't going to teach Hannah Chinese.

Mrs. Chen looked at Esther with encouragement. "You went to Princeton University," she said in Chinese. "Lazarus said that you studied Chinese. You teach Jiejie. Good girl." She set her stack of books down on the kitchen island and sandwiched Esther's hand between her own. Mrs. Chen's hands were smooth and cold; they reminded Esther of the cold poached chicken that her mother would order when she saw it on Chinese restaurant menus.

"You're very smart. Jiejie is very smart," Mrs. Chen said in Chinese, nodding. "Good girl."

Later that evening, when Esther was back in her apartment, she messaged Peipei on Line, the Taiwanese version of WhatsApp that Peipei had made her join. *Good morning*, she said. *Can you call me please? ASAP?*

Waiting for the call, Esther flipped through the first set of books in the series, which she had brought home to inspect. It was a course for children, with instructions in English and Chinese. It seemed basic enough, but there were forty sets of books to go through. Esther was reminded of her own study of Chinese, the painful hours of practicing characters, her teachers scolding her for her Taiwanese accent. Before studying Chinese in college, she had never known that her parents' Mandarin was so incorrect, hadn't understood the difference between Mandarin (the primary Chinese dialect) and other dialects like Taiwanese and Cantonese. She hadn't even known that Chinese characters came in traditional form (used in Taiwan and Hong Kong) and simplified (used in the mainland and Singapore).

Her phone trilled.

On the call, Peipei started with an apology. She had already spoken with Mrs. Chen, who had told her that Esther was unhappy with the Chinese books.

"Whose idea was this?" Esther asked.

"My mom's," Peipei said. "Don't worry about it."

"But are you guys really expecting me to teach her Chinese? I barely know any Chinese myself."

Peipei laughed. "Don't worry about it! If you want to, you can. If you don't, just forget it."

"But you sent all those books..." Esther said.

"I sent them because my mom wanted me to," Peipei said.

"Okay, I guess. I was worried."

"But," Peipei said, "it might be a good idea to try to teach her a little bit. Just in case."

"Just in case what?"

"Just in case, you know, she visits."

Esther groaned. "You said you wanted her to stay here, with Laz. I thought that was the plan."

"Oh, it is, it is," Peipei said smoothly. "But she might need to visit, some time. Maybe next summer."

Esther stayed silent.

"Don't worry about it," Peipei said. "Seriously."

"Okay," Esther said. She felt as if she was being played, woefully unmatched.

"You know my mom," Peipei said. "You know how she is."

I don't know her, Esther wanted to say, not really, and I don't know you either. "I really don't think I can teach her Chinese," she said.

"Fine, fine, no problem," Peipei said. "My mom is leaving in a couple days anyway. It will all be easier when she's gone."

"I hope so," Esther said.

"Don't worry about it," Peipei said again and hung up, and all Esther could do after the call was to lie back down and worry.

Part Two

9

Mrs. Chen was gone, back to Taiwan finally. Esther and Zhang ayi were on their own now, and like dogs in the absence of an alpha, they circled and evaluated each other, trying to understand how they would relate to each other going forward.

"I take Jiejie to park," Zhang ayi told Esther when she arrived a little after ten. It was the fourth day after Mrs. Chen had left.

Esther was grateful that Zhang ayi spoke some English, because then Hannah could actually communicate with her, but that English was sparse and spotty. Did she mean that she already took Hannah to the park, or that she would be taking her later? Mandarin did not have obvious tenses, everything was in context, but the contextless tenseless English was jarring. "You took her to the park already this morning?" Esther asked.

Zhang ayi nodded. "I take Jiejie to park with baby." She was wearing more ostentatious clothes now that Mrs. Chen was gone, with arresting patterns and bright colors—neon pink a recurring theme—as if she had been hiding her true wardrobe from the matriarch. Now, in a loose blouse that looked as if it had been spattered with yellow and orange blobs of paint, Zhang ayi was cutting apples for Hannah. Esther had to admit that she missed the cut fruit that Lin ayi, the confinement nurse, had prepared for her. Lin ayi had always come into the playroom with two plates, one for Hannah and one for Esther. Zhang ayi clearly viewed Esther differently, like another member of the help. Esther didn't warrant cut fruit; she could cut it herself.

"I can bring it to her," Esther said, picking up the finished plate.

Zhang ayi tilted her head in approval, sat down, and took out her phone. With Mrs. Chen gone, Zhang ayi spent a lot of time watching Chinese videos.

In the living room, Hannah was parked in front of the television with vacant and tired eyes.

"Hey," Esther said.

"Hey," Hannah said. She accepted the apples and started eating, eyes back on the screen.

"Make sure you're blinking while you watch," Esther said, and Hannah nodded. This was something that Claire had told her—that Hannah didn't blink enough when watching TV, and her eyes would get tired, and that was one reason why they had wanted to limit screens.

Esther sat on the couch. It was harder than she had expected to fill a day with a nine-year-old girl. She had gained a lot of respect for stay-at-home moms, babysitters, daycare workers, teachers, anyone who had continuous unrelenting contact with children. The most that Esther had ever experienced before this was afternoons with Didi's kids, or very short exposure to her friends' children. Never anything that required stamina.

She opened her phone and checked the *Mathey Girls* chat. Wendy had sent a message asking how Hannah was doing, if Esther needed any help.

Hannah seems fine, Esther said. *I have a question though. How much TV is too much TV for her?*

After a moment she saw that Maggie was typing a response. *The good mom answer is that you should try to get her to limit screen time, maybe to 1-2 hours a day. The bad mom answer is that you should let her have as much screen time as you need to retain your sanity.* Maggie ended her message with a crying laughing emoji.

What if I'm not a mom? Esther wanted to say, but she didn't want her friends to worry even more. They thought she was in over her head, and that's why they kept checking in on her, almost daily, asking about Hannah, Laz, the baby.

"Five more minutes, then let's go play outside."

Hannah nodded absently.

At least the Mathey Girls approved of Esther's visits with Hannah. Her parents did not. Didi had called her the night before, relaying his parents' thoughts like the upstanding son he was.

"Hey Esther, how's it going?" he had asked on the phone, and then gone directly to, "Mom and Dad asked me to call about your work situation."

"What do you mean?"

"Like, why are you babysitting Claire's daughter instead of working?"

Esther groaned. "I knew I shouldn't have said anything when Mom called."

"Can't Laz hire a babysitter?" Didi asked.

"I'm not a babysitter. I'm... spending time with Hannah. Otherwise she's stuck with a Chinese nanny who's taking care of the baby. Laz is only around on the weekends, and he seems pretty, well, shell-shocked still. You get it, don't you? It's important that I take care of her."

"It doesn't have to be you, Esther," Didi said.

"If not me, then who?"

"Anyone—a nanny, a babysitter. You could visit on weekends, still do work during the week. I'm sure Hannah would be fine."

"You don't know that. If Hannah doesn't do fine, she's going to get shipped to Taiwan."

Didi stayed silent for a moment, and Esther knew what he was thinking. Maybe that wouldn't be such a bad idea.

"That would be a bad thing," she added.

"Mom and Dad just want to make sure that you're not wasting your degree and your skills. That you're not killing your career for this," Didi said.

It's already dead, Esther thought.

She considered telling him the truth, that she hadn't been working anyway. Didi would probably understand, wouldn't he? But Didi was, at this moment and always, a conduit to and proxy for her parents, and she wasn't ready to expose herself for the liar she was.

"Are you still there?" Didi asked.

"Yes," Esther said. "I'm not killing my career for this. This is a temporary hiatus, that's all. I could use the break, and more importantly, it's for Hannah."

Didi sighed.

"Are you worried that you're going to go back to Mom and Dad empty-handed after this conversation?" Esther asked, trying to keep her tone light.

"Ha. No... I'm sure you'll be fine, and I guess I can convince Mom and Dad of that. I think they just want something new to worry about. You know how they are now that they're old."

Esther answered with a noncommittal murmur. Her understanding of her parents was frozen in time, back two decades ago when she had gained their approval by graduating from Princeton and becoming a consultant at Centridge. She didn't want to think about her parents growing older, her parents needing help with something that she couldn't help with.

"Maybe you could bring Hannah to Cleveland, a road trip, and she could meet my kids," Didi said. "And Mom and Dad."

"Maybe," Esther said, and then she said she had to go, unnerved by the idea of mixing her adult Philadelphia life with her Cleveland childhood.

When she was fired in February 2021, Esther had vacillated between acceptance and outrage. She hadn't been performing her best, she knew, had survived multiple reviews where she was encouraged to do better if she wanted to reach partnership, and it was a pandemic. Still, she was Esther Hsu, and she had given the best years of her life to Centridge.

While she was in her last two weeks at the firm, she had reached out to the Mathey Girls for emotional support, and as expected they had assured her that she would be successful with or without Centridge. With her family, though, Esther didn't expect that kind of empathy. To avoid hearing their disappointment, she told them that she quit her job to start freelancing. Her long record of obedience in the form of success led her family to believe that she was telling the truth. It was inconceivable that Esther could be considered expendable, that she could be expended. Even Esther herself couldn't conceive of it, and she didn't want to break her family's belief in her, so she had lied.

She did make an effort, in the beginning, to actually provide some freelance consulting to smaller businesses. She had built up some good will with former clients, she had the Princeton network. The resilience of the network was a surprise to her, since she had never associated with the eating club crowd, but apparently the Princeton name was enough to open doors to several short-term projects. The problem was that everyone expected the pandemic to end soon, so there was no need to commit to a long-term remote consultant; they could put off the more substantial projects for winter, or spring, or whenever life returned to normal, and they could have in-person consulting staffed by the big firms. After the initial spate of small projects, Esther entered into a downward spiral of lack of client enthusiasm leading to lack of self-motivation to further lack of client enthusiasm to further lack of self-motivation.

But.

She had never told her family or friends that she had entered the downward spiral—in honesty, when it began she didn't know she had stepped onto that path—and when she found herself at its winding center, alone and hopeless, she dared not admit that she had failed.

So.

In the spring of 2022, when she had been planning Claire's surprise brunch and baby shower and her friends had asked how she found the time, she told them that planning a baby shower was a nice break from the stress of her projects. The truth was that she had left that kind of stress far behind months before, when she had decided that it was hopeless, and she just needed to wait until the pandemic was over to find a real job.

In the immediate aftermath of Claire's death, she had forgotten her lie. Now, being with Hannah was filling empty spaces in her life—she had something to do, someone to think about—and she didn't know how to make her loved ones understand.

***

Hi Esther, my name is Shruti, my daughter Kavi is friends with Hannah from school. Lazarus gave me your number, as I was wondering if Hannah would like to come over for a play date. Separately, please accept my condolences - the entire school community is devastated by what happened to Claire.

"Do you have a friend named Kavi?" Esther asked the next day, but Hannah ignored her. "Hey," Esther said, giving Hannah a poke.

Hannah shut her book and looked at Esther, blinking deliberately.

"What?"

Esther asked again and Hannah said yes, she had a friend named Kavi.

"And would you want to go to her house for a play date some time?"

Esther watched Hannah withdraw into herself, shoulders curling in as she looked down at her hands. It reminded Esther of the days following Claire's death and Hannah's silent phase.

Eventually Hannah shook her head. "No thank you," she said, and she turned back to her book.

"Hey," Esther said, gently prying the book from Hannah's hands. "Why not?"

"I don't feel like it," Hannah said.

"I think she really wants to play with you," Esther said, hoping this was true. She didn't have great child-rearing instincts generally but she knew the importance of friendship. She had asked Lazarus if Hannah had friends, maybe a best friend, and he didn't really know. Claire had always managed Hannah's social life.

Hannah shrugged and held out her hand for the book.

"I think you should go," Esther said. "I could take you."

The ticking of the clock in the playroom was very loud. Esther could see the gears of Hannah's mind keeping time with the clock. She was willing to be patient.

"I think it would be weird," Hannah said finally. "Because of my mom."

Esther sat down cross-legged. "Do you want to talk about it?"

Hannah shook her head and looked away. Eventually, she said, "Daddy asked if I wanted to have lunch with a friend Sunday after church, and I said no. At church everyone treats us different now."

"I'm sorry, Hannah."

"Daddy cries all the time."

"He does?"

"He cries at church, and everyone looks at us."

Esther could picture Laz crying in church—when she saw him these days, after a day of work at the hospital, he looked as if he could break down at any moment. She thought back to the time after Caleb died, how her parents too had struggled with everyday life, and how deeply this had affected her. "You know, when I was a little older than you are, my brother died."

Hannah shifted her body, the beanbag crunching with the movement. "What happened?" Hannah asked.

"He was sick, and he died."

"What was his name?"

"Caleb," Esther said.

"Caleb," Hannah whispered. Then she rose from the beanbag and sat in Esther's lap, cross-legged like Esther, curled up in the hollow under her chin. Hannah pulled Esther's arms around her. They were both looking at the wall, but they were together.

Esther pressed in with her arms gently, not daring to squeeze too tightly. How different it felt holding Hannah compared to her baby brother. Hannah didn't have Jasper's milky smell—she didn't really smell like anything but her shampoo. Her limbs dug into Esther's arms and lap. On impulse, Esther kissed the top of her head.

"Was Caleb your little brother or big brother?" Hannah asked after a moment.

"Big brother," Esther said. "He was a lot older than me. When he got sick, he was in college, and I was just ten. He died when I was eleven."

Hannah didn't say anything; her body felt tense in Esther's arms. Eventually, she said, in the softest whisper, "Were you sad?"

"I was," Esther said. "I was very sad." She felt Hannah soften just a bit. "But I was also very confused, at the time."

Hannah turned her head to look at Esther, their faces closer than they had ever been. Esther could see that Hannah was searching her for something—for truth, for reassurance, she didn't know.

"I wasn't sure how to feel about everything," Esther said. "For a long time."

"When did you feel better?" Hannah asked after turning back to face the wall.

"Well," Esther said, "I felt better, eventually."

"But you're still sad, right?"

"I'm not that sad anymore. I'm a lot better now."

At this, Hannah pulled herself out of Esther's lap and glared at her with her arms down, hands in fists.

"What's wrong?" Esther asked.

Hannah pointed a finger, shaking, at Esther. "Then you weren't really sad that he died, ever. You didn't really care about him." She was breathing hard, trying not to cry.

The accusation in Hannah's eyes was shocking. "Of course I cared about him," Esther said. "But it was such a long time ago."

"I'm not like you. I'll never forget my mama. I'll always be sad. Forever." Hannah ran out of the playroom.

Esther searched all over the house. She called Hannah's name, quietly, so as not to wake the baby. In the kitchen, Zhang ayi paused her video and said she hadn't seen her.

Hannah wasn't in the living room, and she didn't seem to be in the backyard either, though Esther might need to take a closer look at the pirate ship. First though she climbed the stairs to the second floor.

Hannah's room was its usual pink and clean and boring. Esther threw aside the larger marshmallow-pillow-type stuffed animals on the bed, just in case Hannah was small enough to hide underneath them, but of course she wasn't.

She passed Jasper's bedroom; the door was closed. Hannah wouldn't go in and wake the baby, would she? No. Esther moved to the office. Two desks, the larger one being Claire's, an L-shaped monstrosity that Claire had been very proud of. The last time Esther had been in the office, during the baby shower to grab some tape, the messiness of the desk had surprised her. Now the desk was neat and tidy, with two boxes stacked next to the chair.

The guest room still smelled faintly of Chinese herbs, a remnant of Mrs. Chen, Esther supposed. It was empty, as expected—Hannah wouldn't have come here for refuge—so Esther moved on.

She hesitated at the doorway of the master bedroom. There stood the bed that Claire had shared with Laz, unmade. The two side tables, one bare, the other with a Bible, a lamp, a charging station for Laz's phone. She stepped gingerly into the room and peered around. Laz's clothes were in piles on the floor; the room smelled not quite clean. There was trash on the top of the dresser, wadded receipts and some loose change, along with a few ties haphazardly thrown on top with knots pulled wide. Esther felt an ache in her chest. Claire would not have wanted Laz to live this way, and she would not have wanted

Esther to see this either.

Esther moved up to the third floor, where there were another two guest rooms, one being Zhang ayi's. The unused guest room was pristine, lifeless. Zhang ayi's room smelled like Chinese herbs, but different herbs from the second-floor guest room where Mrs. Chen had stayed.

Esther felt like an intruder; she rarely went above the ground floor of the house. You have one job, she told herself. One job. You shouldn't have told her about Caleb. She doesn't need your trauma to add to her own.

She went back down and approached Jasper's door. Hannah usually treated her brother with a cool neutrality, respecting his space and his needs without showing any true interest. If she did go into Jasper's room during his nap, it could only be to wake him up as punishment for Esther, right? But he wasn't crying. No, Hannah wouldn't be so mean.

Still, Esther needed to check. Her hand was on the knob, about to turn it, when she heard a muffled cry coming from somewhere else.

She followed the sound to the master bedroom closet. Sliding it open, she found Hannah on the floor with one of Claire's dresses, a teal knit with chevron stripes, crumpled in her lap. Her face was red, splotchy and wet as she wrung the fabric through her fingers.

Esther knelt down. "Hey," she said.

"Grandma took Mama's clothes," Hannah said. She shuddered as she tried to control her breathing.

Only a few dresses hung on the rod. The long belt of a kelly green wrap dress dangled low and threatened to drag the rest of the dress down to the floor. Without Claire's clothes, the closet looked stripped, Laz's paltry wardrobe inadequate for the space.

"I wouldn't let her take the dresses," Hannah said. "I cried and screamed. I tried to bite Grandma's hand, and Daddy said we would keep some."

No one had mentioned this episode to Esther, and she wondered how many other episodes like this had happened in the hours when she was watching TV or reading news online in her little apartment.

"I'm sorry for what I said," Esther said. "I shouldn't have told you about Caleb."

Hannah sniffled and wiped her face with the dress she was holding.

Esther tried not to look at the other dresses hanging on the rack, because she didn't want to think about Claire wearing them, because she didn't want to cry.

Down the hall Jasper started wailing, and from the first floor Zhang ayi yelled in Chinese that she was coming. They listened to the heavy thud of her feet marching up the stairs, to her opening the door to Jasper's room, to her cooing and comforting the baby. They heard her take him downstairs for a feeding and the second floor was silent again.

"Do you want to go back downstairs?" Esther asked eventually.

Hannah wiped her face again with the dress and handed it to Esther. As Esther was putting the hanger back onto the rod, Hannah grabbed her and buried her face in her stomach. Hannah said something but Esther couldn't quite make it out.

"What did you say, Hannah?"

Hannah looked up. "I said that I know you're still sad. About Caleb."

Esther ran her hands over Hannah's hair. "I think you're right," she said. "I am still sad about Caleb. I will always be sad about him. But my sad feelings are a lot more manageable now than when he first died."

"Do you think Caleb knows how you feel?"

Esther was torn between being honest and providing comfort. "I... I don't know. Maybe. But my feelings are still there, whether or not anyone else knows. And it's okay to be sad or upset."

"Is it okay to be happy?" Hannah whispered.

"Of course it is. That's what your mom would want, for you to be happy."

Hannah sighed a heavy sigh into Esther's shirt and then released her hold. She slid her hand into Esther's. "I'm ready to go down," she said.

10

When Esther and Hannah arrived at Shruti's address, as directed by Google Maps, they couldn't see the house. They were at the bottom of a hill, tucked in a miniature Brixton forest, barred by a tall bronze gate. Esther was surprised to find it had a box with an intercom, a buzzer gate, like in the movies.

Esther buzzed, and a crackled voice asked who it was.

"Esther Hsu, with Hannah Chen, for a play date with Kavi," she said.

"Who?" the voice asked.

"ESTHER HSU, WITH HANNAH CHEN, FOR A PLAY DATE WITH KAVI," Esther said.

"Mummy, it's Kavi's friend. I told you about this," another voice said to the first. "I'm sorry Esther, I'm Shruti. Please drive up."

A buzz sounded, followed by a sharp click. The gates opened slowly, Willy Wonka chocolate factory style. Driving up the hill, Esther wasn't sure if she should expect Versailles-type gardens or magical elves tending the property. All she saw, though, was a very large and well-manicured green. The house was large, larger than the Chen house which already felt unnecessarily large to Esther.

"Does Kavi have any brothers or sisters?" Esther asked Hannah as they got out of the car.

Hannah nodded, nervous and distracted.

"How many? Like twenty? This is a huge house for a single family."

Hannah didn't respond. She hadn't had a play date since before her mother died, and Laz had told Esther that even before Jasper was born, Hannah hadn't had many play dates. First there was the pandemic, and then, after Claire got pregnant, Hannah seemed to lose interest in the few offers that came in, as if she wanted to take advantage of alone time with Claire before the baby came.

The front door opened as they approached. "Welcome, I'm Shruti, please come in," the woman said, and Esther and Hannah walked into a grand foyer, holding hands.

"Kavi," Shruti called. She looked as if she was about to step into a board meeting: polished and professional, with tasteful gold accent jewelry and glossy black hair in a chignon. She gave Esther a pained smile. "She's just finishing up her program. Kavi!"

Two children bounded into the foyer, followed by an elderly woman who Esther assumed was Kavi's grandmother. The grandmother, wearing a loose blouse, slacks and plastic slippers, smiled benevolently at her.

Kavi and her little brother Aiyan stood at attention as Shruti introduced them. Kavi was an intelligent-looking girl with searching eyes and a long braid down her back. She looked at Hannah and offered a small wave, her hand down at her waist, and Hannah did the same. Aiyan had a mischievous grin on his little face, seemingly unbothered by the fact that this was a play date with the girl whose mom just died. The curls on his head bounced as he jiggled up and down, buzzing with manic energy at the opportunity to play with a new friend.

"Kavi, do you want to take Hannah to the basement?" Shruti asked, and Aiyan jumped with his fist in the air, Mario style. "Over the course of the pandemic our basement has transformed into what feels like an amusement park."

"There's a bounce house and a ball pit," Aiyan said.

"A small bounce house and a small ball pit," Shruti said.

Hannah looked up at Esther as if seeking permission. "Go ahead," Esther said.

"Come with me?" Hannah whispered, and Esther shook her head.

"No," Esther said. "You go play."

Hannah hesitated, looking between Kavi, her brother, and Esther, then grasped Kavi's outstretched hand. Without looking back, the kids ran out of the foyer, Aiyan shrieking and squealing.

Shruti showed Esther to the sitting room, and Kavi's grandmother brought tea. The three women sat on the couches—Esther and Shruti awkward and overly polite, the grandmother content to watch them with a placid smile on her face, hands folded in her lap. The room was large and airy and bright, all creams and beiges. A large television hung over the fireplace, just like in the Chen household; there was a baby grand piano in the corner.

"We're a bit rusty with play dates," Shruti said. "With the pandemic and all. It's been ages since we've had people over outside of our pod. I realized I've kind of forgotten how to host a regular play date!" She chuckled.

"Don't worry, this is my first play date, so I have no idea what a regular play date is," Esther said.

Shruti's hand went to her mouth. "Oh, I'm sorry. I'm sorry for your loss. I should have said that earlier."

"Don't apologize, please. I mean, thank you, but I'm doing okay, I'm just trying my best to take care of Hannah right now."

"Lazarus told me a little bit—that you're taking a break from work to help watch Hannah over the summer? That's so kind of you," Shruti said.

"Well, Claire was one of my best friends in college," Esther said.

"Still, that's a big help to him, I'm sure. You know, some of the other moms at school reached out to Lazarus to see if there was anything we could do for Hannah, but he never really responded."

"Oh," Esther said. "I didn't know."

"I mean, it's difficult because none of us know him very well. It was always Claire who took care of the school side of things. It's always the mom, isn't it."

"I suppose so," Esther said. "I think Laz is kind of overwhelmed right now."

"Oh I'm sure he is! I don't mean to belittle what he's going through at all. God knows what my husband would do if something like this happened. I can't even think about that." Shruti turned and patted the grandmother on the leg. "Mummy, can you get those cookies, the biscuits, from Costco?"

"My mother-in-law is visiting from India," Shruti said after the grandmother left. "She came early on in the pandemic to help with the kids, when the schools shut down, and never left."

Esther kept her face neutral. "My brother lives in Cleveland, where my parents are, and they spent a lot of time at his place over the pandemic too. I'm not sure my sister-in-law liked all that extra time with them, though."

Shruti chuckled. "It's had its ups and downs. Overall, I'm grateful for the help, but it's hard to have her expectations constantly in my face, you know?"

Esther nodded and was about to say that her sister-in-law had said the same thing in a much less kind way, but the grandmother re-entered with a tin of European butter cookies. She set them down proudly and opened her hands with a flourish, beckoning Esther to eat.

As they ate their cookies, Shruti talked about how terrible the pandemic had been, how truly wonderful it was to see how resilient children are, how happy she was to see things returning to normal. Esther tried to think of it from a mom's point of view, but she found that she felt more like a babysitter than a parent and she was unable to reciprocate the feelings that Shruti was presenting.

When Shruti mentioned that she was a lawyer for an insurance company, Esther was afraid that the conversation would turn to a detailed discussion of her own work. Lawyers and consultants and bankers were all the same class of professional, in Esther's mind, people who made a lot of money by working for people who made even more money, all in the pursuit of money and nothing better for the world. Of course, lawyers like Serena who did nonprofit public interest stuff were different. Lawyers like Serena wouldn't know anything about management consulting and wouldn't care to ask for details.

Esther braced herself then when she told Shruti that she was a freelance consultant.

"What kind of consulting?" Shruti asked.

"Management consulting, focusing on strategy," Esther said, words flowing from a long-ingrained habit. "But things have slowed down quite a bit with the pandemic," she added, trying to end the work discussion.

"I see," Shruti said. "I imagine that would be quite difficult."

A timer went off on Shruti's phone; she had to leave for a work call. She offered her apologies, gave Esther the Wi-Fi password, told her that she could relax or watch TV or whatever, and that she hoped her call wouldn't last for more than an hour.

"I'm so tired of Zoom calls, aren't you?" Shruti asked, and Esther agreed as if she too had so many Zoom calls that she could afford to be tired of them.

Then it was Esther and the grandmother, alone in the sitting room.

Esther waited to see if the grandmother wanted to chat. It was easy to see this plump little South Asian grandmother being a plump little Chinese grandmother, also sitting in a tufted armchair, also occasionally opening her hand toward the cookies to encourage Esther to eat. Did she speak English? She definitely understood English, because Shruti had spoken it to her. But did she expect Esther to chat with her? A little old Chinese lady would not expect Esther to chat with her; if the little old Chinese lady wanted to chat, she would chat first and Esther would respond.

Esther waited with her hands in her lap and a small, obedient smile on her face. She ran her eyes along the walls, appreciating the spare but luxe aesthetic. The TV above the fireplace was the only obvious thing out of place. When Esther glanced back at the grandmother, she was relieved to see her head leaned against the armchair with eyes closed.

Esther considered whether she too should take a nap. The couch was lush and firm and velvety. But no, she didn't want Shruti to come back from her call and see Esther covered in drool.

She took out her phone instead and munched on a cookie while she scrolled. Facebook, Instagram, Twitter, she did them all. She didn't post—of course not—but she checked them and lived vicariously through her friends and acquaintances. She had given up on ever achieving the levels of peak family happiness and career success of her peers; their achievements didn't make her feel bad anymore. Most of the time.

Then she checked her email and dropped her cookie in surprise. It was a message from her Centridge ex-colleague Jose. The subject line: *Hi.*

It had been how many years since she had contact with him? At least five, no, six. She picked up the cookie and took a comfort nibble. She glanced at the grandmother, still asleep, thank goodness.

The email said: *Hi Esther, long time no talk. Just wanted to check in and see how things are. You might know that I'm with Solutris Consulting now. And I might have an opportunity if you're interested.*

She was staring numbly at her screen when she got a text from Shruti: *I'm so sorry Esther, but do you know where my MIL is? I texted her but sometimes she doesn't check her phone. She will need to take the kids to piano - they need to leave at 4:10. My call is running way over and doesn't look like it will end soon. Apologies!*

Esther replied: *No problem, MIL fell asleep but I will let her know.* Shruti replied with a thumbs up emoji.

Esther tried to wake the grandmother by calling softly, "Excuse me, Grandmother, excuse me." Then she tried to tap her lightly on the shoulder. Ultimately, she had to speak louder than she was comfortable with and push a little harder than she wanted to before the grandmother woke up. "I'm sorry to wake you up, but Shruti says you need to take the kids to piano at 4:10," Esther said.

The grandmother gave Esther her previous placid smile and heaved herself out of the armchair. She patted Esther on the arm and walked out of the room. Esther followed her through the foyer, into a hallway and then down deep plush stairs to the basement.

The kids were playing on a tablet, all three crowded around the tiny screen as toys and entertainment structures surrounded them. Not only was there a bounce house and a ball pit, there were two carousel-type horses on springs and two long raised sine wave tracks with racing carts. There was even an old-fashioned standing popcorn maker, which explained the lingering smell of artificial butter.

"Hannah," Esther said, and Hannah looked up, blinking. "It's time to go."

"Noooooo," Kavi and her brother wailed, and Aiyan wrapped his arms around Hannah.

"But we just started on the tablet," Aiyan said.

"You guys have to go to piano," Esther said, and the grandmother nodded and extended her hand.

Hannah looked at Esther with mournful eyes as Aiyan let go.

"Did you have a good time?" Esther asked as she followed Hannah up the stairs. Hannah bounced her head vigorously and beamed—as if she had shed her grief, for now, allowing herself to have fun—and Esther's heart melted a little bit.

I'm sorry I can't see you off, Shruti texted.

Esther replied: *No problem, thank you so much for having us. Hannah had a lot of fun, and I think it's really good for her to play with other kids.*

Shruti gave her a thumbs up emoji. Then: *We should do it again soon. Next time feel free to drop Hannah off, take some time to yourself.*

That sounds great, Esther said.

On the car ride home, Esther and Hannah were each quiet, in two totally different worlds. Hannah, presumably, was thinking about how much fun she had had with her friend, the bounce house, the popcorn.

Esther was thinking about the email she had flagged on her phone. Jose.

***

Imagine: two mid to senior consultants, diligently attacking their keyboards, sitting on opposite sides of a hotel executive suite table after a long day of client meetings and document review.

Imagine that they see many similarities between themselves, that they both share the burden of being first-generation Ivy Leaguers with immigrant parents, that they both understand what it is to be the only person of color in a room, especially a large conference room, or the only two people of color as they are put on more deals together. They make a striking impression when they present to a client or show up for a diligence meeting. The man is slight, prematurely balding, looks more like a brown CPA than a typical management consultant. The woman is small, but next to the man just seems like a slightly smaller version, neither of them commanding much authority until they start to speak, in tandem, precise and effective. They finish each other's thoughts, not as friends or lovers but as consultants: a psychic connection over metrics and historical data and projections.

Imagine that the woman is single, seems perpetually single, doesn't have the time or energy or skill to keep a long-term partner. Her utility keeps her content, and though she occasionally squeezes in a dinner or date with someone she meets or is set up with, she isn't upset when these fail to develop into anything more serious. Through work, she has finally found validation, finally become confident in her ability to meet or exceed others' expectations. For the first time in her life, she feels effective and capable and suited to purpose, recognized for what she is worth.

Imagine that the man is married, as far as the woman knows he is happily married, with a toddler and a baby. Imagine that his wife is getting so tired of this lifestyle; she knew it would be difficult, but she is finding it harder and harder to be patient. She knows that someday he will make partner and will have more control of his schedule, will be able to send people on his team to the on-site meetings instead of going himself. Imagine that the wife suspects that her husband already could work from New York if he wanted to, but he chooses to go to Dayton or Indianapolis or Tucson because he wants to.

Imagine that the woman knows nothing of what the wife suspects or knows, because the woman is naive enough to think that her work partner is simply a work partner, naive enough to think that this could last.

11

"I'll show you," Hannah said, grabbing Esther's hand.

Esther let herself be pulled up the stairs, and up the stairs again, then through room after room of European art, then room after room of Asian art, and then they had arrived. The teahouse exhibit was a number of buildings, much more sprawling than Esther imagined. It was so real that it looked fake. She read the information placard. The whole teahouse had been moved from Japan; the real deal, right there in the Philadelphia Museum of Art.

Hannah dropped Esther's hand and ran to the bamboo fence. She peered into the interior of the courtyard, resting her head on one of the bamboo slats, contemplative.

"I'm going to walk around," Esther said, and she began her stroll around the structure. The museum was nearly empty at that time, a late Wednesday morning, and it seemed they were the only two in the exhibit.

Over the few weeks that Esther had been watching Hannah, they had grown tired of the Brixton house; tired of the playroom, tired of the living room, tired of the pirate ship in the backyard. While Hannah seemed fine with the parks and playgrounds around the city, Esther disliked sitting in the sun, watching Hannah play, hoping that Hannah played with the other kids. Often the other kids seemed to sense that Hannah was marked by something bad and avoided her.

Esther saw this as a big step, coming to the museum. Hannah had refused to go to the Please Touch Museum — she said it was for babies, but Esther knew that it used to be a favorite haunt with Claire before the pandemic. Claire had taken Hannah to the art museum, but apparently it didn't have the same depth of memory and joy associated with it, so Hannah was willing to see it again. Esther was only somewhat ashamed to admit that she had never been here; she had been busy, and then there had been the pandemic, and she wasn't much of an art person. She honestly hadn't believed Hannah when she heard that there was an actual house inside the museum.

Esther turned a corner. Hannah stood across the small yard, head still on the bamboo slat. She was squinting at something in the garden, unaware that she was being watched. She looked somber, closed, her little nine-year-old body weighed down by sadness.

Hannah was rarely emotional around Esther; the two of them never seemed to talk about Claire. Esther didn't push. She knew what it felt like to be a grieving child, with terrifyingly large feelings, and how at times it felt safer to just keep them at bay. She also knew that after time the feelings would subside, or at least it would be tamped down into something that was acceptable to live with.

Then Hannah looked up, and they locked eyes. Esther felt as if she were looking into a mirror, a portal into the past, the clarity that was impressed upon her as a young girl—the confrontation with death and its finality—shining in Hannah's eyes. Then Esther realized that no, hers was different, because she had had Didi there beside her, even if they had ignored each other. And the death of her brother Caleb was nothing at all like the death of Hannah's mother. When Caleb died, Esther's mother was still there. Her mother had been stricken and withdrawn, fundamentally changed, as they all were, but at the end of the day if Esther went to give her mother a hug she was hugged back, no matter how offhandedly.

She was struck by the weight of her responsibility in guiding Hannah through this, the worst time of her life. She wasn't a child therapist; she had never studied any type of psychology. All she had was her own experience and understanding.

Then Esther was striding to Hannah and enveloping her in a hug, squeezing hard.

"Ow," Hannah said, but she didn't try to push Esther away.

Later, after they had meandered through the other exhibits, Hannah taking the lead and Esther trying her best to appreciate the art despite her turbulent feelings, they ended up in the gift shop and Hannah asked if she could get a souvenir. As she left to look at the stuffed animals, Esther recalled how her own mother would never let her get anything at gift shops. A waste, because things were more expensive than elsewhere, and they didn't need anything, and if

Esther got something then Didi had to get something as well, and Mommy and Daddy worked so hard for them, they shouldn't ask to spend money on such frivolous things.

But Hannah had been raised differently. Claire had bought things for Hannah to show her love and affection; they had the money so why not use it to buy things that were beautiful, useful, educational, whatever.

Esther's gaze fell onto the stationary section with its notebooks, pens, sketchbooks, bookmarks, and she remembered her old diaries. Especially the diary she had kept when Caleb was sick, and after he died.

"Hannah," she called, as if through a fog.

Hannah came to her holding a plush cat, and Esther pointed at the blank diaries. "What are those?" Hannah asked. She picked one up and flipped it open. "It's empty." She put it back and was distracted by a set of rainbow pens.

"It's a diary," Esther said. "So you can write your thoughts."

Hannah brushed her fingers across the top of the rainbow pen box.

"Do you want those pens?" Esther asked, and Hannah nodded yes. "If you want the pens, I'll get them for you, but you also have to get a diary and promise to write in it."

"Like every day?" Hannah asked.

"Yes, if you can. My fourth grade teacher made us all start diaries, and I think it's a good habit."

"Will you read it?"

"No."

"Promise?"

"I promise," Esther said, sticking out her pinkie.

Hannah wrapped her pinkie around Esther's, accepting the promise. "Will Daddy read it?" she asked.

"No, we can ask him not to."

Hannah disentangled her pinkie from Esther's. "Okay," she said. Her eyes roamed the selection, and she asked Esther which one she should get, the one with the yellow flowers or the one with the crazy triangles, and Esther suggested the one with flowers. Hannah shrugged and handed the yellow flowered diary to Esther along with the rainbow pens.

"We'll try to write in it every day," Esther said, but Hannah wasn't listening anymore. As they went to the cashier to check out, Hannah abandoned the stuffed cat at the stationary stand. It lay on a spread of thank you cards, glassy eyes staring upwards.

That afternoon, Esther pretended to work on her laptop as she studied Hannah writing in the new diary. Hannah was hunched over, leaning too close to the paper. Was she trying to shield it from view?

"Hannah," Esther said, laughing, "I can't see from this far away, don't worry."

Hannah looked up, blinking hard. "What do you mean?"

The skin around Hannah's eyes was thin and pink. "Wait, are you crying?"

"No," Hannah said.

"Your eyes are red," Esther said.

Hannah rubbed her eyes quickly and went back to her entry.

Esther started Googling at her laptop: *child eyes red reading tears*.

She stayed for dinner that night, which she usually didn't like to do unless Laz had to stay late for work. But Zhang ayi had bought a fish to steam, and the prospect of steamed fish bathed in a traditional sauce of scallions, ginger and soy was too tempting to ignore.

As Hannah was getting ready for bed, Esther found Laz in the living room watching *Jeopardy*. He was saying answers out loud, sounding calm but sitting on the edge of the sofa, hands on his knees.

"Laz," Esther said softly, not wanting to break his focus.

"Turkey," Laz said. He glanced at Esther, then did a double take, and a red flush bloomed up his neck and face. "I thought you were Claire, for a second."

"I'm sorry," Esther said. "I didn't —"

Laz shook his head. "She never liked to watch *Jeopardy* with me. I always liked it before, to take my mind off of things. I thought I might let myself watch it again, now." He turned the TV off.

"You can keep watching," Esther said, but it was too late, and everything was awkward, so she sat in the armchair next to the sofa. "I wanted to ask about Hannah."

Laz nodded for her to continue.

It was difficult, even now, for Esther to look Laz in the eye. A long ago habit of trying not to seem too interested had conditioned her to always look at a spot behind his head, pretend like she didn't even know he was there. Don't be stupid, she told herself. "I was wondering, for Hannah, if she might need to get her eyes checked."

"What?"

Esther held a shrug. "I'm not a doctor, obviously, so you would know better, but she's been squinting a lot, rubbing her eyes, that kind of thing."

Laz looked at Esther with steady eyes, thinking. "I don't think Claire ever mentioned that... I don't even know when she last had a checkup. I think it was before Claire got pregnant." He grimaced. "How often are they supposed to go for checkups again?"

"I don't know," Esther said. "Don't you know? As a doctor?"

"I'm not a pediatrician," Laz said. He dragged his hand across his face. "You must think I'm a terrible father."

"I don't have any idea how you're supposed to act as a father in this situation," Esther said honestly. "I don't think you're a terrible father."

"I don't even know who her pediatrician is," Laz said. "Claire took care of all of that." He looked at Esther as if Esther might be able to solve the problem if he only waited patiently enough.

"I think you have to find out," Esther said.

"Right," Laz said, nodding. "Yes. I will find out and try to find time to make an appointment. Do you think you would be able to take her, or...?"

At that moment Esther wanted to roll her eyes, or scream, but all she said was, "I guess, if you're too busy."

"That would be great, thanks," he said. "I really appreciate it. I'm sorry I'm so... useless."

"It's okay, Laz," Esther said. "I'll see you tomorrow, I guess."

Esther left him to his *Jeopardy*, telling herself that he really was trying, just like she was. She tried to view him with compassion. It was hard to believe that she had had a crush on him, before he and Claire met. They had all been such different people then.

***

Before he was Laz, he was Hao-lan. Esther met him freshman year, in molecular biology, when she was still pre-med. He was slight, serious and studious, with a kind face. When he asked a question in precept, his faint accent slipped out. When he chatted with others, he rarely blinked, his eyes giving their entire focus to whoever he engaged with; when he was done with a conversation, he would blink rapidly to make up for it. He wore his backpack up high, but somehow it looked normal, like it belonged there.

She didn't understand why she was interested in him. There were other Asian boys in her classes, but she never felt that curiosity, that longing to know them better. He just seemed different, like there was potential for something—for what, Esther wasn't sure. When he saw her, he smiled at her, nodded, presumably because she was Chinese and maybe because he noticed that she was always stealing looks at him. But they never talked. She wouldn't have expected him to speak to her. As a freshman, quiet, out of place and overwhelmed, Esther was used to being skipped over.

All semester she watched him from afar; at the same time, she was dealing with her first real academic crisis, unable to keep up with the rest of the class. She dreamed of asking him for help; he clearly was smarter than she was (though, honestly, she felt that the entire class was smarter than she was), and maybe they could use this as a chance to get to know each other. Instead, she went to office hours, got a tutor through the Mathey academic office, eked out a C-, decided that she wasn't smart enough to be pre-med after all. This boy, while appealing, was less important than her redirecting the course of her life—letting down her parents, her first realization that she might not be able to follow in Caleb's footsteps as she had wanted.

By the end of freshman year, Esther's dreams of being a doctor had been put aside, along with the possibility of taking more classes with Hao-lan. Then, in the spring of sophomore year, he reappeared.

It was a Wednesday night in early April, and Esther walked down the steps to the Mathey library underneath the dining hall for a Study Break. As she reached the entry at the bottom of the steps, two students passed on their way out.

"These are worth their weight in gold," one of the students said to his friend, clutching his pretzel in its paper wrapper and holding it up like a trophy.

Tonight, the special treat for Study Break was Auntie Anne's, so the Mathey Girls had agreed earlier in the day to meet there. By the fall, when they were juniors, they would no longer get the benefit of the residential college system, no more free snacks in the common room or library on a weekday night. They had to take free pretzels while they still could.

Esther's eyes adjusted to the dimness; the library was half underground and very little evening light came in from the windows that lined the upper walls. Students clustered in groups, speaking in low murmurs. Claire and Maggie sat in leather armchairs pulled close to each other, heads together, whispering and giggling, their pretzels already on the table. Serena and Wendy were in line for their pretzels, and Esther joined them before all five women sat around the table with their spoils.

"What are you guys whispering about?" Serena asked.

"Oh, nothing important," Claire said.

Serena rolled her eyes. Esther was used to Claire and Maggie's closeness, their special duo within the larger group, but she knew that Serena resented it sometimes.

Claire turned to Wendy and Esther. "Hey, guys, do you want to go with me and Serena to the City next Saturday for a Manna event? It's dim sum." Manna was the Asian Christian group that Claire and Serena were part of.

"No thank you," Wendy said with a scoff. An avid atheist, she consistently rebuffed what she saw as Claire's attempts to evangelize.

"How about you, Esther?" Claire asked.

"Um, maybe another time," Esther said. Esther had been to a Manna meeting or two as a freshman, enjoying the community, but ultimately decided that she was too far gone from being a practicing Christian to be part of the club. Claire still invited her to events and meetings, and Esther continued to politely decline.

"Can I go?" Maggie asked. Maggie was part of Princeton Evangelical Fellowship, another Christian club on campus, one not tied to ethnicity.

"You can go," Serena said, "but you might be the only white person there."

Maggie laughed and twirled her fingers in a broad circle, indicating the Mathey Girls. "That's never stopped me before." She waggled her eyebrows at Claire. "And I want to see the boy."

"What boy?" Serena demanded.

"Yeah, what boy?" Esther echoed.

Claire blushed deeply and tried to hide behind the pretzel she was holding.

"There's a boy who joined Manna," Maggie said. "And Claire thinks he's cute."

"Maggie!" Claire said.

"I don't remember any new boys in Manna! Especially ones that are cute," Serena said. Serena regularly told everyone how she thought the boys in Manna were unappealing.

"He just came last week, when you weren't there," Claire said.

"We need more details," Wendy said.

The girls leaned forward in their chairs as Claire described him. He was a new Christian, baptized over spring break. He was from Taiwan, a pre-med in the Wilson residential college.

"Wait a second," Esther said. "Is his name Hao-lan Chen?"

"It's Lazarus," Claire said. "Lazarus Chen."

"But he's pre-med in Wilson? From Taiwan, our year? He has an accent?"

Claire nodded.

"Is he good friends with Edward Kim?"

Claire nodded again. "Do you know him? He introduced himself as Lazarus. But maybe his Chinese name is Hao-lan?"

They compared details—it must be the same boy, Hao-lan and Lazarus. He was about Maggie's height, maybe a little taller, with an accent and glasses too big for his face.

"What a small world!" Claire said. "So funny. Is he nice? He seems really nice. Like he's going to take care of you, you know?"

Esther nodded, unsure of how to react.

After the Study Break, she trailed the rest of the Mathey Girls back to the quad dorm that she shared with Claire, Maggie, and Serena as sophomores, their path lit by lamps perched above the successive arched stone entryways of Blair Hall.

Claire was interested in Hao-lan Chen? *Her* Hao-lan Chen? Of course he wasn't hers; she hadn't even ever really talked to him. But she had liked him from afar, before, a secret crush that she had never wanted to share.

"Are you okay?" Claire asked. She had paused in front of the dorm entryway to hold the heavy wooden door for Esther after the other girls had filed in.

"Me? Yeah," Esther said. What else could she say? That she didn't want her best friend to like a boy that she had liked a year ago? A boy that she had never had the courage to approach when she had the chance?

Over the following weeks, it became clear that Claire and Laz were interested in each other, would become a couple, would probably end up getting married and having a bunch of kids. Esther told herself to grow up and be happy for her friend. As she got to know Laz, she saw that he was perfect for Claire and vice versa. They shared a faith, they shared priorities, and they shared a seeming lack of sadness that Esther couldn't relate to.

Twenty years later, Claire was gone, and Laz was struggling to survive without her. Esther felt that she should give him more time, let him find his footing in this new world without his wife. But how long was he going to drift?

12

Therapy. Esther had never seen a therapist, but she knew enough from her friends and popular discourse to understand that this was something Hannah should do. And it was a weekday, so of course she should be the one taking Hannah to the appointment, she told herself as they approached the automatic doors of the medical building. There would probably be ongoing appointments in the future, and she couldn't ask Laz to take off work all the time, right? In any case, here they were, and they would be fine.

Hannah paused and pointed at the sign at the doors: *Medical facility —please remember your mask.* "We aren't wearing masks. We need to get them!"

"Oh," Esther said, "it's fine, nobody is wearing masks anymore."

The automatic doors slid open and slowly, too slowly, a geriatric man shuffled through. He was followed by a similarly aged woman who must have been his wife. Leaning heavily on his cane, the old man didn't look up as he shuffled past them, but the wife did. Both of them were wearing masks.

Esther and Hannah exchanged glances, went back to the car, scrounged around for masks—why did Esther's mask smell like fried chicken?—and went back into the building.

Walking down the third-floor hall they passed an orthodontist, a dentist, then another orthodontist. The placard outside Dr. Winter's office merely stated his name, as if his specialty was better kept a secret.

Esther had found Dr. Winter through Google. He wasn't her first choice; her first couple of choices, all women of color, had been booked at least six months out. By the time she called his office, she was so happy to know that he had availability in June that when they asked about Hannah's insurance, which she didn't know anything about, she had said she would pay out of pocket. But she was prepared now, with Hannah's insurance card in her purse, and hoped that this would be covered. If not, how much could this kind of thing be?

The reception area was small and tidy, but the air felt stale. No one else was waiting there, which was a relief. Esther felt entirely out of place, having never had any kind of mental health issues herself (at least, none that she would admit to, ha ha).

They checked in with the receptionist, a woman who looked to be in her early twenties, with auburn hair in a pert ponytail and fluttery fringed eyelashes. Esther gave her the medical authorization form that Lazarus had signed for Hannah. After the receptionist tucked the form into a folder on the desk, she said, "There's a note here that you'll be paying out of pocket?"

"I brought the insurance card," Esther said, handing over Laz's card.

The receptionist looked at the front of the card, frowned, flipped it over, kept frowning. "Let me just check something," she said, and her fingers went clickety-clack on the keyboard. "No, yeah, this won't work."

Hannah looked at Esther with a question in her eyes and Esther played it cool. "No problem, we'll pay out of pocket then."

The receptionist handed the insurance card back and looked at Esther for a moment. "Credit card please," she said, and Esther gave her the prepaid debit card from Peipei. "Please sit down and I'll call you when the doctor is ready."

They sat and Hannah busied herself with a children's *Highlights* magazine that looked suspiciously new and glossy. The waiting room had a large aquarium and a display case lined with plastic figurines that could have been old Happy Meal toys—some of them looked familiar from Esther's childhood. After a couple of minutes, Dr. Winter came out to greet them.

"Leonard Winter," he said. "Please follow me." He was young, younger than Esther, and his smile showed too many teeth. Hannah looked at Esther, another question in her eyes, and Esther gave her a reassuring nod.

Dr. Winter's office had pale yellow walls with light blue chairs around a low table separate from a couch area with a muted rainbow dotted rug, together creating an atmosphere of carefully controlled playfulness. Esther smelled cedar and then spied a hamster cage on a little table next an armchair.

"That's Mr. Ham," Dr. Winter said as Hannah ran to the cage to take a look. "Hannah, why don't you keep Mr. Ham company while I chat with your aunt for a little bit."

Hannah and Esther froze in their respective places and Dr. Winter's eyebrow shot up. "You know what, I think Mr. Ham might be hungry. Let me find you a treat that you can give him." The doctor went to his desk, took a glance at his computer monitor, and then found a box of treats for Hannah.

"Ms. Hiss-su, is it?"

"Hsu, like *shoe*," Esther said. "Sorry."

Dr. Winter motioned for Esther to sit down in a separate pair of chairs away from the hamster cage. "Please don't apologize for your last name, Ms. Hsu."

"Of course, sorry," Esther said, and she wanted someone to kick her in the face.

Dr. Winter looked into Esther's eyes in a way that she found disconcerting and spoke in a low voice. "I apologize for referring to you as Hannah's aunt. My notes indicated that's who you are. I will speak to Jenny about that."

"No, it's fine, we just aren't used to using that term. I mean, she used to call me Auntie Esther, before her mom died..." Esther glanced at Hannah who was poking her fingers into the hamster cage. "But since I've been, you know, taking care of her, since then, she just calls me Esther." Esther gave him a brief summary of her relationship to Claire and why she was taking care of Hannah—that she was asked to help out, at least for the summer, so that she wouldn't be sent to Taiwan to be with her dad's family—and she was startled to hear herself describe this situation as if it were normal.

"And can I ask where Hannah's father is in all this?" Dr. Winter asked.

"Lazarus is busy. With work. At least during the week. On the weekends I don't go to their house, and he spends time with her."

Dr. Winter stroked the very short beard on his chin. "I see."

"I gave the medical consent form to your assistant when we registered—he's authorized me to bring her to appointments." Esther waited for more questions, but Dr. Winter seemed to be considering, or was he judging, condemning?

"So I understand that you will be paying out of pocket," Dr. Winter said.

"Is that okay?"

"Of course," he said. "Many patients do."

He then called Hannah over. "Hannah, do you mind if I ask Esther to wait outside while we chat?"

Hannah looked from Dr. Winter to Esther and Esther almost wanted to cry from the trust that she saw in Hannah's eyes. Esther nodded, yes, whatever you think is good, and Hannah nodded in return.

Back in the waiting room, Esther flipped through this week's *People*, but her eyes glazed over. Something about the way Dr. Winter looked at her, at Hannah, made her feel very vulnerable. There was nothing sinister there, but it was the way he looked so obviously without judgment that made it seem that he absolutely was judging you. He seemed like he had practiced this look of neutrality, pretending that the words you were saying made sense, that he understood them. Esther realized it was the lack of emotion in his gaze and in his tone that unsettled her. This little girl's mother just died, she was thrown into this terrible situation of loss, and still Dr. Winter had nodded as if to say, yes, go on, I've heard this before.

Esther rose and went to the reception desk. "Sorry, I had a question."

"Sure," the receptionist, who must be Jenny, said. "How can I help?"

"Can I ask—how much are these visits? For out of pocket? And I think you still have the card I gave you." Esther nodded her head toward the debit card sitting next to Jenny's keyboard.

"Oh, yes, we keep this until the end of the first visit," Jenny said. "I hope you don't mind. I'll give it back when we settle the bill."

"Of course," Esther said, though she wasn't sure that this was appropriate. "And could you tell me how much these visits are? It's just that the card is a prepaid debit, and I'm not sure how much is on it..."

"It's $250 per hour session," Jenny said matter-of-factly.

Esther swallowed. "That's a lot," she said.

Jenny again gazed at Esther for a moment, her eyelashes quivering. "Dr. Winter is highly qualified and highly rated by his patients."

"I see," Esther said. $250 an hour. Jesus. She sat back down, mulling over this number. She didn't even know if Peipei's debit card had that much money on it. She took out her phone, was about to ask the Mathey Girls if the rate was normal—she knew that Wendy had her son in therapy to deal with his 'anger issues' and Maggie herself did therapy—and she saw an email notification on her phone. It was a message from Jose.

Just wanted to make sure you got my earlier message, it said. And then it repeated his original email: *Hi Esther, long time no talk. Just wanted to check in and see how things are. You might know that I'm with Solutris Consulting now. And I might have an opportunity if you're interested.*

He had always been so persistent. She still wasn't ready to answer; he would have to wait.

Her mind went back to why she had originally picked up her phone: the $250 appointment. She found that she had lost the will to ask the Mathey Girls for their opinion. What would they tell her, that Hannah wasn't worth it?

Of course Hannah was worth it.

Esther thought back to her own childhood and lack of therapy. And, when she thought about it, her parents' lack of therapy and Didi's lack of therapy. Would they have been happier, or at least less obviously broken, if they had sought professional help? No doubt they would have. Would it have been worth $250 an hour? That was a silly question, though, because there was no way in hell her parents would ever have agreed to pay that, even if they had considered going to therapy in the first place, which they clearly hadn't.

Esther wasn't going to let Hannah grieve in silence, alone. She herself had never been able to talk to anyone about her brother's death. No one. Not until college, when she met Claire and the other Mathey Girls, and she was removed enough from home and family to come to terms with what she had experienced. Maybe she should go to therapy now. No way. It was too expensive. And it was probably too late.

Esther's rambling thoughts were interrupted by Dr. Winter

bringing Hannah into the waiting room. He sent Hannah to the aquarium and sat across from Esther. "She did very well," he said.

"Good," Esther said, feeling proud that Hannah did well but at the same time unsure of what that meant.

"She really loves and trusts you," Dr. Winter said.

Esther flushed. "Thank you," she said, but Dr. Winter wasn't looking at her with praise or admiration.

"It's a very significant responsibility," he said.

"I'm aware."

Dr. Winter held her gaze, his x-ray psychological vision peeling away any barriers Esther was trying to put up with smiling and looking polite.

"I think Hannah will benefit greatly from therapy," he said, and then got up and called Hannah over. "Hannah, it was very nice talking to you today. I hope I can talk to you again soon, and we can continue our chat."

Hannah nodded, and Esther could tell that she liked Dr. Winter, or at least didn't dislike him. Dr. Winter signaled to Jenny and then went back into his office.

"Your card," Jenny said, setting out the card and an invoice for Esther to sign. The invoice had the charge for the first appointment, $250, and then a statement that Esther agreed that future appointments would be charged directly to this card without the need for paper invoicing.

"Actually," Esther said, "can you use this card going forward? I'm not sure how much is on that debit card." She handed Jenny one of her own credit cards; she would work out details with Laz later.

"No problem. And would you like to make your next appointment now?" Jenny asked.

Esther glanced at Hannah, who had again picked up the *Highlights* magazine. "How often are appointments usually?"

"It's up to you," Jenny said. "It could be a week, two weeks, some parents even do a month." Jenny's mouth turned down, presumably at the thought of the negligent parents who only let their children get therapy once a month.

Esther made an appointment for two weeks later, which seemed acceptable to Jenny. She made a mental note to ask Wendy how often she sent her son.

In the car ride home, Hannah sat subdued in the back seat.

"Did you like talking to the doctor?" Esther asked, glancing in the rearview mirror.

Hannah looked out the window. "I did," she said. "I could tell him things."

"That's good," Esther said. "I mean, you can always tell me things, you know."

"It's different," Hannah said. "I can tell him different things."

"Right."

"Don't feel bad," Hannah said.

"I don't feel bad. I'm glad you liked him." Esther gave Hannah a smile in the mirror. He said that she loves and trusts me, Esther thought. Then her mouth stiffened as she remembered Dr. Winter's next statement. It's a very significant responsibility, he had said.

13

Therapy had been a success, Esther thought, and she wished that getting Hannah's eyes checked were as straightforward. She sent Laz two reminder messages about making an appointment for Hannah's pediatric checkup before he finally responded on Saturday afternoon.

I found it. Aaron Chun is her pediatrician. Can you make appt for her? Laz said by text.

Esther gritted her teeth. *Yes.*

She called Dr. Chun's office and found that Hannah was past due for a checkup—they had called and emailed Claire as the parent on the contact list, but no one had made an appointment, and now they were fully booked until late August. All Esther could do was book the earliest available spot and turn to the Mathey Girls for advice.

Something doesn't feel right, she said in the chat. She explained the eyesight problem. *Do we just wait until August? That seems too far away.*

What does Laz think? Serena said.

He is not helping, at all, Esther said, and then she felt bad for saying that. *He's very busy with work.*

You need to get her eyesight checked ASAP!!! Maggie said. *If you don't get it fixed it will only get worse!!!*

Do I take her to an optometrist, or ??? Esther said. *Like an adult optometrist?*

You need to see a pediatric optometrist, and make sure it's covered by their insurance, Wendy said. *Probably don't need a pediatric ophthalmologist at this stage, unless there's a deeper issue involved.*

That sounds complicated, Esther said.

This really should be up to Laz, Serena said.

Wendy gave Serena's comment a thumbs up emoji.

You can't rely on Laz to take care of this stuff. Claire always had the mental load!!! The mothers always do!!! Maggie said.

What do you mean? Esther said.

You know, worrying about feeding, school, doctor's appointments, clothes, play dates, everything else. The mother is the one who has to worry about everything; dads don't think the same way, Maggie said.

That can't be right all the time, Serena said.

It's totally true, Wendy said. *Every mom I know agrees.*

What happens when the mother is dead, Esther thought, but she dared not type it.

What if there's no mom? What if there are two dads? Serena said.

There's always one person in the pair who bears the mental load, Wendy said.

And with Claire and Laz it was always Claire, Maggie said.

Wendy gave Maggie's comment a crying emoji.

Overwhelmed, Esther went through Maggie's message listing everything that moms worried about:

1. Feeding. This was Zhang ayi's responsibility. Thank God.

2. School. It was still summer, so she didn't have to worry about that, right?

3. Doctor's appointments. It seemed like Laz should do this but if it was just checkups Esther could try to keep on top of it. Except for the eye thing. She still didn't have an answer for that. At least therapy went okay.

4. Clothes. Esther had not thought about this at all. She would need to ask Hannah if she needed new clothes.

5. Play dates. Oh yes. Esther needed to arrange another play date with Kavi.

6. Everything else. What else could there possibly be?

Esther tried not to panic.

She panicked.

Because of, and in spite of, her panic, she closed WhatsApp and called Maggie.

Esther was nervous as it rang once, twice, wondering if she made a mistake, this was so awkward, and then Maggie picked up.

"Esther?" She sounded concerned; of course she did. No one ever called anyone out of the blue anymore. "Everything alright?"

"I need help." Then Esther started to cry as she admitted to Maggie how overwhelmed she felt. She didn't know what it took to take care of a kid. They were asking her to do mom things, but she wasn't a mom. She had never even really babysat before, not anyone other than her brother's kids, and even then someone else had always been there. Hannah needed something or someone better than her. She was afraid that she was failing Hannah, and that she was failing Laz, and that she was failing Claire.

When Esther was done panic-confessing, Maggie let out a deep sigh. "Let me think," she said, and Esther waited. The possibility that Maggie could solve everything was enticing.

"This shouldn't all be on you," Maggie said. "I'm sorry that we put so much pressure on you."

"Well, I'm here, in Philly," Esther said.

"But it's not fair that just because you're the one in Philly you have to be the one to put aside your career and your own life to take care of Claire's daughter. I think that we were so happy at this potential solution, we didn't think about whether it was the right thing to do."

"Wait—do you think I can't do it? I mean, I guess I can't. That's why I'm calling."

"It's not that you can't do it, it's just that you shouldn't have to do it all on your own." Maggie was choosing her words carefully, the way that Esther chose her words with Hannah when she wanted to make her feel better about something.

"How about this," Maggie said. "Let me talk with Laz, about the optometrist thing, and in general, try to take some of the load off of you."

"Oh," Esther said, "I wouldn't want to add more to Laz's plate. He already seems so beaten down with everything and busy with work." She felt a sinking feeling, like there was no good solution, that she was dragging everything down.

"He's her father," Maggie said, a sharp edge lining her voice. "Whatever he's going through, he can't just let you take all the responsibility for Hannah. That's not healthy for him, or you, or Hannah. And it's not sustainable."

Esther didn't say anything. Sustainability was not something she had let herself think about.

"Let me speak to him," Maggie said, "and I'll get back to you."

"Thank you," Esther said.

"Esther, don't be afraid to ask for help. Ever. Ask me, ask the girls, ask Laz. You're already doing a lot."

Esther mumbled another thanks.

"Maybe we could have Hannah visit us in California. Maybe you could bring Hannah to visit us! It could be a break for both of you. Oh that might be fun. Oh crap, I've gotta run for soccer pickup. Let me talk to Laz about a trip for Hannah. Talk soon, okay? Don't forget to ask if you need help, Esther."

Esther set her phone down, leaned back against her couch and took a deep breath of gratitude and relief. Maggie was on her side; Maggie was a mom and would get things done.

Esther could never call her actual mother at times like these. She had never had the type of mom who would solve her problems. As a child, Esther was supposed to never create problems, and if problems were created for her, she was expected to solve them on her own. She never talked to her mom about death, or difficult things. As a young adult Esther had thought that her mother had done a good job— Esther and Didi were industrious, committed, and capable people. Then Maggie and Claire had children, and they loved them openly and unabashedly, and Esther realized how different her childhood was.

She wasn't sure though—how much of her relationship with her mom had been affected by her older brother's death? If Caleb had stayed healthy, would her mom have been more like Maggie and Claire? Would she be talking to her mom right now, getting advice and support? She would never know.

***

Caleb had been a freshman at Princeton when he started getting sick. It took several months of worried calls home, visits to doctors and the ER, and their mom going to New Jersey for short sudden trips before he was diagnosed with liver disease. It was fundamentally unfair, he said with a laugh, that he was the one with a failing liver when he hardly drank at all. At age ten Esther had not gotten the joke, but she had remembered it, written it down, like so many other things Caleb had said to her. His absence when he left for college had felt so acute, she had to treasure what morsels he might drop when they saw him.

For a short period of time, Esther was glad that Caleb was sick because he came home immediately after his last freshman final exam and stayed home that summer, turning down his offer at a lab in the chemistry department.

She would think, later, that maybe her personal joy in having him home was the selfish tipping point that made him sicker.

Later than that, she would try to convince herself that that sort of thinking was irrational, that nothing she did or felt had any influence on her brother's sickness and death. Much later than that, years later, she would finally convince herself that that was true.

By the end of the summer after Caleb's freshman year, his diagnosis had been paired with a prognosis, and the odds were only slightly in his favor. If he got a liver transplant, and his body accepted it, he might live to be an old man. If he didn't get a liver transplant, he might die within a year. If he got a liver transplant, and his body rejected the liver, he would die sooner.

All of this Esther learned through overheard conversations, often with her mother in tears, often with Caleb trying to comfort their mother, and once with the roles reversed, Caleb in tears, their mother trying to comfort him in his anger and sadness.

"He might die," Esther told Didi, because she needed to tell someone every time she re-realized what lay ahead.

"I know," Didi said, because Esther had told him before. Didi would then run off to play, or at least run off to get away from her, and she would mull over that fact—Caleb might die—unsure of how she could possibly understand or deal with it.

Caleb wanted to go back to Princeton while he waited on the transplant list. Their father agreed, if that's what Caleb wanted, but their mother thought it was a terrible idea. In the end they compromised: Caleb went back for his sophomore year, and their mother quit her job and lived with a church friend's aunt in New Brunswick, a half hour away from Princeton and just ten minutes away from Robert Wood Johnson, the expected transplant hospital.

For three months Esther and Didi lived with their dad, alone, in limbo. He didn't cook, so they ate a lot of cereal, bananas, and casseroles from church friends. Esther made sure that Didi brushed his teeth and did his homework. In their regular calls, their mom would give updates on Caleb (he's working hard, he's joined the chess club, his bilirubin counts are stable), and their dad would lie to their mother and say that they were happy and fine and there was no need to worry about Esther and Didi. Everyone in the Hsu family understood that Caleb was the priority.

For three months, the family held out a deranged hope that an otherwise healthy man would die, in a car accident or similar, where his liver could be harvested and given to Caleb. The doctors said that Caleb was at the top of the recipient priority list: he was young, he had such a bright future ahead of him.

Ultimately, someone did die, a liver was found, the family went to meet Caleb and Mom in New Brunswick, and he got the transplant. The surgery was successful, but his body rejected the liver within a matter of days. The family was devastated—they had put so much hope and prayer into the doctors finding the donor that they hadn't considered the real possibility that Caleb's body would reject the dead man's gift.

He was put back on the list, back up high, but now Esther's family's hope was tainted with the fear of another success and rejection. Waiting for his second liver transplant, his kidneys failed. He got a new kidney—those were easier to source—no need for his mother's offer to give one of her own.

By the time of Caleb's kidney transplant, the whole family had moved to New Jersey. They lived in an extended stay hotel, a friend of Esther's parents' having helped them get an employee discount. Esther's dad renewed their stay at the end of each week, for three weeks. In the second week, Caleb was back in the ICU. In the fourth week, Caleb was gone.

Somehow, the Hsus packed up their hotel life and went back to Cleveland. It was hard for Esther to remember those days and weeks in New Jersey. What did she and Didi do all day when they were in the ICU waiting room? When visiting hours were over and the family retreated to their hotel room?

In the months following her brother's death, as silence blanketed the Hsu house and each member of the family retreated into his or her own chamber of pain, Esther had a lot of time to ponder serious questions. *Is there a God? If there is a God, why did my brother die? What happened to the livers and the kidney that Caleb's body rejected? Were they thrown away? Or were they given to the other people on the list? How did he get his liver disease? Will I get liver disease? Will Didi get liver disease? Did God give Caleb liver disease to punish him, or to punish us? How do Mom and Dad still believe in God after their son died? Is Caleb watching from heaven, if there is a heaven? But if there is a heaven, then there must be a God, and why would God make Caleb just to let him die?*

These were the types of questions that she wrote in her diary, and as an adult she still didn't have the answers.

There were other questions that were never written down. Questions about what she needed to do to make her family okay again. Questions about whether God had picked the right Hsu child to die, because surely Caleb was a much better person than she was, and what about Didi, he never even tried to be good. These questions she carried, simmering in her subconscious, through the rest of her childhood.

14

"More syrup please," Hannah said. She was enjoying a late breakfast of Eggo Waffles, a treat that Esther had introduced her and Zhang ayi to.

Esther grabbed the syrup from the island and handed it over, and Hannah poured a grotesque amount onto her waffle. Zhang ayi grunted and then Hannah passed the syrup over, and another grotesque amount was poured.

Esther's phone buzzed with a message from Laz. *Maggie invited the two of you to visit her in California this weekend. I think it's fine, if you're interested. Might be good for Hannah to get away. Also, I got Hannah an appointment with optometrist for day after tomorrow. Emailed you the details.*

He'd found a pediatric optometrist, someone at Children's Hospital of Philadelphia. Esther had to ask: *How did you get appt so fast?*

I asked my secretary for help and the optometrist is her friends daughter, Laz said. Esther had forgotten that Laz had a secretary. She wondered what else his secretary might be able to help with.

She looked up to see Zhang ayi swirling her fingertip in the syrup before popping it into her mouth with a flourish. Hannah laughed and did the same.

This is good, Esther thought. She wanted to diversify the people Hannah felt comfortable with. They spent more time with Zhang ayi and Jasper now, going to the park or taking walks together, and Hannah had her play dates with Kavi, drop-offs so that she wouldn't rely on Esther all the time. With a trip to see Maggie, Hannah's world could get even bigger.

At some point, Esther knew, she would have to start working again. Maybe in the fall, when Hannah was back in school. It was already mid-June and Esther hadn't yet replied to Jose's email, though she had looked him up on LinkedIn. In his new profile picture, he looked different—no glasses, shoulders back with a confidence that she hadn't seen before. He had gained weight and looked successful. Corporate.

If she was willing to see him again, Jose might be able to set her up in a good job. They had worked so well together, once upon a time. The Incident (as Esther thought of it) felt so far away now, foggy. And nothing had really happened, after all.

"Help, Esther," Hannah said. She had syrup on her hands and in her hair. Zhang ayi was nowhere to be found—the baby must have needed something.

"Hold on," Esther said. She wet a rag and tried her best to wipe Hannah's fingers and hair. "I think you'll need to take a shower."

"Whyyyyyy?"

"Because you got syrup all over your hair. Hey—it's on the floor too! Gross. Go take a shower, and don't step in the syrup. We can go to the playground when you're done."

Hannah left on tiptoe, holding her damp fingers in the air, trying not to contaminate everything with her mapleness.

Scrubbing the floor on hands and knees, Esther thought again about Jose's email. She couldn't not reply. It had been days; if she really wanted to get a job, if she was really willing to see him again, she needed to reply soon.

Jose and Esther had met when she was an analyst, he was an early mid-level consultant, and their Centridge managers found that they made an efficient team. When put on separate projects, paired with other people, each worked well, but there was a special alchemy when they worked together. The higher-ups recognized this, encouraged this, exploited this. As they do. Their principal Arnold started to use the duo on more of his projects, and he himself started to move up the ranks, and over time they were staffed almost exclusively on Arnold's deals.

Soon Esther was a consultant, Jose a principal, Arnold a partner, and a rotating carousel of analysts was brought into the mix before they found Stella. For a few golden years, they were what Arnold called Team Magic:

Arnold at the top, supporting and developing his talent, not doing much once the client hired the firm;

Jose, doing a lot of the work that Arnold should have been doing in addition to his own, not getting paid enough, but with his sights on partnership;

Esther, the powerhouse of the team, acting as crucial bridge between data and ideas, junior and senior; and

Stella, doing whatever Esther and Jose asked her to do, almost always perfect, never asking questions.

Esther had recognized Stella as a younger version of herself, and Esther wanted to be Stella's Jose. Because eventually Jose would be the partner, and Esther would be the principal, and Stella would be the consultant. It was thrilling to feel that their little group had unlocked the key to maximum efficiency, client satisfaction, and workplace camaraderie.

And now, here was Esther cleaning the floor of syrup, waiting on a nine-year-old to finish her shower, the days of Team Magic long gone. As she rose to take her rag to the sink, Esther admitted to herself how badly she missed that time.

Did she want to work with Jose? She wanted to work, and if it were at all possible to work with Jose the way they used to work, before it all went wrong, she would have jumped at the chance. It was hard to imagine that being the case. Still, she needed to reply, she couldn't just ignore him indefinitely.

She didn't let herself think too much about it; she whipped out her phone and sent him an email: *Jose, Congrats on the move. I'm in Philadelphia and currently between jobs. It would be good to catch up.* Almost immediately after sending the message she started to doubt herself. Could she make this work? Could she speak to him like a normal, emotionally neutral ex-colleague? She would have to. She wanted a job. They were adults. Nothing had really happened between them—right?

***

"Her vision isn't terrible," Dr. Ferns, the optometrist, said. "She definitely could use glasses, but her prescription is mild." She turned from Esther to Hannah. "You have to remember to take care of your eyes, young lady! Blink more, especially when looking at screens, and make sure you take breaks."

"I don't want to wear glasses," Hannah said.

"If you don't wear glasses and you strain your eyes you could start to get headaches, and you wouldn't want that, would you?" Dr. Ferns spoke in a higher register to Hannah than to Esther, her voice lilting as if she thought Hannah wouldn't understand a normal adult voice.

The doctor was young, and in her white lab coat and thick tortoiseshell glasses she looked like she was wearing the uniform of a professional—of what she thought an optometrist should look like.

Hannah shrugged and glanced at Esther for help.

"If the doctor says you need glasses, we should at least give them a try," Esther said.

"Miss—," Dr. Ferns said, glancing at the medical consent form Esther had provided at check-in, "How do you pronounce your last name?"

"It's Hsu, like *shoe*, but you can call me Esther."

"Miss Hsu, I understand that you're helping Hannah with her medical appointments in this... difficult time. Do you wear corrective lenses yourself? Do you have children?"

"I wear contacts," Esther said. "No kids of my own."

Dr. Ferns nodded. "You may be aware of a well-known study of children—they were of Chinese descent—who lived in Singapore and in Australia. In that study, the children in Australia had better eyesight than the children in Singapore, despite all being of Chinese descent. The difference?" She paused and raised her eyebrows. "The kids in Australia spent time playing outside. The kids in Singapore, it seems, spent time inside studying and looking at screens. Are you aware of that study?"

"No," Esther said. Of course not. Why would she be? Was the doctor saying that it was Esther's fault that Hannah had bad eyesight, because she didn't play outside? She did play outside, all the time, well maybe not all the time, but at least some of the time. They went to the park, didn't they?

"Esther tries to make me take breaks from screens," Hannah said. "She tells me to blink."

Dr. Ferns looked between the two of them as if trying to understand their relationship. Eventually she reverted to her higher-pitched child voice and said to Hannah, "Let's try to spend more time outside too, okay? And I bet playing outside will be more fun when you have glasses and can see everything more clearly."

After the appointment, they went to the eyeglass shop in a nearby mall to pick out frames. Esther asked the Mathey Girls on chat for advice, sending pictures with Hannah posing. One picture of Hannah in neon pink sparkly frames, one picture of Hannah in dark brown tortoiseshell.

She looks so cute with glasses! I'd get both in case one gets broken or lost, Maggie said in the chat.

Trusting Maggie, Esther ordered both.

The next day they would be flying to California to see Maggie for a long weekend. Laz had bought the tickets for both of them, even though Esther offered to use her miles or at least pay for her own ticket. It was a nice gesture on his part, she thought.

Immediately after glasses shopping, they went clothes shopping, as Esther had discovered that Hannah didn't have summer clothes that actually fit. From what she gathered, Claire would replenish Hannah's clothes as needed, but she must not have had a chance when she was pregnant.

"What do you think we need?" Esther asked, looking at the brightly colored display. "Like some shorts, some t-shirts?"

"I don't like shopping."

"I don't really like shopping either," Esther said, "but we have to get stuff that fits. How's this?" She pointed to a pink t-shirt that said *Girl power.*

"Yuck," Hannah said. She sat on the edge of the shirt display and crossed her arms.

"Let's make this fast," Esther said. "We'll get a couple of things, and then when we visit Auntie Maggie, we can ask her to take us shopping. She knows all about this stuff."

Hannah pushed herself up like a soldier accepting an assignment and nodded sharply.

They left the store with some shorts, shirts, new underwear, and sandals. Very, very basic wardrobe complete, Esther thought, hoping that this—all of this—was enough.

15

The next day, they were on a plane to SFO to visit Maggie.

"But how long can I watch screens?" Hannah asked, sounding hopeful but tentative, as if not daring to expect too much.

"I mean, there's not much else to do, so I guess you can watch the entire time?"

Hannah squealed, bringing her hands to her mask. "And do I have to wear the mask the whole time?"

Esther scanned the rows around them. "Eh..." The flight was mostly full, with about a third of the other passengers wearing masks. The elderly couple behind them weren't wearing them. Esther was tired of having to make what felt like a moral decision based on the moral decisions made by strangers, and having to make these decisions for someone who trusted her was an added layer of pressure. But she didn't want to get Maggie or her family, or the elderly couple behind them who didn't want to mask, sick. "How about you can watch the entire time, but you have to wear a mask when you're not eating and drinking."

Hannah accepted the proposal and put the cheap airline earphones in her ears.

It was Esther's first flight since before the pandemic. She was supposed to go home to see her parents last Christmas, but then Omicron had happened. She had taken it as a sign. No such sign had happened today, no news reports about record delays and cancellations, rising numbers in hospitals, no new variants to report, and most people weren't wearing masks anyway. No one requested to see the consent form that Laz had signed for the travel, or even asked how Esther was related to Hannah.

In what felt like another lifetime, she had flown many tens of thousands of miles for work, countless flights to countless cities. She had learned to travel light, buy a magazine at the airport that she would leave in the seat pocket when she disembarked, otherwise try to work or sleep on the plane because in those days she needed to be productive all the time and sleep was a contributor to her being productive at her destination. Everything was different now; instead of her work she had a nine-year-old. She settled back into her seat, tried to relax.

She was nervous and excited to see Maggie. Of the Mathey Girls, she had always felt like she related to Maggie the least. Part of it was for the most obvious reason: she was white. Perhaps Esther was being racist, but it was undeniable. Because even though Wendy grew up in Singapore, Serena in New Jersey and Claire in California, all very different from Esther's Ohio upbringing, they were still yellow faces at a university that was largely white in a country that seemed to identify itself as white, Black, or if you really had to mention it, other.

But Maggie wasn't like the white girls that Esther had grown up and gone to school with. Maggie's parents were diplomats; she had lived on three different continents growing up. She was white but she had more experience with life outside of America than Esther did.

From freshman year, Claire and Maggie had called themselves sisters from another mother because they were so similar in their habits and preferences—they both played the clarinet, both swam in high school, they even had the same favorite grape-flavored dental floss. How lucky that they had been assigned as roommates, everyone thought, though Esther was always a little jealous of how easily Claire and Maggie understood each other. Over time, Esther had come to accept that Maggie was just more intelligent, more interesting, more kind, more competent than she was, and therefore much more Claire's equal.

If Claire had left their lives immediately after college, Esther was sure that the Mathey Girls would have lost touch with Maggie. She would have been pulled away by the world that she seemed destined for: successful, white, and privileged, leaving Esther, Serena and Wendy behind. Over the decades, though, they had grown so tight together that despite the fact that their axle had been torn out, the wheel still held and still turned.

Maggie had moved right before the pandemic, and her new house was gorgeous, with an expansive view of the water. Even Hannah, who lived in a community of mansions and pirate ship play structures and buzzer gates, was impressed.

"It's so bright," Esther said as they stepped into the parlor. "So many windows."

"I wanted a place with a lot of natural light," Maggie said. "No, I *needed* a place with a lot of natural light. Because SF can be so gloomy on its gloomy days, I wanted maximum sun exposure at all times."

Maggie was wearing makeup, more makeup than Esther was used to. Esther herself never wore makeup anymore, not since she stopped working. Maggie's makeup seemed to match her house, beautiful and refined. "So we have two extra bedrooms, but one of them has become Jeremy's exercise room, so only one has a bed. We do have air mattresses though, so Hannah can either stay with you, Esther, or she can stay with Rosie." Maggie seemed to register the uncertainty on Hannah's face. "Rosie's at work right now—she's working at an ice cream parlor this summer—but she said she would be happy to have you bunk with her, Hannah."

Esther saw Hannah's drawn-in shoulders, the slight wrinkle on her forehead. "Do you think we could decide later, after we settle in a bit?" Esther asked on her behalf.

"For sure," Maggie said with a smile. "And if you want, you could stay with Esther tonight and then move in with Rosie tomorrow if you change your mind. Whatever you like. This weekend is going to be all about fun."

They spent the day at Golden Gate Park: Esther, Hannah, Maggie and her two boys. They went to the de Young Art Museum first, where everyone indulged Hannah spending too long in the textiles section. Esther told Maggie that the boys—Jeremy Jr. and Tommy, miniature versions of their dad with freckles and strawberry blond hair—were very well-behaved, very patient, and Maggie was visibly pleased by the compliment. When Maggie suggested they go to the Japanese Tea Garden after the art museum, Esther was afraid that it would remind Hannah of whatever sad feelings she might have had at the Japanese teahouse at the Philadelphia Museum of Art, but Hannah didn't seem fazed. She chased and was chased by Maggie's boys, and Maggie and Esther followed far behind like old dowager chaperones.

After Golden Gate Park, Maggie suggested that they go for ice cream.

"Can we go to the place where Rosie works?" Hannah asked.

"No, we shouldn't bother her at her job," Esther said at the same time that Maggie chimed, "Yes, absolutely, that's a fabulous idea!"

Being a mom seemed so easy for Maggie. Esther would never tell Hannah that any of her ideas were fabulous. This was exactly the type of thing that Claire would have said.

Maggie seemed so comfortable, so in her element, with the kids. Esther was feeling lighter and lighter just being with Maggie and the children, as if Maggie was Mary Poppins, effervescent.

***

That evening, Maggie set her wine on the table and sank into the couch with a muffled *floomp*—the sound of air compressing in the bowels of expensive upholstery. She was wearing a dusty pink tracksuit that looked too luxurious to ever be worn in a place as lowly as a running track, and the overall impression that Esther got, seeing Maggie in her soft pink outfit on her soft yet firm sofa, was plush.

Maggie studied Esther for a moment. "Have you ever tried the little wands that you stir into wine to take away the bad stuff?"

"Wands?"

"They're little plastic wands." Maggie made a stirring motion with her pointer finger in an imaginary drink. "They take out the allergens from wine. Not sure if that works with the Asian flush."

"That sounds magical," Esther said, and Maggie laughed. "No, seriously, it would be magical if I could drink alcohol and not get sick."

"Honestly, a glass of wine after the kids have gone to bed has been a simple pleasure that has carried me through many a long night." Then Maggie seemed to let go of her face from the day—the invisible string holding up the corners of her lips snapped, the muscles keeping her eyes wide released. In one moment, Maggie went from bright to burnished.

"It must be exhausting to have three kids," Esther said.

"Well," Maggie said, "I can't say it isn't. But it's not like I do anything else."

"I've heard that being a stay-at-home mom is like a full-time job,"

Esther ventured.

"It's so much harder." Maggie breathed a deep sigh. "But enough about me. Hannah seems really taken with Rosie," she said.

"Oh yeah. It didn't take her long at all to leave me behind in that huge guest bedroom of yours." Esther smiled to herself, thinking of how Hannah had attached herself to Rosie immediately after dinner. "Rosie's a great girl."

Maggie smiled, then hesitated. "She is. Things are going to get so much more... complicated the next couple of years."

"What do you mean?"

"You know, with boys, and hormones, and college."

"Right." Esther's own childhood was so sheltered, attending an all-girls prep school on scholarship from middle school, her parents keeping her from going to dances or anywhere else, really. Her own experience with boys and hormones hadn't started until she was in college, and by then she felt so far behind.

"You know, it's ridiculously difficult to get into Princeton nowadays. It wasn't easy when we applied, but now it's insane," Maggie said.

"But, I mean, you and Jeremy both went there..."

"Half the kids at Rosie's school have parents who went there. The competition is fierce, let me tell you." Maggie took another sip of her wine. "We're thinking of having her start fencing. We should have started earlier, but apparently there's a very good private coach who will have an open spot next month."

"Isn't Rosie just starting high school? You guys have at least a year or two before you need to worry about it right?"

"It's never too early," Maggie said. "It's always been on our minds, since Rosie was little, and the pandemic didn't make things any easier."

Esther couldn't help but think of that scandal in the news, the one where rich people had paid some guy to get their kids into college. The parents had ranged from wealthy actresses to wealthy fund managers to a random wealthy Chinese person. Esther recalled from the news that the wealthy Chinese person had paid the most, and this seemed particularly egregious. Then she thought of her own application to Princeton, and old feelings of shame reared up. It was as if they had been waiting to pounce, having been pushed down for years.

"Are you okay?" Maggie asked, reaching to rest her hand on Esther's knee. "I'm sorry, I shouldn't have brought up Princeton, and in such a glib way."

"No, no," Esther said. "I wasn't..." She didn't want to say that she wasn't thinking about Claire. She didn't want to admit it.

"I was thinking of setting up some kind of fund in Claire's name," Maggie said. "To raise awareness for... amniotic embolisms. You know?"

"Sure," Esther said.

"It seems important to do something."

Now both women were definitely thinking about Claire, each tucked into her own pocket of sadness on opposite ends of the couch.

There was an electronic chime and Maggie jumped up. "That's Jeremy. One sec." She left the room, and Esther could hear their dialogue. *Hi honey, hi honey, have you eaten, didn't get a chance. Oh let me heat something up for you, I thought you would have eaten. Thanks, I'm starving actually. Did Esther and Hannah make it here okay? Yes, Hannah's sleeping with Rosie tonight and Esther's in the parlor, why don't you go say hi. I'll bring you food in a second.*

Esther readied herself as Jeremy's heavy steps thudded down the hall.

"Hey Esther," Jeremy said as he walked in with his arms open wide. Jeremy was a hugger and Esther allowed him his hugs because he was married to Maggie.

"Hey Jeremy," she said to his shoulder. His shirt was stiff, and his cologne was the type of understated and masculine scent that reminded Esther of a high-end leather goods store.

Jeremy released her from his gorilla embrace and put his paws at his sides. "I'm so sorry I couldn't make it to the memorial service," he said. "I'm so sorry for your loss."

"It's all of our loss, really," Esther said. "And it's okay, about the memorial."

Jeremy looked at her with worry in his eyes, the same way that Maggie had looked at her earlier, and Esther let herself be examined. He motioned for her to sit, and she sank back into the cocoon of the couch.

He sat as well, in the armchair that matched the couch, though the seat was not quite as robust—this must be his usual spot—and the armchair gave a slight wheeze as he sat down. He had been a wrestler at Princeton and graduated before the Mathey Girls even arrived. When Maggie had showed them pictures of this guy she met at an alumni event, this brawny wrestling champ who was a teddy bear at heart, Esther hadn't understood the appeal. But he was a good guy. Esther knew this now, though many years ago she and the other Mathey Girls had resented him for allowing Maggie to give up on her PhD and her career ambitions because, Maggie had argued, being a mom needed to take priority given his busy work schedule.

"It's really great, what you've been doing for Hannah," Jeremy said.

"Oh..." Esther said, "I mean, any one of us would have done the same thing if they were in Philly."

"Maybe," Jeremy said. "But still, you're doing it, giving up a lot for Hannah, and I know Maggie is very proud of you."

Esther flushed. Take the damn compliment, she thought. "How is work?" she asked, to change the subject.

"Work is work. Busy, but I can't complain." Jeremy did something with funds. He had been doing something with funds since he had met Maggie all those years ago, and while his job titles had changed and the fund names had changed, it was always the same. Wendy understood—when Wendy and Jeremy were in the same room, they would always pair off to talk finance and whatever big money makers talked about. "You know," he added, "I think this trip will do Maggie a lot of good."

"What do you mean?"

"She's been so torn apart by Claire's passing. In a way it's to be expected, but she really has been a different person since she heard the news. It's been hard on the kids, seeing their mom like that, and I could tell this past week she was getting really excited for this trip. So thank you, for coming." Jeremy looked into Esther's eyes, and she wanted to hide. This much bare emotion coming from Jeremy of all people was too much.

"Here's some pasta, and some of that bread you like. The salad was wilted so I didn't think you'd want it," Maggie said, bringing in the food. "Do you want to eat in the dining room or...?"

"I'll eat here, if you guys don't mind," Jeremy said. "You girls can catch up while I eat." He tucked a napkin into his collar and began scooping up pasta, the fork looking tiny in his hand.

Esther watched Maggie look at Jeremy with steady fondness. She tried to imagine Maggie torn apart, a different person, just days ago. Now that Jeremy had said it, Esther could sense the fatigue and sadness hiding in plain sight on Maggie's face.

"Now what were we talking about?" Maggie smoothed her hair behind her ear and settled back down on the couch.

"Oh... Princeton," Esther said. Not Claire. We weren't talking about Claire.

Maggie grimaced. "You know, I can't bear to think that we're not allowed to think back to our time in college anymore."

"I know exactly what you mean," Esther said.

Jeremy looked up from his food. "You guys are absolutely allowed to think back to your Princeton days. In fact, you have to." He looked at each of them, Maggie and Esther, before continuing. "What you guys have is so special, and Claire might be gone, but that doesn't mean that what you guys have is gone."

Esther wasn't sure she agreed, but Maggie seemed convinced by what Jeremy said, throwing her arms around him and kissing his bald head. Then Maggie started sniffling, and Esther started tearing up, and she realized that he was absolutely right.

"Remember that time when Claire tried to cook that post-Thanksgiving sale turkey, and we set off the fire alarm and all of Spelman had to evacuate?" Maggie asked.

"And then the firemen came out with the charred bird and all the plastic stuff was melted inside because she didn't take it out beforehand," Esther said.

"And how one fireman had the audacity to pat Claire on the head because he thought she was so cute!"

"I remember how our apartment smelled like burnt plastic and turkey for a week after," Esther said.

"It was revolting."

"Claire felt so bad, and remember how we had to pretend that we didn't mind—we bought all those air freshener things to clean up the smell."

"And then it was even worse," Maggie said, and by then the tears in her eyes were from laughter.

Maggie and Esther looked at each other and understood that this was what they needed to do—resurrect the good stories, the funny stories, and never let them go. And so they started telling more stories, Jeremy joining the laughter. Many of these were new to him, and some of them were so ridiculous. Like the time Maggie wanted to pet that squirrel who was so close and then it turned on her and they all ran away shrieking. And the time that Serena went into the wrong lecture, late, and the professor called her out, and she realized with everyone watching that she was actually in the wrong building.

By the time Esther went to bed, she was sated with emotion, and grateful that, for the first time in weeks, she had laughed so hard that she cried, that her emotion had been a rainbow of sad to happy rather than just a tsunami of grief. She was grateful to Maggie for helping talk to Laz, for inviting them to visit, for still being alive and reminding her that she was alive as well.

16

The next day Maggie surprised them with a boat ride in the Bay. It was sunny but windy, and the boat swerved wildly on the water. Esther's knuckles turned white as they gripped the rail. The captain let Hannah hold the wheel; the wind whipped her hair, and she screamed in delight. Maggie had brought fried chicken to eat on the ride but most of it got thrown overboard, at first just one piece whipped off Jeremy's paper plate and then the boys tossed their pieces into the water.

After the ride they disembarked, wobbly, with crazy hair and delirium in their eyes. They went back home to rest, and Esther got to see Rosie's room. It was on the third floor, the attic converted into an entire living space with den, office and bathroom. To call it an attic was misleading though—no slanted roof or dark interior. Like the first floor it was airy and bright.

"Is that... a Princeton wall?" Esther asked, pointing to the wall behind the TV.

Rosie rolled her eyes. "Yes, yes it is. Obviously it's Mom and Dad's doing."

Esther went to take a closer look. It was as if Maggie had bought out the U-Store and transferred it all to this particular wall. Flag pennants, framed paintings of Nassau Hall, Blair Arch, Firestone Library. There were personal items as well: pictures of their family on campus, Maggie's diploma. Maggie's diploma?

"Dad has his diploma hanging in his office," Rosie explained. "Mom wanted her diploma hanging somewhere. So it's right where I can see it whenever I watch TV or hang out with my friends."

"Ah," Esther said. She saw, also, pictures of the Mathey Girls back in their college days. Fresh-faced, impossibly young. They were just babies then. She had seen copies of these pictures before, but she had never felt quite so old when looking at them.

"Are you going to go to Princeton for college?" Hannah asked as she nestled into one of Rosie's giant beanbags.

Rosie shrugged. "Obviously, my parents want me to go there. They went there. My Pop Pop and his dad went there too. But it's really hard to get in nowadays. Much harder than when my parents got in." She looked at Esther. "I might start fencing."

Hannah asked what fencing was, and Rosie started to explain the little she knew about it, while Esther let her eyes wander across the Princeton wall. She took a closer look at one of the framed pictures—a man and girl in front of East Pyne; the man's hand rested on the girl's shoulder. At first, she had thought it was one of their family pictures, but no, the man was older, lanky, definitely not Jeremy. The girl looked like Rosie, but the clothes were dated, and the picture had the pixelated feel of a 1980s drugstore Kodak print enlarged with twenty-first century technology.

"Is this your mom?" she asked, pointing.

"Yeah, with Pop Pop. My great-grandfather."

Esther felt a tinge of betrayal. Maggie had never told them that her grandfather and great-grandfather had gone to Princeton. None of the other Mathey Girls were legacy kids; Esther had only ever met one non-white person in her class at Princeton whose parent had gone there as well, and it had been for grad school. None of the other Mathey Girls' parents had gone to college in the United States, and Serena's dad hadn't gone to college at all. Esther suspected that this would have made a difference to them, knowing that Maggie's grandfather had attended Princeton, and that this was why Maggie didn't tell them. She would ask Maggie about this later, she thought.

"Esther, is that Mama?" Hannah asked. She had approached from behind and was pointing at a picture of Claire and Maggie in their freshman year dorm. They were wearing Mathey sweatshirts, arms around each other, sitting on the cushioned windowsill. Maggie's eyes were completely red from the flash, only a pinprick of yellow in Claire's dark eyes.

"It is," Esther said, reaching her arm around Hannah to pull her closer. "There's a couple of pictures of your mom here." She pointed them out one by one as Hannah followed with rapt attention.

"She looks so happy," Hannah said.

"Yes," Esther said. "She loved Princeton."

"Maybe I'll go there when I'm a grown-up," Hannah said.

Esther glanced over at Rosie, in the beanbag watching videos on her laptop. She didn't ever want Hannah to feel the kind of pressure that Rosie must be feeling. But she also knew that without parental pressure and dedication and possibly soul-destroying levels of stress, the likelihood of Rosie or Hannah getting into Princeton these days was minuscule. "You don't need to worry about that now," she said to Hannah.

Hannah nodded. She contemplated the wall for a moment longer, then slipped away to join Rosie.

Esther remained standing at the wall. She couldn't help but contrast Maggie's enthusiasm for the University with her own ambivalence. Princeton, storied for both its academic excellence and its elitism, the home of Albert Einstein yet the country club of the Ivy League. She knew she was amazingly lucky to have had the chance to go there. She appreciated the University, the academic experience, the future it opened for her, and of course the Mathey Girls. But ultimately, she had never been able to rid herself of the idea that she went there not for herself but for her parents. It had been her attempt to realize her parents' dreams, to fill the hole of Caleb's death the only way she knew how.

***

Maggie and Esther sat in deep Adirondack chairs on the back deck, looking out onto the water. The bottom of the sun had reached the horizon, a churning orange column beneath it as if the ocean were on fire. The waves crashed and slapped, discordant yet rhythmic, soothing.

The kids were playing inside, and Rosie had promised to get Hannah asleep by a decent hour, as Esther and Hannah were flying back the next morning.

"It's been a day," Maggie said. The light reflected off of her hair, giving her a crimson halo. She picked up her wineglass and took a sip. "A lovely day."

"Thank you so much for having us. And for finding all of those clothes for Hannah—I really didn't know where to start."

"No worries, I've had lots of practice buying kids clothes!"

The two friends let themselves be silent, lulled by the sounds of the surf. With someone else, the silence between them might have felt awkward, but their long friendship was like a blanket shared between them.

"Maggie," Esther said softly, "why did you never tell us that your grandfather went to Princeton? And great-grandfather?"

Maggie tilted her head, a small grimace on her face. "I felt like it was a dirty secret when we were in college. Like people, you guys especially, would have thought that I only got in because of my family. I know you thought that about a lot of the people we went to school with."

"I didn't think that."

"Serena definitely thought that. And maybe you didn't think that specifically about certain people, but we all knew it. Princeton has always been that kind of place, right? And I didn't want you or the other girls to think of me like that. I wanted to prove that I was smart enough in my own right."

"I never thought of you as anything less than brilliant," Esther said. "Honest."

"Oh Esther. You always thought everyone was smarter than you were. But in any case, I realized later that it didn't matter anyway. I didn't prove anything to anyone."

"What do you mean?"

"I made it so close," Maggie said, her fingers pinching together. "If I had hung on a couple years more, I could have finished my dissertation, and who knows? Maybe I would have been a professor, written a book, won a Nobel prize. Ha!" For a moment her eyes gleamed with what might have been, then she settled back into her chair.

"Do you regret—"

"No," she said. "No regrets."

"Maybe it's not too late," Esther said. "Maybe you could go back to school? Now that your kids are bigger."

"No, no," Maggie said with a laugh. "In the trade-off of career versus family, family wins hands down. And the field of biochemistry has evolved and grown so much over the last two decades that I don't even recognize it anymore. The stuff that I was working on, cutting edge stuff twenty years ago, that's like basic now. They explain it to school kids with YouTube videos."

The sun continued its slow descent past the horizon and a breeze brought cooler air. Esther zipped up her jacket.

"What about you? Do you ever wish that you had done things differently?" Maggie asked. "I mean, that you had…"

"Had kids?"

"I suppose, or just hadn't focused so much on career right out of college."

"It didn't feel like I had a choice," Esther said. "Once I started working, things didn't slow down for years. And I guess I never really wanted a family, or kids. I used to really like my job."

"Really? You always sounded so busy and stressed out by everything."

"I guess I just liked being good at something. Seriously good. I didn't mind the stress."

Maggie nodded. "I know what you mean, about being good at something. I miss that too."

"But you're a great mom, Maggie. That's a lot."

"It is," Maggie said. "But I wonder if I could be doing more."

"Whatever it is you end up deciding to do, you'll be great at it."

"Thanks Esther. And you—"

"MOM!"

"Mommy!"

Maggie's boys came bounding out onto the deck in their pajamas, with Hannah and Rosie behind.

"They wanted to say goodnight," Rosie said. The boys took turns hugging Maggie and giving her goodnight kisses.

Hannah walked onto the deck in her nightgown with hesitant steps. Esther saw Hannah eying Maggie, whose arms were wrapped around her youngest son.

"Good night, Hannah," Esther said, offering a hug as well.

Hannah considered for just a second before throwing herself into Esther's arms and planting a kiss on her cheek. "Goodnight, Esther," she said, before disengaging. "Goodnight, Auntie Maggie." She turned and ran after the boys back into the house, Rosie following like a sheepdog herding a young flock.

Esther turned to look back at Maggie, who was watching her with a wistful eye.

"What?" Esther asked.

"You're so good with her, you know. She adores you."

Esther flushed. "Hannah's great. I adore her too."

"I think Claire... I think Claire would be really happy to see how you're taking care of her."

Esther wanted to protest, to say that she was just helping watch Hannah, not really taking care of her, but stopped herself. She was invested in Hannah in a way no babysitter could be. She loved her.

17

Esther couldn't judge Maggie for wanting to be her own person in college, without the assumptions and expectations that came with being a legacy student. Esther herself hadn't been completely open with the Mathey Girls about her brother.

She hadn't felt able to tell anyone when she first arrived at Princeton. It was too complicated, too deep, and she was already too overwhelmed with navigating her present to dig up her past. As her freshman year and friendship with the Mathey Girls progressed, she realized that her family history was too important to keep from her friends and she regretted not saying something when they first met.

She resolved over freshman winter break that she would tell Claire first. But when Esther returned to Princeton for "reading period," the week-long study period before final exams after winter break, she couldn't find a good time. She carried her secret day to day like an engagement ring hidden in a pocket until the right moment, anxious that she might miss it.

On the last day of reading period, the two of them were studying in the basement of Firestone Library. They sat across from each other at a long wooden table amongst the shelves, one of many scattered throughout the massive building.

Esther, trying to build up the courage to unburden herself, watched Claire alternately flip through her econ textbook and scribble in her notebook.

Claire raised her head. "What's up?"

"I need to tell you something," Esther whispered.

Claire scooted her chair closer to the table and leaned forward. "What is it?"

Esther's fingers were clenched together in her lap. She forced herself to loosen them. "So this is weird. And I should have told you before. But I had a brother, who went to Princeton, and he died. He was a sophomore. I was eleven."

"What?!" Claire rushed to Esther's side of the table and wrapped her in a fierce hug. "I'm so, so sorry," she cried. Her voice echoed through the stacks and someone unseen told them to hush.

Claire pulled a chair close and put her hand on Esther's back. Her eyes were wide and starting to water, and seeing her friend almost cry was enough to make Esther cry as well. "What was his name?" Claire asked in a whisper.

"Caleb." She saw Claire struggling with how to respond, what to say. "I'm fine. I just wanted you to know. Maybe we shouldn't tell anyone else."

"Why not?"

Esther couldn't give a reason.

"I won't tell anyone," Claire said. "Or if you want, I can tell the other girls, if you don't want to do it."

"Thank you," Esther said.

"Why didn't you say anything sooner?"

What could Esther say? That she considered herself extremely awkward, that she never really understood her feelings until it was too late, that she was afraid that her friends would view her differently? She shook her head. "I thought it wasn't important, at first."

"Of course it's important!"

Someone directed another shushing sound at them, and then a male voice said, "I'm trying to study here!"

"Do you want to talk about it more, now?" Claire whispered.

"No, I just wanted to tell someone. I'm good, I think."

After a moment, when it was clear that Esther was done, Claire moved back to her side of the table and they resumed their studying, Claire throwing occasional reassuring glances (you will be okay) and Esther trying to throw them back (yes, I will be okay).

They didn't discuss Caleb further until several months later, when the Mathey Girls had decided that they were going to room together sophomore year (except Wendy, who wanted a single), and Esther had told Claire she was ready to tell the others, but she didn't know how to do it. A few days after that, the Mathey Girls held a surprise dinner for Esther, to say that they were there for her, always, and she could talk about her brother, or not, and they weren't mad that she didn't tell them, they understood, they would always understand. And that night, at that dinner, Esther had told them about Caleb. About how she had idolized him as a little girl, and how even when he was sick in the hospital, he would go around to other patients to give them encouragement and check in. How the nurses had told her that he was their favorite because he was so kind and had such a good attitude.

What Esther never told the Mathey Girls, not even Claire, was how fundamentally she was an impostor. She never told them how during the entirety of her childhood, people treated her better, cut her slack, because they knew about her brother. How she tried so hard to fill his shoes, but could never, because she just wasn't as intelligent or outstanding as he was.

And of course, she never told them how she got into Princeton, how she had used her brother to be admitted as a legacy, and how even her application essay was about his death. When she wrote the essay she had felt catharsis, but as she went over it, removing extraneous words and honing the description of her pain, she had let a clinical and cynical detachment take over. She let her brother's death become a tool. The only logical conclusion, as she understood it after she got accepted, was that she didn't deserve what she got. If Caleb hadn't died, and she hadn't exploited his death in her application, she wouldn't have gotten in.

***

When Esther stretched her arms, eyes closed, the sheets rustled with a sharp starchy sound, as if she were at a five-star hotel. For a moment in her post-sleep delirium, she wondered what project she was working on, what city she was in, and her heart quickened because it did not immediately come to mind. Then she opened her eyes and took in the muted pastels of the wall and the light coming in through the curtains. She breathed in notes of lavender and bergamot. No, she wasn't on a work trip; it had been two years since she had been on one of those. She was in Maggie's guest room. She swept her fingers along the duvet cover and wondered how it was possible that the sheets were so soft and still made that scruffy sound when she moved.

Another soft crackle as she turned to get her phone from the table. She had a notification of a Line message from Peipei: *Hi Esther. Lazarus said you took Hannah to California. Hope you have fun. My cousin Tingting will be going to stay with Lazarus and Hannah. Please tell Hannah.*

Esther went downstairs in her pajamas, and Maggie greeted her with a point toward the dining table.

"I made breakfast," she said. "I'm guessing you guys won't get a good meal on the plane."

Hannah was at the table devouring a Belgian waffle piled high with whipped cream, strawberries and chocolate syrup. She saw Esther approach and raised her eyebrows to say *look at these waffles!!!*.

Esther pulled a strip of bacon off a mound on a raised platter and surveyed the adjoining spread of eggs, waffles, hash browns, and fruit. "This is so fancy, Maggie, thank you," she said.

"Oh, you know, we don't use our waffle maker very often. And if we're doing the waffle bar we might as well make sure we have everything else, right? Let me get you a cup of coffee."

Then it was just Esther and Hannah and a table full of food.

"Hannah, do you know your aunt Tingting?" Grabbing a spoon, Esther popped a bite of scrambled eggs into her mouth.

Hannah shook her head.

"Mm. I think she should be your aunt, it's Auntie Peipei's cousin. Well, she's coming from Taiwan to stay at your house."

"When?"

"I don't know."

"How long is she gonna stay?"

"I don't know that either," Esther said, "but Auntie Peipei told me to tell you."

Hannah shrugged and went back to her waffle.

Maggie came back with two cups of coffee. She also was still in her pajamas, and her cheeks were flushed with what Esther guessed was happiness and the glow of accomplishment.

"These eggs are amazing," Esther said.

"Ah," Maggie said. "I've read a lot of cookbooks. And watched a lot of shows. I know all the secrets."

"And where is the rest of the family?"

"Jeremy's at work, so lame right, that he has to work on a Sunday. Not usually, but today there's some urgent something something. The kids are still in bed. I let them sleep in on weekends, you know they're so busy during the week. But I'll go get them—so at least they're up to say goodbye." Then Maggie was off, before Esther could tell her there was no need.

The Maggie that lived in this house was a different Maggie, Esther realized. Fully mother and wife, fully grown-up. When the Mathey Girls got together, she was the old college Maggie, pre-husband and pre-kids, pre-cooking and pre-hostessing. Out of all of them, Esther supposed that she herself had changed the least since college. Maybe not the greatest thing, she thought as she grabbed another slice of bacon.

The airport security line was horrifically long, but it was moving.

"Did you have fun?" Esther asked.

Hannah nodded vigorously. "Can we come back to California again soon? And maybe next time we can go to Disneyland."

"I think that would be a great idea," Esther said. "I've never been to Disneyland. Maybe when Jasper is a little bit older, your daddy can take both of you."

Hannah's eyes narrowed at the mention of her little brother back at home.

"Hey," Esther said. "Didn't you have fun playing with Tommy?"

"Yes," Hannah said with suspicion in her eyes.

"Well, when Jasper is bigger, he'll play with you like that." Esther watched Hannah consider this. "I used to play with my little brother all the time when I was young," she lied.

"Were you best friends?" Hannah asked.

Esther was about to say yes and then felt that this was a lie too far. "I wouldn't say we were best friends, but it was good to have someone to play with." In the face of loss, yes, it was good to have someone else.

"But," Hannah said.

"But what."

"But by the time Jasper is six like Tommy, I'll be fourteen, no fifteen. And Rosie and Tommy don't play together, and she's fifteen."

Esther looked at Hannah's obstinate little face. "Okay, okay, you win," she said.

Hannah smiled grimly, then said, "I still want to come back to California. Before I get old."

"Got it. I'll let your dad know."

"Oh, Esther," Hannah said, "we have to get postcards. At the airport shop."

"What for?"

"For the scrapbook."

"Oh," Esther said, and her heart sank as she remembered that Claire used to make scrapbooks of their family trips, using photos and postcards and ticket stubs. Esther hadn't thought to save any physical reminders of their trip. She was surprised that Hannah even remembered the scrapbooks from before the pandemic.

Hannah took Esther's hand. "We don't have to do a scrapbook," she said, shuffling forward and pulling Esther along with the line.

"No, no, we'll do it," Esther said. "We'll try."

On the plane, Hannah was again excited for five hours of screens, already scrolling through the options.

Esther sent Laz a text: *we boarded, will take off soon.*

Soon her phone chimed with his reply: *Have a good flight. Peipei told you that our cousin Ting Ting will be coming tomorrow? We are getting the guest room ready.*

No, she didn't mention it would be tomorrow, Esther thought, but she gave his message a thumbs up emoji.

And then Laz sent another text: *Thank you for everything.*

"Aw," Hannah said when her cartoon was interrupted by the security briefing. Still, a screen was a screen; she continued to stare through the seat belt and oxygen mask instructions.

Esther nudged Hannah and reminded her to blink, then put her phone in her lap and relaxed back into her seat. This time she was sitting in between Hannah and a scrawny teenage boy whose massive red over-ear headphones and shaggy hair obscured much of his face. She closed her eyes, content and placid. This had been a good trip. Her relationship with Maggie was closer now than it had ever been, and she felt a sense of relief that the trip had drawn them together instead of showing them how different and incompatible they were without Claire. No, they could be just as close, closer, even without her. Because, Esther was realizing, this was the only way forward. Claire wasn't coming back, and none of them could afford to feel sadness or guilt whenever they were together.

And Hannah. Hannah had had fun. She had not once this weekend withdrawn into sadness, which she still did occasionally in Philly. Esther had seen how Maggie's overt motherly happiness buoyed Hannah's spirits, and she thought yes, she could do this, she could try to be happier around Hannah. Maggie's happiness around the children wasn't fake; it was a calculated decision to set aside the darker realities of life for later when the children were asleep. Esther would try to do this. Ironically, she realized, she had done something similar when she was young after Caleb died. She had put on a brave face and acted happy when she was around her parents, so that they would be less sad. And hadn't it worked? Eventually they had all pushed past the grief. For the sake of others of course she could act more positive, more uplifting, more nurturing.

"Look," Hannah said, poking Esther's arm and pointing to her screen. "Pokémon!" Maggie's boys had introduced Hannah to Pokémon, with their cards and their toys and their games, wielding their encyclopedic knowledge to impress her.

This was healthy, Esther thought. A nine-year-old girl being interested in nine-year-old things. She bent down to get her water bottle from her purse and saw the postcards Hannah had picked out in the airport. The Golden Gate Bridge, the Japanese tea garden, Fisherman's Wharf. *Wish you were here*, the last one proclaimed in yellow block letters.

Esther took a sip of water and looked again at Hannah. Yes, Hannah looked more like Laz, but her spirit was Claire's. And Esther would do whatever it took, as long as it took, to nurture that spirit.

Part Three

18

"Esther, we're making Tingting try waffles," Hannah said as Esther set her bag down on the kitchen island.

"*Auntie* Tingting," Esther reminded her. She waved to Jasper, fat and happy in his bouncer, a little reclining Buddha with his hands reaching for the rays of sunlight as they passed through the window. "What do you think, Tingting?"

"Tastes delicious," Tingting said.

"Yummy," Hannah corrected.

"Yummy," Zhang ayi echoed.

"I'm going to make coffee. I was running late. Tingting, do you drink coffee?" Esther asked, rummaging through the cabinets.

"Yes, I drink coffee," Tingting said, her English halting and forced. When they had met two days ago, Tingting was embarrassed, but Esther had reassured her that her English was very good, and that she could understand just fine.

She looked like she was in her twenties, though her cherubic round face meant that she could be anywhere from college-aged to her mid-thirties. The thin wire glasses indicated trendy and young. She covered her mouth when she smiled, and she had the high nasally voice that Esther associated with young Taiwanese women who didn't mind being categorized as cute. Tingting was congenial and accommodating and on the whole reminded Esther of a steamed sweet bun.

Yes, Tingting was a pleasant addition to the household routine. But was she staying for just a little while? Forever? It was unclear. She was going to start work the following week at a pharmaceutical startup that was, of course, run by one of Peipei's Taiwanese friends. What was she going to do there? Unclear.

Esther had been surprised to learn that Laz had never met

Tingting before. She was a cousin, but not really, only somewhat more factually than the way that unrelated friends of parents were aunts and uncles. She was someone's cousin's spouse's daughter, or something, originally from Kaohsiung, smart enough to have gone to a university in Taipei that was, according to Laz, very good.

Esther poured two cups of coffee and handed one to Tingting. "I think there's creamer in the fridge. Do you want sugar?"

"I drink black," Tingting said, taking a sip.

Esther raised an internal eyebrow.

"Can Tingting come with us to get the glasses?" Hannah asked.

"*Auntie* Tingting," Esther said again. "And sure, she can come with us, if she wants. But then we need to go to Dr. Winter."

"My therapist," Hannah told Tingting.

"Sera-pist?" Tingting looked at Esther for explanation.

"Therapist," Esther said. "Um." She pulled up Google Translate and showed Tingting.

"*Zhiliaoshi*?" Tingting asked. She looked Hannah up and down, inspecting her body. "Hannah is sick?"

Before Esther could think of how to explain, Hannah said, "I'm not sick. The therapist is because my mama died. So I can talk to him about special things."

"Special things," Tingting said, processing, but neither Hannah nor Esther volunteered to give her any more information.

In the eyeglass shop, Hannah turned her face side to side, up and down. "I look weird," Hannah said.

"You look very cute," Esther said. Like a little librarian, but she wouldn't say that part out loud.

Hannah took off the brown glasses and put on the sparkly pink.

"So cute!" Tingting said. She gave Hannah's shoulders a squeeze, putting her face next to Hannah's in the mirror. "We have glasses, cute together."

Yikes. But Hannah laughed, so whatever.

"How does everything look?" Esther asked. "Less blurry?"

"It feels a little... strange," Hannah said. "But it's better."

They left the shop and Esther checked the time. Then she saw the naked longing in Tingting's eyes as they roamed the length of the mall.

"Tingting, did you want to do some shopping?"

"Oh yes!" Tingting said. "We can go shopping?"

"Well, if we wanted to take you home before the appointment, we should leave now," Esther said. Tingting nodded sadly, unable to draw her eyes away from the storefronts. "But maybe you could shop while we go to the appointment. It's only five minutes from here, and we could pick you up when we're done."

Tingting clapped her hands together. "Thank you, yes."

"Esther," Hannah said, "then we can shop too, right, if we don't need to drop Tingting off?"

"*Auntie* Tingting," Esther said. "And yes, we can, but didn't we already get enough clothes with Auntie Maggie last weekend?"

"Can we go to Claire's?" Hannah asked. "We didn't go to Claire's with Auntie Maggie." Both Hannah and Tingting were looking with urgency at Claire's.

"Sure," Esther said, relieved that Hannah didn't seem to make the connection between the shop and her mother's name. Hannah grabbed Tingting's hand, and they trotted to the store. Esther sauntered over, in no rush to look at beaded hair clips and stuffed animals with giant eyes. She followed Tingting and Hannah through Claire's, and then Justice, and then they decided to take a pretzel break.

Now, not only did Hannah have her sparkly pink eyeglasses, she was wearing a tufted pink kitty headband and had a set of flimsy crystal-studded bangles on her wrist. They clattered as she took a long draw of lemonade and handed the cup to Tingting, who tried it and pronounced it "So yummy!" before handing it back.

"We should head out," Esther said. She tried her best to wipe cinnamon sugar off her fingers. "Tingting, did you still want to shop?"

"Yes, if okay."

"No problem, I'll text you when we're on our way back from the appointment." Esther then realized that Tingting hadn't paid for anything yet. "But... do you need money?"

Tingting chuckled. "I have. Peipei gave me this." She opened her Hello Kitty wallet and pulled out a card that looked just like the one Peipei had given Esther.

"Great," Esther said, though this felt weird.

As Esther and Hannah left, Tingting drank from the giant

lemonade, eager eyes scanning the stores near the food court.

Hannah bounded out of Dr. Winter's office after her allotted hour. "Let's go back to the mall and get Tingting."

"You mean *Auntie* Tingting," Esther said. "Gimme a sec." She directed Hannah to the chairs in the far corner and went to speak with Dr. Winter next to his office door.

As usual, they lowered their voices, as if Hannah wouldn't hear. "She's doing well," Dr. Winter said. "She's opening up."

"I thought she opened up last time," Esther said.

Dr. Winter let out a benevolent grunt. "The process of a child opening up to a mental health professional is not a one or two visit endeavor," he said. "Especially after a traumatic event."

"Of course," Esther said. This was why people like her parents hated the idea of therapy for their kids.

Dr. Winter seemed to sense Esther's annoyance. "But she is definitely improving, and I expect she will continue to improve over time. I suggested that she write down her thoughts and feelings in a diary or journal, a safe space outside of our visits. She said that you bought her a blank diary at the art museum, and she's been writing in it?"

"That's right. I try to remind her to write."

"Very good," Dr. Winter said. "Please encourage her to express her thoughts when she feels like it. And also remind her that it doesn't matter if she spells things correctly or writes neatly, as no one will be reading it." He raised one eyebrow. "She likes things to be perfect," he said.

Esther looked back at Hannah, who was paging through an issue of *Time*. "She's a smart girl," Esther murmured.

"Indeed," Dr. Winter said. He then held his hand out, directing Esther towards Jenny to make the next appointment, and slipped inside his office.

***

"TGIF! TGIF!" Hannah sang as Esther came in through the door.

"Wow," Esther said. "Someone sounds cheerful this morning."

Hannah pranced up to her and started leading her to the kitchen. "We have a surprise for you! Shh!"

Bops and high-pitched tings of Chinese pop music echoed from the kitchen. When they reached the entrance, Hannah planted herself legs apart and thrust jazz hands towards the kitchen island. There, alone on the broad expanse of marble, stood a cup of coffee and a waffle doused in syrup.

"We made you breakfast!" she shrieked.

"Wow, thanks Hannah!" Esther said, plastering a smile on her face.

Tingting popped out from behind the refrigerator door. "Surprise!"

"Thanks, Tingting. This is really nice," Esther said.

Hannah gestured frantically again to the food at the island, and Esther sat on a stool. "Did you eat already?" Esther asked.

"Yes, I had Lucky Charms," Hannah said. "Two bowls."

"That explains the energy," Esther said, taking a sip of coffee.

"I can make the coffee now," Tingting said. "Is it right?"

"It's perfect." Esther looked down at her mug. "Actually, I feel like it's better than when I make it. What's your secret?"

"I watch YouTube," Tingting said. "In Chinese."

"Esther, guess what," Hannah said, sidling up to her.

"What?"

"Auntie Tingting is going to teach me Chinese."

"Oh, really? That's great," Esther said. "You can finally use those books Auntie Peipei sent over."

"I know!" Hannah crowed. "I showed them to her yesterday, and she said she'll teach me. I told her you couldn't do it."

Esther smothered the instinct to defend herself. She looked at Tingting. "Thank you—that will make Peipei very happy."

"No problem," Tingting said.

Hannah did a little shuffle with her feet. "Did you like your surprise?" she asked, wagging her head to the beat of the music.

"Yes, of course, thank you."

"It's to thank you for coming every day," Hannah said.

"Thank you..." Esther saw a look pass between Hannah and Tingting. "But I'm still coming next week, right?"

Hannah laughed. "Yes, Auntie Tingting has to work."

"Afternoons only," Tingting said.

"What? Really?"

"I only work in afternoons. So you can come here in afternoons only. You can work in mornings now." Tingting's eyes were bright and guileless, as if she was genuinely happy that Esther had time to work.

"Oh," Esther said. She turned to Hannah. "Is that what your daddy said?"

"Yes," Hannah said. "He said that I was very lucky that you gave up your working time for me. And that now you can have your mornings free. And that I should say thank you. But I had a better idea —the surprise." She did her jazz hands toward the waffle again.

"Great," Esther said, taking another sip. She kept a smile on her face. She understood that this was a gift to her, a show of gratitude, and she needed to accept it with grace. She ate her waffle and willed her face to remain pleasant as Tingting and Hannah chattered about the plans for the rest of the day. Tingting needed to go shopping again to buy clothes for work, and she asked if Hannah and Esther wanted to come.

"I'm tired of shopping," Hannah said.

Bless you, little one, Esther thought.

"Okay, no problem, I go by myself," Tingting said.

"Do you need us to drive you? We could drop you off at the mall," Esther said.

"No need," Tingting said. "I drive green car."

"The Prius," Hannah said.

Esther looked at Hannah. "You okay with that? Your daddy's okay with that?"

"It was Daddy's idea," Hannah said. "It's just sitting there, and no one is using it."

"I have keys," Tingting said. "I drive in Taiwan."

"Daddy checked," Hannah said. "She can drive with her Taiwan driver's license."

They were explaining this to Esther as if she were a small stupid child. And of course, it all made sense, a car was just a car, and it was sitting there, and Tingting had a drivers' license, and she needed to buy clothes for work. And the mornings—of course Esther wouldn't need to come in the mornings. Zhang ayi had always been there;

Esther probably wasn't needed anyway, but now if Tingting was there of course she could watch Hannah. And of course Tingting could teach Hannah Chinese. It would be easy since Tingting spoke both Chinese and English, and if Hannah was willing to learn of course she should learn the language if given the opportunity, and of course, and of course, and of course.

Later that day, Esther and Hannah went to the Westover Reservoir to see the ducks. Westover sat a couple of towns over from Brixton, the radius of their adventures together having grown as time went by. The last time they had gone to the playground nearby, Hannah had seen a large group of ducks in the pond, and now Esther was fulfilling her promise that they would feed them.

It was late afternoon, but the day was still bright, and light shimmered on the slowly moving water. They sat on a bench under the shade of a dogwood tree as Esther rummaged through her bag for the bread.

"Hey, I was thinking, would you want to visit Chicago?" Esther asked.

"Why?"

"We could go visit Auntie Wendy."

Hannah shrugged and hopped off the bench, bread bag in hand.

"It would be fun," Esther said. "Like our trip to California."

Hannah started throwing out small pieces of bread a few yards from the water's edge, and the ducks came out of the water to meet them. There were about twenty of them, and the sedate air with which they glided on the pond was lost as they waddled in chaos to the bread.

Esther and Hannah had sneaked the loaf out of the kitchen when Zhang ayi wasn't paying attention, as they knew she wouldn't approve of throwing good food to ungrateful animals. Esther distracted Zhang ayi and Hannah grabbed the bag, trying to keep a crinkling to the minimum while dashing out of the kitchen, and they reconvened in the hallway, hands clamped over their mouths to smother their laughter.

"Does Auntie Wendy have kids?" Hannah asked.

"She has a son, Kingston. He's thirteen, in between Jeremy Jr. and

Rosie."

Hannah shrugged again, unenticed by the idea of visiting a teenage boy. "Kingston is a weird name."

"He has a lot of Pokémon stuff," Esther offered.

Hannah perked up, considering.

Suddenly, a mallard pecked at Hannah's foot, and she yelped and hopped backward. "No thank you!" she shouted to the duck, and as a group they took a collective waddle backward.

Hannah thrust the bag of bread at Esther and went to examine the other side of the pond, far from the ducks.

Slowly, the ducks advanced toward Esther, heads swiveling between her eyes and the bread in her hands. She put the rest of the loaf in her backpack. The ducks continued their approach, eying the backpack.

"No! Bad ducks!" she hissed, and they paused.

The mallard, the one who had pecked at Hannah's foot and was clearly the most foolhardy of them all, ran towards her, and the other ducks joined in a frenzy. Out of instinct and fear Esther kicked out. Her foot seemed to make contact with something but she wasn't sure because now the ducks were a mass of indignant squawks and honks and flutters and feathers.

"Esther!" Hannah called. "No! Ducks! No!" She ran over, spinning her arms like a deranged windmill. The ducks scattered and she threw herself into Esther's arms. "Are you okay?" Hannah asked.

"I'm okay," Esther whispered.

"Maybe we should go get some ice cream," Hannah said into Esther's shirt. "I don't like the ducks after all."

Esther's pounding heart began to slow. "No more ducks," she said. "Let's get some ice cream." As they walked toward the car, Esther squeezed Hannah's hand. "Thanks for saving me from the ducks," Esther said.

"You're welcome," Hannah said, adding a grim nod, like a soldier who just completed a fraught mission.

19

Guys, can we do a group Zoom sometime soon? Esther and I had such a great weekend together and I really miss everyone. Thank you Esther for bringing Hannah (and bringing yourself), it was really good for my soul, Maggie said in the *Mathey Girls* chat.

Jealous, Wendy said. *When are you going to bring Hannah to Chicago?*

Maybe this can be your summer itinerary, Serena said. *You can bring Hannah to visit each of us in turn. I vote NY next - we're the closest.*

No! Come to Chicago, Wendy said. *Kingston needs a friend. And I need a friend to help me deal with Kingston. :(*

Kingston was thirteen, Wendy's only child, and according to Wendy he had decided that this was the summer that he was going to start hating his mother and asking to move to Singapore to be with his father.

It's true, I think Kingston and Wendy need us more than Serena and Val, Esther said. She got a thumbs up emoji from Wendy and a thumbs down emoji from Serena.

My kids all miss Hannah already and are asking when she can come back, Maggie said. *Especially the boys. They want to teach her more Pokémon.*

She loves Pokémon now, Esther said.

OMG Kingston has a million Pokémon cards and figurines that he no longer plays with. Tell Hannah that if you two come visit us, she can have all of them, Wendy said.

In any case, we need to do a Zoom. It's been too long. Let's find a time where we can spend an hour or two looking at each other's beautiful faces, Maggie said.

It was evening and Esther was back in her apartment alone. She had been reluctant to leave the Chen house, and when Laz had asked her to stay for dinner, she had said yes, sure. With Tingting at the dinner table, the family seemed happier and more complete. And Esther was trying to be more upbeat around Hannah, more like Maggie. They had laughed at dinner over the four pairs of shoes that Tingting had managed to buy in the hour that Hannah was with Dr. Winter, a silly thing but at least they were laughing.

On the drive back to her apartment, Esther found herself deflating. That afternoon she received yet another email from Jose. She had written that she would be going to California and would be busy for a few days, and he had gamely waited until they were back to follow up. *Hope your trip went well. Are you free to chat this week? Really looking forward to reconnecting.*

"Reconnecting"—as if The Incident hadn't happened and they had simply lost touch over the years.

The Centridge Christmas party (officially the Holiday Party, but everyone knew it as the Christmas party) was held each year at a different swanky hotel ballroom or bar. 2015 was a special year for Jose, because he was positioning himself for the upcoming spring's preliminary partner selection pool.

It was the end of the evening. They had worn their extrovert masks for hours, Jose sidling up to partners, one after the other, introducing and re-introducing himself. Esther had played the part of wing woman, supporting his efforts to be visible. While they were known as part of Arnold's Team Magic, if Jose was going to get promoted, he needed to be seen as distinct from Arnold. That was Jose's thinking, anyway, and Esther had been happy to assist.

But Esther had barely slept the night before. Running on fumes, she would have skipped the Christmas party if Jose hadn't asked her to come help. She had promised to be there for him, so she went.

They had to tackle the event as a team. How else to get noticed, make their way up the food chain? And they had earned it, hadn't they? They deserved to be recognized. And this was their (Jose's) chance to get drunk and chummy with the higher ups—it's not like he was invited to drinks on their personal time.

Toward the end of the evening, Esther and Jose sat in a curved booth, worn out from all the chitchat.

"Did you talk to everyone you needed to talk to?" Esther asked.

"I think so," Jose mumbled. "Everyone's too wasted for it to make any difference now anyway."

Esther knew Jose himself was pretty far gone at this point, after downing shot after shot with various partners. While she hadn't had any alcohol, she herself felt under the influence of something. Maybe the combination of fatigue and the energy drink she had gulped down before the party, the two cigarettes she had smoked trying to be social, the Cokes she had been sipping throughout the night. All that plus the energy of the evening filtered her experience as if she wasn't quite there.

"Look," Jose said, nodding his head toward the door.

Esther saw their partner Arnold leave with a young analyst, his arm around her waist, the two stumbling against each other. From behind, it almost looked like Arnold and his wife, except the analyst's blond hair was wavy instead of straight.

"He definitely has a type," Jose said.

"Gross."

"What about you?"

"Do I have a type?"

"No, are you seeing anybody these days?"

Esther snorted. "When would I have time to see anybody? I'm too busy working or helping my friends get promoted."

"Thanks, though, for tonight," Jose said. "I really appreciate it. You're always there for me."

"Yeah, no worries."

"When I make partner, I'm going to help you too, you know."

Esther understood. No one else was going to help them, so they had to help each other.

"Sometimes I feel like it's so close," Jose said, "but other times it seems like it will never happen."

"Partnership?"

"Partnership and, you know, happiness."

Esther turned to look at him. "You're not happy?"

"I don't think so," he said.

"But you have your wife, your kid..."

"I work all the time."

Esther's eyes followed another couple as they walked toward the door. "I work all the time too, and I don't have a family or kids. This is all I have. And I think I'm happy. Happy enough."

"You deserve more than *happy enough*," Jose said. "You deserve to be with someone who appreciates how amazing you are."

A thin layer of silence settled at their table, and Esther turned to see Jose looking at her with large and limpid eyes.

He leaned toward her and time both slowed down and rushed forward as she felt his lips on hers.

She didn't pull back from the kiss. She leaned into it, into him, and when he put his hand on her neck, she didn't push it away. He tasted like alcohol. He was sloppy, his tongue roving in her mouth. For a moment this felt right, in this dark bar, music loud, everyone having thrown their inhibitions away. For a moment she allowed herself to explore, to see what it might be like to be someone else, someone who didn't think about what was right and wrong. Then his other hand was on her back, pulling her toward him, and as she raised her hands, she found herself pushing him away instead of succumbing to his embrace.

"What?" he asked.

She scooted back toward the far end of the booth, glancing around. It was dark and loud, and she couldn't tell who might be watching.

"What?" he asked again, and his eyes traveled from her face to her neckline and back again.

"We can't," she said.

He tried to lean toward her again, but she stopped him with a hand on his shoulder. "It's not right, Jose."

At this he seemed to sober up, for just a second, and he moved back.

"Don't we deserve to be happy?" he asked. He didn't take his eyes away from her as he reached for his drink.

She didn't know how to answer. She had thought she was fine, that they were both fine, but there was a naked hunger in his eyes that scared her. Not because she was afraid of him, necessarily, but because she was afraid of whatever existed between them now.

"I think I'm in love with you," Jose said.

"I think you're drunk," Esther said, trying to keep her tone light. "I think you should go home now. To your wife."

"I'm drunk, but I'm also in love with you."

Esther knew that he was being sincere, even though his words came out slow and slurred. She felt adrenaline coursing through her; the distinction between her clarity and Jose's lack of control was painfully stark. "Jose, here's the plan. You're going to go home to your wife, and we are going to pretend that tonight didn't happen."

Jose's shoulders slumped. "I don't want to go home," he said.

"Then I'll see you tomorrow," Esther said, and she slipped out of the booth.

She didn't look back as she left the hotel and managed to hold herself together until she was in a cab. She let the tears fall then.

Back at her apartment, Esther tried to understand how she had misread her relationship with Jose that badly. They had always been so professional despite how closely they worked together; she had never suspected any flirtation or subtext. Thinking further though, maybe they had shared too many inside jokes, spent too much time alone together.

Should she have been smarter, more careful?

She told herself that nothing had actually happened; a kiss, yes, but she stopped that and then he just said something stupid. This was nothing like other experiences she knew of, lecherous principals taking advantage of young analysts, of actual physical assault, of rape.

She was safe.

Why was she so upset, then?

She had respected him as a brilliant and decent man. She thought that he had respected her as a hardworking and capable woman.

She thought she had found a place where she was valued for who she was, that brought out the best in her, and that this was a pathway to personal fulfillment. That the hours of stress and fatigue were worth it, not for the salary she earned but for the sense of purpose it gave her.

Her thoughts whirled around their relationship before, their teamwork with the partners tonight, the kiss, the part after before she escaped from the hotel bar.

The kiss—she hadn't pulled away immediately. She had been reckless in kissing him back. She had been sober, and he had not. She should have known better.

And the fact that Jose had said he loved her—when had she last heard that from someone? This was a moment stolen, beautiful words that she had thought she might hear again, someday, when the time was right.

What if the reason that Jose had wanted to work with her wasn't because she was *just that good*, as she liked to think, but because he was attracted to her?

The morning after The Incident, Esther was brave. She put on a blouse and slacks and makeup and went into the office and sat at her computer. She thought that Jose might want to clear the air, but he called in sick. She tried her best to get work done but her hands trembled at her keyboard.

That afternoon she went to Arnold's office and asked to be put on a new project in Tulsa she had heard about. She gave him an excuse about wanting more responsibility, and Arnold praised her for her initiative—she could go on-site immediately for due diligence. When she finally saw Jose in the office again, it was almost two weeks later. They barely acknowledged each other, Esther turning quickly away as Jose gave her a silent nod.

That was the end of Team Magic, a swift slit to the throat. Esther considered it humane at the time, both to herself and to Jose.

After The Incident, after Esther had been moved to deals with various other principals with whom she didn't mesh quite so well, Jose had never tried to contact her at Centridge. He must have known that she had asked to be put on different projects. He had always known her too well.

Now, six years later, she took a deep breath and replied to his latest email. *Let me know if you are in Philly. We can meet for coffee.*

20

It was Monday morning and Esther had wanted to sleep in, but her body insisted on waking up at eight. Sleep more, she told herself as she lay in her bed. No one needs you right now.

She flopped over and buried her face in her pillow, thinking of her text conversation with Laz the night before.

Laz: *Hi Esther, I wanted to say thanks again for all the time you have been spending with Hannah. I can't believe how happy she's been the last few days. I think the Cali trip was really good for her.*

Esther: *I'm glad to hear that! I think she had fun with Maggie's kids. She told me she wants to go back to California before she gets old. I think that means in the next couple of years.*

Laz: *Lol. I will keep that in mind.*

...

Laz: *I also wanted to say that since Hannah is doing so much better, you really don't have to come in every day anymore. I know this has taken up so much of your time, and I assume you need to get back to work!*

Esther: *Oh, I'm not in any hurry to get back to work. I've really enjoyed hanging out with her.*

Laz: *I feel like you've given so much, you deserve some time for yourself. Zhang ayi is here all day and Tingting is here in the mornings, and Hannah should be fine for a couple hours in the afternoons on her own. If you have the time, you could come one afternoon a week or something? I know Hannah does enjoy her time with you.*

...

Esther: *I'd still like to come in the afternoons, for now, if Hannah wants the company.*

Laz: *You sure?*

Esther: *Yes.*

Laz: *If that's what you want, we can still do that.*
Esther: *Great.*

It was almost as if they didn't want her anymore.

She had done good things for Hannah, right? Esther thought back to a month ago when Hannah didn't talk at all. Esther was the first one she had talked to, and now it sometimes felt as if Hannah couldn't stop talking. And she had encouraged Hannah to write in her diary every day, reminding her that it was a 'safe space', though she suspected that Hannah was doing just fine without any additional safe spaces.

And it had felt good to feel useful. For Claire's sake, not for hers.

Maybe, Esther thought, having her mornings back was a positive thing. Maybe now she could really start the job search again. Eventually Jose would want to meet up; if she could get a start on updating her resume, even looking for other opportunities, this would only be to her advantage when she spoke to him. So far, it seemed, Jose's emails indicated that they could forget The Incident and be a platonic super-duo again. Maybe there might be a place at Jose's new job which didn't involve directly working with him. No matter what emotional wreckage lay in their past, she had always done stellar work for him, never been anything but the best.

Be hopeful, she told herself. She got out of bed and made a cup of coffee. She would be productive; she would make use of her morning. Sitting at her laptop, Esther realized that she was looking forward to seeing Hannah after lunch, and she smiled to herself as she opened her LinkedIn profile.

She was surprised to see a new suggested contact: Didi, with twenty-seven mutual connections. Didi, who hated social media, and who had made Esther feel like a corporate shill when she had asked him if he had a LinkedIn profile years ago. She clicked to add him as a connection and checked his profile. Princeton University for undergrad, Johns Hopkins for med school, Residency at the Cleveland Clinic and now his current position as Attending there. What a star.

Esther sent Didi a text. *I found you on Linkedin. I thought you didn't like social media?* She knew he wouldn't reply until the evening or whenever he was done with work. When Esther was working, she had been the same way—conscientious, focused, diligent, unrelenting.

She clicked on her own profile and saw how meager it looked in comparison. Yes, Princeton for undergrad, but then what. Just Centridge for an embarrassing number of years, then the last few years as a freelance consultant. It was embarrassing—her failure of a career just waiting to be discovered by anyone who happened upon her page.

Hannah greeted her with a hug when she arrived at the house. "Did you eat lunch?" Esther asked.

"Peanut butter and jelly," Hannah said. She was the kind of kid who could have waffles for breakfast and PB&J for lunch every day. No wonder Zhang ayi liked her so much.

The playroom looked as if it had been tidied by an adult hand. On the art table were Hannah's diary and two of the Chinese books in a neat stack.

"How's the Chinese going?" Esther asked.

"*Hen hao*," Hannah said. *Very good.*

"And did you write in your diary this weekend?"

"Yes."

"But," Esther said, raising a single eyebrow, "did you write in your diary... in CHINESE?"

Hannah giggled and collapsed backward onto the beanbag chair. "What are we going to do today?"

"I don't have any plans—maybe the park?"

"We went to the Please Touch Museum, yesterday after church," Hannah said quietly.

Esther sat on the floor and traced her finger on the edge of the rug. It stung to hear this, because Hannah had so categorically shut down Esther when she had suggested it before. But surely this was a sign that Hannah was doing better, that she would go to the museum with her family, if not with her. "And did you have fun?"

"I did," Hannah said. Her voice dropped even lower. "But it wasn't the same without Mama." She turned onto her side, peered at Esther. "At least Jasper can have fun at the museum without thinking of her when he's bigger."

"Oh, Hannah," Esther said. She opened her arms. "Do you need a hug?"

"No," Hannah said, turning back to gaze at the ceiling. "Jasper's not going to remember Mama at all. That's really sad."

"I agree, it is sad."

"I'm lucky because I remember Mama." Hannah heaved a sigh, and her voice began to quaver. "But I'm going to forget."

Esther went and knelt next to the beanbag chair. Fat tears rolled down the side of Hannah's face. She wanted to hug her, give her some comfort, but Hannah was still supine, staring at the ceiling.

Eventually Hannah dragged her arm across her face. "I'm lucky and unlucky, I guess." She extricated herself from the beanbag and crawled into Esther's lap.

Esther stayed quiet, unsure of what to say.

"Daddy says that Mama is in heaven," Hannah said.

"She is," Esther said.

"No, she isn't. You don't believe it. I know you don't."

Esther thought back to what she might have said. Yes, a while back they had discussed what Esther did on Sundays, whether she went to church, and she had told Hannah that she used to be a Christian and go to church, but she didn't believe in that any longer. Hannah must have held that nugget of information close.

"I'm not sure what I believe about heaven," Esther said.

"I don't think she's in heaven," Hannah said. "I don't think she would be happy in heaven, knowing that I was still here. And leaving Jasper behind. I don't think she'd be happy, and if she was unhappy in heaven, then it wouldn't be heaven, would it?"

Esther stroked Hannah's hair. "I think... I think there are some questions that we can't know the answers to. But I know that your mom and dad believed that after you die you will see your family again. So maybe your mom is happy, in heaven, waiting to see you."

Hannah looked up at Esther. "That doesn't make any sense. That means she's waiting for me to die."

For the love of God, Esther thought. "I mean... I don't think..."

"It's okay, Esther," Hannah said. "I know you don't know the answers." She got out of Esther's lap and stood in front of the bookshelf. Esther couldn't see her face, but she could see Hannah sighing, again, and then standing very still. When Hannah turned around again, her face was back to its normal composed self, and she was smiling. "Maybe we can go for a walk and then reward ourselves with ice cream?"

Esther nodded, glad that the spell was broken and Hannah was back to being a little girl again. "Yes, good idea, let's go."

***

That night, at home, Esther received a text from an unknown contact: *This is Jose. In Philly Thursday and Friday —when/where can we meet?*

She had deleted him from her phone contacts, and he had guessed that she would. Hence, the *This is Jose*. In his emails he had steered clear of hinting of past discord but of course he knew, she was the one who cut him off after The Incident, and he was the one who never tried to contact her again. A part of her had hoped that he wouldn't be in Philly for weeks, months, maybe never.

She had suggested coffee in her previous email. Not a meal, from which it might be hard for her to make a sudden exit, and definitely not drinks. She checked Yelp for a coffeehouse that she had never been to, would likely never go to again. *Can you do Halcyon Coffee 10:30 am Friday?* Maybe he would have another meeting at that time.

Sounds good, see you then, he replied.

Well shit.

Maybe they could work together again, not closely like before, but in a relationship based on mutual respect and trust. She could restart her career, make money again. The "freelance consulting" on her LinkedIn profile would be just a minor gap in her resume. With her career back on track she could rejoin the life that her friends and peers were living. This was what she wanted, wasn't it?

***

I accepted your connection request, Didi texted. *I know I hated this kind of stuff before, but I realized after Claire's passing that I really need to make more of an effort to keep in touch with people.*

And you chose Linkedin?? Esther asked.

It was the least social of social media, Didi said. *Getting my toes wet.*

Esther was ready to let that be the end of the conversation, but on

167

her screen were the three pulsing dots of Didi preparing a reply. She waited for what seemed like minutes, curious as to what he was writing.

How are you doing? he asked at last.

She started writing a reply, then she realized that he too would see the pulsing dots, be waiting to see what she would say. *Okay. You?*

Quickly this time, he replied with *Okay*, and that was their agreement that the conversation was over.

People asked whether Esther and Didi were close, and she would answer truthfully: not really. In the fundamental dichotomy of Esther's childhood, pre- and post- Caleb's illness, Didi had somehow remained constant, an afterthought, while everything else changed.

She had a clear mental image of her life before Caleb got sick. She was oblivious, happy, curious. She had a role model—her big brother who was universally acknowledged to be brilliant and outstanding, and she had proof of this every day in her lucky younger years when he was still home. He let her do puzzles in his room, read, be near him without ever telling her to leave him alone. When his friends were around, they told her to scram, but she remembered Caleb telling them it was fine, on more than one occasion. Where was Didi in those days? Running around outside, playing by himself. He was too loud, too wild to sit still in Caleb's room. She herself would tell him to leave because he wouldn't stop fidgeting. Caleb is studying, she would tell Didi, go play outside.

Caleb's illness ended Esther's life as a kid.

In her early childhood, Esther had been only vaguely aware of her parents' emotions. They were very proud of Caleb, and they were proud that while Esther wasn't as bright as he was (Asian parental honesty always unsparing), she was obedient like her brother. But when Caleb got sick, she saw anxiety rising to the surface of her parents' relationship, like the vein that started to pop out on the side of her father's face. They began to fight more in front of Esther and Didi. Her mom started crying during the day, though she held her tears until her calls or visits with Caleb were over. After Caleb died, there was no need to censor themselves anymore and Esther's parents fought, and her mom cried, with abandon.

Then, eventually, Esther's parents seemed to give up on the world around them. Her father grew withdrawn—quiet but in a way that was so different from the quiet of the before times. Quiet as if beaten down, not quiet as if satisfied. Her mother stopped crying, but she also seemed to stop caring. The family stopped attending church, and this meant that Esther's parents no longer had any contact with their old friends.

Esther too felt herself changing, resisting the abyss into which her parents seemed to have fallen. She was willing to do whatever it took to have them engage with life, to feel some sort of pride or joy again. She pushed herself at school, at piano, to be the best, to win awards, to drag a wan smile onto her father's face when she showed him her report card, or onto her mother's face when she strode back to her seat after playing in a recital.

In all this, Didi lagged behind, usually out of sight and out of mind but occasionally intruding by being too loud, too unconstrained. As Esther succeeded beyond her parents' expectations, she felt that she was giving Didi a gift. She got As and got into Princeton so that he didn't have to. He never showed any recognition of her sacrifice, and in her mind, he never showed any of the promise that Caleb had shown or the tenacity with which she too had succeeded.

And yet, somehow Didi got 1580 on his SATs, almost a perfect score. And somehow Didi got very good grades, and somehow he was also on two varsity sports teams, and somehow he too was hoping to get into Princeton. By the time Didi was applying to colleges, Esther was on campus making merry with the Mathey Girls, and her mom's updates surprised her. 1580? Didi? But Esther herself had only just broken 1500. And he had barely studied, if he studied at all, her mom said, and Esther had felt the first of many pangs of jealousy.

The great irony was that Didi became a doctor, just like Caleb wanted to, just like Esther wanted to before she realized she couldn't. Somehow Didi had been the one to establish himself as the model child, living near his parents with his lovely family and successful medical career. Didi, the afterthought, eclipsed and surpassed Esther decades ago. She had always thought of him as a caboose on the train that was her childhood and young adulthood, but the truth was that they had always been two separate trains, running on parallel tracks, and he had been waiting to overtake her.

So no, when asked if she and her brother were close, with being only two years apart and both having gone to Princeton and both having gone through the same familial trauma, no, she and Didi weren't close. How could they be?

Esther shook her head, trying to put her brother out of her mind, just as she had done so often before. It was time for the Zoom call with the Mathey Girls. She opened her laptop and propped it on her knees, then pulled a throw around herself. It was summer, but she needed comfort.

Wendy and Esther were on time, as usual. Esther peered at her own face on the screen. The first couple of times they had tried the Mathey Girl Zoom, early on in the pandemic, she had been shocked at how terrible she looked. Was her face really that puffy? And was her skin really that dusky? And did she generally look that flat, dull, lifeless? Then she got used to the fact that yes, she was hideous, it was okay, it was a pandemic, and they were all stressed out and terrified. Fairly quickly, though, they started compensating for their haggard appearances with makeup, better lighting, face blurring. Everyone except Serena, who didn't give a shit how she looked whether around her friends or at work or amongst the general public.

Today, Esther felt like she looked presentable, perhaps even healthy—maybe all that time being attacked by ducks at ponds was good for her skin.

"How's it going?" Esther asked.

Wendy grunted. "My son just told me he hates me, and that wasn't the worst part of my day, if that gives you any indication."

"Oh no," Esther said, inviting her to vent.

Wendy proceeded to describe her terrible incompetent underlings and how she was trying her best to get them to come back into the office so that she could mentor them face to face, because she was ready to put in the time if they were. She wanted them to lean in, to take advantage of their resources (the office, but also her time and willingness to engage), but the Gen Zers were resisting. "It's so aggravating," she said. "And now my dentist says that I need to wear a mouth guard for the stress."

"And it sounds like things aren't going well with Kingston?"

"Oh, it's a perpetual nightmare. You can't imagine. If I had known that he would be like this, I would have shipped him off to Singapore years ago." Wendy paused. "Scratch that. You know I don't mean it." She leaned in toward the screen. "I hope he didn't hear that. Kingston's dad would love to hear me say that."

Kingston's dad was no longer identified by name. He had absconded to Singapore, with his mistress but without his son, when Kingston was a toddler. True to his Asian patriarchal roots, he later demanded that Kingston be sent to live with him, and Kingston wielded the screaming hot antagonism between his parents as a weapon.

Maggie joined the line and flashed them a wide smile. "Hi ladies! What are we talking about?"

As Wendy again started talking about Kingston and the young rebels at work, Val joined the line. "Hey all! Sorry for being late. Serena is… hold on. Serena, are you coming? I think she's on a work call. She said she'll be done soon."

They started their updates in earnest, each taking their turn as they always did. They didn't wait for Serena, because who knew if Serena would really ever be done with her work call, and Val could always catch her up afterward. One by one, they talked about what was new in their lives and identified any problems where the Mathey Girls could give support or offer solutions. Esther realized as Maggie was describing Rosie's new fencing instructor that this was the first Zoom they had had since Claire died. She decided to keep this observation to herself.

As in their real-life get-togethers, Esther was usually the last to speak, and always only after someone urged her to share. By the time Esther was giving her update, Serena had joined the line, only forty minutes late.

"So Esther, your turn, what's new with you?" Wendy asked.

"Well, I feel like you guys know, we went to California," Esther said.

"And we had such a good time!" Maggie said.

"Yes, we really had a good time. And now we're back, and Hannah is doing really well. And oh, Laz's cousin has come to stay at their house."

"To do what?" Serena asked.

"She has a job at a pharma company nearby, and she's staying there."

"Is she nice?" Maggie asked.

"Yes, she's very nice. Very cute, Taiwan cute, if you know what I mean."

"And she's staying on a permanent basis?" Wendy asked.

"I don't know," Esther said. "Hannah likes her."

"That's good, that Hannah can spend time with someone she actually likes from Laz's family," Val said.

"Yeah. Though I don't think Tingting is actually related to Laz. They say they're cousins, but I think it's super distant if anything."

"Wait a second," Wendy said, waving her hand at the screen. "How old is she?"

"I'm not sure. Maybe mid-twenties?"

"Huh," Wendy said.

"What are you thinking?" Val asked.

"Is she single?" Wendy asked.

"I don't know," Esther said. She saw the skepticism on Wendy's face. "I never asked."

There was a pause.

"So a 'distant cousin' comes from Taiwan to stay with Laz, and she's cute and maybe single," Wendy said. "Are you guys thinking what I'm thinking?"

"I think so, but I hope it isn't true," Serena said.

"Esther just said this girl is in her mid-twenties, guys," Maggie said.

"Did Mrs. Chen send this cousin from Taiwan?" Wendy asked.

Esther blanched as she realized what they were implying. "Oh—no, no it's not like that. Peipei just told me she was coming, but no one mentioned Mrs. Chen sending her," Esther said.

"Hold up—are we thinking that this 'distant cousin' was sent as some kind of replacement wife for Laz?" Valerie asked.

No one said anything.

"I mean, there are so many things wrong with this if it's true," Maggie said finally. "Claire's only been gone, what, a month? And Esther you said this girl is in her twenties? His family wouldn't possibly try to set Laz up so soon, with someone so young, would they?"

"That's ridiculous," Val said. "Right?"

After a moment, Wendy said, "I wouldn't put it past Mrs. Chen to try to set Laz up with someone who might be able to have more kids."

"That's horrible," Maggie said.

"I don't know," Esther said. "Tingting doesn't seem like she's here to... date Laz." Even saying the words made her feel sullied. "She's more like a kid, a big sister to Hannah."

"I think we're jumping to conclusions," Val said. "I mean, Mrs. Chen is terrible, but she's not that terrible, right?"

"I would keep an eye out, Esther, just in case," Wendy said. "These Asian family power dynamics are no joke. I wouldn't put it past her."

"Esther, are you okay? You look like you're about to cry," Maggie said.

Esther nodded quickly. "I'm fine. I think Val's right; we're jumping to conclusions. Tingting seems sweet, really." As she said it, though, she thought of the fact that Tingting was teaching Hannah Chinese, and the fact that Tingting was driving Claire's car, and the fact that Tingting really was pretty cute. She was afraid to tell her friends about these facts, because they painted what seemed to be a very damning picture. "But Serena, what about your updates? Anything new?"

Serena seemed reluctant to change the subject but she must have sensed Esther's fervent desire to take away the spotlight and so she started to talk about changes at her job.

Esther's phone buzzed. It was a separate message from Wendy: *I still think you should keep your eyes and ears open, about that 'cousin'. Let me know if you want to chat.*

21

The next day, Esther arrived at the Chen house earlier than usual. Not, she told herself, to spy on Tingting. Just to make sure everything was... kosher. After the Zoom the night before, Wendy had called, riled up by the idea of the Chen family trying to find a replacement for Claire. A young, presumably fertile, Taiwanese Chinese replacement.

Esther had tried to hold her ground, finding it hard to believe that families would be that manipulative. Granted she didn't have much personal experience with wealthy Chinese families—her parents were in that 1960s generation of immigrants from Taiwan who arrived with college degrees but no money.

Wendy told her that she was being naive if she thought Mrs. Chen would be any different from any other traditional Chinese woman. Chinese mothers had survived through thousands of years of scheming to get the best for their sons, and Taiwan was even more traditional than the mainland.

"Think about it," Wendy said. "He's the only son of the family, a doctor, the prince. How could they let this opportunity pass?" The opportunity, unspoken, being Claire's death.

Esther had been too unsettled in the morning to sit still. She needed to know, and so she arrived before noon, before Tingting left for work.

She let herself in the house. She had almost hoped the door would be locked, but it never was. If the door was locked, she could ring the doorbell, and her presence would be obvious and announced. As it was, the door opened too easily despite its massive weight and Esther walked in feeling very much like a thief.

"Hello?" she called, but no one answered. As she stepped into the foyer and took off her shoes, she caught a whiff of something delicious in the air. Could it be? She followed her nose toward the kitchen and yes, she was sure now, it could only be Taiwanese beef noodle soup. The smell was meaty yet delicate, rich beef broth enhanced by star anise and other Chinese spices that elevated the soup to ethereal. Her mouth watered.

In the kitchen Hannah and Zhang ayi were working at the island, Hannah perched on a stool. They were both wearing aprons (where had those come from?) and their hands were covered in flour as they pinched and pulled a white dough.

"Esther!" Hannah said. "We're making noodles!"

"Wow! That's awesome," Esther said, in genuine admiration.

Tingting was at the stove, stirring the contents of a tall steel pot. "Beef noodle for lunch," she announced.

"It smells so good," Esther said.

Baby Jasper was far from the flour flying through the air, happy in his bouncer. Still, Esther felt the need to be useful, so she picked him up. She held his neck carefully, as she knew she needed to, and admired his pudgy heft in her arms. She bounced him and observed the domestic tableau in front of her. The traditional three generations of women in the kitchen, working together and passing knowledge down, creating nourishment for the family. The modern update: the Sub-Zero refrigerator, the marble island and bright lighting, the happiness on their faces.

Soon the noodles were done, dropped into another large pot to cook, and Esther set Jasper down so she could sit at the table. Each of them got a bowl with steaming hot noodles, then two or three pieces of bok choy that had been quickly cooked in the soup, then chunks of beef, then a crowning of broth bringing it all together. The women added liberal scoops of pickled radish from a bowl in the center.

The noodles were thick and toothsome, substantial as only hand pulled noodles could be, the meat so tender that it was falling apart, and as Esther chewed, she could not help but let out a small moan. "It's so good," she said, mouth full. "Just like Taiwan."

Tingting slurped broth from her spoon. "When you go to Taiwan?"

"When I was a kid," Esther said, holding her face over the bowl and letting the steam from the soup infiltrate her pores.

"Yummy," Hannah said.

"Yummy," Zhang ayi said, and they laughed.

"And I thought you ate peanut butter and jelly every day," Esther said. "Is this how you eat when I'm not around?"

"I was going to eat PB&J," Hannah said, "but then I smelled Tingting's soup."

"Tingting, you should cook more often," Zhang ayi said in Chinese, and Tingting demurred. The two of them always spoke in Mandarin, their preferred language.

"Can you make scallion pancakes?" Hannah asked.

Tingting seemed unsure so Esther translated, *cong you bing*.

"Oh, yes, scallion pancake," Tingting said.

"I make those too," Zhang ayi said in Chinese.

"We should have a contest," Hannah said. "We can see who makes better scallion pancakes."

Zhang ayi and Tingting laughed, but Esther could tell that Hannah was serious.

"You cook a lot, Tingting?" Esther asked.

"I like cook."

Esther thought back to what Wendy had said. Cooking skills would definitely be relevant. "Do you have a boyfriend?" she asked, unable to stop herself.

"No boyfriend," Tingting said, blushing.

"Girlfriend?" Hannah asked.

Tingting laughed. "No girlfriend."

"How old are you? Almost thirty?" Zhang ayi asked in Chinese.

Esther leaned forward. She had wanted to ask this question but had never found the right moment. Thank goodness for Zhang ayi.

"Thirty-one," Tingting said in Chinese.

"You look young. You take good care of your skin," Zhang ayi said in Chinese.

"What are they saying?" Hannah asked.

"Tingting is thirty-one years old," Esther said.

"Almost as old as you."

"Not quite. But closer to me than you."

"You need to get married soon," Zhang ayi said in Chinese, and again Esther paused her eating to watch and listen. She felt like her work was being done for her.

A forced smile appeared on Tingting's face. "Yes," she said in

Chinese. "You can find me a boyfriend!" Then she laughed and continued to eat.

Esther's soup had started to cool, with small specks of fat congealing on the surface of the broth. She stirred slowly with her chopsticks, re-incorporating the fat into the whirlpool of soup. Tingting was thirty-one. In certain circles, thirty-one might be the perfect age for someone like Laz. Mature enough to match a man in his late thirties, still of childbearing age. Esther put her chopsticks down. But no, the beef noodle soup was so good, she would force herself to finish everything. She couldn't let it go to waste.

Later that afternoon, sitting at the table while Hannah wrote in her diary on the opposite corner, Esther texted the Mathey Girls: *Tingting is 31. No boyfriend. And she can cook.*

Holy shit, Maggie replied, almost immediately.

Holy shit indeed, Wendy said. *In a meeting now but will call you in twenty minutes.*

How did you find this out? I still don't believe that Laz's family would do this, Maggie said.

It's hard to believe, Esther said. *But maybe we don't understand Chinese families.*

Aren't you Chinese? Maggie said.

Not Chinese enough, apparently, Esther said.

"What are you doing?" Hannah asked. "You look very excited."

Esther pulled her eyes from the screen to Hannah and refocused. "Just texting with my friends," she said.

"Your Princeton friends?" Hannah asked.

"Yes, how did you know?"

"You never talk about any other friends." Hannah put down her pen and closed the diary. Esther's phone chimed but she dare not look, not when Hannah was observing her like this. "Do you have any other friends?" Hannah asked.

Esther blushed. "Of course I do."

"Like who?"

"Okay, not many. And no one you know." Her phone chimed again.

"Mama had a lot of friends," Hannah said. "But her Princeton friends were her favorites."

"Did she tell you that?"

Chime.

"No," Hannah said. "But she talked about you the most, and she was really happy whenever you had your Zooms or when you came."

Chime. Esther put her phone on silent, a quick flip of the side switch downwards, and shoved the phone into her bag.

"I don't think Daddy has any friends," Hannah said.

"I'm sure he does," Esther said.

"Not like Mama, and you, and your Princeton friends." Hannah put her chin in her hand.

"Well," Esther said, "we're very lucky."

Hannah stared, and Esther feared that Hannah was about to say that no, her mother wasn't lucky at all, because she died. Instead, Hannah looked down and traced her finger on the spiral of her diary, careful and controlled. "Daddy is probably lonely."

Esther once again wished she had trained as a child psychologist so that she knew the right thing to say. She was sure that it existed, but she had no idea what it was—the magic words to reassure Hannah and also change the topic, so that they could think about happier things. "Well," she said, "he's probably feeling a lot of things right now."

"Sad."

"Yes, sad."

"And lonely."

"Maybe lonely. But," Esther said, "I believe he also feels very happy and proud that he has you as his daughter."

Hannah gave Esther a weak smile. "Maybe."

"I'm sure of it."

"I need to pee," Hannah said, getting up. "You better check your phone." She hurried out.

Esther grabbed her phone from her bag and read the messages she had missed.

Serena: *This is definitely not looking good.*

Val: *Again, I think we may be jumping to conclusions.*

Maggie: *Someone should ask Laz. Serena you should ask him.*

Serena: *Ask him what? Whether his 'cousin' that's staying at his house is actually some sort of mail order bride??*

Maggie: *Esther you said you don't see Laz very much, right?*

Maggie: *Esther you still there?*

Serena: *Maybe the 'cousin' has kidnapped her.*

Val: *Serena....*

Serena: *jk jk*

Maggie: *Poor Laz. Whether or not this girl is here to be some sort of replacement Claire or not, this must be very awkward for him.*

Wendy: *Done with my call. I think someone needs to talk to Laz. Serena can you talk to him?*

Maggie: *That's what I thought too!*

Serena: *Why does everyone think I should do it? Maybe Val should do it.*

Val: *No thank you.*

Maggie: *Serena it should be you, because Val thinks we're being crazy and because it would be hard for Esther.*

Serena: *???*

Hannah bounced back into the playroom. "Is it time to go to Kavi's yet?"

Esther left WhatsApp with a guilty swipe. "Oh, yes, let's get going." She tried to act relaxed, because she knew how easily Hannah picked up on her energy.

"Did you tell your friends I said hi?" Hannah asked.

"No, I—"

"Tell them I said hi," Hannah said.

Esther opened WhatsApp again, standing and holding her phone high so that Hannah couldn't see. *I've got to deal with Hannah right now. Let's table this - all of this - for later. Hannah says hi (and obviously does not know what we are chatting about).*

Hi Hannah, Maggie said.

Hi Hannah, and yes let's discuss later, Wendy said.

Tell Hannah Aunties Serena and Val send their love, Val said.

Will do, bye, Esther said, and she locked her phone before she could see anything else.

22

Peering through the Halcyon Coffee window, Esther realized that arriving fifteen minutes early wasn't enough. Jose was already seated, typing on his phone. Shit. She quickly stepped back, turned around and started walking back down the street. She had wanted to get there first, to prepare herself, but she had spent longer than she wanted putting on eyeliner and mascara—she was out of practice trying to look professional.

She stopped at the end of the block and examined her reflection in a print shop window. She looked different from when he last saw her, she supposed, healthier maybe. She actually spent time in the sun now. She actually had time to eat. She was wearing a blouse, skirt and heels, a necessary step down from her original plan of a full business suit—her old pre-pandemic suit jacket didn't fit anymore.

Now that she knew that Jose was waiting, it made more sense for her to arrive on time, or even late. She could do a power play, arrive at 10:20, make him sit. But no, she wouldn't, this was for a potential job, and she shouldn't play petty games.

"Hey pretty lady, *nihaoma*," someone said behind her.

Without thinking Esther turned her head, finding a man handing out leaflets, leering as he held one out to her.

"*Konichiwa!*" he said.

She shook her head and started walking back. Dammit. She never knew what to say in these situations, and they happened often enough that she should have a stock response ready by now. She was always too nice, too polite. And what good would it be to tell him that it was rude to assume that she was Chinese or Japanese, that he wouldn't act the same way if she were a man or not Asian. Serena would know the right thing to say; she should remember to ask her the next time they chatted.

Now she was in front of Halcyon, looking in the window again, and now Jose was looking back at her with his hand raised in greeting. She steeled herself and walked in.

"Hey," he said, rising.

"Hey," she said. At the table they shook hands, awkwardly, probably the first time they had ever shaken hands, but at least he didn't try to give her a hug.

"Can I get you a drink?" he asked. It sounded weird, but Esther played it cool.

"I'll get it," she said. "One sec."

She went to order her coffee and didn't look back. Hopefully he wasn't looking at her. She had made a mistake, surely, coming here and meeting him. There was no way that this wouldn't be painful.

"Can I have a tall latte please?" Boring. "No, actually, can I have a, what's this, a mint shaken cold brew?" She felt on the edge of something, and the atmosphere of the shop didn't help.

The coffee shop interior was blinding white. The counters, chairs, walls, even the floor were the white of movie star teeth. The tables were bleached wood, maybe because 100% white would have been a little too institutional, but even with that concession Esther still felt vulnerable, as if under a spotlight. The song playing in the background had a soft but thumping bass line, like the heartbeat of someone much cooler than Esther, and she realized how much she preferred the bad lighting and placid music at Starbucks.

While waiting for her coffee at the end of the counter, she stole a glance at Jose. He was looking at his phone, thankfully. His hair had more gray in it, but for him that was an asset. When they had worked together, both of them had looked young, and people had remarked on it. He was wearing clothes that actually fit, a crisp wrinkle-free button-down and—this was new—gold cuff links.

She sat down with her drink and smiled her work smile, a mask that she had perfected over the years for when she needed to be neutral-positive, but then she saw that he recognized that look. She blushed and took a sip.

"So. I know this is kind of weird," Jose said. "And I'm sorry for that." He opened his hands in a gesture that she had seen a million times, and she knew that he was being honest, and she felt herself relax the tiniest bit.

"It is," she said, "and I'm sorry for that too."

"I say we let the past be the past, and look to the future."

Was it that easy? To just dust your hands of feelings you had, words you expressed, actions you took, that may have derailed someone else's life? "Okay," she said.

"I was afraid you might not want to meet, but Stella said you would."

"You're still working with Stella?"

"Ha. No," Jose said. "We're together. A couple. Didn't you know? She works for PwC now, in their finance department."

"I didn't know," Esther said. Gross. "Congratulations."

"Thank you. I mean, we're not married or anything. I don't think I want to do another marriage any time soon." The color rose in his face. "Can I get this out of the way? I really just want to say sorry for what happened, that night at the Christmas party. I was... I was going through some things, personally, and I may have lost it a little bit."

Esther took another sip.

"I may have gone a little bit insane," Jose murmured.

Esther tried to keep her face steady. What to feel—relief that he clearly was no longer 'in love' with her, so they could move on? Disappointment that he maybe was never 'in love' with her? Panic because maybe no one would ever be in love with her, because she was fundamentally unlovable? Or maybe it was all of these things, and regret that a single night had played such a devastating role in her life, for no reason at all.

He was waiting for a response, eyes hopeful.

She put her work smile on. "I understand. Thanks for the apology."

He nodded, paused as if considering whether to keep going down this line of discussion, then cleared his throat and said, "So. Moving on. How would you feel working with me again?"

She listened as he gave his spiel. He grew more excited as he talked, hands more active, his body loosening up:

He jumped ship to Solutris at the end of 2019, and he had to be honest, the first couple months were really tough, as the pandemic hit and the world fell apart as he was trying to build business. But in a way it was a good time because everything was shifting, people were looking for new ways of doing things, and he had made a name for himself while at Centridge. People like Arnold ended up struggling more than he did because they couldn't adapt to all remote, they couldn't address the existential fears that companies were facing at the time. He had heard that Esther was laid off—he was really sorry but at that time he was just getting his footing and didn't have the capital to try to get any hires of his own. Things were different now, he had so much good will and capital at the firm now, the problem was finding good people. Too many people had been burnt out by the pandemic, senior consultants especially, everyone had realized that they had other things to live for, which he understood, but he still loved the work, and he needed to bring in people who still loved the work the way that he did. He had never forgotten about their time working together, it was the highlight of his time at Centridge. What he was getting at was that he would love to have her join his team. Solutris was dynamic, flexible, really promoting people based on merit. It was the opposite of Centridge with its old boys' network, and Esther could really shine.

"I mean, I've laid it all out on the table, because I'm not gonna lie, I could really use you, and Solutris has given me a lot of discretion in terms of hiring. I'm sure you know how hot the market is, how valuable you are. I don't want to play games, I don't think I need to." Jose looked at Esther expectantly, hands again open wide.

The lights in the coffee shop bounced off the walls, the chairs, the counters, the cups. Esther suspected that if she just didn't say anything, or move for a while, she would feel less affected by it.

"I suppose you've been doing well, with the freelancing," Jose said.

Esther kept her face neutral as Jose continued.

"To be honest, when I saw that on your LinkedIn, the freelancing, I kind of suspected that it was just you taking a break. But Stella said, and you know Stella is always right about these kinds of things, she said that no way would you not be working. If you were freelancing, you were killing it, she said, and I realized she was right."

If Esther were indeed a killer, a shark, this would be her moment to strike. This would be the moment to make an outrageous demand as part of her negotiation, to make it seem like he had to give her the moon to woo her away from her successful freelance work. She considered it. What would she even ask for? More money? A part time gig? Remote work?

"I need —" she said, and stopped.

"What do you need?" He was leaning forward now, optimistic.

"I need to think about it," she said.

Jose seemed to deflate, a little bit of air seeping out through some unseen hole. "Yes, yes, understood. I wasn't expecting you to commit right away. I mean, as soon as you're willing. I have to be honest; I've been trying to get the right talent for months and if I thought you might be interested, I would make sure there was a position for you."

Esther nodded and gave him a work smile.

"Remember those days when we would, like, just get each other? Clients were always so blown away. I'd ask you to pull some numbers from a random place in the report and before I even finished the sentence, you'd have them projected on the screen. Before I barely even finished my own thought you'd have them up there."

"That did happen, more than once," Esther said.

"That's the kind of vibe I miss so badly. I haven't been able to work with anyone else like that in a long time."

Esther did, in part, share his nostalgia for those days, but she doubted they could ever have that type of synergy again.

"So," Jose said, "should I get back in touch next week? After the holiday?"

"The holiday?"

"Monday. July 4th," he said. "Don't tell me you were planning to work on Monday! If you come to work for us, I'll make sure you don't have to work on public holidays." He chuckled nervously.

Don't make promises you can't keep, she wanted to say. Instead, she checked her phone. "I need to go," she said. "I have a meeting." Let him think it's a meeting with a client, or even another consulting firm looking to hire, she thought. He doesn't need to know the meeting is with a nine-year-old.

"Always busy," Jose said. He was smiling now. "I'm really glad we got to talk, and I really appreciate you thinking about what I said. I'll get in touch next week, or feel free to reach out whenever."

They got up and left the coffee shop together. "I'm going left," he said. "You?"

"I'm going right," she said. To be polite she asked him whether he was going to another meeting.

"Oh," Jose said. "No, I'm going back to my hotel." He held out his hand, and she shook it, and it was a little less awkward this time. "I wasn't going to tell you this, but I came down to Philly to meet with you. I thought it best if we speak in person, after all this time."

Esther said goodbye, work smile on her face, and walked away.

***

The following night, Esther was folding laundry with the TV on. The streaming service had already asked her once if she was still watching. Yes, she was still processing her meeting with Jose and yes, streaming service, she needed the comfort of this low stakes comedy series on her screen. Sometimes she thought better when there was a separate story happening in the background. Sometimes she needed to do slow motion repetitive tasks like folding laundry, augmented by the separate story happening in the background, to let her brain slow down so she could wade through her mental slush.

She placed a t-shirt in the basket. All of her clothes looked the same these days. T-shirts and shorts, t-shirts and jeans. I'm not boring, I'm consistent, she told herself.

She had tried to tweak her LinkedIn profile to make it less boring, to better sell herself. In response, the internet job search gods had deemed her fair game, and now she was getting random emails about positions that were only tenuously related, if at all, to her skill set or employment history. She had added health care consulting onto her profile, and today she got an email about a job as a physical therapist with Children's Hospital of Philadelphia. It seemed that everyone was hiring and everyone was desperate.

Desperate. The look in Jose's eyes when he thought that Esther was considering his offer. The inflection in his voice when he tried to imply that she could pretty much ask for anything and his firm would give it. Maybe she should ask for a salary of one million dollars, over the phone in a supervillain voice, and see how close he could get.

The problem was, the prospect of working with Jose was still too unfathomable for her to view it rationally. She had spent years thinking of Jose with a painful, awkward red X stamped across his being, and now here he was, X-less, asking her—no, begging her—to try to make things like they were before.

He was not in love with her. He had probably never really been in love with her. He was dating Stella, for God's sake, which was skeevy and off-putting. But it also meant that something like The Incident wouldn't happen again, and wasn't that the ultimate problem that she had been trying to avoid?

She was bound to disappoint if she actually started working with him. She wasn't that good, really, because if she was that good, she would never have been fired. Or maybe, it was as Jose said, it had been a problem with Arnold and the pandemic and the world on fire. Not her after all. But she didn't really believe that.

The thing that Esther knew about herself, that no one else seemed to recognize, was that she was very good at seeming intelligent and competent. If she didn't try hard enough, though, anyone who was paying attention would see that she actually wasn't very smart, and the only reason she was so 'capable' was because she worked so much harder to seem that way. There was no natural gift there, not like her friends, or Jose.

After her last pair of underwear was folded and placed in the basket, Esther considered the actors on her screen and found their office antics, at this particular moment, entirely insufficient. She turned the TV off and grabbed her phone for solace.

She missed Claire.

Esther had never told anyone about Jose. She had thought about confiding in Claire after The Incident, but something held her back. Was it fear that Claire would judge her, suspect Esther of leading Jose on? Probably not. Why not then, why didn't she tell her old friend, who might have knocked some sense into her, who might have told her, "He must be having problems with his wife. It's not really about you"? Claire might have encouraged her to have confidence in herself, to keep fighting for her career, to not let a single incident ruin everything. But Esther hadn't told her, and it was too late, and Claire was gone.

Esther opened WhatsApp and the *Mathey Girls* chat. *Is anyone around?*

No one replied.

She texted Laz. *I realize that Monday is July 4th and you probably have the day off. Should I still come over?*

After a moment she texted Didi. *How are things?*

186

She scanned her Instagram feed and waited for someone to reply, to verify that she existed and had relationships and had a meaningful life. A real-life Captcha: if someone replies to my message that means that I am not a robot.

She could call her parents, but then they might think something was wrong, because she never called them. Her calls back home had dwindled as her work situation deteriorated, and she didn't want to lie and say things were okay.

She went to Claire's Instagram page. It was still there as if she were alive but hadn't posted in a while. As Esther scrolled through the pictures, she saw herself with her friends at the surprise brunch, half of them holding up their champagne flutes. She remembered how Maggie had purposely asked a younger waitress to take their picture because, in her words, 'they know all the secrets to getting good shots.' And yes, they did look good, no closed eyes or hideous shadows or double chins. There were some pictures from the baby shower as well; Esther wasn't in any of those. Someone must have sent them to Claire because she was in most of them with her huge belly, her warmth radiating from the screen.

Esther scrolled further back in history, to get as far away as possible from this year.

She saw Laz, carefree and making goofy faces at the camera at a wedding, in a tux with his bow tie askew. A half smile came to her lips. This was the Lazarus that she had a crush on all those years ago.

And Hannah. So many pictures of Hannah. She was a cutie when she was younger with an open and curious face. Esther had seen all of these pictures before, thought they were cute, and felt happy for her friend. Now that she knew present-day Hannah so well, the pictures meant something else altogether. Like seeing baby pictures of a good friend or a beloved; in the pictures Esther could trace the evolution of Hannah and felt like the window into her earlier childhood was comfortingly familiar.

She sat back, phone on her chest, and brushed the tears from her eyes.

After a moment her phone chimed with a reply from Laz. *I do have the day off. If you want to take the day off, feel free. A colleague invited us to his house for a barbecue but I am not sure I am up to it. Will probably do burgers at home. Hannah would love for you to come.*

23

Happy 4th! Maggie said in the *Mathey Girls* chat. *Any special plans? We're busy with our annual barbecue, we're back to our first big bash in three whole years! Full house!*

No big plans for us, Valerie said. *But I don't have to work today! Fingers crossed it stays that way.*

I'm working, Wendy said. *International markets don't celebrate July 4th.*

Boo, Maggie said.

I hope you aren't making all your staff work too??? Serena said.

Just a skeleton staff, Wendy said. *I'm working so that others don't have to.* Serena gave her a thumbs up emoji.

I'm going to see Hannah and Laz, Esther said. *Laz said that he was invited to a friends place but he 'wasn't up to it' so just doing a small thing at home.*

Poor Laz, Maggie said.

I called him over the weekend to check in on him, Serena said. *He seemed okay, all things considered.*

Did you ask him about the cousin???? Wendy said.

No! And he didn't mention her, Serena said.

Well @Esther today's your chance to see the two of them together, Wendy said.

It was a bright day; the clouds were stingy, grouping in fluffy cliques or not there at all. This was going to be a big July 4th, bigger than last year when people were still wary of the pandemic. This year, people understood that it wasn't over, maybe it would never be over, but most everyone had given up on caring. Fireworks had already been going off the past several nights, as if people just couldn't wait to celebrate.

Esther had woken up anxious, then downed two cups of coffee before she thought better of it, and now her heart was racing as she stood in front of the Chens'. She patted her fingertips to her chest to calm it down. Just as she was going to push the doorbell, Hannah opened the door with a grunt.

"Esther! I've been waiting for you all day!"

"Impossible! It's not even lunchtime," Esther said.

Hannah threw her arms around Esther's waist. "Guess what," she said, bouncing on her toes. "We have scallion pancakes."

"So that's what smells so good," Esther said, disengaging herself from Hannah to remove her sandals inside.

"Yeah, Ayi and Tingting made them, and there was a contest. We saved some for you so that you can be a judge too."

A chorus of cheers greeted them when they entered the kitchen. Zhang ayi wiped her hands on the dishtowel at the sink and beckoned to Esther. "Come in, come in," she said in Chinese.

There were two plates of scallion pancakes on the table, cut into wedges, and Tingting was already standing behind them, eyes open wide. "Scallion pancake!" she said in English.

Laz was sitting at the table with the baby in his arms. "You have to be the tiebreaker," he said.

"Oh no," Esther said.

"It's a blinder test," Hannah said.

"A blind test," Laz said.

"You don't know who made which one," Hannah said.

"Oh dear," Esther said, approaching the table. "They both look great."

"They're already cold," Zhang ayi said in Chinese.

"Sometimes scallion pancakes are even better cold," Laz said in Chinese.

"Yes, yes," Tingting said in Chinese. She turned toward Hannah and said, "*Ting de dong ma?*" *Do you understand?*

"*Ting de dong,*" Hannah said. *I understand.*

Everyone watched Esther with eager eyes as she sat. Zhang ayi set a cup of tea in front of her; the steam rose, the fragrance of Oolong cutting through the smell of grease.

"The tea is a pellet cleaner," Hannah said.

"Palate cleanser," Laz said.

"You take one bite, then drink some tea, then try the other one.

Then you drink more tea and do the same thing backwards. Then you choose the winner." Hannah tapped the table. "Go."

Esther was overwhelmed by the caffeine coursing through her system, the smells of the tea and the greasy pancakes, the attention of everyone around the table. She closed her eyes to settle for a moment.

"Is she praying?" she heard Hannah whisper. "She doesn't pray."

"Shh," Laz said. "You okay, Esther?"

Esther nodded as she examined the two plates. One pancake was browner than the other, indicating a crispier edge. The less brown one had fewer scallions and seemed to have been shaped by a more delicate hand. Esther looked from the paler pancake to Tingting, who maintained an admirable poker face. She looked at Laz and he was smiling, encouraging, and Esther grabbed a piece of the paler pancake with her chopsticks and stuffed it into her mouth.

It was cold, a bit rubbery, but the pleasure centers in her brain lit up at the umami and the hint of salt. With each chew a tiny bit of oil was released from the pancake, complemented by wispy scallion undertones. It didn't taste greasy at all, just moist and chewy.

"Holy crap," she said. "That is an excellent scallion pancake." Tingting covered her mouth with her hands, hiding her pleasure, and Esther pretended not to notice.

She took a sip of tea and picked up a piece of the other pancake. She glanced at Zhang ayi, who wiggled her eyebrows conspiratorially. Before taking the bite, Esther took another sip of tea.

"Pellet cleaner," Hannah whispered.

The second pancake had, as expected, retained more of its crunch, and as flakes shattered against her teeth a shiver ran down her spine. Compared to the first pancake, this one was more toothsome; it took more effort to chew but the flavor reward was stronger.

"Very... robust," Esther said.

"What does that mean?" Zhang ayi asked in Chinese, but no one answered. They were all watching Esther, intent.

She finished her bite. "*Hen hao chi,*" Esther said. *Delicious.*

"Which one you like better?" Tingting asked.

"No, she can't decide yet. She has to do it again, backwards," Hannah said.

"Do I really?"

"Yes, otherwise it's not fair." Hannah put her hands on the table.

"Hannah was very taken with the idea of testing, and controls," Laz said.

"Yes, controls. Otherwise the data is flawed," Hannah said, drawing out the last word. She pointed to the darker pancake. "So you have to start with this one this time."

Esther sighed. "For you, Hannah, I will eat more of these delicious scallion pancakes." She took another gulp of tea.

The second time around, the darker pancake was markedly less delightful—it was too salty, too greasy. She tried to keep her face placid, even offering a smile to Zhang ayi, as she mashed the pancake with her teeth. She followed it with more tea, hoping that the bitterness of the tea would wash away the oil.

"I'm very full," Esther whispered, but everyone just wanted her to finish and be done. She took the second piece of Tingting's pancake, for she had no doubt whose was whose, and now it was limp and rubbery, the subtlety of the flavor lost to her discomfort.

She looked back at the faces waiting for a verdict. "*Yiyang hao,*" she said, weakly. *Both equally good.*

A collective groan. "Which one do you like better though?" Hannah wailed, punching her fist down on the table and causing Jasper to cry.

"How about we all take it down a notch," Laz said, shushing the baby. "They're both good. *Yiyang hao.*"

"You must choose," Zhang ayi said sternly in Chinese, and then she took the baby from Laz. Secure in her arms, Jasper settled, and now even he seemed to be looking at Esther with expectation.

"Okay, okay," Esther said. She really didn't want to do it, but she pointed a limp finger at the paler scallion pancake.

Tingting erupted in a squeal of joy and, to Esther's horror, gave Laz a hug that felt two seconds too long. "*Hao bang!*" Tingting said, *Awesome,* letting go of Laz to give Hannah a series of high fives. Hannah too was jumping and shouting in excitement.

Esther was awash with regret as she watched Laz, a blush fading from his cheeks, resting his eyes on Tingting and Hannah together.

Zhang ayi stalked away with Jasper in her arms, muttering in Chinese about how the scallion pancakes were already cold and when they were hot hers were better tasting by far.

191

"Laz—you better say something to Ayi," Esther hissed at Laz, tearing his attention away from Tingting and Hannah.

"Oh, yes," he said, and he called out encouragement to Zhang ayi in Chinese—he thought hers were so good, restaurant quality, and he would love it if she could make them for dinner some time, but Zhang ayi had her back toward them and she simply waved his compliments away.

***

After the excitement of scallion pancakes, Hannah asked when they could see the fireworks. She had never been allowed to stay up and watch them, but Laz had caved this year. Esther reminded Hannah that fireworks wouldn't start for another ten or eleven hours. Hannah considered, and decided then that everyone should watch a movie, together, as a family—without Jasper, who needed his nap—and the adults all agreed, so Hannah picked one about a squirrel forced to find a new home after his forest neighborhood was razed.

Tingting perched herself at one end of the sofa and Laz wavered before sitting in the armchair next to her. Hannah sat in the middle of the sofa and patted the space next to her.

"Sit here, Esther," Hannah said.

She sat, the farthest from Laz, and she saw Laz and Tingting smile at each other.

"*Dage, kanwan dianying women haiyao chi hanbao ma?*" Tingting asked Laz. *Big brother, after we finish watching the movie are we still going to eat hamburgers?*

Laz replied in Chinese that they could make hamburgers later, but they needed some time to digest the scallion pancakes. As he fiddled with the remote, trying to find Hannah's movie, Esther pondered Tingting's calling Laz *Dage*. *Big brother*—theoretically harmless, theoretically neutral. She wasn't sure if in Chinese that could translate into something flirty, though that seemed incestuous to her American mind.

Esther had watched the movie with Hannah before, twice, but Laz and Tingting hadn't seen it. It was charming, in a family movie kind of way, but Esther couldn't be invested. Tingting kept turning to Laz during the movie, at funny parts, to laugh together, or to ask a question. The level of familiarity between them made Esther uneasy. He seemed so much older than she was. And frankly she was so much cuter than him. But he was a doctor, widowed, and a good person.

I'm not jealous, she told herself. I'm protecting him, and I'm protecting the little girl beside me who is staring at the TV like a zombie.

When Tingting laughed, she covered her mouth like an anime schoolgirl, and Esther started to feel annoyed.

Zhang ayi came in while they were watching and announced that Jasper was asleep. She leaned against the doorway, watching the movie, and Esther took the opportunity to offer her seat on the couch so she could get some air. No one seemed to notice when she left the room.

The kitchen still smelled like grease, so Esther went to the playroom and sat at the table; as usual Hannah's diary and Chinese workbooks were in the corner. Her phone buzzed and she saw a message from Wendy to the *Mathey Girls* chat: *Sometimes I detest my clients. @Esther, how is it going with the cousin?*

Esther pondered how to reply, but Serena answered first. *Wendy, leave her alone.*

What do you mean? Wendy said.

She doesn't need to be spying on Laz at his house, Serena said.

I'm not asking her to spy, Wendy said. *Aren't you curious?*

I trust Laz, Serena said. *I think we should all give him a little bit more credit.*

She's right, Esther thought. Then she thought of Tingting hugging Laz, of her calling him *Dage* as if they had known each other for years, the look on Laz's face when he was watching Tingting and Hannah jumping up and down.

She silenced her phone and set it on the table face down. Resting her head in her hands, she was overcome with a feeling of displacement, as if she were a library book accidentally shelved with someone's permanent collection. What was she doing here?

Her eyes landed on the diary to her right. She could tell by the way the pages lay that Hannah had already filled more than half of it.

Esther's childhood diaries had been wide ruled, single subject spiral notebooks, because that's what they had at home. Bright primary colors disguising the muddle of emotions inside. She remembered how strong her feelings were, in the months before and after Caleb died. But she didn't remember exactly what it felt like to feel those feelings. Not anymore.

If Caleb were still alive, he would be almost fifty years old by now. Who would she have become if she hadn't gone through his death when she was eleven? If her family had continued, strong and secure, her parents filled with pride at their three successful children. The three of them: Caleb, Esther, Didi forming a tripod on which their parents could lean as they made their way through their older years. Instead, all they had was the lopsided pairing of Didi and Esther, each damaged by Caleb's death but one obviously more damaged than the other.

Hannah would be damaged as well, Esther knew. She would grow up being the girl whose mother died when she was just a kid, no matter how much the people around her tried to support her. This loss would attach itself to Hannah's identity, never to be shaken off or overcome.

There was so little Esther could do to help.

Esther imagined Hannah writing in her diary, expressing all the strong feelings she must be feeling. Feelings that she dared not share with anyone, just as Esther had never dared share hers with anyone. How lonely Esther had felt back then. How lonely Hannah must feel now.

A brazen impulse overtook her, and Esther put her hand on the diary. She could help Hannah in a way that no one else could, she thought. She just needed to know what Hannah was feeling, so she could help. She glanced up at the open door, making sure it was clear, and then pulled the diary close and opened it to a page near the beginning. She saw, in Hannah's nine-year-old scrawl:

Dear Mama,

Esther took me to ice cream today. She had pistasheo and I had coton candy. I miss you.

Esther turned to a later page.

Dear Mama,

A new cuzin is at our house to stay. Her name is ting ting. I think she is ok but she is pretty. Daddy said yes she is pretty and then I felt mad. Realy mad. I miss you every day. I wish you would come back and be with me.

Esther flipped further through the diary and found that they were all letters to Claire, except for the first few entries.

Dr. Winter says I can rite to you if I want.

Dr. Winter says it's ok to feel sad and it's ok to cry.

I miss you.

I miss you.

I miss you.

Esther closed the diary and put it back on top of the Chinese workbook, hands shaking. As she was about to get up to find Hannah, Laz appeared in the doorway.

"Hey," he said.

"Hey."

"I was wondering where you went."

"I... I had a call I had to make," Esther said.

Laz sat at the table. "You know, I really appreciate what you've done for Hannah," he said. It was difficult for Esther to look him directly in the eye. The sincerity with which he spoke was overwhelming.

"She's a great girl," Esther said, and she glanced at the diary.

Laz followed her gaze and picked it up; it looked small in his hands. "This is her safe space, Hannah says. She tells me I'm not allowed to read it."

"Of course not," Esther said. She could feel her cheeks start to flush.

"Do you think she's doing... okay?"

To have Laz's heart distilled in his eyes and directed at Esther was too much. She wrenched her head to the side. "She usually seems fine, with me."

"But...?"

"But..." Esther eyed the diary again.

Laz looked at the diary, and at Esther, and at the diary again. "Did you read this?"

Shame flooded her face. "I just took a quick look," she said. "Just now."

Laz studied Esther. "That's... disappointing."

"I know."

"And what did you see?"

"I'm not sure I should tell you. I shouldn't have looked."

"Esther, what did you see in the diary?" Laz leaned forward, and his eyes were fearful.

And then, from the doorway, Hannah yelled "YOU READ MY DIARY?" She ran in, a banshee, and clutched the diary to her chest. "HOW COULD YOU?" she wailed.

Esther looked at Laz, as if he could save her from the unavoidable. But he didn't care about her at this moment; he went down on his knee to soothe Hannah, telling her it was going to be okay. Hannah was now sobbing, gulping air.

"Hannah, I'm sorry," Esther said, her voice raised in a yell to overcome the crying. "I'm so sorry!"

"IT WAS MY SAFE SPACE!" Hannah screamed. She pushed Laz's hand away. "NOW I DON'T HAVE A SAFE SPACE!"

Hannah started tearing at the diary. She tried to rip the cover, wasn't strong enough, so she started wrenching out pages, a half page, a handful of pages, and throwing them to the floor.

"No, Hannah," Esther shouted but Hannah ignored her.

"Hannah," Laz said, "please stop!"

Almost all of the pages were out now, and the cover dangled from Hannah's hand. She hurled the empty diary at the wall, and it ricocheted off a pile of board games, knocking them to the floor.

"No," Esther whispered as Hannah ran out of the room.

Laz bent down and started picking up the pages. "Dear Mama," he read, and his face paled. Another page, and another page. "These were letters to Claire?" His hand shook as he slumped onto the floor and buried his face in a fistful of pages.

"I'm going to find Hannah," Esther said. "I'm so sorry." She left him alone in the playroom with the evidence of her crime.

She ran, following the sound of Hannah sobbing. She could fix this, she thought, she just needed to explain, and Hannah would understand. But when she entered the living room Tingting was rocking Hannah in her lap, smoothing her hair, murmuring comforting words in Chinese as Hannah's chest heaved in and out.

Tingting looked at Hannah with a question in her eyes. What happened?

"I screwed up," Esther said. "Hannah, I'm sorry."

Hannah rubbed her face against Tingting's shirt, tears and snot leaving a wet trail. "Go away," she said without looking up.

"I can explain," Esther said.

"No," Hannah said. "I don't want to talk to you. Go away."

A hand landed on Esther's shoulder; it was Laz. His face was a flashback to the days after the memorial service. "I think you should go," he said in a low voice.

***

Please tell Hannah I'm really sorry, Esther texted to Laz. She had made it home, somehow, surviving two near accidents on the way, swerving just in time for one and braking just in time for the other. Now she was on the couch in her apartment and her right leg wouldn't stop bouncing up and down.

Why did she look at the diary? What was wrong with her? Did she think that she was some kind of savior for Hannah, that anything she did could possibly help this little girl who was dealing with an impossible loss? Of course she fucked it up. Of course she took it for granted, Hannah's love, and Laz's gratitude. She always made things look fine, on the surface, but she was always the same underneath. A mess. Useless. She buried her face in her hands.

Her phone buzzed and she snatched it up. It was a message from Didi: *Happy 4th! Mom and Dad say hello.* He had attached a picture of their parents with his family, in his backyard, a family selfie. Esther was grateful, greedy for the distraction. Her dad wore a ridiculous foam Uncle Sam hat, but her nephew holding his hand clearly made it worthwhile for him. Her mom shaded her eyes as she looked at the camera from a lounge chair. Didi held the selfie stick, Ray-bans on, and behind him his wife Crystal held Esther's niece Bonnie, whose chubby legs poked out from a yellow sundress that Esther had ordered for her in the spring. Esther remembered why she had bought the sundress — she had seen Hannah in that dress on Claire's Instagram and thought it so cute that she had found out where Claire bought it and ordered one for Bonnie.

Just three months ago Esther could pick up the phone, message Claire, and find out where she was buying Hannah's clothes. Jesus. And now look what she had done with Hannah. She had made everything worse.

She threw her phone back onto the couch and started pacing in her living room. What could she do to fix this? Surely there must be a way to make this better again.

A buzz again, and she saw a text from Laz:

Esther, I spoke with Hannah and I realize that I have made a mistake. Lots of mistakes but the biggest one being so removed from her at this time. I had no idea that she was hurting so much, and I wish you had told me. I could have done more for her if I had known. I am going to take a couple of days and spend some time with her; I should have taken longer before. I understand that it's not your fault that I went back to work, that's on me. And I'm sorry to put you in the position of taking care of her. I think it would be best if you don't come for a while. It seems that we have collectively broken Hannah's trust and I need to earn it back.

Esther wasn't surprised that Laz wanted her to stay away from the house, but it still stung. *I understand,* she texted. *Please know that I didn't know that Hannah was struggling this way either.*

Almost immediately she received Laz's reply. *Hannah told me that she tried to talk to you about her feelings, but she couldn't. I don't know if you knew this. In any case, what's done is done and I need to do my part going forward.*

Another blow. It was as if the last six weeks with Hannah were all a mirage, a simulation, a joke. Esther thought back to the parks and playgrounds, the ice cream, the puzzles, the trip to Maggie's. Hannah had seemed fine for most of those moments, even happy in many of them. Esther tried to recall a time when she and Hannah talked about harder, potentially sad things, where Hannah had tried but failed to say something. Hannah had always seemed so sure of her words — even when talking about Claire she had never seemed to be hiding anything.

Then Esther recalled her own experience with her parents after Caleb's death, how she had hidden the saddest parts of herself away. Only revealing her true feelings in her diary, or at night alone in her bedroom crying in the dark. She had wanted to be strong for her parents, she remembered, because she knew how sad they were. And as an adult she had resented how they had let her bear this burden on her own, that they must have guessed that their daughter was suffering but chose not to address it.

And yet, despite her own experience, she did the same thing to Hannah. She let her own personal grief overshadow Hannah's need to grieve; she looked for the happiest Hannah to make herself happy. How could she have missed this?

Esther lay on the couch in the dark. She had been lying there for hours; as the daylight had faded, she hadn't bothered to turn on the lights. I don't deserve light, she had told herself. I don't deserve anything.

She had turned her phone off and she guessed that by now Wendy would have asked for an update about Tingting and Laz. Maybe Wendy would have forgotten; maybe instead Maggie would have sent around a picture of her kids, allowing her friends to revel in their domestic perfection, wishing everyone a happy 4th. But Wendy wouldn't forget, she wasn't the type to forget. She would demand an answer, and Esther wouldn't know what to say.

Yes, maybe there was something between Laz and Tingting. Yes, maybe it was disturbing and gross, but Hannah had turned to Tingting for support when Esther had ruined everything. Tingting would never read Hannah's diary. Tingting made delicious scallion pancakes. Tingting fit in their family in a way that Esther never could and honestly would never want to.

She hadn't asked for this, to take care of Hannah. They asked for it. The Chens. It was their plan, and she had agreed out of a sense of grief and loyalty. Maybe she had been flattered that they trusted her, but she should have known better. She should have known that this was more than she could handle, and she shouldn't have let them expect anything more than the truth of what she was—a nobody, a nothing.

Suddenly, a faraway boom. Then another, and a closer series of booms, the apartment quivering. The fireworks were starting now that the sun was down. Esther went to the window and gazed at the night sky, the flares of color shooting up and out. She thought of Hannah watching fireworks with Laz and Tingting. Would Hannah be able to overcome the disastrous day and enjoy the show? Would Tingting be clapping her hands in wonder, looking up together with Laz at the shimmering shards of light? America, the beautiful, for their small family to enjoy together, as Esther stood alone in her darkened apartment.

24

Esther woke up on the couch, still in yesterday's clothes, her body stiff, a brackish taste in her mouth. The sunlight shone through the window like an accusation.

She reached for her phone to check the time before remembering that she had turned it off the night before. She decided against turning it back on. If she didn't check her messages, she could remain innocent of the aftermath of yesterday.

Now, she didn't have anything to do. She wasn't going to see Hannah, obviously, not now and maybe never again.

A separate part of her brain recalled Jose and his offer over coffee, but she was miles away from being able to deal with that right now.

A walk. The sky outside was blue and beckoning. A walk would do her good.

It would be an adventure, taking a walk when she had nowhere in particular to go. She would wear a sundress and sandals. She would be cute. She would remember to bring sunglasses and first she would remember to put on sunscreen because who knew how long she would be out? Today was going to be a psychic cleanse; she was going to engage with the world around her.

Esther kept her optimism wrapped around her like a blanket (though no blanket needed today! It was going to be sunny!), got dressed and left her apartment building. She started walking, where should she go, not Rittenhouse Square Park in front of her; she didn't want to think about Hannah or parks or playgrounds. She needed coffee, and there was a Starbucks a couple blocks down, and that seemed like a reasonable place to go first.

There were more people on the sidewalk than she would have expected, or maybe she never noticed before. They were all looking at phones or listening through earbuds, talking with whomever they were walking with. She didn't see a single person as she was, unadorned and alone, except a homeless man sitting against the brick of the next apartment building. He was mumbling to himself, staring ahead, squinting from the sun.

Did she have cash? No ones or fives but she had a ten. When she was close enough, she stopped and held out the bill in her hand.

The man looked at her, up and down. She offered him a hesitant smile, and the bill in her outstretched hand wavered. He was older than she was, white, scruffy, his hair greasy and matted against his head. It was hot but around his legs was a tarp, so he might have looked like a Buddha if not for the malcontent in his eyes.

And then: "Go back to where you came from, China virus." The man snatched the bill from her hand and then leaned far back against the wall as if she were a walking Covid specimen, menacing and contagious.

Esther recoiled, mirroring his movement, stricken by the venom in his voice. She glanced around to see if anyone had noticed. If they had, they pretended they hadn't. Without saying anything further she trotted away from him, keeping pace with her pounding heart. She was filled with shame—because she had thought she was being magnanimous, because she had left herself unguarded, and maybe even a little bit because her very distantly related peoples in Wuhan had let the virus mutate and issue forth from their wet market? Damn it.

No, she wasn't retreating from him, she was rising above him, she tried to tell herself. There's nothing to be ashamed of. Still, her hands were shaking and her face was burning. She clenched her fingers together, taking deep breaths, slowing herself down.

She thought about that Vanessa Carlton song about making your way downtown, faces past, something homebound. She remembered back when she was young, she thought that song was about her. She hadn't suspected at the time that that song was for cute white girls who weren't going to get Asian hate when they tried to do good things. Maybe someone needed to write a song about how Asian hate could pop out when you least expected it.

Safety—Starbucks. She pushed the door open with a whoosh and was greeted by a cool blast of air. It was busy, every Starbucks was always busy. She would get iced coffee, not hot because it was too hot, and maybe she should get some seasonal summery drink to match her dress, or maybe she should get just a black cold brew to match the darkness of that homeless man's soul. No no no, she told herself, don't let him take over this experience. She couldn't afford to let revelatory walks be associated with hate, not right now.

Esther got her drink, and they even spelled her name right. Should she sit? She sat and then remembered that she had neither her phone nor a companion. Her eyes wandered around the shop; everyone else at a table had other people or electronics to keep them company. She saw one guy with a book. Ah yes, books. This is what people did when they didn't have phones, or friends; she could do it too. She could go to the bookstore and find a book and sit somewhere with her book and her coffee and read. Maybe she could gain some kind of deep epiphany in doing so. Maybe she would find her true self! Maybe, at the very least, she could distract herself from yesterday, from this morning.

But she didn't have her phone, so she couldn't check where a bookstore was. She considered asking the guy with the book, but what if he didn't live nearby, or what if he thought she was insane. Was it insane to ask where a bookstore was?

Screw it. At this point she had lost all sense of equilibrium; she had nothing to lose. He was a youngish Black guy, maybe early thirties, wearing hipster thick framed glasses and a loose plaid button-down.

"Excuse me," she said.

He looked up, stuck his thumb in the page where he was. "Yes?"

"I'm sorry to bother you, but I'm looking for a bookstore." Esther recognized the tinge of mania in her voice and blushed. "I don't have my phone, but I need to find a bookstore nearby, and I thought... because you have a book... I realize now that this sounds really stupid."

The guy gave her a smile. "No problem," he said. "I'm pretty sure there's a Barnes and Noble down a couple blocks on Walnut."

"Great, Walnut," Esther said. She hesitated. "I'm sorry, but I also have a really bad sense of direction, and again I don't have my phone to use Google Maps. Any chance you could give me more detailed directions?" My God, she thought, what is wrong with me.

The guy looked her up and down in a way that made Esther edge back a half step in preparation to flee. But, instead of telling her to go back to China, he pulled out his phone, opened the Maps app, and showed her on the screen.

"It's easy. You'd turn right out the door, walk down two blocks, then it'll be on your right side, across from the park."

"Right," Esther said. "Of course, that Barnes and Noble." She blushed. "I have a terrible sense of direction."

"Would you... would you like me to walk with you?" he asked. "I was just killing time before meeting a friend." Now his face was hopeful, and Esther realized that he probably thought they were the same age. "My name is Tony."

"Tony, hi, I'm Esther," she said. Tony was about to get up, but she motioned for him to stay seated. "No, I'm sorry, I'm fine on my own. I wasn't trying to hit on you or anything, I swear, I just needed directions to the bookstore. My God I realize that I sound like a mess. I'm sorry."

"No worries," Tony said. "Hey, can I give you my number? In case you want to call sometime?"

Jesus. "Oh, sorry, I don't have my phone..."

"Here. I have a card." Tony pulled out a card from his wallet. He laughed. "I swear I don't keep these cards to give to women who don't have their phones."

Esther forced out a laugh in response. Then she glanced at the book he was holding. *Cultures and Conflicts in East Asia*. Oh God.

He saw her looking down at the title and held her gaze for a second too long. "I've been trying to learn more about Asian culture," he said, as if this was an appropriate thing to say to an Asian person, as if the Asian person who heard it was supposed to be appreciative and grateful.

"Awesome," Esther said, and she backed up, knocking into an empty chair behind her. "Well, thanks so much Tony, I appreciate the directions."

"Wait, but the card?"

"I'm good, thanks. Enjoy... your book," Esther said as she turned to escape. She didn't look back as she left the store. She headed toward home. Fuck Starbucks. Fuck Barnes & Noble. Fuck attempts at being free from technology, and fuck Tony and all the men like him who were 'trying to learn more about Asian culture.'

In college and beyond, she had experienced the peril of men interested in Asia, in Asians. White men in particular who had studied Chinese or Japanese or, rarely, Korean, some majoring in East Asian Studies or similar, their summers abroad in Asia having granted them the gift of White Man in Asia Syndrome. WMAS, where an utterly ordinary white man found himself the center of attention from Asian girls in Beijing, Seoul, Taipei, Bangkok, who for whatever reason (Trying to get out of poverty? Social prestige among their friends? Wanting to see what a white boyfriend might be like? Trying to piss off their parents?) threw themselves at him. WMAS, where that utterly ordinary white man returned to the US after his summer abroad believing himself a sexual god to all women of Asian descent, even the ones who were clearly smarter, more successful, and/or more attractive than he was. Even the ones who had been born in the United States, didn't speak any Asian language, were practically white themselves. It had been a while, though, since Esther had come across one of these guys in the wild. The guy in Starbucks couldn't have had WMAS, first because he was Black, and second because he was still learning about Asian culture. He didn't think he was an expert, not yet. But surely reading about Asian culture and trying to pick up Asian women was a variant of WMAS.

Walking back to her apartment building, Esther crossed the street and back again to avoid the homeless man. What was worse—the guy who hated Asian women and stayed clear of them or the guy who loved Asian women because he thought that Asian women loved him? Sometimes it was hard to tell where any particular man fell on this spectrum, if it was a static position at all. Then there were the guys to whom Asian women were nonexistent, irrelevant, and this might be the most humiliating because it meant that a woman like Esther wasn't even worth any kind of emotion.

This, Esther thought as she entered the building, this was why she had always liked guys like Laz. Laz was the opposite of the WMAS guy. He was humble, ordinary looking, not an alpha in the traditional sense. He was the type of guy who was safe. She had always felt at ease with this kind of guy. Jose had been that kind of guy, until he had shown that he wasn't.

Back in her apartment, Esther threw off her sundress and changed into a t-shirt and shorts. She collapsed onto her couch, grabbing her lifeless phone off the table. As she waited for it to power on, she understood that however much she dreaded what she was going to see with her phone on, she didn't want to face the world outside with her phone off.

***

Laz hadn't texted her. She deserved more, she thought, more reprimand, more warning to stay away, more shame. Instead, she received silence.

Right now, Laz and Hannah and Tingting were probably eating lunch. Maybe beef noodle soup, Laz praising Tingting's cooking skills, Zhang ayi starting to grow resentful that this young pretty thing was taking a starring role in the kitchen. Tingting would soon go to work, and then Laz and Hannah would have an afternoon together, alone, getting to know each other. There is nothing wrong with this picture, Esther told herself. This is a good thing, for Hannah, and there is absolutely no reason for you to be there.

She opened WhatsApp and found a string of messages from the Mathey Girls. Early on Wendy had asked for an update on Laz and Tingting, but Esther hadn't seen it, and then Wendy's question had been buried in the subsequent messages. A picture of Val, asleep on the bed (Serena: *the one day she doesn't have to work and this is how she spends her time*); a picture of Maggie and her kids (Maggie: *hope you all are enjoying the 4th. My house is bedlam but look at how cute my kids are!*); chatter about how cute Maggie's kids were; a picture of Kingston with his headphones on, glaring at the camera (Wendy: *look at how cute my kid is! Lol*).

Esther's thumbs hovered over the keyboard on her screen, circling slowly before coming to a stop. The thought of telling the Mathey Girls what happened with Hannah made her feel ill. She locked her phone.

A chat group isn't a real conversation, Esther thought. Just banter, throwaway text on a screen, the group telling themselves that they have a meaningful relationship based on acronyms and emojis cast into the chat like fishing lines into water. There were so many things Esther couldn't say over WhatsApp, or over Zoom, things that were too difficult for a group conversation in any context. She had so many feelings she kept to herself, so many layers she kept hidden.

But, she knew, the parts of her that she hid—there was no one else she would want to show. If she would reveal herself to anyone, it would be to the women in this group. The chat was just a chat, yes, but it was reflective of a shared history, a longer story than whatever anyone happened to be typing about at any moment. The *Mathey Girls* chat was like a bit of land jutting out of the surface of the water, hiding an island that stood solid and immovable deep under the sea.

It reminded her of a Bible verse from when she was little, before her family stopped going to church. *Faith is the assurance of things hoped for, the evidence of things not seen.* Her mother had framed a print of this quote, purchased at some cheesy Christian bookstore, and hung it in the kitchen above the sink. Little Esther had known that it was beautiful, had understood in a vague childhood way what it meant. Later, she had considered the circular reasoning of it all. Faith was evidence of something unseen, but because faith was so personally experienced and defined, the something unseen was similarly personally experienced and defined, so the idea of it being evidence of something objective didn't make sense.

After her brother died, her mother had still made everyone go to church every Sunday, even though everything had changed. The fundamental contract with God had been severed; this was obvious to Esther, and she thought it should be obvious to her mother. Her father had started to lose faith even before Caleb had died, Esther had witnessed this, but no one acknowledged it. Her mother had held strong, for years, clinging to some remembrance of surety and comfort. And then by the time Esther reached high school, the family had stopped going to church, her mom had stopped talking about prayer or the Bible. The print in the kitchen had been taken down, the wallpaper behind the missing frame slightly darker than the wallpaper surrounding it.

How strange that her parents and Didi were all Bible-loving Christians again, decades later. Because Crystal was a born-again Christian, converting during college, and she brought Didi back into the fold when they were dating, and he had brought their parents back into the fold. They probably thought that this was the greatest gift that Didi gave them, greater than him being a doctor and marrying a Chinese American woman and having lovely Chinese American kids. Esther didn't need to give her parents anything; Didi was more than enough.

She stood at the window and tried to see what she saw before her walk. The sun was still bright, but the earlier feeling of promise was spent. She rested her forehead against the glass and closed her eyes. What am I even doing in this city, she thought. An old feeling arose: she missed her mom, and her dad, and maybe even Didi. It had been so long since she had allowed herself to need her family.

She dialed her mom's number, expecting to leave a voicemail, but her mom picked up. "Esther-ah? You okay?"

"Oh, hi mom," Esther said. "I'm okay, was just thinking of you."

"Everything alright?"

Esther wanted to shout CLEARLY NOT, I'M CALLING YOU IN THE MIDDLE OF THE DAY WANTING TO CHAT, but she didn't. Was it even possible to be honest to her parents when things weren't alright?

"Yeah, don't worry."

"Okay," her mom said. "I'm making lunch for Daddy."

"Nice," Esther said. Another long-forgotten feeling arose in her heart. Why can't my mom be one of those moms who actually talks to me? Esther had put away that line of thinking years ago, but she felt it now, that longing to have an honest conversation with her mother.

"You busy with work?" her mom asked.

"No, not right now," Esther said. At least this was true. Esther stretched to see if she could see the homeless man from her window, but her view was blocked by the facade of her building. "I saw that picture, Didi sent it, of you guys together for July 4th. It made me think of you." Esther took a breath and before her mom could say anything, she added, "I miss you guys."

"Oh," her mom said. "We miss you too."

Esther nodded, even though her mom couldn't see.

"If you're not busy with work," her mom said, "you could come home. To visit."

Esther considered. "It has been a while," she said.

"Your room is all cleaned," her mom said, as if a messy room was what had kept Esther away for the last two years.

Esther started pacing her living room. Why not go home? There was nothing keeping her in Philly. It might be nice to get away from her apartment, get some distance from the Chens.

"I mean, I could drive—I have a car now," Esther said. "I could leave now and get there tonight."

"Tonight? Why?"

"I have some time... Are you and Dad busy or something?"

"We have a prayer meeting tonight, home after nine."

"I wouldn't want to bother you," Esther said.

"No bother."

A hopeful smile sat on Esther's face. "Okay... Well, I'll text you when I'm getting closer, with my exact time."

"Okay, okay, we'll leave the door unlocked."

"Thanks Mom. I love you. I'll see you tonight."

"Okay bye," her mom said, and hung up.

Esther went to her bedroom to pack, a little nugget of hope blooming inside. She still had her family, her real family, even if she had messed everything up with Claire's family. Her real family could never push her away or keep her out. They had to accept her for whoever she was, or at least whoever she told them she was. Maybe, like her friendship with the Mathey Girls, her family was another island hidden under the surface of Esther's turbulent life. Maybe it was just waiting to be rediscovered and reclaimed.

A part of her wanted to share this revelation with the Mathey Girls. *Hey guys!* she could say, *I'm going to Cleveland!* But no, if she told her friends she was going home, they would ask about Hannah, and she wasn't ready to tell them yet.

Part Four

25

Esther lay in her childhood bed (twin), under her childhood comforter (white, with yellow ducks in faded rows), looking at her childhood ceiling (off white, popcorn, stipples still menacing after all these years). She glanced around her room, trying to understand why it felt different. Right—her mom's pandemic de-cluttering phase. The knickknacks she had accumulated throughout her childhood, the droppings of her college and young adult years, all put away or thrown away, so even though the furniture was familiar, the fact that it was bare was not.

She scrunched the comforter between her fingers. She remembered picking it out at the store when she was little. The fabric had been washed so many times that it had gone from rough to deliciously soft to so soft that it was falling apart. The stuffing clumped in haphazard knots, the comforter thick in some places and thin in others.

Her neck and shoulders were stiff from the drive the day before. In college she cultivated her tolerance for the drive between Cleveland and the East Coast; eight hours in the beat-up Camry her parents had bought from an old church friend, the sugar and caffeine of three bottled Frappuccinos coursing through her veins. She had thought a lot during those eight-hour drives, especially during the mostly flat and unchanging expanse that was middle Pennsylvania. But now she was older, and her body didn't want bottled Frappuccinos, it wanted more caffeine, less sugar, and more opportunities to pee. And there was only so much thinking that she wanted to do at this time in her life, especially at this particular moment, but she had pushed through with the help of a playlist of early 2000s alternative hits and multiple bathroom breaks and the knowledge that she was leaving Philly and its problems behind.

Coffee. She needed coffee. She padded to the kitchen, rolling her neck and shoulders to get them loose.

"Morning," she said, and started to rummage through the cabinets.

Her mom was at the small table, a Chinese newspaper spread in front of her, reading glasses perched on the end of her nose. She looked smaller than Esther remembered, but her polyester blouse was familiar on her tiny frame. She had stopped dying her hair over the pandemic, and this made her look older—at least, it made her look her actual age.

"What you looking for?" her mom asked.

"Coffee."

"Oh. We might not have any."

"I thought last time I came I bought some instant Starbucks to keep here."

"Last time you came was years ago." Esther's mom continued to squint at the tiny characters, decidedly not making eye contact.

It was true, and Esther accepted the admonishment. The last two years the pandemic had excused her from visiting, and her parents hadn't given her a hard time for it, and she had been grateful without telling them so.

The newspaper rustled as her mom turned the page. "You want tea?"

"Do you have American tea?"

"No," her mom said. "Only Chinese tea leaves."

"I guess I'll go out and get coffee in a bit." Esther sat at the table empty-handed. A new print of the same old verse on faith hung above the sink. This one was written in blue calligraphy on a cream background, adorned with curlicues in two of the corners. Esther imagined a never-ending supply of faith prints, ready to be consumed by Christians as their aesthetic tastes and religious inclinations waxed and waned.

Her mom saw her looking at the print. "You going to church, Esther?"

"Nope," Esther said. "You?"

"Every Sunday," her mom said. She patted Esther's hand. "Everything okay at work? Why are you home?"

"Everything's okay," Esther said, a reflex, but her mom was looking at her for more. "Well, actually I haven't been working very much. For a while."

Her mom frowned, took her reading glasses off and set them on the table. "Because of Claire?"

"Before Claire, actually." Seeing the concern on her mom's face made Esther's heart constrict. "But don't worry, it's my choice. I have some job stuff lined up, it's just when I want to take it."

Her mom's face relaxed somewhat and Esther's relaxed with it. "Where's Dad?" Esther asked.

"Church. Seniors' Bible study."

"I didn't realize Dad was so into church now," Esther said. It had always been her mom's thing, when she was younger, and it struck Esther again how little she actually knew her parents.

"It gives him something to do. Usually I go too."

Of course. Her parents were comfortably retired, supported by their pensions and their kids, but they didn't enjoy retirement the way regular Americans were supposed to—they weren't interested in golf or fishing or white lady mahjong or whatever else elderly Americans liked. They must be so bored. Esther remembered how during the worst times of the pandemic her mom had sounded almost giddy, with all her energies directed toward feeding and caring for their little bubble with Didi's family. Now, that bubble had burst, the kids back to daycare and camp, life back to boring and normal.

"Do you still go to Didi's often?" Esther asked.

Her mom shook her head. "No... Crystal..."

Esther knew it was Crystal's prerogative to take care of her children the way she saw fit, but it still hurt to see her mom be relegated to seniors' church activities to fill her time instead of spending it with her grandchildren. Esther's mom saw the look on her face and rushed to ameliorate. "Crystal is a good mom," she said.

"You're too nice," Esther said. "Maybe you and Dad could take a trip or something."

A smirk crossed Esther's mom's face, briefly.

"Would you want to go back to Taiwan? It's been a long time since you went back, right?"

"Too hot," her mom said, "and they have the quarantine."

Esther had heard about this, but she had also seen news that Taiwan had reduced the quarantine period to only a couple of days. She knew her mom would know this. "Maybe when they relax the quarantine rules you and Dad should go," Esther said.

Her mother shook her head again. "Too expensive," she said.

"I can buy your tickets," Esther said. "I would love to pay for your trip to Taiwan."

"*Ni dou meigongzuo!*" her mom said in Chinese, *you're not even working,* and Esther blushed. Her mom patted her hand again. "You save your money." Then her mom got up and started taking out food from the fridge. "I make your favorite for lunch. Shepherd's pie."

At some point in Esther's youth, she had rebelled against Chinese food and her mom had started making shepherd's pie. She didn't recall which came first, but it had become her favorite dish. This was in the years after Caleb died, and she remembered the brief joy that it brought her mom to see her devour it. It was true, at the time it was her favorite, the savory coalescence of mashed potatoes, beef and corn. And Esther had let it remain a favorite, so that she could give her mom the pleasure of making it and serving it and watching her eat it.

"Thanks, Mom," Esther said. "And can we have Chinese food for dinner?" She knew her mom preferred cooking Chinese food, that once the kids left the house that was all her parents ate. Esther had never appreciated it when she was growing up, and she had never learned how to cook anything Chinese, or anything at all, really. "Maybe you could teach me how to cook some things while I'm here."

Her mom turned to her with a smile that Esther couldn't help but mirror. "*Hao a,*" her mom said. *Sure.* "How long you staying?"

"Forever," Esther said, just to see the momentary shock on her mom's face. "Just kidding. Just a couple days, I think, maybe go back this weekend."

Her mom turned back to her food prep. In Chinese, she said, "You tell me what you want to cook, and I'll teach you."

***

After lunch, Esther tried to digest her shepherd's pie while watching Chinese TV with her parents.

"How did you get this again?" she asked, pointing at the TV.

"Didi set it up," her dad said. He looked the same as when Esther had last seen him; with his skinny frame and protruding belly, his high hairline stuck in early phase recession, his hair and bushy eyebrows long gone gray.

It was so easy to fall back into this couch, this house, Esther thought. She should do it more often. Then her dad asked, "How's work?" and she stiffened. He looked at her through his thick glasses, expecting her to tell him that it was good, she was doing well, it was busy, but she was happy keeping busy. The same answer she had given him so many times over the years.

Esther glanced at her mom, who kept her face neutral.

"I haven't been working," Esther said. "For a while."

Her dad's gaze took a slow loop from Esther to her mom and back again. "But your money's okay?" he asked. His English had always sounded better than her mom's, the same accent and same limited vocabulary, but his delivery was less hesitant and so he sounded more fluent.

"Money's okay," Esther said.

"You didn't... get fired, right?" her mom asked.

"*Buhuiba*," her dad said. *No way.*

"Actually, I did," Esther said. Her parents were staring at her now, as if this was hard to believe. It *was* hard to believe. Esther had had a hard time believing when it first happened. "Remember when I stopped working for Centridge and started doing freelance? During the pandemic? That was me getting fired."

Her parents glanced at each other. "And, actually," she continued, "I said I was freelancing but I haven't really done any work. I mean, recently, I haven't been able to get any work. At all."

Her dad switched off the TV, brow furrowed. The ticking of the clock on the wall, oppressively loud, filled the room.

Esther felt very Chinese—that she had failed in a way that only a Chinese child could fail her parents. Her parents had never been the type to overtly demand the best from her, but they had expected it, and she had always delivered.

"It's fine," her dad said, quietly.

"What?" Esther asked.

"It's fine for you take a break," he said.

Esther looked at her mom and she too hadn't expected this—she could see her mom processing and rearranging her own thoughts to match her dad's, mental calisthenics honed after decades of marriage.

"You're okay with all this?" Esther asked. "Just to clarify."

"Money's okay?" he asked again.

"Yes, for now."

"Then it's good you take a break."

"What if I never work again?" Esther asked.

"You're a smart girl. You can get different job. You went to *Princeton*." Her dad was nodding to himself, and her mom was nodding too.

"It doesn't... it doesn't work that way," Esther said. "Just because I went to Princeton doesn't mean I can get a good job."

"No?" her dad asked, and Esther thought that maybe he had a point. Deep down, perhaps she had recognized this herself. She was fired, and her freelance work had died, but she never believed that her career was over. She knew that she could do *something*, when she wanted to, whether it was because she went to Princeton or just because she knew herself enough to know that if she wanted to work, she would work.

"Daddy always hopes that Crystal stops work," Esther's mom said.

"Take care of the kids," her dad added.

"Crystal is never going to stop working," Esther said. "She loves her job." She didn't point out that not only did Crystal seem to enjoy working at the Clinic, she was also the breadwinner in the family. She was a more prestigious doctor than Didi, an anesthesiologist as opposed to an internist.

"Well, Didi said you would never stop work, and look, you stopped work," her dad said.

Esther understood then that her parents must have talked to Didi about Crystal taking a break from work to be with the kids, and that Didi must have used Esther as an example of a free-thinking Chinese American woman who had a successful career instead of focusing on family. It was flattering, kind of, but also damning that Didi thought of her that way.

"Did you see the pictures?" Esther's mom asked, pointing to the collection of framed photos hanging above the couch.

She stood up to take a closer look at the arrangement of various sized photos in simple black frames, laid out like a mosaic oval, unusually artsy for her parents' house. She recognized some of the old school pictures of Didi and her that used to sit elsewhere, but now there were also pictures of Didi's kids. In the center of the oval was a blown-up print of a picture from Didi's college graduation. Her parents stood proud, flanking their two children. Didi was jubilant, his face flushed, and Esther was smiling but she remembered being stressed out about work on that day, wanting to finish up with the picture so that she could return a client call.

There weren't any pictures of Caleb in the mosaic. Esther wasn't surprised; after his death his pictures had been stored away. Her dad had told her at the time that it made her mother too sad to see them, and Esther had assumed that this was the normal thing to do, to store away whatever made you sad rather than acknowledge it.

She considered asking her parents whether they might want to put some pictures of Caleb on the wall now, but her mother was looking at her with expectant eyes, hoping that Esther would enjoy the photos as her mother enjoyed them.

"It's very nice," Esther said.

"Crystal designed it," her dad said, using his finger to paint circles in the air. "Put this picture here, that picture there."

"And did you see how clean your room is?" her mom asked. "We threw away so much junk."

"Yeah, I saw," Esther said. "I was thinking of getting a new blanket for that bed."

"You can, but no one uses that room," her dad said. "You never come home." Esther's mom swatted his arm and told him in Chinese not to say that; Esther was here right now after all.

"Maybe I can stay longer this time," Esther said. She thought about Philly, and what was not waiting for her back there. Not Claire, not Hannah. "Wait—Mom, you didn't throw away all my old stuff, right?"

"I did," her mom said. "You said it's okay."

"What?"

"I asked if I could throw away your old stuff. You said it's okay."

Esther tried to remember that conversation. It must have been early in the pandemic, she was still at Centridge then, she had likely been too busy to even register what her mom was asking.

"But my old notebooks—you wouldn't have thrown them away?"

"What notebooks?" her mom asked. "I don't know —"

Esther was already running to her room.

The accordion hinges creaked in protest as Esther yanked the closet door open. She gasped at the near emptiness before her. Her closet used to hold decades of Things Left Behind—clothes, shoes, trophies, letters, schoolwork—and now there was almost nothing. On the rod there were only the dress that she had worn as a bridesmaid in Claire's wedding and her Princeton beer jacket, received on graduation day and meant to be worn at Reunions but instead abandoned in her Cleveland childhood closet.

There were two plastic storage bins on the shelf above the clothing rod, one small and transparent—filled with hard copy photos —and one large and opaque blue. She dragged her desk chair over to the closet to see what was in the blue box. Her diaries might still be there.

Tottering on the unstable seat as she reached up, her finger caught on the side of the bin, and she faltered. She scrabbled again, her fingers desperate for purchase on the smooth plastic, and as she took hold of the bin it slid down and she fell under its weight.

Esther hoisted herself up and rubbed her back. The hallway echoed with thumping sounds; her mom came in with frightened eyes.

"You okay?"

Esther grunted as she righted the bin.

"You fall off the chair?" her mom asked.

Kneeling on the carpet, Esther undid the latches of the bin to reveal a jumble of documents, folders, binders and notebooks crammed together. She began to lift pieces out one by one.

"Philosophy 101 paper. Econ 102 exam. Graduation program," she muttered.

"We kept all your A papers," her mom said.

"Is this all college stuff?" Esther asked. "No, here's my SAT scores."

"You said that we could throw your stuff out, but Daddy and I thought you might still want some," her mom said, anxious.

"But did you keep my diaries? From when I was kid? Please tell me you kept them."

"There's a diary," Esther's mom said, and she came to stand over the box. "There." But the diary she pointed to was from eighth grade, when she graduated to using a real book with the word Diary on the front cover.

"They were in notebooks, Mom, like this." Esther lifted up her Organic Chemistry notebook, which her parents had inexplicably thought worth saving.

"Oh," Esther's mom said, and Esther paused, a sparkler shooting out filaments of hope inside her. Her mom was standing right next to her, and Esther tried to manifest her mother saying yes, I saved them, of course I did.

But her mom didn't say anything else, and Esther had reached the bottom of the bin, and her old diaries weren't there. She sank back onto her heels.

"I think we threw them away," her mom said. "We didn't know about any diaries."

"Oh Mom," Esther said, trying to rein in her disappointment.

"Was it important?" her mom asked, wringing her hands.

Yes, it was important, Esther wanted to say. She wanted to say that her diary had been one of the few places—no, the only place—where she could say how she was really feeling after her brother died. How her parents had never given her any space to open up to them, how they never offered the possibility of processing their grief together instead of in their separate silos. How the diaries never gave Esther any answers, but at least they let her ask the overwhelming questions that arose after Caleb's death.

Her mother had no idea, of course she had no idea, she would never have thrown the diaries away if she had any idea.

"I'm sorry," Esther's mom said. She crouched down to start putting the papers back into the bin.

Esther held out her hand. "No, I got it," she said. "I'll put it away."

"I didn't know," her mom said.

"It's okay."

"It's okay?"

"It's okay."

Esther placed notebooks and binders and folders back into the bin, slowly, without looking up. She heard her mom leave the room.

Her mom was fragile, Esther reminded herself. Esther could be strong, she could keep the feelings of grief and loss for herself and protect her mother. Her mom had suffered enough.

The diaries had never offered Esther any solutions anyway. They were just notebooks, just paper and wire. They had never taken away any of her grief, and whether she had the diaries now or not, the grief would remain.

If only, though, if only she were holding one right now, in her hands—maybe she could have taken it back for Hannah, to show her that she had gone through the same thing, that she understood what she was going through and never wanted to hurt her. Even if Hannah didn't forgive her, at least Esther would have a little bit of her old self back. If only.

Esther snapped the latches of the bin shut and shoved it back into the closet, leaving it on the floor. She pushed against the protesting closet door then rested her head against it, eyes closed.

26

Esther didn't allow herself to wallow after she learned that the diaries were gone. She told herself that she had lost enough over the last few weeks, months, years—her job, Claire, even her relationship with Hannah—she wouldn't let the loss of an object like a notebook take equal space in her panorama of despondence.

Instead, she watched Chinese TV with her parents. She bought a new bedding set for her room to show that she was still invested in her family home.

She didn't tell the Mathey Girls that she was in Cleveland.

She waited to hear from Laz, and she was left waiting.

After two days at home, she met Didi for drinks at a bar on the lake shore. The patrons were mostly white with a sprinkling of melanin interspersed through the crowd. This was still much more colorful than the Cleveland of her childhood. You would think that by her age she would be used to it, but living on the East Coast for so long had increased her sensitivity to how white this side of Cleveland was.

"You're looking for the minorities, aren't you," Didi said with a smirk on his face.

"I'm looking for the people of color, yes," Esther said.

"And?"

Esther just gave him a smile and looked at the drinks menu. Her intuition told her that she was going to order cranberry juice, but sometimes high-end places would have interesting mocktails. Nope.

"You're looking well," she said. This was not a lie. Compared to the last time Esther saw him, for Claire's memorial service, he looked like a new man. "And where's Crystal? Working?"

Didi grimaced. Crystal was always working.

"It's nice to have Mom as your babysitter," Esther said. "I wish we had had that kind of relationship with our grandparents, you know?"

"Sure," Didi said. The waitress came and they ordered drinks. Didi looked out over the water. "You know we wanted to get an au pair, but Mom was so offended at the idea that we dropped it."

"Why?"

"Because then we wouldn't need her, I guess, and she thought it was a waste of money." Didi shrugged, burying any further complaint. "And how's Philly? Mom told me that you were fired and that you haven't been working."

"Wow. Word travels fast."

"I'm impressed that you kept it from us for so long. But seriously, are you okay? Financially?"

"I'm okay, financially, for now," Esther said. The sun was setting but it was still hot, and she welcomed the breeze wafting in from the lake. Didi waited for her to continue, and Esther realized how much he was starting to look like their dad. The long face, the bushy eyebrows. But her dad never carried himself with the *Born in America, I'm a doctor* confidence that Didi had. Mom and Dad must be so proud looking at him.

"You know, I could ask around if you're looking for a new job." Didi didn't make eye contact as he said this. Maybe he thought she would be offended.

It came out quickly, before she had a chance to think about it: "Thanks, I'm good." Then Esther shook her head. "No, actually, I will keep that in mind if I need the help," she said, and Didi looked at her in surprise. Yes, she thought, I might actually ask you for help. So far, her only lead on a job was Jose, and she still wasn't sure she could handle working for him.

"If you want to come to Cleveland, we know a lot of people here," Didi said. "It's not just doctors and stuff. Crystal has her Harvard Club, and I'm active with the Princeton Association."

"I know, I know," Esther said. "You guys love your alumni associations. But don't forget, I was the one who got you into college." It was an old joke, a not funny one, because ultimately Caleb was the one who got both of them into Princeton and they knew it.

"Well," Didi said, "it would be a waste of these networks if we don't use them to help people like us."

"People like us?"

"You know, *people of color,*" Didi said in a low voice, as if saying a bad word.

Esther considered the layers of privilege she had witnessed, had touched, and was now embedded in. The students at Princeton had been a spectrum. On the far end were the kids who shared last names with the residential halls, descendants of generations of Princeton-associated wealth and prestige. On the other end were the kids whose parents hadn't gone to college, kids who had made it to the University by their sheer genius or talent or whatever it took, the kids who worked in the dining halls serving the kids whose names were on the buildings. And somewhere in the middle there were kids like Esther, children of college educated immigrants, raised by parents who prioritized their children's education over their own health and well-being, desperate to shove their offspring into the elite of American life.

"We visited Caleb's grave last weekend," Didi said suddenly.

The bar around them was loud, with music and chatter and the sound of the water, but a halo of silence descended on Esther and Didi. They rarely, never really, talked about Caleb or his death or its aftermath.

"I haven't been there in forever," Esther said.

"We went as a family. Ben and Bonnie were just running on the grass as if it was a park or something, and I couldn't help but think of how we would cope if something happened to Ben." Didi shuddered.

"Remember when we were little, and I would hold your hand so that you would stay still?" Esther asked.

"What do you mean?"

"Mom and Dad would be so sad and quiet, and all you wanted to do was run down the hill to the flowers, and I didn't want to ruin things for them, so I held your hand and kept you with me."

Didi shook his head. "I don't remember that at all."

Esther remembered Didi pulling on her arm, crying. She remembered clamping her hand over his mouth so that his shouting wouldn't bother their parents. Maybe it was best that he didn't remember.

"Were Mom and Dad there, when your family went to the cemetery?"

"Yeah. Nobody cried or anything, I was surprised at how easily we all kept things light and happy for the kids. I guess it's been too long to be really sad about it anymore."

Esther wanted to say that this couldn't possibly be true, but she knew he was right. Time always, always smoothed over the hurt of death. Even with Claire, who had only passed two months ago. Esther had already felt the diffusion of her acute grief, the inevitable consequence of continuing to live her life in the face of loss.

"I really messed up, with Hannah," Esther said, and she explained how she had read the diary, how she was afraid that Laz and Tingting were being set up and that Hannah would have to go back to Taiwan, how she felt that she had failed the memory of her best friend by hurting her daughter and not stopping the changes to her family.

She waited for Didi's judgment, at the same time hoping that he could somehow find a way to absolve her from the damage she had done.

"And that's why you came home?" he asked.

"I guess. I needed to get away," Esther said. She didn't tell him about her failed attempt at a walk, because she was ashamed that she was almost forty and apparently couldn't even take a walk like a normal person.

"I think," Didi said, eyes looking up as he searched for the right words, "I think that you need to try harder."

"What do you mean?"

"When you think you fail at something, you give up and run."

"No, I don't," Esther said slowly.

"Sure you do. Like in undergrad, you got a C in what, mol-bio, and decided that you weren't cut out for pre-med and majored in economics instead? And became a consultant?"

Esther wrinkled her nose. "I didn't..."

"And then you got fired, and essentially just gave up on working."

"I tried freelance..." Esther said, but she knew that she had not tried very hard.

"And when freelance didn't work out, you just gave up entirely."

Esther shook her head. "I don't think you can equate my college major and my career with what's happening with Hannah."

"Sure I can," Didi said. "You think you messed up with Hannah, and yes it was a shitty thing to do, reading her diary, but in the scheme of things it's not that bad. It really isn't, don't give me that look, and there's no reason you can't fix things."

Esther didn't know what to say. When Didi said it, it made sense, but she wasn't used to receiving wisdom from her little brother. It was humbling.

"I can give Lazarus a call," Didi said.

"No," Esther said. "I can deal with it."

"Why don't you let me help you, just this once," Didi said. "I know you don't need my help, that if you decide you want to fix all of this, you totally can. But if it feels hard, I can step up. You don't need to handle everything on your own."

Esther wanted to hug him, like she would hug a friend, but something held her back. All of the years they had lived on the earth together, in the same house, at the same school, and they had never really been friends.

She squeezed her fingers together. "I think... I'm sorry I wasn't there for you, when we were younger, with Caleb. I'm sorry we didn't talk more, and that I was such a shitty sister."

Didi took a sip of his beer. "Hm," he said. "I mean, it wasn't a total loss. You did get me into Princeton."

***

Hi Laz, I hope everything is going well with you and Hannah. I hope she's happy. I want to explain myself, but I'm not sure I can, but just know that I am truly sorry for the breach of trust. Also, she has an appointment with Dr. Winter scheduled for Tuesday 2:30 pm. Let me know if you want me to cancel it, or move it, or maybe you or Tingting might be able to take her.

Saturday afternoon at Didi's; a ten-minute drive from her parents' house that transported them from mid-middle class to upper middle class, from pothole-riddled streets lined with deteriorating houses to new developments with stately McMansions in gated communities, from near the highway to near the Lake.

Didi's household was built on a foundation of concessions and compromise, starting with the decision to live in Cleveland to be near his parents. Crystal's parents had their own son in Los Angeles, an hour from their Alhambra home, and then there was that old Chinese saying: *Fushuinanshou. Water thrown to the ground is hard to recover.* When a woman marries a man, she leaves her birth family forever. Crystal, the thrown water, and Didi, the ground, got jobs at Cleveland Clinic. Their house in Avon, Ohio was a new build when they moved in, larger and more ostentatious than they might need, and awkwardly far from the Clinic by Cleveland standards, but Crystal deserved a *really nice house* given, well, Cleveland.

From a distance, Crystal might be seen as a doppelganger of Esther and the Mathey Girls. Asian American, Ivy League, successful. If she had gone to Princeton instead of Harvard, maybe she would have been one of them, perhaps if Claire had befriended Crystal and over time softened her edges. Instead, there was a fierceness to Crystal, a keen-edged ambition that Esther never related to. The Mathey Girls were smart, they were capable, but they weren't sharks like Crystal was.

Crystal was also a different type of Chinese American than Esther and Didi. Her family was more traditional than the Hsu family, and unlike Esther and Didi she had grown up speaking Chinese at home, having Chinese friends, regularly in touch with Chinese language and Chinese culture—at least, the version of Chinese culture that existed in the San Gabriel Valley in the 80s and 90s. Didi had assured Crystal that his mom wasn't a traditional Chinese mother-in-law, that she didn't need to worry about the horror stories of over-attachment to the son, micromanaging the children, criticizing the cooking, etc. etc. Still, despite how nice their mom was, she and Crystal continued to abrade each other.

Now, Esther had left the rest of the family in the living room to text Laz about Hannah's upcoming therapy appointment, trying to restrain herself from a word vomit of apologies and good wishes, and Crystal came in.

"Oh, hi, I didn't realize you were in here. I was going to grab a kombucha. You want one?"

"Sure," Esther said. "You still very busy?"

"Yup," Crystal said. She took two bottles from the fridge and handed one to Esther at the table.

They opened their bottles and drank. Esther noticed that Crystal was hovering between leaving and staying. "Do you want to sit?" she asked.

Crystal eased herself into the chair with a grateful smile. One thing that Esther had always appreciated in Crystal was how little she seemed to care about how she looked. She never wore makeup and always kept her hair in a low ponytail. Now she looked more weathered than before, the pandemic having taken its toll on her just as it had on everyone else. Esther assumed that she too looked more weathered, more gray in her hair, and she no longer wore makeup or got her hair straightened now that she wasn't working. Shit. We're morphing into old Chinese ladies, Esther realized with a grimace.

"Andrew told me about your job," Crystal said quietly.

"Yeah," Esther said.

"I'm sorry that you didn't feel like you could tell your family, at the time."

It was unusual to speak with Crystal so intimately, but Esther accepted her invitation. "In hindsight it looks pretty stupid, doesn't it? Like what difference does it make if I tell my parents that I was fired versus I quit. It doesn't really change anything—I'm out of a job," she said. "But at the time the thought of telling them, or Didi, or you, or anyone really, was terrifying."

"You told your friends, right? Your college friends?"

Esther nodded her head. "I mean, I couldn't keep it all to myself."

Crystal's face was marked with pity.

"This is the thing," Esther said. "I was fired, but I had stopped trying long before then. It was almost as if I was testing them. Like, how long would they keep me employed when I was dialing it in, when I didn't really care."

"I thought you loved your job," Crystal said.

"I loved being good at my job. There were things I didn't like," Esther said. "But I always did an excellent job anyway, until the end. And then I got fired, which I probably deserved." She ran her fingertips across her eyebrows. "I probably sound very defensive right now, but it's true."

"Oh, I believe you," Crystal said.

"Really?"

"We haven't talked a lot, the two of us, but I know you. I know Andrew—Didi—well enough, and your parents, and from everything

I've seen of you, I know that there is no way in hell you'd get fired if you were actually trying."

A rueful laugh escaped Esther's mouth. "Thanks, I guess." She leaned back in her chair. "Maybe the Esther that everyone thinks they know is someone totally different from me. You think you know me, even Didi and my parents think they know me, but I'm not really who you all think I am. I'm really not that confident, or competent—"

"Stop right there." Crystal leaned forward, eyes locked on Esther. "I think you're wrong. I know myself, and I know how good I am at sizing people up. I think the problem isn't that we don't know the real you. I think the problem is that *you* don't know the real you."

"No," Esther said, shaking her head.

"Yes," Crystal said. "Sure, you're going through a rough patch. It's to be expected. I would guess that something happened at your old job, something that caused you to lose confidence, or lose faith in the work, and that's why you started to slide. Because you couldn't commit yourself to it anymore, and yes, maybe a part of you was testing them to see how far you could let go."

Esther found this disconcertingly accurate.

"And then," Crystal said, "when you got fired, you thought it was a reflection of you as a person, when it really wasn't. It was a reflection of the pandemic, and the market, and the fact that you weren't performing like you used to, and they could see that."

The kids were screaming in the other room, but Crystal didn't seem to register. She took a long swig of her kombucha and then continued. "The thing is, strong women like us, we can't get bogged down with impostor syndrome and all that nonsense. It's so easy to take on that mantle, you know? Especially Asian women. We're brought up to be successful and competent, but at the same time demure and obedient, and where does that leave us? We don't allow ourselves to be proud of our achievements, our skills. Fuck that shit."

"Damn, Crystal," Esther whispered. "I can't say you're wrong in any of that."

"Like I said, I know people. Especially people like us."

Esther considered her sister-in-law with a new respect. Then, breaking the rarefied air, Crystal burped loud and long, and Esther couldn't help but smile.

"That's some spicy kombucha," Crystal said, and they were both laughing.

It felt so satisfying to laugh, then Esther remembered why she was back in Cleveland again, and she found herself wiping tears from her eyes.

"I'm sorry," Esther said, seeing Crystal's look of concern.

Crystal put her hands on Esther's. "We have all been through way too much the last couple of years, and these last couple of months have been brutal to you."

Again, she couldn't disagree.

"Andrew —Didi—told me not to mention it, but he also told me about what you've been doing for Claire's daughter, and what you said to him last night about Caleb." Crystal pressed on Esther's hands, the pressure a comfort instead of a burden. "I think, and remember —I know people—I think you need to recognize that despite all the shit that you've gone through, you're still giving yourself to other people. That's a lot."

Esther didn't know what to say.

The kitchen door swung open, and in came Esther's mom. "Bonnie wants crackers," she said, and then she saw Crystal holding Esther's hands at the table, Esther's eyes wet. Esther pulled her hands away, hid them on her lap, and Crystal went to the cupboard to get the crackers.

"*Ni dui jiejie neme hao,*" Esther's mom said as Crystal handed her the box. *You're so good to your older sister.* Esther knew, and she knew that Crystal knew, what her mom wanted to convey. Her mom was recognizing Crystal's kindness, praising the fact that she was helping Esther.

Crystal's face flushed, red spots appearing on her cheeks above the corners of her upturned mouth. It was hard to believe that two minutes ago Crystal was giving her a pep talk; now she was, indeed, demure and obedient as she had been raised to be. This is the paradox, Esther thought.

27

The next day Esther dropped her parents off at church for their seniors' Bible study, picked up a bouquet of flowers at the grocery store and drove to Lakewood Park Cemetery. It was her first time going by herself, the first time she was sitting in the drivers' seat, as she went up the sloped path past the cemetery gates. Nothing looked familiar from where she sat.

She last came here, what, at least a decade ago, yes, it was around Didi and Crystal's wedding, when Didi made it a thing for their newly enlarged family to visit Caleb's grave together.

Now, Esther drove slowly, making her way along the winding cemetery road. She hadn't appreciated the beauty of the cemetery when she was younger. The expansive green, the long slopes down into miniature valleys, trees spreading wide to provide respite from the summer sun. It was a weekday morning, and there were only a few scattered visitors. Esther didn't let her eyes rest on any of these people, as if her looking at them might distract them—in an unwanted way—from their grief.

She saw the sign for section fourteen and parked her car close to the grass. Caleb's grave was in a lot far from the path and, flowers in hand, Esther stepped gingerly around the marble slabs embedded in the ground. Things were looking more familiar now; the clearing down the small hill, the thick-trunked tree on her left and the slope down to a ravine past the gravestones. Esther felt a force guiding her to her brother's grave. *This way*, it said. *You remember.*

The air was thick with the smell of cut grass and the sound of lawnmowers and bird chatter; it was almost hot enough to be stifling.

Soon, too soon, she was standing over his gravestone. The flowers that Didi and her parents must have brought on their last visit had been removed. She unwrapped her bouquet, crumpled the cellophane and tissue paper and rubber bands into a wet ball and stuffed them into her bag. As she put the flowers in the cup under the gravestone, they leaned haphazardly in every direction. She should have bought two bouquets; she had never been the one buying the flowers before.

Esther wasn't the type to talk to the deceased at the grave—her parents had done it, and she had always felt a kind of embarrassment when she heard them speaking to the stone as if speaking to their son. His body is in a box, down there, she had wanted to tell them. It's just a body. He's gone, he can't hear you.

Still, Esther knelt down and passed her hand over the gravestone, tracing her fingers along the Bible verse carved into the stone. "I have fought the good fight, I have finished my course, I have kept the faith," Esther read in a whisper. She remembered once, coming to the cemetery with her mom, during college. Her mom had also read the verse aloud, rueful and hard—this was after the family had stopped going to church. She recalled her despair at hearing the disappointment in her mom's voice that day.

It was hard to believe that that was two decades ago, that Esther was now twice as old as Caleb was when he died. He wouldn't recognize her now, would he? Maybe he would see that she was starting to look like their mom, with her mouth beginning to curve down and sun spots, stubborn, at the tops of her cheeks. Maybe he would be proud of her, that she had been successful, somewhat, that their family was still intact, mostly. He would definitely be proud of Didi for finishing what he, Caleb, had started. And Esther had helped Didi get to where he was, because she had helped to carry her parents emotionally through those first worst years, she had paved the path for Didi to succeed, kept everyone and everything afloat for Didi to excel.

No; she shook her head. Didi's accomplishments weren't hers to claim. She needed to stop thinking like this, as if she carried everything for her family, as if it was her job to make things okay. It wasn't fair to herself, and it wasn't fair to the people whom she claimed responsibility for.

She let herself sink into the grass, surrendering to the heat and summer's drone around her.

She could try. That's all she could do. She could take what gifts had been given to her, accept what misfortunes were thrust upon her, and try her best. Not in terms of success or failure, but in terms of maybe ending at a net positive on the cosmic ledger of her life, maybe being a good friend, a good daughter. She didn't need to save anyone. But still—she could try to help.

A car honking on the road outside the cemetery broke the chain of Esther's contemplation.

She stood and dusted strands of cut grass from her knees. "Goodbye," she said, unsure of exactly who or what she was saying goodbye to. "And thank you."

Esther spent the following several days with her parents, mostly her mom. She could tell that her dad wasn't too happy with the change in their routine; he wanted to watch his Chinese TV and do his church activities in peace. Her mom, though, was excited to teach her how to cook some of her basic Chinese recipes. Eggs and tomatoes, Russian soup that wasn't actually Russian, minced pork with garlic shoots. As they spent time at the Chinese grocery store and in the kitchen, Esther's mom dropped ingots of information about her early years in the US. How in Taiwan her family had had a helper who did all the cooking, so when she married Esther's dad after grad school, she had to teach herself from cookbooks, trying to cobble together food that reminded them of their homeland with American ingredients bought in overwhelming American stores. The Chinese grocery store that Esther had taken for granted as a child had been a miracle to her mom when it first opened. Esther had never thought to ask her mom about those early days, or perhaps her mom had never seemed open to being asked. She realized that when the pandemic hit, she had never even considered moving home to Cleveland, joining the pod with her parents and Didi's family, and she couldn't remember if her parents had ever asked her to.

Tuesday after dinner, sitting on the couch with her dad watching TV, Esther saw a text from Laz: *Can we meet? I can come to Rittenhouse.*

This was what Esther was waiting for. When she was listening to Crystal, when she was visiting the cemetery, when she was chopping garlic for her mom, when she was sitting with her dad, she had tried to force herself to be in the moment but all she really wanted was this. An invitation to offer penance to Laz, do whatever it took to fix things.

Her fingers tingled as she replied: *I'm not in Philly today, but tomorrow night or the day after works. I hope everything is okay?*

Things are okay, Laz wrote after a long couple of minutes. *Tomorrow night would be good.*

"I need to go," Esther said aloud, startling her dad.

"Go where?" her dad asked.

"Back to Philly," she said. "Tomorrow."

"Your mom will be sad."

Esther blushed. "I'll come back, soon."

Her dad nodded and turned his attention back to the screen. Esther jumped up and went to the kitchen where her mom was cleaning up.

"Mom—I need to go back to Philly tomorrow."

Esther's mom turned, wiping her hands on a dish towel. She looked at Esther as if searching. "You okay?" she asked.

"Yes," Esther said. "And I'll be back to visit soon, I promise."

Esther's mom gazed at her for a moment longer and then, after patting her on the shoulder, went back to the dishes.

28

Esther was back in Philadelphia, back at Starbucks, squeezing her fingers together, pressing each one in towards her palm, pinkie to pointer. She was surrounded by layers of sound. The inoffensive singer-songwriter crooning, the harsh buzz of bean grinders, the hiss of espresso machines, the jagged whir of the receipt printers, the chatter of people.

"Esther," a barista called, and she got her drink. *Ester*, it said.

She had come way too early; the walk from her apartment had passed in a blur though she had definitely noticed the absence of the Asian hate homeless man. She hoped that he was okay, somewhere getting whatever help he needed to get. She hoped that he wasn't antagonizing some other Asian on some other street.

Laz had suggested bubble tea, and Esther had suggested Starbucks instead, thinking that bubble tea seemed too intimate, too friendly. Now in the purposeful banality of the coffee shop she wondered if this was the right decision. But it was too late, Laz was entering the shop, walking over, he was here.

"Hey Esther," he said.

"Hey Laz—Lazarus," she said.

He glanced at the table. "You already got a drink? I'll go get one." And then he went to the line, looking back as if to check that she was still there. She raised her cup, then looked away to give him some space.

Soon a barista shouted "La... Lasteers? La-stare-us?"

"That's me," Laz said. "I'm Lasteers." He brought his drink over and showed Esther the side of the cup. *Lasteres*.

"It's like they're trying to get people's names wrong," he said. "I mean, Lazarus isn't a common name, but I don't even know what this means." He shook his head, smiling.

Esther braced herself for judgment in his gaze but when he sat and looked at her, she found herself unjudged.

"So. This is weird," he said. He cleared his throat.

Esther could have left him hanging, forced him to say whatever he was having trouble saying, but this was Laz and she didn't want him to suffer. "How has your time with Hannah been?" She knew from the relaxation of his face, his shoulders, that it had been going well, and this was a safe question.

"Good," he said. "It's been good. Better."

"And Hannah? She's been okay?"

"She… she has her ups and down. But she's mostly been fine. Now that I'm back to work she's going to go to her friend's house twice a week."

"Kavi?"

"Yes," Laz said. "How did you know?"

Shruti had reached out to her about a more regular playdate, and Esther had rerouted her to Laz, but she didn't mention this.

"I've also set up some visits from some of Hannah's other classmates, in the next couple of weekends. It took me a while to get my act together, but I finally responded to some messages that other parents had sent after Claire's passing. I guess I hadn't thought Hannah needed anyone else, at the time, since you were around."

"That's good. I mean, it's good that she's getting to see other kids."

"But yesterday, I took off work to take her to her therapy appointment. And that's why I wanted to talk," Laz said. "I spoke with Dr. Winter after the appointment. I hadn't realized that you were paying for the sessions. I'm sorry, I should have thought about it more."

"I should have asked you," Esther said. "It seemed easier to use my card, at the time."

"It's kind of… inappropriate," Laz said. "Dr. Winter thinks so too. He had assumed that the credit card was mine, or that I was at least paying you back." He paused to chuckle. "I didn't know therapy is so expensive!" Then his face reverted to serious. "I'll pay you back."

"I'm glad you took her to the appointment. Did Dr. Winter say anything about… how she was?"

"We talked about the diary. He called it a setback, and I think we can all agree that that's what it was."

"I'm sorry," Esther whispered, and recognized that she had apologized too many times already, that each apology carried less weight, like smoke dissipating into the air.

A woman at a nearby table cackled, her laugh cutting through the current of noise and distracting Esther and Laz for a moment before they turned back to each other.

"I've been thinking about it a lot," Laz said, "trying to really put my mind and heart with Hannah. For once. The diary thing was a setback, yes, but we couldn't really expect this process to be, you know, linear. I mean, there are moments when I'm totally fine, and then moments when I just want to throw myself in front of a bus when I think about Claire."

"Please don't throw yourself in front of a bus, Laz."

"What I'm trying to say is, we have to expect ups and downs and setbacks, but over time things get better. Claire's gone. Yes, she's gone. And we somehow have to press forward. We don't have a choice. And Dr. Winter confirmed what I had been thinking, which is that Hannah's life is so much better with you in it, why should we, the adults, deny her your presence in her life?"

"Really?"

"Really. Dr. Winter thought that when Hannah is ready, and eventually she will be ready, maybe sooner rather than later, we should get together again. We can move forward together, right?"

"I would love that," Esther said. "Truly." She reveled in the possibility that Hannah might trust her again, might want to spend time with her.

While Esther and Laz were looking at each other in mutual relief, a voice said, "Hi, Esther." She looked up and it was that guy, Tony, that guy with the book. He was wearing a t-shirt with some kind of math equation on it and had another book under his arm. "Nice to see you again. Hi, I'm Tony," he said, turning to Laz.

"Hi," Laz said, standing to shake his hand. "I'm Lazarus, Esther's friend. From college. My wife is—was—Esther's best friend."

"We don't know each other," Esther said to Laz. "I mean, Tony and I met once, here at Starbucks."

"I think I offended her because I was reading a book on Asian history," Tony said.

Laz looked between Esther and Tony as if awaiting an explanation. Esther just shook her head in embarrassment.

"Well, anyway, this was a nice surprise. I was afraid that I'd scared you away from this Starbucks forever. Good to see you," Tony said, and then he was off to order. Esther kept her eyes on the table, cheeks burning.

"He seems nice," Laz said after Tony left.

"We really don't know each other, at all," she said.

"He's looking at you," Laz said, and he gave a wave to Tony. Esther didn't turn back to look. "He's a little young."

"For the love of God, Laz," Esther said. "Don't be ridiculous. And you, you're the last one who should be talking about someone who's too young."

"What do you mean?"

"I mean, you know, Tingting..."

"Esther," Laz said, serious now, "I'm not... interested in Tingting. Not interested in dating anyone, for that matter, but definitely not Tingting."

"Oh."

"How could you think that? Claire was the love of my life." Anger and disappointment flashed across Laz's face.

"I'm sorry," Esther said. "I know, of course I know that Claire is the one, was the one, always. I guess I misunderstood. Not from anything you said or did. Of course."

"I suppose it's odd that she's at our house," Laz said. "It was a favor for Peipei—that's why Tingting is with us. Tingting's aunt is Peipei's good friend, and she wanted her to get a job in the States, eventually find full-time work, maybe apply to grad school."

"That... makes sense," Esther said.

"It makes a lot more sense than me trying to date a what, thirty-year-old, two months after my wife passed away." Laz reprimanded Esther with his eyes. "I'm not that heartless."

"I know you're not, Laz, I swear. That's why I was so... confused, I guess."

Laz considered her for a long moment with his spotlight gaze. "Maybe you should see a therapist," he said.

"Me?"

"Yes, you, it might be good for you."

Esther bristled. "I mean, maybe, but maybe you should see one too."

"I'm going to. Dr. Winter gave me a recommendation. I need all the help I can get, I guess."

"I'll think about it," Esther said. There would be a tragic irony if she went to therapy now, having avoided it for the last thirty years. Then again, she was a shitshow. Maybe therapy could fix that.

The two of them sat in silence, contemplating the inestimable distance each needed to travel to even glimpse the finish line of okay.

"I should go, but let's keep in touch," Laz said, and then the two of them were standing, not sure whether to hug goodbye, instead exchanging awkward waves across the table.

"Let me know when Hannah is ready to meet," Esther said as Laz was turning to go. He looked back at her, and said he would, but looked away quickly as if to avoid making any promises.

She watched the door swing shut after him, the shop suddenly loud again, when she felt a tap on her shoulder. She turned and, of course, it was Tony.

"I don't want to come off as too forward, but I thought I would really regret it if I didn't try to give you my card again. I mean, if I didn't scare you away the first time, maybe that's a good sign, or maybe now you'll never come back, and that would be a terrible loss." He smiled at her, confident, and then his smile faltered as he saw the look on her face. "Hey, you okay?"

"I'm fine," Esther said, and then "no, I'm not, but I'll be fine, I think." She let out a long exhale. "That guy, Lazarus... his wife was my best friend, and she passed away a couple months ago."

"Oh, I'm so sorry," Tony said, putting his hand on his heart.

"And, I was helping to watch their daughter, and I massively screwed everything up, and now she hates me."

Tony raised an eyebrow.

"And, I mistakenly assumed Laz was dating a woman a decade younger than he is, even though I know he really isn't that type, but I guess I was scared that things were falling apart and I wasn't able to glue everything together."

"You know, Esther," Tony said, "it sounds like you'd like to talk. I'd be happy to listen, no strings attached, if you need it." He looked at Esther and she didn't see anything leering in his eyes. Just a little curiosity, with an ocean of generosity underneath.

"Okay," she said, and she sat down.

"One sec," Tony said, and he bounded to his table to get the book and drink he had left behind. When he was back, sitting across from her, she glanced at the title. *A Little History of the World,* by E. H. Gombrich. He saw her looking and handed it to her. She flipped it open—there were pictures on almost every page, surrounded by lengthy passages of prose.

"It was written for kids," Tony said. "In the 1930s. But it's a really excellent overview of modern world history, actually even longer than that, it starts from the time of the dinosaurs if you can believe it. But anyway, it's very accessible. I've been trying to broaden my knowledge base." Esther handed him the book again and he chuckled. "This was recommended by my colleague, the same one who recommended *Cultures and Conflicts in East Asia* actually, but I told her that one was too much, too soon. I need to start from the beginning, though I didn't necessarily mean all the way to the time of the dinosaurs. Anyway, speaking of colleagues..." he took out his wallet and handed his card to her. A new one, not the wrinkled one from before, and this time, she took it.

Anthony Richards
  Senior Software Engineer, VZB Robotics

"I think I owe you an apology," Esther said, and when he tried to wave it off, she said, "No, I wasn't... I wasn't myself the day we met." She proceeded to tell him about the man who had called her China virus, and then her fear of WMAS when she had seen his book.

"But Esther," Tony said, "I don't know if you can tell this, but I'm not white."

She laughed a grateful laugh, and he told her that he accepted her apology, and that he was all ears for her to talk about whatever she needed to talk about. So she started with that day, the day they met, and went backwards from there to her reading the diary, and her days with Hannah, even the duck attack, and her conversations with her friends and her suspicions with Tingting, and Claire's memorial service, and as she was about to describe how Claire had died, a barista approached their table and told them it was closing time. Esther glanced around and was surprised to find that all the other patrons had left, that the music had been turned off.

"Sorry, we lost track of time," Tony said to the barista. They got up to leave, apologizing to the staff, and walked outside where the sun was still up.

"They close earlier now, because of Covid," Tony said.

They stood looking at each other and Esther felt a wild impulse to ask him to go back to her apartment, but she didn't want to have sex or anything, she just wanted to keep talking. For him to keep looking at her and listening and asking questions. She clenched her fingers.

"Bubble tea," she said. "Do you want some?"

"I've never had it," Tony said, "but I'd love to try."

***

Esther knew she had sat on it for long enough, and she had to respond to Jose's emails. His follow-up messages over the past two weeks had become increasingly desperate. She sat on her couch with her laptop on her knees, finalizing her reply. In her draft she noted that she had considered his messages, taking into account his need for urgent assistance, and was glad to begin discussions on a position with Solutris provided that her conditions were met. For salary, Esther suggested an amount that was 50% higher than what she had been making at Centridge with commensurate proportional bonus, 100% remote except for necessary on-site trips. In other words, unsaid, she would never need to be in the New York office with Jose unless she wanted to be. If he agreed to her terms, she would be willing to start immediately.

Her proposal was ridiculous, over the top, but she was feeling pretty ridiculous and over the top these days, as if she was on a precipice and she didn't really much care what happened when she fell over. Part of this was the fact that while she and Laz had reconciled, Hannah was still unwilling to see her, and this left her days empty and aimless. She was willing to be a little crazy for a happier reason as well. Tony. They had met twice now since their

Starbucks and bubble tea night, and the second time he had spent the night at her place. It was the first time that anyone had slept in her apartment, except Didi for Claire's memorial service.

A smile crossed her face as she thought of waking up to Tony's arm flung across her midsection, his hot sleeping breath on the back of her neck. She had forgotten how delicious it was to be touched by someone who was attracted to her, by someone she was attracted to.

She had told Tony about a lot in her life, going all the way back to Caleb. He had an amazing ability to listen, to ask the right questions, and she never felt judged. She had not, though, told him about Jose, other than that he was an ex-colleague who was trying to recruit her to his new firm. Tony encouraged her to reach high, to go for it even though he could tell that she wasn't excited about the opportunity.

Esther reviewed her draft to Jose one more time. Her eyes narrowed and she increased the proposed salary by another 10%. There was a lot of implication in the email, but she trusted Jose to read between the lines. She also knew that he would never accept her proposal as drafted, that either he would counter with a more reasonable number or reject her outright. Either way, she was moving forward, and this was a good thing, for now. She hit send.

Her phone chimed with a message in the *Mathey Girls* chat.

@Esther, how are things with the new BOYFRIEND? Maggie said.

He's not a boyfriend, Esther replied immediately. Then, just to get Maggie even more excited, she added: *Yet.*

Maggie gave her a heart emoji. *I'm so happy for you.*

The Mathey Girls seemed starved for good news. It wasn't a secret anymore that Esther had stopped seeing Hannah. Laz had told Serena a sanitized version of what happened—Hannah had an emotional setback and he was spending more time with her one-on-one—and after some questioning in their group chat Esther admitted that Hannah didn't want to see her anymore.

She had also told them that Laz was most definitely not interested in Tingting, which was met by relief and *I told you so*'s and just one skeptical *of course he would say that* from Wendy. This was good news, but it was also boring news. Maybe her friends weren't starved for good news; maybe they were just starved for exciting news. And dating Tony was exciting, for Esther and for the friends who loved her.

I looked him up, Wendy said. *He's cute.*

241

Wait how did you find him? Maggie said. *What's his last name?*

It wasn't that hard, Wendy said. *Esther said his name was Tony and he worked for a robotics startup.*

I literally tried looking up "Tony Philadelphia robotics startup" and didn't find anything, Serena said, jumping in.

Wendy gave her a ha ha emoji. *But you didn't think to check for Anthony? His last name is Richards.*

!!, Serena said.

Esther blushed, imagining her friends Googling Tony as she watched the blue dots hovering on her screen.

OMG, Maggie said almost immediately. *He is cute.*

I mean, if I were into boys, I would think he's pretty cute too, Serena said.

Is he tall? Maggie said. *Please tell me he's tall.*

He's pretty tall, Esther said. *But everyone is tall to me.*

Taller than my husband? Maggie said. *Please tell me he's taller than Jeremy.*

Esther gave her a crying laughing emoji. *I think he might be taller than Jeremy.*

Jeremy's going to be so jealous, Maggie said with the same emoji.

When are you meeting him next? Wendy said.

Tomorrow, Esther said.

Didn't you guys meet like twice in the last week? Maggie said. *Sounds very promising.*

Esther hadn't told them that she had slept with Tony, and she knew they wouldn't ask. Tony had betrayed a moment of surprise when Esther had asked him to go back to her apartment after their last date, which made Esther feel like she was being too forward, but she reasoned that if a normal date was two or three hours, their three dates together were the equivalent of four or five dates, and he had by then heard more of her life story than almost anyone she knew, and she was almost forty years old, and really who cared at this point? But she still wouldn't tell the Mathey Girls, unless asked, because that just felt weird. Tony was hers, and while she was happy to share excitement with her friends, she wasn't ready to share her sex life.

Just saw the messages, Val said. *And just saw the google pic. He's Black?*

Yup, Esther said.

That's a first, Serena said. *For some of us.*

As far as you know! Esther said.

Keep us updated, Maggie said. *I need more fire in my life.*

We know, Serena said.

No one replied after that, the chat settling down once again, leaving Esther with her thoughts.

She thought about Tony.

He was perfect, for this moment in her life. She knew she should treasure this sensation of perfection for as long as she could, tamp down the specter of future arguments and incompatibilities. Still. He was younger than she was, five years younger, and this felt like a lot. He liked kids, she knew, but he told her he didn't care if he had kids or not, a coded reply to the unspoken question of whether he would want to pursue a serious relationship with an almost forty-year-old woman who wasn't particularly interested in kids, and now, if she was being honest, was a little afraid of childbirth and the possibility of a sudden unexpected death.

Then there was the fact that he was successful but he hadn't gone to a fancy private college, didn't have an Ivy League pedigree. So far, he seemed confident enough in his intelligence that he wasn't intimidated or put off by Esther's resume, but by experience—hers and others—she knew that most men just weren't secure enough to be with a woman who looked 'better' on paper. If she did go back to consulting, she would make more money than him, would travel for work, be a jet-setter again, and this would make the disparity more obvious.

Also, he was Black, and she didn't know how this would sit with her parents who, as far as she knew, were not as racist as some of the other older Chinese people she knew, but she had never had a Black boyfriend. She also didn't know if his family would approve, and eventually she would need to go to Pittsburgh to meet them, and what if they thought that she was too old, or too not-Black, for their son? Chinese parents wouldn't like that she went to a fancier school, that she might make more money (case in point: Didi and Crystal). She didn't know if his family might feel the same way.

She considered all of these things, trying to be dispassionate, and decided that these were all issues for some day down the line. Right now, she was going to enjoy this new love in her life. If the last few months had taught her anything, it was that she needed to appreciate her happy days however she found them.

And then, just as Esther was sitting at her table in a dreamy daze, head in one hand and a ghost of a smile on her face, her laptop chimed.

It was Jose. She hadn't expected him to reply so soon.

Esther, thanks for the email. I get it. I will have some discussions internally and get back soonest.

Holy crap. This might be happening after all.

29

July melted into August. Sitting on a bench at the Westover Reservoir, Esther stuffed a receipt into her book and put her sunglasses back on. She was reading *A Little History of the World*, because Tony had given it to her after he finished it and insisted she read it so they could discuss. It was very Tony, and she missed him. He was in Connecticut for a conference this week, and he had made her promise that she read it by the time he came back. Don't worry, she said, I'll finish it. I don't have anything else to do.

Her job discussion with Jose was still ongoing; every couple of days he would send an email reiterating that he was still in negotiations with his partners, but he was optimistic. Esther would reply with a noncommittal thanks, implying that he could take his time, she didn't need him, but she appreciated his effort so he should keep working at it. This kind of corporate non-speak was still second nature to her, and she knew that Jose spoke the same dialect.

She had chosen Westover to get away from her neighborhood, and there was that bubble tea shop nearby. It was far from the Chen house, but Esther had done a visual sweep just to be sure—no Chens in sight. The ducks were in the pond now, having abandoned her after first checking whether she had brought any goodies for them. Only bubble tea, and it's mine, she had told them, and they had waddled away in seeming offense.

Esther glanced down at her book. Hannah would love it, she knew. If she were still visiting Hannah every day, she would have said the same thing that Tony said to her: you have to read it, so we can discuss. It was written for kids, maybe for kids a little older than Hannah, but Hannah was clever and an information sponge. There were still a couple weeks of summer left; it would be good for her brain. Esther could text Laz and recommend it. Or maybe order it online and have it sent to their house, a no strings attached peace offering? But if it came from her, Hannah might immediately reject it.

She took out her phone and began typing a text to Laz, *How's it going? I've been reading a book (written for kids, long story) that I think Hannah would really like. Its—*

She heard a distant chorus of children behind her, kids squealing in that way that only kids do, giving voice to their excitement. They were, no doubt, running, chasing each other, getting worked up at the playground. She turned to look, a lazy smile on her face, and then quickly spun around, back towards the pond. It was Hannah.

Hannah.

Running with Kavi and Aiyan, faces lit with happiness and freedom, and they were still screaming, taking turns, their voices blending together. Hannah hadn't seen her, Esther was sure, they were far enough that Esther only recognized them because she recognized Hannah's yellow sundress and her glasses and skinny arms and by extension Kavi and her little brother.

Esther sank down, neck flush with the back of the bench. They weren't heading towards the pond, but still. Laz had told her, just a couple of days ago, that he had asked Hannah if she wanted to see Esther and she had seemed uninterested. Not adamant, or angry, but still on the negative side of neutral, so he thought maybe it wasn't the right time yet. Why had she chosen this stupid park? If Hannah saw her, and told Laz, he would think that Esther was stalking her or something. And the way that she was trying to hide her body by the bench was objectively suspicious. Shit.

She went back to her phone, deleted her previous draft to Laz and started a new text. *Hey I'm at Westover reservoir, and I realize that Hannah is here. Do you think its okay if she sees me?* She considered whether to send it, realizing that it sounded a little bit too desperate, and her finger hovered over the send button on the screen.

"No, not the ducks!" Esther heard Hannah yell, still far.

"But we have crackers!!" Aiyan screamed. Esther could tell he was running toward the pond, nearing her bench. She tried to sink down even further.

"I'm not going over there!" Hannah shouted.

"Don't be a scaredy cat!" Kavi yelled, close like her brother, and then in a moment both Aiyan and Kavi ran past Esther toward the pond. The ducks started mobilizing at the sight of the little boy with a bag of crackers, gathering at the edge of the water. Esther recognized the big bully mallard, the one who had nipped at Hannah, leading the charge.

"Careful Aiyan!" Esther yelled out, on instinct, and then Kavi and Aiyan turned back to her. The ducks, too, paused, unsure whether Esther meant to do them harm.

"Hi Esther," Kavi said, waving as she turned to head to the bench. She was panting from running.

Aiyan had stopped, scared now, clutching the bag of crackers to his chest as if to hide them, but the ducks continued to advance foot by webbed foot toward him like a squad advancing toward battle. He was much smaller than Hannah, and the mallard jutting his head back and forth seemed much more menacing in comparison.

Esther got up and sprinted toward the flock, waving her arms to force their retreat.

"Hi Esther," Aiyan said, in what sounded like a mixture of disappointment and relief.

"They bite," she said, and Aiyan's eyes opened wide.

"Esther?"

She wheeled around and there was Hannah. Behind her were Kavi and her grandmother, who raised her hand in greeting and then settled herself on the bench with a grunt.

Hannah was shading her eyes with her hand, squinting under the bright sun, and it was hard to see what she was thinking. Esther felt herself being examined. She got down on one knee, proposing a hug, or maybe just forgiveness. She didn't dare open her arms.

Hannah approached slowly. She looked older than a couple of weeks ago, somehow, longer and leaner than Esther remembered.

"Hey," Esther said.

"Did you come to feed the ducks?" Hannah asked.

"No, I just came to read." Esther motioned to the bench, but Hannah didn't look back. Instead she just stood, staring, evaluating, just like when Esther first started spending time with her at the beginning of summer. This was a step back, maybe many steps back, but it was infinitely better than the rage and betrayal she had last seen on Hannah's face. "I'm reading a book that I think you'd really like," she added.

Hannah cocked her head to the side and narrowed her eyes. "A grown-up book?"

"It's like a grown-up book but written for kids. Or a kids' book but written so that grown-ups would like it. Here, let me show you." Esther grabbed the book and handed it to Hannah. "I really think you'd like it."

Hannah considered the book briefly, but then her gaze found its way back to Esther's face.

"Hannah, I'm sorry about the diary," Esther said.

"I know. Daddy told me. A lot."

"And are you... are you still mad?"

Hannah looked past Esther at the ducks who were now settled at the far side of the pond, far away from Esther and her flailing arms and shouting voice.

"Aiyan, too close to the water," Kavi's grandmother called out, and Aiyan moved one step back from the water. "Too close!" the grandmother said, and Aiyan left the water's edge to join his sister in inspecting a tree near the bench.

"Daddy got me a new diary," Hannah said eventually. "We went back to the Art Museum and I got a different one. It's the one with the triangles."

"That's good," Esther said.

"I don't write letters to Mama anymore," Hannah said. "I just write my feelings."

"Oh, Hannah," Esther said. "I'm sorry that you felt like you needed to do that, to change how you write in your diary."

"It's okay," Hannah said. "I know she's gone."

Esther wasn't sure what to say.

"Dr. Winter said that it was up to me how I wanted to get my feelings down, that any way was okay, but I didn't think Mama would like the new diary as much, and so I stopped writing her letters." Hannah shrugged her shoulders, unwilling to explain further.

"And... how's Jasper? And Tingting and Zhang ayi?" Esther asked.

"They're okay. Tingting is busier at work now, she's gone some mornings, and then Ayi watches both me and the baby."

Esther wanted more than anything to wrap Hannah in her arms, to offer to go to her house whenever she wanted, to fill any gaps of time where Hannah might feel bored or alone. But Hannah was standing with arms crossed, hesitant, untrusting.

"You happy?" Esther whispered.

"I watch a lot more screens," Hannah said. "I like that."

Kavi ran up and grabbed Hannah's arm. "She fell asleep," Kavi said, giggling, and they all looked to see Aiyan jumping and making silly faces in front of his grandmother. Kavi and Hannah ran to join him, giggling.

"Don't wake her up," Esther called, softly.

"But my mom said she shouldn't sleep when she takes us places," Kavi said.

"Er... But I'm watching you, here, so you can let her rest for a little bit. It's probably exhausting taking the three of you out."

"It is!" Aiyan said, triumphant. His grandmother stirred but didn't open her eyes.

"Guys, come over here," Esther said. "I have an idea. Bring the crackers."

The ducks watched with interest from the far side of the pond. Esther parceled out the crackers, which the children held in their hands, pockets, and skirt. Then they distributed them in the grass, some distance away from the water's edge, where Esther stood guard. The ducks began swimming toward her, and she careened her arms to stall their approach as she urged the kids to hurry up. Aiyan was the first to finish, having scattered fistfuls of crackers around the field, but the girls took longer—splitting the crackers into smaller pieces and then arranging them in some kind of circular shape.

As the ducks approached the shore, Esther confirmed with the kids that they were done, and they all ran to the bench. From the safety of their perch, the sleeping grandmother a talisman to protect them, they watched as the flock scrabbled out of the water and waddled furiously to the crackers. The big mallard busied himself with one of Aiyan's cracker dumps while other ducks picked piece by piece at the girls' creation.

"It's a heart," Hannah said, seeing Esther try to decipher her work.

"A heart," Esther murmured.

They watched the ducks devour the crackers, quacking and

squawking with purpose, hunting through the grass to make sure that no pieces were missed. Eventually they seemed to realize that the crackers were gone, and the big mallard looked at Esther with calculating eyes.

"No," Esther said. "Go away." The mallard seemed to understand and led the flock back into the water.

"That was awesome," Aiyan said. "Can we do that again?"

The girls laughed, waking Kavi's grandmother. "Oh, did I fall asleep?" she asked. She checked her watch. "We need to be heading home."

"I need to go potty," Aiyan said. "Bye Esther." He pulled on his grandmother's hand, helping her up so that they could go.

"Bye guys," Esther said, looking at Hannah.

Hannah lifted her hand goodbye and then she and Kavi started running back towards the parking lot, Aiyan dragging the grandmother behind. As she was running, Hannah looked back at Esther and waved goodbye again.

Esther waved back with big arms crisscrossing above her head. Bye Hannah. See you soon. I hope.

30

Esther expected a message from Laz after seeing Hannah—she assumed that Hannah would tell him—but by the next day she hadn't heard anything. She craved some validation that yes, there was hope in reconciling her relationship with Hannah. Sitting on her couch, she typed with buzzing fingers: *Hi Laz, don't know if Hannah told you, but I saw her at Westover yesterday during her playdate.* She paused. She changed it to: *Hi Laz, I met Hannah accidentally at Westover yesterday during her playdate, she seemed better. I hope this is the case.* Send.

She debated whether to send a follow-up message asking if she might be able to visit their house, whether her pride would allow her to be that needy. What she really wanted to say was MY GOD I'VE MISSED YOUR DAUGHTER AND EVERY PART OF ME IS HOPING THAT WE CAN REPAIR OUR RELATIONSHIP TO BE A FRACTION OF WHAT IT WAS BEFORE but that was, of course, off the table. Ultimately, she went with: *Also, I found a book that I think would be great for Hannah. It's called A Little History of the World by Gombrich.*

She turned to Twitter because Tony did Twitter. His tweets were jokes about coding or computers, and she liked the fact that her boyfriend (she was, by now, thinking of him as her boyfriend but she hadn't told him as much) interacted with other people in such a normal way. This morning he had sent two tweets related to the conference he was in, and he had what seemed to Esther a lot of likes. There was something comforting in dating a nerd, a nerd with a soul. Tony was just more substantial as a human being than just about any guy she knew. Definitely more substantial than any guy she had dated before.

She had new emails and opened the app, assuming it would be the usual mix of ads and political donation requests. But one of the emails was from Jose, under a new subject line: TERMS OF OFFER. She held her breath as her eyes scanned through it. They had accepted her proposed salary and bonus provisions, her over-the-top set of numbers which she had presented as a starting point for negotiations rather than an honest expectation. They would like her to start as soon as possible.

Her eyes narrowed as she read the last paragraph: *While Solutris Consulting is supportive of remote working where appropriate, we have found that in-person working results in greater efficiencies and work quality. As such, we would expect you to follow our current Covid policy which is for every employee hired by the New York office to be on premises at least three days a week unless the employee is on-site at a client location for those days.*

As she considered, her phone buzzed in her hand, ringtone blaring. It was Jose. She answered on instinct, some long-buried impulse to always answer a phone call from a work colleague, even when it was against her best interest, because they might need her for something.

"Hello," she said.

"Hey, it's Jose," he said. "I just sent you the offer terms."

"I was just taking a look," she said.

"Okay, great, look, this call is off the record, just between friends, but I just wanted to get your initial reaction." Jose chuckled. "I'm pretty proud of myself, getting you this deal. When I saw your numbers I thought it was pretty ballsy, but Stella thought you were doing the right thing by being aggressive—"

"Wait. You told Stella? Isn't that a breach of confidentiality?"

"I mean, I didn't tell her the exact numbers," Jose said.

"Uh huh."

"I was impressed that you were advocating for yourself like that, and I mentioned to Stella that they were higher than market. That's all. And she thought it was the right move on your part."

"Right," Esther said.

"But anyway," Jose said. "Any initial thoughts? I have a couple of projects lined up and it would be huge if you could start by mid-August."

"That's like two weeks away," Esther said.

"Exactly."

Esther started pacing by the window, trying to focus. It was so much easier to sound like she knew what she was doing when she was writing an email. "I appreciate you helping get this through—"

"It was a battle, let me tell you."

"Let me finish, please. I appreciate you helping get this through, but the remote working was a key term, I thought you understood that."

"Listen, that Covid policy isn't strictly enforced, just come in and show your face a couple days a week and you can spend the rest of the time in Philly."

"This is important to me," Esther said.

"I mean, it's only when you're not on-site, so it won't even apply most weeks."

"I don't want to go to New York, Jose." *I don't want to see you.*

"Shit," Jose said. "I mean, I thought that the remote working thing was just a negotiating point. You got the numbers you asked for! There's no way Solutris is going to give you an exception to their Covid policy on top of those numbers."

Esther looked out onto Rittenhouse Square, people wandering around on their lunch breaks, tourists posing for pictures.

"Are you there?" Jose asked.

"I'm thinking."

"I bent over backward to get you those numbers," he said in a quiet voice. "It's not a good look if I go back and say that you refuse to come in. They think they're getting a team player with that level of salary."

"I *am* a team player," Esther said. *I just don't want to play with you.*

"It doesn't seem like it, if you're not willing to come into the office."

He had a point. The salary was very high. Shit. Esther pressed her head against the window.

"Why don't you want to come to New York? You don't even have to move if you don't mind commuting. It's not too far."

"It's not just the commute."

"Can I ask? Is it a guy thing?"

Esther wanted to punch Jose in the throat, but that would require being in New York, exactly what she was trying to avoid.

"Scratch that," he said. "Forget I asked. I get it. Remote working is important. Let me talk to some people. It's awkward, because I'm sure the numbers will have to go down. Are you okay with that? Tell me before I throw myself out there again."

He really had no idea. He wasn't trying to be an idiot, she knew. He just was. And she didn't hate Jose; she didn't want him to destroy the goodwill he had at his job if she wasn't going to seriously consider his offer.

"Give me a couple of days. Let me think about it before you do anything else."

"Okay," he said, sounding relieved. "But it would be great if we could get you signed on by end of next week so that we can get going by mid-August. I'm sure that once major terms are agreed we will make everything happen quick. Team Magic, right? And oh, I can tell you something, but you have to promise that I didn't say anything. At least not for another... eleven days. Stella is pregnant. We're not telling anyone yet, not until she's at three months, but that's one of the reasons I really want to bring you on as soon as possible. I'm going to be a better father, this time around, I know it."

"Congratulations," Esther said. She suspected that he wanted more, some kind of assurance that he was a good person or something, but she wasn't ready to give him that. "For the offer, I'll think about it and be in touch."

After the call ended, Esther tossed her phone on the couch. She couldn't imagine being that confident in herself, ever. Where past actions, actions that derailed careers and lives, could be mentally erased by an apology over coffee. Where it was never your fault, whatever it was, and you always made sure that everyone knew you were trying your best.

***

But here, Tony was back, and he took his Uber straight to Esther's apartment, and then it was a shower, and bed, and food, and bed. He stayed with her through the entire weekend, a ridiculous record, washing and wearing the clothes that he had taken to the conference. Looking at her boyfriend in his button-down shirt Esther thought — but didn't say — that maybe he should stay with her forever. They could keep rewashing his conference clothes, an eternity of button-downs, and they could keep ordering in and never leave the apartment.

Imagine if she had had Tony during those endless pandemic days. Imagine if she had had Tony years ago, the way that Maggie had Jeremy and Serena had Val.

"You can't change," Esther told him, in bed. "You're perfect."

"Nobody's perfect," he said, but then he kissed her, and she knew he was wrong.

Tony thought that she should take the job. You don't know the whole story, Esther said, and when pressed she finally told him about The Incident as they ate Thai takeout at her little table.

"You really didn't know he had feelings for you, before he told you?" Tony asked.

"I really didn't know," Esther said. "We were so driven, so focused on work and advancement and all that, or at least I was. I thought he was too." She put a piece of fried tofu onto his plate. "Would it bother you, if I went to work for him?" she asked.

"I mean, if I thought something might happen between you two, maybe. But it doesn't sound like you were ever really into him."

"I wasn't. And won't ever be."

"And he sounds really desperate to have you as an employee. I can't imagine he would jeopardize that again." Tony took a bite, contemplation on his face. "I think the question is whether you would *want* to work with him. He seems like a pretty shitty guy."

"Yeah."

"But just because he's a shitty guy doesn't mean you should turn down a really good job offer." Tony tapped his fork on his plate. "Maybe you should take the job. Tell him that if he wants you in the office, he has to put you in a five-star hotel three days a week. They'll say yes if they're willing to pay you that enormous salary, hotel costs would be nothing to them. And then," and here he gave her a little wink as he added more curry to her rice, "I'll come up with you and we can have five-star hotel sex when you get back from the office."

Esther laughed, and she gave him some more pad Thai, making sure he got the last shrimp.

After dinner, Tony said, "I think I'm ready to leave the apartment. It's been, what, three days? I could use some bubble tea."

They decided to go to a new place, a half hour walk, and warm air greeted them as they left Esther's apartment building. Hand in hand they strolled down the street, and as they passed the spot where the man had called Esther "China virus" she pointed it out.

"I never saw him after that time," she said.

"What would you do if you saw him again?" Tony asked.

"I don't know," she said. "Probably try to avoid his attention. Probably not give him more money."

"I would say something to him, if I saw him."

"What would you say?"

"I would tell him to leave you alone."

"You wouldn't need to do that. I think he's maybe mentally ill."

"I want you to feel safe walking down the street though." Tony squeezed Esther's hand.

"He didn't make me feel unsafe. It was just surprising, that's all, that he was so... hostile. I was pretty unstable that day."

"I remember," he said.

Esther saw the grin on his face and punched him gently on the arm. "My instability is part of my charm," she said.

"Absolutely."

There was a line out the door of the bubble tea shop—always a good sign in Esther's view. "Let's take a selfie," Esther said as they waited.

Tony sighed dramatically.

"I know, I know, you're not a picture person. Indulge me," Esther said.

"Okay, but you take it."

"You have way longer arms. It has to be you."

"Can't argue with that," Tony said.

The picture he took was terrible; they were looking at different places, her eyes half closed, his face blurry with movement.

"Wow, I'm really bad at this."

"Do you want me to take a picture?" the girl behind them asked. She looked like she was twelve, too young to be waiting for bubble tea by herself, but Esther knew better than most how misleading Asian faces could be.

"Sure," Esther said, "thanks."

The girl took pictures of them, a regular picture and a silly picture because they were all standing in line anyway. She handed the phone back to Esther.

"You guys are such a cute couple," she said.

Esther turned to Tony, eyebrows raised. No one had ever said that to her before, no stranger at least.

"What?" Tony asked. "We are."

The pictures that the girl took were nice, as expected from someone who looked the age that she looked.

"Aw," Tony said. "You can send that one to your friends." Esther had told the Mathey Girls how he wasn't much of a picture person.

"Okay, but only if you don't look at the chat," Esther said. She posted the photos, normal and silly, in the *Mathey Girls* chat. *I'm smitten,* she wrote, turning her phone away from Tony who seemed to be trying to look. As they passed through the doorway of the bubble tea shop, she slipped her phone into her pocket.

Tony was old school; he liked to pay when they ate together, and Esther let him, but she knew that once she started working again, they would have to change the rules. Because once she was working, she was going to treat him to decadent steak dinners and weekend trips in between projects, and massages and all the nice things that she was able to enjoy by herself when she was employed. She actually hadn't had much chance to do those things, because she had always been working, but she hoped it would be different now.

She ordered a lemon yogurt drink, and he got a bubble tea. He didn't like to stray from the standard milk tea with boba because, in his words, it was the nectar of the gods, and why would he want to drink anything other than divine nectar? Give it time, she had said, there's a whole universe of drink options to discover.

The shop was loud with high-pitched conversations, blenders and shakers almost drowning out a background of Asian pop music. It was pleasant, though, with the smell of waffles in the air and pastel decor inviting people to take pictures and post them online.

They were able to grab a seat when an angry Asian girl stormed out of the shop and her pleading boyfriend followed. The seat was warm from the pleading boyfriend's butt, and Esther felt a little bit like she had stolen something as she sat down. She took out her phone as Tony went to get their drinks.

You guys are too cute, Maggie said. Heart emoji heart emoji heart emoji.

So he does exist! Finally, evidence! Serena said.

Esther had a text, too, from Laz. It said: *Peipei is coming into town this weekend for business. She'll be here for a week, most likely, and maybe then we could all get together.*

Of course, Esther replied. *Just let me know when.*

Tony returned to the table and they sipped their drinks. Esther looked at him through the dreamy filter of new love. "What's up?" he asked.

"I'm just glad you're back," she said.

"Me too," he said. "But I think I have to go back to my apartment tonight, or latest tomorrow morning. I need to pick up some stuff before I go into the office."

"Boo," she said.

"I know. It's been nice, this weekend." He chuckled.

"What's so funny?"

"I used to spend a lot of my weekends, a lot of my free time anyway, reading. Alone. When I was at the conference, I was able to do a little bit of reading, but this weekend I haven't done any."

"I'm dumbing you down, Tony," Esther said. "It's been my plan all along."

"Who would have guessed that my Ivy league girlfriend would be the one to take me away from my pursuit of—are you okay?"

"I'm fine. It's just that you called me your girlfriend."

"That's what you are, aren't you? That's how I've been describing you to my friends and stuff."

Esther brought her hands to her flushed cheeks.

Tony laughed. "Not only are you my girlfriend, but I love you, Esther Hsu. You know that, right?"

It slipped out then, before Esther had a chance to think about it: "I love you too." As soon as she said it, she knew it was true.

31

It was unsettling to be standing at the Chens' imposing front door again, waiting for someone to answer the doorbell. The house had not changed, Esther would not have expected it to, but her relationship to the house and the family inside had.

Tingting opened the door, already squealing, jumping on her toes and clapping her hands together.

"Esther *jiejie!*" *Big sister!*

"Hi Tingting," Esther said, giving into a jumpy hug and being pulled into the foyer.

"Come in, come in, the food is ready," Tingting said in Chinese.

Esther took off her sandals, the nice ones with two sets of buckles around her ankles that forced her to awkwardly unhook one, then the other, then move to the other foot and do it again. Tingting watched with an expression of delight on her face.

"How have you been?" Esther asked, pulling the last hook open.

"Very good," Tingting said. "I got promotion."

"That's great," Esther said, and they went to the dining room that the Chens rarely used. Esther hadn't even really been in that room since Claire's baby shower, and she was relieved to be able to walk in and sit at the table, between a seated Peipei and Laz, without some kind of internal breakdown. They greeted her, friendly, and Esther marveled at the food. The long table was covered with dishes, greens and browns and whites, soups and braises and stir fries, enough for a banquet.

"Is that... Peking duck?" Esther asked.

"We ordered in," Laz said.

"My favorite Chinese restaurant here," Peipei said. "Usually I don't like Chinese restaurants in America but this one is good as long as you ask them *shaoyou, shaoyan.*" *Less oil, less salt.*

259

"Ah," Esther said.

Zhang ayi came in with a platter containing a steamed fish. "Nice to see you again!" Zhang ayi said in Chinese, and Esther was very happy to see her too.

"Zhang ayi, sit with us," Laz said in Chinese, and Zhang ayi tried to resist, saying that she would eat in the kitchen, but they all cajoled her into sitting down, at least until Jasper needed his bottle. For now he was in his swing in the corner, hypnotized by the rocking back and forth.

There were still two empty seats and Esther looked at Laz to see why. "Girls!" he shouted. "Dinner!"

"Okay!" Hannah said, from another room, and Esther tingled with excitement to see her.

They heard the thumping of little feet and Hannah and Kavi bounded into the room.

"That's a lot of food!" Kavi said. "Hi Esther!"

"Hey," Esther said, looking at the two girls. Hannah gave her a small wave before sitting down.

"Let's eat!" Peipei said, and the adults busied themselves with offering food to others—the girls, and the other adults, and lastly helping themselves to whatever was in reach.

"You need one of those things," Peipei said, half rising to reach some pork with her chopsticks. "The round things."

"A lazy Susan?" Laz asked. "I don't think that would work on this table."

"Then you need to get a round table," Peipei said. "A big round table with a lazy Susan."

"That would definitely give this room a Chinese restaurant vibe," Esther said, and she received a spattering of laughter for her effort.

Hannah was sitting directly across from Esther, relaxed and happy, unaware of how important it was to Esther that this go well. The food was a good distraction, as was Kavi and the general chaos at the table.

"You are such a good eater," Peipei said to Kavi. "And you can use chopsticks!"

Kavi nodded vigorously. "I love Chinese food. Also sushi." She was shouting, because it was loud at the table, and because she was nine and she was excited.

"Sushi is Japanese food," Hannah shouted.

"I know that! But you use chopsticks for sushi!" Kavi shouted back. The girls laughed in their loud and happy way.

Zhang ayi was the first to leave the table with Jasper, then the girls, and then Esther was surprised that Peipei turned to Tingting and said, in Chinese, "The adults have some things to discuss." Esther was even more surprised when Tingting replied in Chinese, yes auntie, and slunk out of the room. She had never seen Tingting look cowed before.

It was a good thing that the table was long, so that while Esther was sitting between Peipei and Laz there was space between them. Now Peipei pushed her chair from the table and eyed Esther, then Laz, then Esther again.

"Lazarus told me about the book," Peipei said.

"The book?" Esther asked.

"Hannah's book," Peipei said, and Esther realized that she meant the diary. "So you aren't visiting Hannah anymore."

"No, I'm not," Esther said.

"You understand Chinese, right?" Peipei asked.

"I understand, yes. Most of it."

"But you can't speak."

"I can't speak very well, no," Esther said.

"Well, I speak in Chinese, you speak in English, okay?" Peipei asked in Chinese, and Esther had no choice but to agree to her terms.

Freed from the shackles of English conversation, Peipei launched into her diatribe. From the looks she gave to Laz while she was saying it, it was clear that she had already had a similar conversation with him. The gist was that she wasn't happy with how Laz's house was running, and more importantly, Mrs. Chen back in Taiwan was not happy with how Laz's house was running. The list of specific complaints was long. Lazarus spent a lot of time at work. Hannah spent a lot of time in front of a TV and now she needed glasses because of it. Hannah was too skinny; the baby was getting a little too fat. Zhang ayi was too loud and her Chinese was too mainland, which could only be a bad influence on the children if they were ever to learn Mandarin. Tingting was a distraction.

"Big sister," Laz said in Chinese, "it was your request for Tingting to come here."

Peipei snorted. "There's no use for her being here anymore; she'll get her own place sooner or later."

"Wait a second," Esther said in English. "Just to be clear, why exactly did you think it would be useful for Tingting to be here, in this house?"

Peipei flushed and brought her fist to her mouth. Then she threw out an answer in Chinese about helping around the house, playing with Hannah, being a companion.

"You said that she needed to be here to help your friend," Laz said in Chinese, his voice rising. "You said that it was for your connections."

Peipei was rubbing her hand on her neck, trying to loosen an invisible noose. "That's right, don't make an issue out of it. You're overreacting." She turned her attention to Esther and continued, in Chinese, "I mean, she's young and pretty, right? What's the harm in Lazarus meeting someone new?"

At this point Laz said something in Chinese that Esther had never heard before. It sounded as though it fell somewhere on the spectrum between go to hell and fuck you, but not to the point of get the hell out of my house right now you bitch. Esther could see the shock on Peipei's face, and now she was really riled up.

"Little brother," Peipei shouted in Chinese, "you're raising your family like a ghost family. There's no love here, no happiness. You think Hannah's better here, watching TV all day while you're at work, than back in Taiwan with her family? She doesn't even have Chinese friends! And your son, how is he going to grow up speaking Chinese if his sister only speaks English? You want to keep the nanny from the mainland forever? You want to raise a mainland son?"

"You don't know what you're talking about," Laz said in Chinese. "Hannah's happy here. She would be miserable in Taiwan, and you know it. Hannah and Jasper are American kids—" and here Peipei scoffed a very Chinese scoff, but Laz ignored her, "and we are an American family. Taking them to Taiwan won't change that."

"Wait. Hold up," Esther said in English. "You aren't planning to take the kids back to Taiwan? Are you? Seriously?"

"They would be happier in Taiwan," Peipei said, reverting back to

English and losing some of her power in the process.

"NO, WE WOULDN'T!" Hannah said from the other side of the wall.

The three of them looked toward the door, and Hannah appeared. Tingting had her hands on Hannah's shoulders, shushing her and trying to guide her back out.

"No thank you!" Hannah said, pulling free from Tingting's grasp.

"How much did you hear?" Laz asked, in Chinese, and the question was meant for Tingting.

"A lot," Hannah said, in English. "You forgot that I've been learning Chinese too. And I understood enough to know what you're planning to do, and I won't go."

"See!" Peipei said in Chinese. "This is an American child, little brother. Is this what you want? If you don't teach her now, she will never learn. And you will be stuck with this."

"Hey!" Esther said in English. "She just told you she can understand you, Peipei."

Hannah glared. Yes, she understood, if not all of the words, then at least what Peipei was trying to say. "I'm not going to Taiwan," Hannah said again, and she ran out of the room.

"I'm sorry, auntie," Tingting said in Chinese, bowing quickly in apology then fleeing as well.

There was a long moment where each of Peipei, Esther and Laz looked at the table, their hands, the clock on the wall. Anywhere but at each other.

"I'm just thinking of what's best for the family, little brother," Peipei said eventually, in Chinese.

"I know," Laz said in English.

"No," Esther said. She stood up and walked to the other side of the table and leaned forward, so that she was facing Peipei and Laz, looking down at them. "You can't do this to Hannah. She's already gone through so much."

Peipei tried to say something, and Esther raised her hand to stop her.

"Let me finish." She took a breath. "At some point in the future, Hannah might want to go to Taiwan. She might want to re-discover her roots, learn Chinese, whatever. But right now, she needs her family. Here. She needs her father and her little brother. Peipei, you're not her family, I'm sorry to say, not in the way she needs. She needs this house, and her playroom, and her best friend Kavi, and the ice cream shop down at the bottom of the hill. She needs her therapist. You have to give her that chance, to be happy here, even though her mom has died. You can't take that chance away."

"Esther is right," Laz said. "And Hannah needs Esther too, whether she is willing to admit it right now or not."

Peipei threw her hands up in exasperation. "You think it would be easy for me to have Hannah come back?" she asked in Chinese. "My kids are already almost grown-up and out of the house. You think I want a baby and a disrespectful girl in my house? You think I want to take care of them? At my age?"

"But then why take them back to Taiwan?" Esther asked.

Laz and Peipei looked at each other. "My mother," Laz said.

Peipei nodded.

Fuck your mother, Esther thought, but all she said was, "Well that's bullshit." She watched Peipei scowl. She didn't act like Mrs. Chen at all, Esther realized. Peipei was fire and heat, whereas Mrs. Chen was ice. Cold. Maybe this was why Peipei had to try so hard to please her mother.

"She honestly believes that this is the best way forward," Laz said. "But she's wrong."

"Maybe," Peipei said, reverting back to English.

Silence settled on them again, and Esther started to feel that the ravaged dishes on the table, some of them not even half eaten, were becoming grotesque. She felt a strong urge to start cleaning them up.

Laz broke the silence. "I can talk to Mom," he said. "Again. Even though she won't listen. She shouldn't have sent you here, Peipei."

"Wait, you didn't have business here?" Esther asked.

"Ha," Peipei said. "Why would I fly all the way here for business?"

"But you thought she had business," Esther said to Laz.

"I believed her when she said it," Laz said. "Because I'm an idiot."

"No," Peipei said. "You're a smart doctor. You're just too... trusting."

"Would your mother listen to you?" Esther asked. "I mean, really listen? And give up the idea of taking Hannah and Jasper away, once and for all?"

Peipei looked at Laz with raised eyebrows, skeptical.

"I have to try," Laz said. "I'm in a very different place than I was when—last time we talked about the possibility of the kids going back to Taiwan. I'm much stronger now. I'm sure I can make it work..."

A misting of doubt hung in the air, everyone wishing that what he said was true. Then Peipei tapped her nails on the table. "Esther, will you start taking care of Hannah again? It would make it more easy to convince my mom."

Laz looked between the both of them, tentative.

"Oh," Esther said. "I mean, I would, but I can't."

"Why not?" Peipei asked.

"She has her own life, her own work," Laz said.

"I would love to, really, but I'm probably going to be starting a new job soon and it will be busy. Really busy."

"We can pay you," Peipei said, immediately, throwing it out as if this was something she said all the time.

Esther tried not to bristle. She wanted to say that they couldn't pay her enough, that soon she would be making more than Laz was making, but all she said was, "I'm not a babysitter, Peipei. And I'm not for hire."

Peipei considered her for a moment. "Of course not," she said. She stood up. "I talk to my mom. Laz, you talk to her too."

A flash of relief crossed Laz's face, and Esther wasn't sure if it was because Peipei was going to talk to Mrs. Chen or because this conversation was over. Probably both. Laz looked exhausted. Peipei was exhausting.

Esther started to pile plates on each other because the grease was congealing, and it was clear that they were done talking.

"Let Ayi take care of that," Peipei said, and she left the room.

Esther continued to clear the table, and Laz joined her. "Thank you," he said.

32

Two days later, Esther was eager to update the Mathey Girls: *Holy crap guys*, she said in the chat. *Peipei got sent back to Taiwan. She left today.*

!!!!, Maggie said.

What happened?? Valerie said.

Mrs. Chen was NOT happy, Esther said.

I thought she was doing Mrs. Chen's bidding? Valerie said.

She went too far, Esther said. *Mrs. Chen wanted her to bring the kids back. But Laz told his mom that Peipei had tried to set him up with Tingting, and his mom went ballistic, apparently.*

Good riddance, Wendy said. *Serves her right.*

Turns out that Mrs. Chen knows Tingting's family too, and thought that Tingting was way too young, and that it was way too soon, and basically the whole thing was totally inappropriate, Esther said.

Damn straight, Serena said.

Then did Tingting get sent back too? Maggie said.

She's still here, Esther said. *It's not her fault that PP did all this. I feel bad for her. I think she had no idea what was really happening.*

Jesus, Valerie said.

The important thing is that Hannah and Jasper are staying, Wendy said.

Yes, Esther said. *For sure.*

It's almost too bad that Peipei is gone, Maggie said.

?? Esther said.

Because I was hoping to see her next week, Maggie said.

???? Esther said.

I'm coming to Philly!! Maggie said.

Yes, it was true, Maggie was coming to Philly next week, she had just bought her tickets. It was too complicated to explain over chat, and so

Maggie called and Esther, keeping an eye on Hannah, Kavi and Aiyan at the playground, gave space for Maggie and her big reveal:

"Do you remember when you came to California and I mentioned a memorial fund, for Claire? Well, I did it. I set up the memorial fund, and it's so much bigger than I had originally imagined. These last couple of months I've been consumed by it, really. I've been on *so* many calls, Esther, but it's happening. I've set up meetings in Philly with Penn next week to iron out the details of the fund distribution, and then meetings in New York the week after. We're going to have a fundraiser, sponsored by the Princeton Club and Valerie's law firm and the initial fund contributors, so I need to check out the venue, make arrangements and all that."

"Holy crap, Maggie," Esther said.

"I know, it's kind of amazing, but it's really all coming together and I'm so excited. We're planning to distribute funds to families affected by maternal mortality. Funeral costs, hospital bills, education and other funds for children who lost their mothers. But also community engagement and awareness; the hospital has been wanting to increase outreach and we're going to help fund that."

"I mean, how did you do all this without us knowing? But wait — you said Valerie's law firm, so she knows?"

"Well," Maggie said, hesitating, "actually everybody knows about it."

"What do you mean?"

"I mean, I could never have done this on my own. I asked Serena for help setting up the nonprofit, and she was the one who was spearheading with Laz and discussions with Penn. And Wendy, she's the largest donor, so far, along with what my family has put in. She's also helping me put together the board."

"Wow," Esther said, trying to understand how she could have been oblivious to all of this. "I could have helped, somehow, maybe."

"You had so much on your plate, with Hannah and everything," Maggie said. "I knew that when I needed your help, all I needed to do was ask. Like, now, for example. Could I stay at your place when I come to Philly? Ha ha. But only if you're okay with that, I know it's really late notice. I'm happy to do a hotel if that's easier."

"No, no, of course you can stay with me," Esther said.

The kids ran up to Esther.

"Can we get ice cream after this?" Hannah asked, breathless, and Kavi and Aiyan nodded behind her, willing Esther to nod as well.

"Sure," Esther said, "after I'm done with this call."

"Was that Hannah?" Maggie asked.

"Yup, but she's already run away now," Esther said.

"I'm so glad that you guys are back together," Maggie said.

Like a band, Esther thought. A band that had fought, broken up, and now were together again, a little bit fractured but slowly restoring their original camaraderie. She took a breath. "I'm really proud of you, Maggie," she said. "This is huge."

"Thanks. I'm really proud of myself, if I'm being honest," Maggie said. "Part of me wasn't sure I could do something like this, but another part of me absolutely knew that I could. It's just that the latter part has been, you know, *dormant* for so long. Do you want to hear the name of the foundation?"

"Of course," Esther said.

"The Claire Chen Foundation for Maternal Mortality Awareness. I know, it's kind of a long name, but there are other foundations for maternal health, but we really need to increase awareness of maternal mortality. And provide support for families affected by it."

"Wow, Maggie, you sound..." Esther wanted to say that she sounded like a brochure, but in a polished way, but she didn't want to actually say that. "You sound really passionate about it."

"Oh, I am," Maggie said. "I know I sound like a PR person right now, but I'm the CEO of the foundation."

"That's amazing, Maggie."

"I'm actually thinking of getting an MBA now. It's crazy, isn't it."

"It's not crazy—I can see you as a CEO with an MBA. But I can't believe you kept me in the dark this whole time."

"In the beginning, I was doing everything on my own, and then I started to bring people in on a need-to-know basis, because I really didn't have any of the right expertise. And you know how I said half of me didn't think I could do it and the other half knew I could? The first half definitely dominated, in the beginning. To be honest, I was really scared of failure. Terrified."

Esther tried to imagine Maggie being scared of anything, let alone being scared of not being able to succeed in something, given who she was and all the resources she had access to. Her friends probably thought the same of her, Esther realized, and she wondered how many shared fears and insecurities they had all left unacknowledged over the years.

"Oh, crap," Maggie said, suddenly. "I have a call in five minutes that I need to prepare for. Ha ha I sound just like you guys now! No, but seriously I need to go. I'll forward you my flight details and we'll talk later, okay?"

As soon as Esther took her phone away from her ear, the children came running up again. "Ice cream!" they chanted, and Aiyan pumped his fist as he jumped up and down.

Esther held up a finger. "One second. I need to send one more text, and then we're going to ice cream, I promise."

"Aww!" Aiyan said.

"Let's do the spinning thing one more time," Hannah said, and they ran away again, screaming.

Esther pondered her screen, fortifying herself. This could be a very expensive mistake. *Jose, off the record: I can't accept your offer, not yet. I have some family obligations through the end of August that I have to attend to, and I have to assess where I am closer to the end of the month. I can let you know then, if that works.*

She sent it, and then drafted a follow up. *I recognize that this puts you in a difficult position, but I will let you know as soon as I can.* No, she thought, changing it to *I recognize that this puts you in a difficult position, but I will let you know as soon as I am ready. I understand this may affect the availability of the offer; please let me know if this is the case.*

She sent the message and then waved to the kids who had been concurrently playing and throwing pointed glances at her.

"Ice cream?" Aiyan shouted, and Esther nodded yes, and they started running towards her again.

Hannah was going to start school in a few short weeks, and Esther wanted to soak her in. It wasn't clear how Laz was going to manage everything once school was in session, and now Hannah wanted to start swim lessons again, and the therapy appointments would continue, and she had her pediatric checkup scheduled for early September, and and and...

Laz would figure it out. Esther would help him, she would always help him when he needed help, but he was learning to do more and be there more, he had told her. Still, when he had asked if she wouldn't mind coming over a couple afternoons a week again, to spend time with Hannah before she started her new job, she had said yes of course when can I start. When Peipei asked, it was one thing, and when Laz asked, it was another.

But now, it was time to get the kids their treat. Now, Aiyan was chanting "Ice cream!" over and over again, tripping over himself in excitement. Now, Hannah was slipping her small, sweaty hand into Esther's as they walked toward the car.

***

So, I've been filled in on Maggie's work, Esther wrote in the *Mathey Girls* chat later that evening as she sat in bed. Tony was reading next to her, a massive tome about the conquistadors.

It's not that we wanted to keep a secret. Maggie said. *I promise.*

I know. I believe you! Esther said.

You were giving more than any of us, taking care of Hannah, Serena said. *We didn't want to burden you even more.*

And we didn't want Hannah to lose you to the work in the foundation, Maggie said. *Because there was a lot of work to do.*

Wait a second, Esther said. *Did you guys have a separate foundation chat? Like the MG chat but for the foundation?*

No, Maggie said, adding a smiley face emoji. *That was all one on one chats.*

And calls, Serena said.

And emails, Wendy said.

I hope you're not upset, Serena said.

I'm not, Esther said, and she wasn't. She recognized that this was a good thing, and she didn't have to be involved for it to be a good thing.

I'm upset, Valerie said.

?? Esther said.

I'm upset that Maggie is going to Philly and she gets to meet Tony before the rest of us, Valerie said. Esther gave her a laughing crying emoji and Maggie gave her a heart.

It's probably good that Tony is meeting Maggie first, Serena said. *Meeting all of us at once might be too much.*

It's true. We are formidable, Wendy said.

OMG Jeremy said the same thing, Maggie said. *I told him I was excited to meet Tony, and he said that Tony was lucky that he was just meeting me first, because we as a group can be very intimidating.*

Ha, Serena said.

FORMIDABLE, Wendy said.

Esther was about to type a response when Tony turned towards her.

"Hey, are you chatting with your Mathey Girl friends again?" He leaned over to sneak a glimpse at the screen.

She turned her phone toward her chest. "Don't peek," she said. She set her phone down on her bedside table and turned back to him. "You ready to take a break?"

"Yes, ma'am," Tony said, and heaved his book aside. As Tony reached his hand toward Esther's hair, she caught it and said, "I have to warn you, my friends are formidable."

"I can only imagine," he said. "I can't wait to meet them."

33

With Maggie on the East Coast, the Mathey Girls were in Manhattan Chinatown, all of them, and it was a celebration. They were celebrating the fact that Maggie had had a successful round of meetings with Penn, that Wendy moved a work trip up a week so that she could accompany Maggie in seeing potential donors in New York. They were celebrating that Tony was able to join and meet the group, that they could all be together.

"I hear that in Hong Kong, a lot of places don't have carts for dim sum anymore," Serena said.

"It's true," Wendy said. "Luckily we're not in Hong Kong." She raised her hand, and the nearest waitress came by with her cart. The waitress started rattling off names in Cantonese, and Wendy asked her to show the table what she had. The waitress obliged, flipping open the bamboo steamer lids, one by one, just fast enough for them to catch a glimpse of each.

"Ooh, chicken feet," Wendy said.

"Don't scare Tony!" Maggie said.

"Nobody likes chicken feet," Serena said.

"I like chicken feet," Wendy said, and she told the waitress to give them an order of chicken feet, an order of spareribs and an order of squid tentacles.

Tony leaned toward Esther's ear and said, "Do you like chicken feet?"

"No way," Esther said. "But I love the squid." Like the considerate Chinese girlfriend she was, she picked up a long squid tentacle and set it on Tony's plate before helping herself. "Try a bite. If you don't like it, I'll eat it."

Tony considered the squid, shrugged, and jammed the entire tentacle in his mouth. He was clumsy with chopsticks, but he was getting better with practice. His cheeks contorted as he tried to tame the appendage, and the Mathey Girls watched him with varying degrees of glee, bemusement, skepticism, and anxiety.

Some chomping, and then a labored swallow.

"More please," Tony said, and at least two of the women squealed with delight.

"Take smaller bites with these," Esther said, putting two more pieces of squid on his plate.

"You guys are really the cutest couple," Valerie said.

Esther rolled her eyes, and Tony gave her a kiss on the cheek with his greasy squid lips.

"Aww," Esther's friends chorused.

"Stop looking at us and eat," Esther said, and her friends obeyed, because it was dim sum and how could you not want to stuff your face with dim sum?

They ate their way through squid and spareribs, chicken legs and pork buns, rice rolls and turnip cake, and eventually egg tarts and mango pudding. Tony tried almost everything, but Wendy had to finish the chicken feet by herself, which she was happy to do.

After dim sum they went for bubble tea, even though they were all full. They found a shop where the six of them crowded around a little table, where the chairs were just a bit too small but the boba had just the right amount of chew.

The women chattered away, making jokes, asking Tony questions, trying to embarrass Esther. She let them have their fun. She was happy, and every so often Tony would look at her, just her, to make sure she was good. She could tell he thought her friends were funny and interesting, and this was a relief.

Her phone chimed; it was a text from Crystal back in Cleveland. *Ben and Bonnie say thank you*, the text said, and it was followed by a photo of the kids holding up their new copy of *A Little History of the World*.

Esther sent Crystal a laughing face emoji. *That was for you because you said you wanted to brush up on world history — too complicated for little kids.*

I'm reading it to them before bed, Crystal said. *Never too early to learn.*

Esther smiled to herself and put her phone back in her bag. This was new, being friendly with Crystal. It was as if she were discovering a sister out of nowhere, and she guessed that Crystal felt the same way about her.

She turned her attention back to the discussion around her; Maggie was talking about the dinner at Laz's house the night before.

"I thought Tingting was very sweet," Maggie said. "But like, in a little sister way."

"Just to be clear," Serena said, "you were extremely wrong, Wendy."

"My bad," Wendy said. She shrugged and took a sip of her drink.

"But is Tingting going to stay at Laz's house? Forever?" Val asked.

"No, she's looking for an apartment," Esther said. She exchanged a glance and a sly smile with Tony.

"Wait, what was that?" Wendy asked. Esther and Tony hadn't been sly enough.

Go ahead, Tony communicated with his eyebrows.

"We're thinking of seeing if she wants to take over Tony's lease," Esther said.

The Mathey Girls looked at each other, verifying that they heard what they thought they heard.

"Dang," Serena said. "You guys move fast."

"A younger me might have counseled Esther to wait to move in together," Wendy said. "But I can tell that you were made for her, Tony."

"I mean, her apartment is a lot nicer than mine," Tony said.

"Ha ha," Esther said. Her friends were happy for her, excited, and she felt very loved.

Tony noticed it too. "So I think it's fascinating that you guys are so close," he said to the Mathey Girls. "I thought I was the only one who could draw her out of her shell, the only one who saw her as she really is, but now I see that she's the real Esther all the time with you guys, if you know what I mean."

"No one else makes Esther as happy as we do," Wendy said. "I mean, other than you."

"It's true," Esther said.

"And you guys have been this way since college?" Tony asked.

"Pretty much," Maggie said, and the others agreed.

"And do you think it was because you went to Princeton that you guys are so tight? Because when I went to college, I barely knew anyone even though there were literally tens of thousands of students there. A lot of that was on me, but still."

"Princeton is really small," Maggie said. "You've been to the campus, right?"

When Tony said no, Maggie groaned and eyed Esther with exaggerated accusation before turning back to Tony.

"It's, what, less than an hour from Esther's—soon to be your—apartment! You have to go visit," she said.

"It's beautiful," Wendy said.

"Yeah, beautiful... like a country club," Serena said.

"I can take you on a tour," Maggie said. "You'll see—it's very small, very close knit."

"If you go, you should definitely have Chuck's," Serena said, and the women chorused in agreement.

"The best buffalo wings," Wendy said. "I still crave them."

"Makes me want to go to Princeton right now," Serena said. "I mean, not the campus. Just Chuck's."

The women allowed themselves a collective moment of nostalgia for Chuck's buffalo wings, the sauce pooling at the sides of flimsy paper plates that threatened to collapse under the weight of the wings, that initial first bite into crispy skin slathered in hot and tart neon orange sauce. They had gone almost weekly when they were undergrads, indulging in plate after plate of wings.

Wendy let out a sigh, a dreamy smile on her face. "What were we talking about again?" she asked. "Before Chuck's."

"About the campus and why the Mathey Girls are so tight," Valerie said. "But I don't know... I went to a small liberal arts college, tiny compared to Princeton, and I made great friends, but nothing like this."

"We were just really lucky," Esther said, "to find each other, and grow up together."

"We've all been so lucky," Serena said. "All of us."

The women fell silent. Tony looked at their faces, trying to understand why the atmosphere had changed. Esther leaned her head on his shoulder.

"I wish Claire could have met you," Maggie said quietly.

"I think she would have loved you," Wendy said.

"I know she would have," Esther said.

"I wish I could have met her too," Tony said, and he drew Esther closer to him. "She sounds amazing."

"She was the best of us," Serena said.

"Don't say that, hon," Valerie said. "She wouldn't want you to think like that." Serena nodded, and Val put her hand on Serena's.

"But hey," Wendy said, gently. "Look at what we've done, what we're doing. We've got the Foundation, and think how many families that's going to help."

"And Esther single-handedly saved Claire's kids from being shipped off to Taiwan," Maggie said.

"Not single-handedly," Esther said.

"You kept Claire's family together," Maggie said. "Laz told me that, last night, when you were in another room. He said that without you, they would have fallen apart."

"I don't know," Esther said. "I did what any of us would have done."

The Mathey Girls told her no, that she had done something special, that she shouldn't discount herself like that. And then Tony changed the subject, because he could tell that Esther didn't like this particular kind of attention, and she nuzzled gratefully into his shoulder.

Soon the rest of them were debating and joking again, and Esther let herself be carried by the energy around her. Today, this day, right here in this bubble tea shop, she let herself enjoy the company of her best friends and her boyfriend. There was so much still unsettled in her life, but there was also so much promise. She had the people she needed, whether they were in the room with her or on a chat on her phone, and if she had these people, she was pretty sure that things were going to be okay.

34

Esther pulled her car into one of the last few spots in the small lot on University Place, across the archway into Mathey.

"Why is it so crowded?" she asked, and Tony shrugged in the seat next to her.

In the backseat, Maggie hummed with excitement. She was back on the East Coast again, three weeks after her initial trip. This time she had meetings at Princeton Medical, which was now part of the Penn hospital network. It had been her idea to come to campus after her meetings and she had insisted on giving Tony a tour.

Maggie led the way from the parking lot to the campus side entrance. Before they could turn into the archway, she spun around and held her hands up.

"Okay. Tony, we're about to go into Mathey courtyard. Imagine Esther and me, eighteen years old, living here. It gives me the chills when I go through this arch. Every damn time."

Tony gave Esther a hopeful smile and she slipped her hand into his. Maggie was coming on strong today, but she had been like this since she arrived in Philly, and Esther couldn't deny her friend the pleasure of success.

They turned into the archway and walked into the courtyard. "Oh, it's move-in day," Maggie said, wistful.

The Mathey buildings surrounding the courtyard were busy with parents and children moving into the dorms. The stolid beauty of the Gothic buildings, with their long light stone studded with windows and wooden doors, was overshadowed by the frenetic energy of the students. Sophomores squealed and cheered as they reunited after the summer, and nervous freshmen with their nervous parents struggled with boxes and suitcases, altogether like a colony of ants, carrying their loads to their separate tunnels, hands and heads touching, lingering before they went their disparate ways.

In the presence of their parents, the students were very obviously children, and Esther understood that this was why most of them seemed so eager to shrug their parents off, shedding a layer of skin. The parents, too, seemed to sense their imminent discard, that they would be sloughed off of their children and nothing would ever be the same. Esther felt as if they were intruding, but Maggie seemed unfazed as she walked into the courtyard.

"This is Blair Hall," Maggie said, turning to the right. "And this one is where Claire and I lived freshman year," Maggie said, gesturing at the first-floor window, her hand faltering for a second before it fell.

The three of them tried not to peer too closely into the uncurtained window.

"And you lived here too?" Tony asked Esther. She could sense that Tony was trying to engage her, to let a little bit of her light shine.

"I lived over there, in Campbell," Esther said, pointing across the courtyard. "Then sophomore year I moved to Blair."

"I wonder if we could sneak our way in," Maggie said. "Maybe we should wait for someone to open a door. I heard they changed the layout of the dorms. When we lived here, it was two quads on the first floor and two quads on the second floor, with a shared staircase for each entryway. I would love to see what it's like now."

They waited for some freshman or sophomore to come out of the entryway, like a magical dwarf coming out of an enchanted portal. Maggie and Tony chatted about the Mathey buildings and Blair Arch, and Esther moved towards the center of the courtyard to get warmed by the sun.

She hadn't been back to campus in years, and her heart was heavy with loss. Coming back here, knowing that Claire was gone, felt wrong. She realized, for the first time, that her parents might have felt something similar when they brought her to Princeton as a freshman. Did it feel wrong to them to come back here without Caleb, when they helped her move into her dorm those decades ago? At what point did they think of Princeton as Esther and Didi's college, and not Caleb's college?

It's just a campus, she told herself. Just some buildings, just a place.

On the other side of the courtyard in one of the Campbell

entryways, a mother held the heavy wooden door open, looking at her son with pride and sadness as he carried a large box past her. Esther glanced over at Maggie and Tony and could hear enough of their conversation to understand that Maggie was talking about how badly she hoped Rosie would get into Princeton someday. Tony listened thoughtfully, as he always did, his arms folded as he took in Maggie's concern, nodding as if he understood exactly how she felt.

Esther walked back to them. "Let's keep going," she said.

"Right," Maggie said.

Maggie gave one last longing look at her old entryway and then she and Esther's eyes met. They were both about to cry, Esther realized, and then she felt Tony's arm around her shoulders.

Maggie walked on ahead, talking loudly so they could hear as she pointed out Nassau Hall, Whig and Clio, occasionally spinning to give Tony a bit of campus lore. They reached the clearing in front of the Chapel and Maggie suggested that they go in.

As they started up the steps, Esther said, "Maggie, you should have been a student tour guide. Did you know all this stuff back then?"

Maggie paused, and Esther and Tony stopped behind her. "You don't remember? I wanted to do it," Maggie said. "I wanted to be an Orange Key guide. I even applied to be one."

"Really?" Esther asked.

"Really," Maggie said, and the three of them stood aside to make way for a family entering the chapel. "But then Serena and Wendy gave me so much grief about it that I didn't. I'm surprised you don't remember."

"I'm sorry, somehow I've forgotten all about that. That's kind of... terrible." Esther looked at Tony, his slightly raised eyebrows. "Sometimes we could be pretty harsh, back then."

"But why would they care if you were a tour guide?" Tony asked.

Maggie laughed dryly. "It was very important to some of us that we weren't *Princeton* Princeton, if you know what I mean."

Tony nodded, as if he knew what Maggie meant, but Esther wasn't sure. She wanted to explain to Tony how different it was back then, how white and rich and elite it had felt, how they had clung to each other, a band of outsiders taking refuge in their little group where they were free to be different.

As they followed Maggie into the Chapel, it struck Esther that Maggie could have been *Princeton* Princeton, she probably should have been, but she had chosen to stick with them, the Mathey Girls, instead.

The Chapel was mostly empty, the few groups of people walking slowly and talking softly. Esther left Maggie and Tony and sat at the end of a pew. The air felt sanctified, as it always did, in a way that the air in her childhood church never had. She closed her eyes and listened to the murmurs and whispers echoing, melding, floating in the air. The sound was both ancient and familiar.

She remembered how she used to come to the Chapel when she was a freshman. She had been so homesick at first. She called her parents every day, pretending like she was fine but actually wanting to beg them to come and take her home. She never told them how much she missed the safety of her family. They probably guessed, Esther realized now, that she wasn't happy, but they had never indulged her in the possibility of coming to get her. So she had started going to the Chapel when she felt overwhelmed by a longing for home, because the Chapel had felt quiet and sacred and constant.

Claire had found her in the Chapel one day in late September freshman year. Why was Claire in the Chapel? Esther couldn't remember. She could, though, remember exactly how she felt as Claire slid next to her in the pew and asked if she was okay. Esther remembered wiping her eyes, even though she had already stopped crying, and saying that she was. Claire could have walked away, could have accepted Esther's lie, but she didn't. Instead, Claire asked if they could sit together a little while, and while sitting next to this new friend, Esther had drawn encouragement and strength from her without Claire even saying a word.

"Esther." Esther felt Tony's hand on her shoulder, and she opened her eyes. "Esther, you okay?"

"Yes, yes, I'm fine," Esther said, and she brushed her hand over her eyes just to make sure they were dry.

"Maggie's waiting outside. We're finally going to eat those wings you told me about."

Esther smiled as she took Tony's hand and rose from the pew. No trip to Princeton was complete without Chuck's. Somehow, since the early 2000s, every time the Mathey Girls went it was the same two Latino men behind the grill counter, the same members of the Korean family at checkout, everyone growing older together. Over the years, wings at Chuck's were constant in the same way that the hallowed air of the Chapel was constant. Today Maggie had looked online and yes, Chuck's was still open, so of course they were going to get wings, and Esther was hopeful that the pandemic hadn't changed anything. That they would see the same two Latino men and the same Korean family, eat the same wings off the same paper plates.

Esther felt a moment of disorientation as she stepped out of the sacrosanct Chapel, back into daylight, back to new and returning students and the collective air of expectation. Again, she and Tony followed Maggie, who led them past the library and down the path toward FitzRandolph Gate, the official entrance to the University.

"All the squirrels are black," Tony said.

"Princeton colors are orange and black, didn't you know?" Maggie asked. "But it's only a myth that we imported black squirrels to match our aesthetic." She chuckled to herself.

They passed more clusters of students, with parents and without, and Esther wondered at the potential that each of these children held. Did they have any idea of the infinite possibilities of their futures? Like stepping on thin ice, new cracks appearing and branching out with each stride. It was impossible to be here and believe in fate, that there was a strict path already set in place for each of them.

She considered her own path and wondered what different futures might lay before her. She had already taken the most difficult step and accepted Jose's offer, finally starting at Solutris the next week. It would be a challenge, commuting, working full-time again, working with Jose. She was only 80% sure she could handle it, but she was 100% sure that she was ready to find out if she could. After all, Hannah had started school again, and didn't really need Esther anymore. Esther had learned to be glad for her.

They stopped at the head of the path leading to the Gate and took in the view. "On graduation day, the seniors process through FitzRandolph Gate, the middle one there," Maggie said. "The journey through the Gate represents the transition into adulthood."

"Very... metaphoric," Tony said.

"You see those students? How they're going through the smaller gates on the side of the main one?" Maggie asked. "Students never go through the main gate before graduation. The legend is, if you exit

Princeton from the Gate before Commencement, you'll never graduate." She smiled. "I think Serena went out through the Gate when we were juniors, just to prove the legend wrong. But she's Serena."

"Did you go through the Gate? Before graduation?" Tony asked Esther.

Esther shook her head. Of course she hadn't. She didn't believe in silly legends, but she had never been the type to take that chance.

"I mean, if you think you might ever go to Princeton for grad school, we can take the long way," Maggie said to Tony. She was being earnest, Esther could tell.

Tony laughed. "I'm not a Princeton kind of person," he said. "But thank you."

Maggie frowned briefly. "Well," she said, "you'll have to explain more when we get to Chuck's." She paused, considering, and Esther took the lead down the path.

She thought back to her graduation day. She remembered that it had been a hot, sunny afternoon, and everyone was sweating in their caps and gowns. The Commencement ceremony had finished, they were officially graduates of the University, and the procession to the Gate had begun in the orderly lines of their Commencement seating. The Mathey Girls and Laz had sat together, and now they would follow each other one by one through the Gate. Maggie had insisted on being first, followed by Laz, Claire, Esther, Wendy, Serena. Time seemed to slow as the Gate neared; they were surrounded on both sides by cheering family and friends, the feeling of celebration overwhelming.

Esther had tried to look for her parents and Didi in the crowd near the Gate—Didi had said they would try to get as close as possible. She didn't see them, though, and she was afraid that they would miss the moment when she finally stepped through. The Gate grew closer, and she wanted to stop, or slow down, uneasy. Then, as she was about to reach the Gate, Claire turned around.

"Ready, Esther?" she asked, a grin on her face, and she held out her hand.

That was all Esther had needed to regain her equilibrium, to let herself feel excited instead of overwhelmed.

"Ready," she said, and taking Claire's hand they made their

metaphoric transition to adulthood together.

Now, at the Gate, Esther paused and placed her hand on the wrought iron at her side. She turned to look back at Tony and Maggie behind her. Maggie raised her eyebrows—everything okay?—and Esther nodded.

She was ready. She let go of the Gate and reached her right hand out to Tony. They walked through together, fingers interlaced, out of the University and into the thrum of Nassau Street.

Acknowledgments

Thank you to Yin-mei Lim, Chingwin Pei, Pantea Yashar, Theresa Brown, Julia McAuley, Jane Liu, Lisa Moon, Sharon Chaitin-Pollack, Galit Askenazi, Elaine Tso, Andrea Corsi, Chen Feng Ng, Melissa Velez, Donna Lee, James Iddins, Betty Chu, May Lo, Dan Gilbert, and Carol Kuecker for your consideration and feedback throughout the many drafts of the novel.

Special thanks to each of Lorie Owens and Jane Hartsock for help with, and inspiration for, publishing this book myself.

Thank you to my MWW Zoom writing group: Dennis, Jane, Lynn and Scott for providing encouragement, critique, and virtual shoulders to cry on.

Thank you to my Shaker/library/Friday writing group: Kristen, Mara, Yelena and Kate. We don't actually get a lot of writing done, and we still don't have a name for the group, but your support has been invaluable. Thanks in particular to Mara and Kristen for marketing pep talks and support.

Super specific thanks to Kruti Trivedi for age-appropriate names; to Aaron Chen for discussion of Philly environs and duck ponds; to Peter Chen for help with colorblindness testing for the cover; to Joseph Chu for author photos; and to Zachariah Yeh for tech help.

In addition to and including the above, I wanted to thank all the friends and family who have supported me throughout the journey of writing this novel. Thanks for listening to way too many updates about drafts and queries and agents and publishing. I am so grateful to have such good people in my life.

To my real-life Mathey Girls: I can't imagine who I would be without you. You are all the best and I can't wait for our next Turkeyfest.

Lastly, and most of all, thank you to my husband and my kids for providing support and inspiration and joy every single day. I love you.

A special request

Thank you for reading Mathey Girls.

I would really appreciate if you could take a moment to rate Mathey Girls online and provide your thoughts. Ratings and reviews are extremely important to indie authors.

Also, if you enjoyed the novel, consider signing up for my newsletter at melodychuauthor.com for the occasional email and updates on when my next book is coming out.

About the author

Melody Chu is a writer and attorney. The daughter of Chinese immigrants from Taiwan, she graduated from Princeton University and Harvard Law School and has practiced as an attorney in Hong Kong, Beijing and the United States. She lives in her hometown of Cleveland, Ohio, with her husband and three children.

Photo by Joseph Chu